AMERICAN CORRUPTION

AMERICAN CORRUPTION

A Story of Boston Corruption under J. Edgar Hoover's FBI

Edward Anthony Gibbons

iUniverse, Inc.
New York Bloomington

American Corruption
A Story of Boston Corruption under J. Edgar Hoover's FBI

iUniverse books may be ordered through booksellers or by contacting:

iUniverse
1663 Liberty Drive
Bloomington, IN 47403
www.iuniverse.com
1-800-Authors (1-800-288-4677)

ISBN: 978-1-4502-3306-4 (pbk)
ISBN: 978-1-4502-3308-8 (cloth)
ISBN: 978-1-4502-3307-1 (ebk)

Printed in the United States of America

iUniverse rev. date: 5/25/2010

To the wise reader in the Book of Life, joy, sorrow, weal, and woe are all alike. Since good and ill alike must have their end, it matters little whether our portion be good or evil.

Omar Khayyam.

Corruption: Evil; depraved. To make, or become corrupt. *Webster.*
Urbi et Orbi

And we surely must acknowledge that the average American contributed to the greatest era of the American Corruption with their individual and collective *violation* of the Volstead act of 1919 that began prohibition and theref115ore fostered crooked police, judges and legislators.

Thus I bring you the life and loves of Edward "Teddy" Sheerin. A hero of World War Two who chose a different life style than that of his returning fellow veterans. He, like many of the 'Post prohibition' era males, when it comes to himself, he believes in the adage:

"Might makes all things right."

A story of Boston Corruption under J. Edgar Hoover's FBI

Chapter One

Many months before the Japanese December 8, 1941 dastardly sneak attack on Pearl Harbor Hawaii, President Franklin Delano Roosevelt, on July 7, 1941, orders a United States Army Military unit shipped to Iceland to relieve the British Infantry troops stationed there so that they could see military action elsewhere.

President F.D. Roosevelt's action, in retrospect, indicates that while the isolation attitude was dominant in the United States the country was more prepared for military action than most Americans realized, behind the scenes the United States was indirectly already involved in the war by this date. F.D.R. kept a lot of secrets from the voters including the evil corrupt fact that Francesco Castiglia, a.k.a. mobster Frank Costello, backed his election while mobster Charles 'Lucky' Luciano, who is deep in the Hollywood scene with his movie star mistress Thelma Todd and dinner companions such as Jimmy Durante and Ed Wynn, backed Al Smith for President. Corruption on the part of Democrats as well as the Republican candidates still prevails.

Sunday December 7, 1941 at 7.55 a.m., the Japanese send 360 planes to attack Pearl Harbor killing 2117 civilians and military personnel. On Monday December 8, Roosevelt declares an act of war against the Axis. By this date the Japanese Army's evil atrocities and killing orgies have slaughtered and murdered over 12 million Chinese civilians. Most were cruelly killed by sword, shovel or bayonet. All this is well known to the Americans.

Plus they heard of the German atrocities in Europe. However, up to this date Americans are severe isolationist in their beliefs, it wasn't their war. However, when it hit home, they banded together in firm resolve to stop all this cruelty on the part of the Axis. And so it is with Edward Teddy Sheerin

In spite of F.D.R.s' October 1941 speech, "No American boys will go to war." Boys like Teddy and his brother Stanley decide it is time to do something and each enlist in the military.

Monday February 19, 1945, under the command of Lt. General Holland M. *Howling Mad* Smith, part of the United States Army 5th Division's attempt to conquer Iwo Jima begins. It is to become the toughest Marine battle in one hundred and sixty-eight years.

Participating in the attack on Iwo Jima, in the air is twenty-one years old United States Army Air Force, Lt. Colonel Edward *Teddy* Sheerin flying an all American made P51 Mustang. (However its engine is a British Rolls Royce 12 cylinder Merlin).

On the ground on the island of Iwo Jima, as part of 30,000 United States Marines, on the south east beach of Okinawa is the 3rd and the fourth Marine Division's 506th Fighter Group. Twenty-year old Marine Sergeant Stephen *Steve* Ryler is leading his *Grunts on land.* It is a suicidal but successful attempt by United States forces to successfully invade and conquer this Japanese held island.

On this historic date of1945, Steve, is crawling on his belly over the shiny black lava pebbles, and in the sky, Teddy is flying his Mustang pursuit plane low above the inching Marines. The two are within one thousand feet of each other. Little do they know that both their lives will later become emotionally entangled around a most beautiful female?

It is a very costly battle, with a great loss of life, and injuries, to the Japs and the Marines. Four days after their landing, the Marines raise the American flag on Mount Suribachi. Moreover has become an extremely vital step on the threshold of the 1270 mile 'road' to Tokyo that the allies will follow to invade Japan.

The Japanese military realize the importance of their need to retain control of this island, it is imperative for them to be able to protect their homeland from a future Allied invasion that could begin here. It is so important to them that in a few hours they fire twenty thousand deadly shells into Ryler's Marine held area. No larger than 9000 sq. yards in size the Japs mount deadly suicidal attempts to hold this area of the island Iwo Jima. In return, the enemy held areas of the island sustain seventy-two days of U.S. aerial bombardment.

Every war results are reflected by dramatic changes in the attitudes and even to how people relate to the times and moral concepts. After WW1 ended, morals were low; Americans degraded and castigated the Germans. When WW2 ends, moral concepts were high and the Americans helped to rebuild Germany and Japan to the great countries they become.

After the Korean Conflict ended, the morals of women declined to a new low with the advent of the birth control pill. No longer would a woman fear unwanted pregnancy, no longer will she remain chaste until marriage, no longer just one or two men in her life. The sky is the limit, the more the merrier. As a result of the women's free sex, sexual diseases proliferate.

Thus the path is set, the lowering of moral options, leads to more allowable corruptions to prevail. In a little over two years after their tours of duty are over, Steve and Ted's paths will entangle their lives and careers with an adorable Monroe look-a-like very 'girlie girl' named Catherine Jane Brooks.

Cathy and Steve are Roslindale High School students at the time they bond. He is the team quarter-back and she a Cheer leader. She obviously fits *Thackeray's* observation:

> *'A pair of bright eyes with a dozen glances, suffice to subdue a man, to enslave him, and inflame, to make him forget: they dazzle him so he would give his life to possess them.*

Stephen Ryler born Wednesday June 6, 1925, is just two days short of his eighteenth birthday when he graduates from high school. Three days later on June 11, 1943 the 5'11", 165 lb blonde with a flat top hair cut, decides he will not wait to be drafted into the military, enlists in the U.S. Marines. (*Wednesday's* child,-*full of woe*).

Eamon Sheerin is born on Saturday March 4, 1905 on Inishmore (Inis Mor) one of the three Aran Island off the shore of western Ireland. From hearing from relatives abroad, his goal is to live in Boston. At sixteen years of age and having no formal education, nor financial power, he earns his ship passage by laboring as a deck hand aboard a liner traveling from Cork Ireland to Boston. The selection of Boston is twofold, first because with his limited knowledge of English, it is the only area in the U.S.A. where there are many Irish folks that speak Gaelic. Second it is the only U.S. port of call for this ocean liner.

Boston, at this time, is the home of the wealthy Brahmans the aristocrat Bostonians, Italians, and Shang e-tighe (shanty) Irish that were born in Ireland or the second generation of Irish ancestry that are born in Boston.

At first it was the Italians who in the early 1800's, flooded in to Boston from overseas, settling mostly in the Boston's land bound North End. Then in the early 1850's, due to the terrible persecutions, and hunger caused by the British, the Irish immigrated to Boston to settle mostly in isolated, almost an island, South Boston. They soon outnumbered the Italians – two to one.

In 1921 the Irish dominated the Boston population of 650,000. However, during the Great Depression (1930-1941) both groups must scrape for a living. To even graduate from high school is a great accomplishment. A job is more important than an education, only the sons of the very few wealthy men go to college. Moreover, the N.I.N.A. signs in the windows of businesses made less employment opportunities for the Irish.

However, at the advent of the Volstead Act in 1919, (prohibition – the greatest *contributor* to the *American Corruption)* the Mob rule and actions or lack of, by corrupt police, judges and legislators gave some unemployed Irish, and Italians, underworld crime job opportunities that continue still.

At eighteen Eamon Sheerin meets and marries French Canadian born, sixteen year old Margaret La Chappelle. Due to the fact that she only speaks French and he only Gaelic, it becomes a cold relationship. She does not become a United States citizen, on his twenty-first birthday Eamon does.

Rough hewn Edward *Ted, Teddy* Sheerin, now 6'1", 189 lbs, was born on Saturday 4/19/1924 to Irish immigrant Eamon and Canadian Margaret Sheerin, a *three finger* Catholic. Ted's philosophy, while growing up, is might makes right and it continues throughout his life.

Ted's older brother Stanley *Stan* is born on Wednesday January 4, 1923. (Another Wednesday child). Edward 'Ted, Teddy' is born Saturday April 19, 1924. Sadly their mother dies giving birth to Teddy

Growing up with no maternal relationship and an inexperienced alcoholic father, Ted and Stanley do not receive the love and affection that normal parents give to their off-spring. This lack of parental affection becomes especially so when, because of the circumstances of Margaret's death, Eamon becomes even less than affectionate.

With their dad working as a day laborer, their survival relies mostly on his income. As the boys get to the age of eleven, they go house to house selling the Saturday Evening Post, Liberty magazine and the Ladies Home Journal. For each sale they receive two or three cents. Summer times they mowed grass and in the winter shovel snow for twenty-five cents. On weekends they get five cents for carrying a bucket of illegal beer from the speakeasy to the church lunches.

The depression era has less work available. Less income, means less food, thus the majority of young recruits for WW2 show physical signs of malnutrition.

The Sheerin boys are often left alone, or occasionally are attended by various female friends of Eamon. It does not help when Eamon, in spells of self-pity, spends his meager wages for prohibition style booze – *Bath-tub gin – to drown his* sorrows. Especially so each year, when Teddy's birth date is a reminder that Margaret died birthing him. Teddy grows in to his teen years, unemotional and cold, and when the time comes, he does not seek romance, he just seeks lustful sex.

Eamon believes that Gaelic is a dying language and to be sure that both his boys are fluent in that language, most of the time he speaks to them in Gaelic. He firmly believes that Gaelic is the language of patriots and English – the language of traitors.

Stanley is among the first men drafted in 1940 and the military is his first experience at three meals a day. On Monday January 26, 1942, just seven weeks after FDR declares war on the axis, Stan's AEF 34TH Infantry division, under Major General Russell P. Hartle, lands in Belfast, Northern Ireland, and Stanley's war duty begins. His *V-mails* to his brother, tell of his excitement at becoming a buck Sergeant.

Stanley Sheerin becomes one of the first and original *Army Rangers.* A group of soldiers secretly trained to participate in ultra-dangerous missions. The Ranger uniform can be easily identified from other soldiers by the green *tam-o-shanter* style cap they wear instead of the usual soldier hat. Prepared for any type of combat, they specialize in pre-invasion reconnoitering as well as infiltrating enemy held territory.

On such a mission into the Ploiesti oil fields of Romania Friday February 4, 1944, Stanley steps on a land mine. It does so much pelvic damage that it castrates him. Being deep within enemy lines he could bleed to death before friendly Partisan could get him to a safe zone. However Michael the guardian angel must be with him.

The temperature has fallen to a low ten degrees, freezing the blood, temporarily stopping the flow from his wound. He is brought to a nearby farm of a local Partisan and a veterinarian takes a piece of skin from a new born calf and temporarily seals the damaged area of Stanley's crotch. U.S. Ranger Medics, looking after wounded fellow Rangers, air lift him from the farm to a military hospital in Palermo. This hospital gained much experience in repairing those types of injuries from having aiding those wounded in the capture of Sicily. Here the Army Medics perform a non-penis urinary exit, on Stanley.

After a three month stay in the Palermo Military hospital Stanley travels on a hospital ship, along with dozens of other wounded soldiers, to a military hospital back on his original base at Belfast, Northern Ireland.

Numerous operations follow before Stanley can comfortably sit down to urinate, as well as several pelvic operations so that his walk would not have a significant awkward motion.

Chapter two

As with most committed couples, Stephen and Cathy experiment with heavy petting. Their sexual activity is limited to fondling, and fingering, to experience an orgasm. They vow to wait until married before *going all-the-way*, but war changes everything.

The evening before he is to report to Camp Lejeune they are both nervous. "How do I know you will wait for me? I know you are very passionate and enjoy our love making. How will I be sure you will always remain only just mine?"

"I have something for you." She reaches into her purse and removes a photo of herself in a bathing suit. "No other boy will have this, and I promise I will not go out with any boys, I will wait for you. I am only passionate when you are. I love you. I will also say a Rosary every night before I go to sleep, to pray for your safety, and to keep me from temptations. You know, deep in your heart, that I am – and always will be, just yours. Keep this photo close, and it will always be a reminder that I am just yours."

"I may get killed in the war and never have completely enjoyed your body. Cathy, I need you to prove your love for me. Our usual horny heavy petting is not showing you are mine."

Without further persuasion, she surprises him "I want you in me right now."

A jolting surprise to Steve, but typical male, it is all that is needed for him to react. Placing his full lips upon hers, he takes her hand and places it at his crotch. She needs no further encouragement. She maneuvers his zipper to firmly place her warm soft hand upon his now exposed erection. With her other hand she raises her skirt and spreads her French style wide leg panties, then her nervous, shaking, hand guides his penetration.

The first thrust is like an ant sting to her vagina, rough and clumsy, but what follows is like nothing she has ever imagined. How can any girl imagine the rapture and prophetic exaltation of an orgasm from the strong flow from her lover's manliness? All of this occurs just twenty-six days before September 9, 1943, her sixteenth birthday. Like all females, her first venery experience will always be remembered.

The day, the time, the place, even the color of her panties, will remain in her romantic brain forever, Saturday June 15, 1946 the E.T.O. war operation is finally over. The European part of the world is temporarily at peace.

Saturday June 15, 1946, while on a furlough, Steve and Cathy are married in St. Columba's Church. With stiletto heels Cathy stands an exquisite feminine five foot seven at one hundred twenty-nine pounds. Her wedding gown is of elegant white linen that flows from her shoulders past her twenty-two inch waist, accenting the curvature of her pleasantly rounded torso prominence and ends in a short trailing train on the floor.

The French *mantilla* style veil is thistledown of a delicate *broderie anglaise* of gossamer weave snowflakes in Irish lace that is a tiara over her braided long blonde tresses. It finalizes enchantingly on her derrière.

Underneath all this elegance she follows tradition, something old, something new, something borrowed, something blue –an *old* high school ribbon, a *new* bra, *borrowed* her sister Jeanne Marie's ankle bracelet, and last but not least, the pale *blue* panties that she wore the night she lost her virginity to Steve.

The church has a flowing essence of the perfume of many floral arrangements. The organ music is adding to the enchantment of the bride to be. For her it is a thrilling exciting moment, so exciting and heart racing that when Father Timothy Coughlin says, "Do you Catherine Jane Brooks, take Stephen J. Ryler" and before he can continue the excited Cathy exclaims, "I do, I do, oh yes I do." There is a loud roar of laughter from the congregation.

During the reception there are some anxious moments when the slightly inebriate Steve gets into an argument with the orchestra leader because he does not play any Irish music. Grabbing the man by the necktie, Stephen begins choking him until the victim's face begins to gain a bluish hue. The wedding's best man, Phil Brennan, and Cathy's dad Art, pull Steve away and sit him down. This incident should have warned friends and family that alcohol is already a problem for Steve. After subduing the aggressor, Art returns to the head table and whispers to his wife Marie, "His drinking is becoming more of a problem than ever."

Steve's father Donald, very embarrassed, starts to go to the fracas when his wife Eileen grabs his arm, "Sit down, sit down, you will only make matters worse. They are doing a good job of handling our drunken son."

After their honeymoon, the young couple begins their partnership ecstatically happy. She works as a secretary for a young handsome lawyer, turned politician, Suffolk County District Attorney Lawrence Cameron. For a lad with a shortage of funds and having a difficult time working his way through Suffolk Law School, he now has an expensive condo in the very secluded Beacon Hill Louisburg Square. For enhancement to the décor, there is an exclusive grassy square, enclosed by a wrought Iron fence. It is the street next to the State Capital, for Cameron it is just short walk to the Suffolk County Court house.

Cameron shares Louisburg Square with many historical personages associated with the square. Louisa May Alcott's father lived at #10, while at the funeral of her father, she died there. In 1852 the world famous singer Jenny Lind was married in #20.Years later Senator John Kerry bought a residence in Louisburg Square.

Last, but not least, it is just a few blocks down Beacon Street to the famous *Cheers* Pub

Steve has his own ideas on re-acquainting himself to civilian life; he decides to just take the 52/20 that all veterans can receive until they obtain employment. He does not seek employment; he just wants to enjoy his new found freedom.

July of 1946, Ted's Uncle Mattie hires him to tend bar in his Quincy cafe called Mattie's Tap. It is here that Ted's seeds of his future are planted. The café is quaint, lace curtained windows, soft music; linen draped, candled lit, tables and an excellent Italian menu that draws nurses and doctors from a nearby hospital.

Thursday evening September 12, 1946 about eight, a heavy set man wearing an American Legion cap, comes into the Café. "I coach a little league baseball team. I wonder if you would mind putting this small poster on your bar. It is telling about my kid's baseball team playing a week from Sunday at Fenway Park. "

"No problem friend. I see on your cap you have a Jewish Chaplain emblem. One Vet to another, we must help each other. Where were you stationed?"

"I was in the E.T.O; stationed in Germany I am Rabbi Alvan Waterman."

"I was in the South Pacific, I'm Ted Sheerin. How about a complimentary drink Rabbi, you look a little overheated."

"I'd appreciate a beer, thanks," the stranger says, taking off his hat. "I am a little sweaty from walking around to the business establishments to ask them to display these posters."

"The way the dark clouds are beginning to form Rabbi, you won't be sweaty too long; the rain will cool things down a bit."

"You may be right; I better finish this beer and get going."

"When you finish with those posters, come on back and spend some time bull shitting about the military."

"I'd like that Ted, but I will be quite a distance away from here after I put out my last poster. How about my coming back some evening and we can swap stories?"

"I'm tending bar here every night except Mondays; pick your time my friend."

The clouds soon broke into a deluge, slowing business. Customers are few, and far between as the thunder storm progresses in the night.

Ted is doing a cross word puzzle when just before closing, a rain soaked female, the image of Liz Taylor, enters the Café. She removes her drenched trench coat, revealing a starched white nurse uniform. She gives the dripping coat a strong shaking, then hangs it over the nearest bar stool.

Turning towards Ted, "Double scotch neat, please," and she sits on a barstool. Using her handkerchief she begins wiping the rain drops from her forehead and around her strikingly purple blue eyes. The heavenly scent of her perfume is accented by the moisture.

Placing the drink in front of her, Ted comments, "You took a hellava nasty night to honor us with your presence," he teases, as he hands her a clean, dry, bar towel.

"Had no choice, my car stalled when I went through a large puddle a couple of blocks from here and it won't start again. I am going to have to use a hackney for transportation."

In his usual closing time schedule, Ted goes about getting the bar area ready to shut down. Conversation is lacking until the misty eyed beauty observes aloud. "Is that photo –on the back mirror –a picture of you standing next to a P51 Mustang?"

"Wow, lady, it is of me; but how the hell do you know that is a Mustang? Ninety percent of the males that have been in the service don't know that is a Mustang, how do you?"

"I was a nurse at Okinawa and they flew out of there to Iwo."

"Jesus Christ woman, I flew out of Okinawa to Iwo. I'm Ted Sheerin; I was a light Colonel stationed at Oki. I miss flying those babies. I could get the speed up to 445 MPH and with six .50 caliber guns blazing, I could dominate the sky. I was in the last group to strafe Oki on Friday June 22, 1945 the day the battle for Oki ended with the allied victory."

"Well you outranked me a bit; I was a Captain in the nurse corps at Oki. I'm Anne Marie Nevins."

"It is so nice to meet you. You are the first Vet I've met that was affiliated with the war in the South Pacific."

After additional reminiscences, "Time to drink up, I need to close down the place."

"May I use your phone, I need that taxicab."

"You've got to be kidding, no cab for you, you're a buddy. I'll drive you where ever you want to go."

"Slow down Colonel Ted, I may be a buddy to you but there is such a thing called *fuck your buddy week* and I do not want to give you any ideas. I have been in autos with *Fly boys*. If you plan to run outta gas, let me tell you to forget it, I don't even shake hands on the first date."

"Well lovely one, you have just set the rules, so, I will shake hands with you next Monday night when I take you dancing. Then the following Monday on our third date I will kiss you once. The fourth date will be the Labor Day and I will hope for the best."

While slowly shaking her head in a negative fashion, she grins. Helping her don her now semi-dry raincoat, her smile gives Ted the impression that the thought of cohabitating is a strong possibility

Each of the following Mondays the couple spend romantically dining and dancing, and a few light passion moments of kissing that ends while standing in her front doorway saying good night. That is all but the Monday September 30, 1946.

After attending an Ethel Merman/Arthur Treacher stage play of *Panama Hattie* at the Colonial Theatre and a few imbibed cocktails, they head to Anne's apartment. As they approach the doorway, she hands him her key. "Let's not stand in the doorway tonight."

Puzzled and curious, Ted takes her key, unlocks, then opens the door, and steps into the apartment living room. Assisting in removing her coat, he lays it on the nearest armchair. In typical female gesture, she removes her hat, runs her fingers through her hair, then pulls Ted close and gives him a tantalizing kiss. She then steps back four or five steps, runs her hands down her hips, "Do you lift my skirt or do I?"

He can only compare the *cock-a-hoop* euphoric rush of blood to his brain as being like the first time he shot down a Jap Zero. He unbuttons her blouse, then skirt and lets it fall to the floor, revealing a red bra and panties, all trimmed with black lace. Before him stands a full bodied, estrogen loaded, aphrodisiac. Then like a first time sixteen year old boy with a Mrs. Robinson, he doesn't know where he should put his hands. His thoughts rage. *Do I go for the breast, or do I remove the panties next?*

Anne solves the problem by undoing his belt, then his zipper, and his pants drop to the floor. She kneels, pulls his boxers down, and begins to kiss his pubic area. Time for some manly action as he bends her backward onto the carpet, straightens her legs; kisses her left then right inner thigh while removing her panties. Kneeling between the parted thighs and with her cooperation, his manhood is encased by her vagina. There will be no *coitus interruptus.* In fact, it is so enjoyable that he delays his withdrawal after the orgasms.

There is no rush to be modest, or to don the discarded clothing, it is a time to lie there and ponder the *shouldas.* Time enough to do things a little more logical the next time, both realizing that it was good enough to enjoy doing again soon.

However, a still confused male, has questions. "Do you mind telling me what this all about?"

"Not at all, Teddy boy. You were so sure of yourself in telling me about the four Mondays, I needed to show you that it is all masculine bullshit. The female is always the one in charge. It is she who decides when and for whom she will spread her thighs. From the way you helped me that rainy night, I felt that you were a compassionate type of guy and I liked you from that first night. I had not had any lovin' in months, I could have been yours on the first date, but I wanted to show you that I was in charge, and I will remain in charge. I will not cater to any scrotal excesses."

"So how do I know when?"

"My *when* will be based on my moods, my needs, and my ovulations. I use the *rhythm method,* to determine my safe periods to prevent pregnancy. So you can see that my passion moments are not based on romance, just on my emotional, physical need of satisfaction."

"I have never met a woman that is so outspoken, and this frank, before. You believe in telling it as it is, don't you?"

"I don't want any misunderstandings; you now know how I feel and *if or when* will be decided by me. If that doesn't suit you, so be it."

"Oh baby, you are great. I enjoyed it a hellava lot. I'll abide by your decision as to the *will and when.* You are worth the wait. I just hope it will not be too long a period, *between the drinks.*"

"How about the night after tomorrow, my *safe period* lasts for a couple of days, so it will be periods of feast and famine sexually?"

The monthly *Déjà vu's* continue, moreover – man proposes – woman foreclosures.

When a woman wants a man and lusts after him, the lover need not bother to conjure up opportunities, for she will find more in an hour, than we men could think of in a century.

Abbe di Brantome

Men are so credulous, so naïve! When they believe that they are about to make a sexual conquest and the female allows him to undress her, revealing red silk panties and bra trimmed in black lace, it should then dawn on him that he had not made a conquest, instead she had. Getting dressed in her sexy undies indicates the woman is anticipating a liaison with him.

Chapter three

Enjoying the new civilian life and a fifty-two week government stipend of twenty bucks a week, and while Cathy is at work, Steve wanders into to Mattie's Tap to quench his thirst. Sits at the bar and says, "Draw me a cold one fella."

"Tap or bottle?" responds Teddy.

"Tap."

Enjoying a few sips, Steve's eye notes the fighter plane photo tapped to the mirror behind where Teddy is standing. "Is that you beside that plane in that photo?"

"Yeah, I flew a Mustang over Iwo."

"No shit! I was a gyrene that landed on Iwo," and he reaches over the bar and shakes hands with Teddy.

After minor memory exchanges and another beer, Steve leaves. This immediate rapport with Teddy has interested Steve and he begins to come back to Mattie's weekly. They compare war stories and realize their close proximity on that memorable day at Iwo Jima, and how near they were to death. It bonds them to a new friendship.

In one visit to Mattie's, maybe in a bit of anti-military officer rank that Teddy had above non-com Steve, Steve uses Teddy's military title to tease Ted. "You intend to be bartender for life Colonel?"

"No way, no way at all, with the minimum wage at forty cents an hour, I want something secure. I intend to take the exams and become a cop. Their wage starts at fifty cents an hour but I hear there is some easy money to be made. If that doesn't please a guy, the job allows cops enough *off time* to have a side job or business. I will study and rise up in the ranks. Police lieutenants and captains, make good pay, but the best position would be as a Deputy Superintendent. That is a high rank and pay –but not the responsibility of a Superintendent."

"Not bad thinking Teddy, so dream on and I'll give it a try also. My grandfather was on the Boston force when they went on strike in September of 1919. Governor Alvan Coolidge fired all the cops and a few Lieuts and Captains. So that year all the regular cops are replaced by mostly World War one vets. He also gave them the jurisdiction of law enforcement in the entire Commonwealth of Massachusetts, the only city with state wide law enforcement powers."

"Now it is twenty-eight years later Steve, and all those replacement cops are nearing their thirty years and will retire with a pension. So about two thousand new cops will be needed to replace them in the next two years and it will mostly be world War two vets. It will become a brand-new police force. That means we stand a hellava good chance of getting on the force."

"We veterans are owed a lot; we should take advantage of every opportunity. Speaking of vets, Steve, another vet just walked in the door."

With a wave of his hand, "Alvan, come here and meet Steve Ryler, Steve this is Rabbi Alvan Waterman. Al, you are just in time to join in on our plans."

"Glad to meet you Steve. What plans are you talking about Ted?"

"We are talking about joining the police force, how about you Al?"

"Thanks, but no thanks guys. With my religious duties, my little league coaching, dabbling in real estate and a few used car sales, I am comfortable."

"That sure is a heavy schedule Alvan, do you mind telling us what the real estate and used cars have to do with you?"

"As far as the real estate goes, I own some land in Pembroke that was given to me by my grandmother and I am trying to sell some of it. As you know Teddy, rabbinical duties do not pay enough, so I buy and sell a few used cars a year to supplement my income."

The two men put actions to their ideas and on Friday February 14, 1947 they take the Boston Police exams and on Wednesday February 16, the take the State Police examination. With the veteran's bonus of

5% exam credit, they each score a high grade on both the State Police and Boston Police exams.

Coincidentally they both choose the Boston Police because it is only forty-eight square miles and any transfers would be no further than a trolley car ride from home. The Statsies could transfer a trooper across Massachusetts as far away from home as much as two hundred miles.

March of 1947, Sheerin and Ryler are enrolled in the Boston Police Academy under Lieutenant Mark Andrews. Again by coincident, they both, upon graduation, are assigned to the Jamaica Plain Division 13.

Thursday May 8, 1947, Captain O'Halloran at roll call, "We are in need of motorcycle officers. Some of you patrolmen may have had motorcycle duty while in the military. If any of you has that experience and wish to go on bike duty, please step forward."

Steve and Ted are the only policemen who step out from the ranks.

"You two patrolmen go down to the garage. Sergeant Joe Friel from H.Q. is waiting there to give you a test run."

Upon their arrival Friel introduces himself, "If you rode in the military, this is no big deal for you. Ryler you take the first run, you can take your pick, the Harley with a side car, or the Indian."

Steve takes the Harley with the sidecar attached. Ted takes the Indian cycle and each pass the test run. Jamaica Plain now has a pair of motor vehicle traffic enforcement officers. A time for them to discover how many people are willing to pay to corrupt, rather than pay for the consequences of their actions.

CHAPTER FOUR

IN SEPTEMBER, TED stops eighteen year old Edward *Teddy* Kennedy for a traffic violation. Examining Kennedy's drivers license, he asks, "You any relation to U.S. Representative John F. Kennedy?"

"Yes sir," is the respectful reply. This courtesy from a person that is obviously *well connected* is unusual. That typical violator usually shows *bully power,* such as "Do you know who I am?" Or some other angry retort.

"Since we are both known as Edward or *Teddy*, I won't give you a ticket this time; just go a little lighter on the pedal."

As he remounts his motorcycle a good example of attempted bullying occurs. Ship building tycoon William B. Murphy races by with a speed going 20 M.P.H. over the legal limit. In a fast high speed chase, Sheerin overtakes and stops the culprit.

"You're wasting time giving me a ticket. I will be down in Judge Casey's court before you can get to the precinct to write up the ticket, and then your ticket will be thrown out."

Never the less Ted gives him a ticket then speeds down to the Suffolk County District Court and is in the Clerk's office and has obtained a court summons to hand to Murphy as he arrives.

"Welcome to the court house Mr. Murphy, you save me a trip to your office." As he hands Murphy a formal summons to appear in court in two weeks, for a motor vehicle moving violation,

Murphy takes the summons and angrily storms out of the courthouse.

The next day, Murphy again goes down Morton Street even faster than the day before. When Ted goes in pursuit, Murphy increases his speed and a chase is on. Finally along side of the speeding Cadillac Ted yells, "Murphy pull your car over and stop or I will shoot out your tires."

Now aware of how Ted's mind works, Murphy stops and is ticketed not only for over speeding but plus a new charges of driving so as to endanger and failing to stop for the police officer.

The irate Murphy yells, "I anticipated your harassment and I made an appointment with my friend Judge Casey to *clip your wings."*

Ted arriving at the scheduled hearing is greeted by the Court House Clerk, "Officer Sheerin, Judge Frank Casey is waiting for you in his private chambers."

Entering Ted sees Murphy sitting in a chair near the Judges' desk. "You wanted to see me your Honor."

"Yes I do. Have a seat Teddy. You know our friendship goes back to before the war and I now have a ticklish position that has occurred between two of my friends. I want your opinion of how we can resolve this issue that Mr. Murphy has created."

Murphy jumps up, "Frank, I didn't create the situation he did it."

Judge Casey, whose normal façade is similar to a *father knows best* style man, suddenly flushes an angry crimson. The color contrast is accented by his gray hair and black robe as he quickly rebukes Murphy. "You let out a burst like that again and friend or no friend Billy, I will fry your dumb ass. Do you hcar me Billy?"

The chagrined Murphy sharply becomes aware of his mistake, friend or not, realizing Casey's position, he apologizes, "I am sorry your honor."

Turning to Teddy Casey again says, "I am sorry for William's comments Teddy. Please try to put that incident aside and tell what you think is a fair solution for my errant friend Murphy."

"Your Honor, I will abide with any decision you make, but I would recommend that Mr. Murphy be instructed to hold his trouble making tongue. He appears to me, to believe that he is above the law and all others. I for one will not take his abuse and any future show of stupid arrogance by Mr. Murphy; will be met by me, with enforcement to the hilt."

Turning to Murphy the Judge admonishes, "Billy Murphy, what

the Sam hill is wrong with you. Your actions, your attempt to abuse our friendship, all this indicates a stupidity or even a mental illness on your part. You will pay the court clerk a $500.00 fine for the first ticket from Officer Sheerin. I will hold the second ticket open, in the event such abusive actions reoccur. That will allow me to order a trail and send you to prison for Contempt of Court charges. Now leave this court and never drive down Morton Street again."

While the Judge's order appears to be followed by Murphy, a few weeks later a very odd situation arises. Ted is driving his cycle on the totally dark Morton Street at 11.30 p.m. As he reaches the intersection of Circuit Drive, a dark black sedan zooms out of Circuit Drive slamming into the right side of his motorcycle. He is thrown about thirty feet through the air and lands in the concrete gutter on the opposite side of Morton Street from Circuit Drive. The ominous dark sedan makes a wheel screeching u-turn to escape the scene and go with tire rubber burning burst of speed, heads back up Circuit Drive.

Because the police motorcycle does not have any communication device such as a radio, and because motor vehicle traffic is very low at this time of the evening, Ted lays painfully gasping for breath and is moaning as he tries to move from the gutter on to the abutting grassy area. One or two autos pass without seeing the wreckage slightly hidden behind bushes and it is approximately fifteen minutes before he is noticed.

In a semi-conscious daze Teddy hears a speeding auto, and the screeching of suddenly braked tires, then silence. An alert young fellow has spotted the crashed bike. Not sure of what the situation is going to reveal, he stealthily comes over to the damaged motorcycle and is startled at hearing Sheerin's agonizing moan.

"Jesus Christ officer, what happened?" Not waiting for an answer he again questions, "Can you get up so I can take you to the hospital?"

"I don't know, but if you will give me a hand I will try to get up."

With the driver's assistance, Ted, in agony, struggles and gets up. With great effort Teddy is laid down on the back seat of the sedan. He spends a week in Boston City Hospital for repairs to his many broken ribs and extensive bad bruises to his shoulder, arms, hips, and legs.

While the circumstantial evidence indicates that it is no accident, it appears to defiantly be a pre-meditated design to permanently damage

Ted. Is this incident a Murphy's revenge? On the other hand, is this coincidentally some other miscreants diabolical doings?

In the long run, some culprit wins. Because the motorcycle is damaged beyond repair and the Police Department Budget does not allow funds to purchase a new cycle. On his return to duty, Ted is assigned to the Division 13 Sector A&R patrol car.

Meanwhile, it is going well for Steve Ryler until the following July Fourth 1949. It is one of the first sign of Steve's potential for alcoholism. Taking a right turn at an intersection at too high a speed, his cycle slides on loose gravel and tosses Steve against a curb.

The precinct patrol wagon doubles as an ambulance; (To refer to it as a 'Paddy wagon' is an insult to the Irish) it picks up Steve and carts him off to Boston City Hospital. At BCH emergency room, the doctor determines that most of the injuries are just sprains, and Cathy is phoned to come to the hospital and pick him up.

Patrolman John Tosko is the ambulance/ patrol wagon driver, Charles *Chuck* Lafferty, is the cop that rides in back with a prisoner or patient. He is an alcoholic himself, thus to protect a fellow drinker, in his report to the station, he neglects to mention that Steve has been boozing. By the time Steve is seen by the E. R. doctor, some of the booze has worn off and because he is not now a falling down drunk the doctor makes no note of it. The policy of cover-up thus rules. The unwritten *Blue rule* in regards to the police still is alive.

With no damages to his Harley, a few weeks after the accident he is back on the bike. August the thirtieth, by his boozing he has a near collision with a fire engine and avoiding a collision skids the motorcycle into a ditch. This time he breaks an arm and is off duty, followed by limited duty, until late October. Since the cycle is severely damaged thus out of operation and no funds to purchase a new bike. Steve is permanently assigned night foot patrol duty walking a beat, business door shaking and Jamaica Plain no longer has motorcycle traffic enforcers.

Chapter five

With the police budget cut by City Hall, the use of motorcycles is financially limited. Saturday evening August 20, 1949 Sheerin is assigned, with Patrolman Woosley, to Sector A & R squad car. At about 9:00 p.m., they are driving along Circuit Drive in Franklin Park when suddenly in their headlight beams appears a naked young female walking on the painted white line traffic divider. She is in her mid-twenties with beautiful body proportions, a true lustful male eye-catcher.

Carefully pulling aside of the ambulatory five foot five inch lass, Woosley stops the cruiser and Ted gets out. Ignoring the officer she continues down the road, one naked foot after the other as she maintains her balance walking the white stripe.

Getting between she and the patrol car, Sheerin tries to engage her in conversation. Question after question she ignores, she just keeps walking. Finally in apparent exasperation with Sheerin, and keeping her eyes on the white line, she says, "I am following the line that will lead me to my Savior Jesus Christ."

"But you have no clothes on, where are your clothes?"

"I have shed my clothes because they were covering this sinful body."

The only sinful thought that came to Ted's mind he softly relays to his partner, "What a waste of symmetrical magnificence. Those tits are at least a thirty-eight."

However any further thoughts are interrupted by Woosley, "Teddy, better get her in, radio turret just said that she is missing from Mattapan State Hospital."

This presents a huge problem, by now traffic has stopped in both directions. The warm summer evening has many strolling couples on the walkways of this Franklin Park area. A large crowd of observers are now following and watching every move Ted may make.

How should he handle a naked female in a manner that would not be misinterpreted by the *on-lookers*? Grabbing a person with clothes on is simple; just grab anywhere. Where should he take a hold of a naked one, especially a female one?

He could grasp her waist length shiny jet black hair that is covering her back simulating a silk shawl. But that might cause a ruckus as being brutality. Maybe some of the female observers could put her into the back seat of the cruiser. The way that the men are lecherously ogling this beautiful naked female, they would gladly give a hand.

Teddy, always the charmer, it is time for persuasion, holding open the back door of the vehicle, "It will be quicker to meet your Savior if you allow us to drive you to him."

The Savior must have been watching and decided to aid Sheerin, in a surprise move, she turns and climbs into the back seat. With Ted along side of her, they head the short distance up Morton Street to the sanitarium.

They are met by the security at the gate of the hospital and led to the admittance area where a matron, who resembles the sister of King Kong, meets them. Built like a fullback, dressed in black dress and reeking of cigarette smoke while carrying a baton, "What did you do with her clothing," she berates Sheerin?

"She was fully clothed when she escaped from here; we will examine her to see if you men molested her." And she continues to rant, "You should have had a police matron bring her in."

The insinuation and verbal abuse is more than Ted is willing to take. Lashing back at her, "You dumb bitch," he shouts. "We could not leave her in the middle of a dark, heavy traveled road. How the hell could we hold her in the middle of a street even if a matron was available? She was as naked as a jay-bird when we found her. Was I supposed to leave her for some guy to drag her into the woods?"

"And for your god damned information," he continues. "Females in the police department are scarce. There are only three matrons on the entire police force and none on duty tonight. We do not carry blankets and as you can see; our summer uniform is a shirt and tie, no jacket."

"If this hell hole was secure, she wouldn't have escaped. So don't blame your guilt laden shit on me madam. Give me the papers showing that we returned her to your care and I will get the fuck outta here," he demanded.

Returning to the cruiser Woosley observes," Teddy I could hear you way out here, you were pretty rough on that old bitch, and maybe she'll complain to the captain."

"Fuck that *butch* and the tribe she came from! No, take that back, I wouldn't fuck her even using your pecker," he jokingly added. "However, I wouldn't mind banging the one we brought in, now that is a far different story."

CHAPTER SIX

THE PATROLMEN THAT go off-duty at midnight meet their relief man at their route police call box. Then they use that phone to report of being relieved, to the police division desk clerk Harry Manson.

The route assigned to Steve this evening, has a Ballantine brewery and he spends most of his tour of duty in the guest pub room of the brewery. About nine p.m., each evening, the station patrol wagon is sent to the brewery to pick up a couple of buckets of ale for the men on duty in the precinct. If Steve is there at that time, *Chuck* Lafferty will chat a few minutes with him. Returning to the precinct, he will tell Manson that Steve is okay. Realizing all this, Harry fills in the forty minute duty calls whether or not Steve phones in. Thus the cops protect each other, the code of the force.

After duty on Saturday December 24, 1949, the off-duty Ted is entering his apartment when his phone begins to ring. Hoping it is Anne in one of her horny moods and wanting a liaison, he rushes to answer.

"Hello."

"Ted, I hate to call you at this hour but when it comes to Stephen you are the only one that I can turn to," is the worried voice of Cathy.

"What's wrong Cathy?"

"I went to the usual spot that I am to pick Stephen up after his tour of duty is over and he wasn't there. He promised he would be sober and that we would go to Midnight Mass at Holy Cross Cathedral. I did not phone the precinct because it might have got him in trouble. Can you help me find him Ted?"

Ted had not seen Cathy since her Anniversary party last June. "I'll sure try Cathy. I'll make some calls and call you back. I have your phone number. Better still Cathy, you go to that police *callbox* and wait, I'll meet you there after I've made some info calls."

Phoning the precinct, Ted gets C*huck* Lafferty who is filling in as relief for the Mason the call box switchboard officer. "*Chuck,* have you heard from Ryler?"

"I sure have, I was worried how I was going to handle it. I tried phoning you, but you weren't home. I'm damned glad you phoned. Phil Brennan in the O-sector squad car phoned in and said Ryler was passed out in the brewery pub room."

"Thanks, I was afraid of that. Check him out as finished tour and I'll take care of it."

Ted arriving at the pre-arranged meeting spot, Cathy excitedly greets him. "Oh Teddy, I am so glad to see you, did you find Stephen?"

"No, but I'll take you to where he is, get in your car and follow me."

Pulling up to the brewery, they go around to the guest door on the side of the building. Entering a twenty by thirty foot pub room Cathy is amazed. It looks like the friendly neighborhood pub. It is nothing as she imagined it would be.

The walls are paneled in dark mahogany. There are five tables, each with four chairs. Protruding out of one of the walls are four kegs of beer or ale. In the center of the four kegs is a sign reading ***In need of service – ring bell.*** From ten to ten, an attendant keeps checking the room, after ten *p.m.,* for service ringing the bell is required.

A neon blue colored clock is over the entry door, and on the room right wall are three huge Olympic style circles with the *Ballantine* logo blinking across the middle. Along the other walls are large photos of *The Boston Braves, Boston Red Sox, Boston Celtics, Boston Bruins,* and other such local sport insignia around the walls.

A long bench leans against the third wall. Lying prone on the floor beneath the bench is the hardly conscience drunk policeman who had evidently fallen off the bench. As usual, no one is in attendance. After-hours, this is a *help-yourself* operation for select visitors who know the proper code numbers to punch on the outer door lock to gain entry.

The drunken, prone individual does not respond to either Cathy's

"Stephen, Stephen." Nor, Ted's, "Steve, Steve." Too big and heavy to cart out to the autos, Ted suggests, " We are going to have to wait a little while till we can get him alert enough for us to help him into your car, so let's sit down and have a beer while we wait on him."

In about an hour of trying to get his attention, Steve finally half-heartily sits up on his own. With a slurred voice, "What the hell are you and Ted doing here Cathy?"

"We are trying to get your stupid arsse sober enough to get you the fuck outta here and home," Ted responds.

"Oh, Stephen you went to the priest and took '*the Pledge*'. You promised me, that you would not touch alcohol again. You promise that we would go to Midnight Mass, how could you be so inconsiderate?"

Bending over from the chair he is now sitting on, he slaps Cathy a cruel blow across her face that knocks her down on to the floor. Stunned, she doesn't make an effort to get up.

Stephen's only remark is, "Where's your modesty woman? Pull your skirt down woman, you are showing Ted all of you that is privately mine."

Ted normally might have enjoyed the view. From the blow Cathy is slow to react. Her pale pink panties are high up on her slender white thighs. Teddy is too stunned by Steve's actions to give further thought to the aphrodisiac scene he is witnessing.

Irate, he yells, "You want to duke it out with somebody, I am here," and he reaches over and lands a tight fist on Steve's jaw. In seconds Steve is down on the floor in the same spot that he was in when Ted and Cathy came in. Lifting the stunned Steve up from the floor, "You fuckin' moron, if you ever hit Cathy again I will whip your arsse so badly you will need to be hospitalized."

Cathy struggles to cover her exposed area and then to get up. A Strong female, she brushes a tear from her cheek but refuses to cry even though her jaw has already begun to swell.

"How do you feel, do you feel like you can drive home?" Ted asks.

"Oh, yes Ted. Get him into my car and I will head home?"

"No way lady, no goddamned way is he going with you! He is going to suffer a long lecture as I berate him while I drive him to your house. If he gives me any shit along the way, I'll stop my car and give him a going over he won't forget in a hurry."

Obviously Steve does not like what he hears. "Don't do this to me Cathy, you know I love you."

"How do I know that you love me? Your actions, you're drinking, your abuse belies your rhetoric. I am just second fiddle in your heart. I have a better chance of knowing your love if I go to fantasy land, pick a daisy and while plucking each petal and canting love me, love me not; maybe I will get my answer."

The fist blow to his head doesn't help to stabilize him. Realizing Steve hasn't regained his equilibrium, Ted rings the service bell and a husky bib-overall warehouse man comes into the room. With his help, they get Steve into Ted's auto.

Chapter seven

Thursday March 2, 1950, Rabbi Alvan Waterman needing a monthly income, arranges a term purchase agreement and sells Ted a large parcel of land on the lake Pembroke. It is land that Phyllis grandfather purchased eighty years ago. At that time he operated a fish and game camp on the lake.

The lot Teddy Sheerin purchases is a thousand feet on the lake front by one hundred feet inland. An excellent ten degree slope from its back edge gives good drainage down to the lake. On one side of the lot, a rustic trickling creek stream is gurgling over small stones all the way to the lake.

The acreage has many trees, whispering pines, birch, but most notable are two, hundred-fifty year old oaks. Although eighty feet apart, their overlapping branches meet and form a huge canopy that Ted plans to take advantage of. He sets his house in between the trees to enjoy the oaks over-lapping tent. The house faces the southwest, thus giving the winter advantage of some sun warmth, but not the direct hot western rays of the summer sun. Due to the fact that the only access to the property is by boat, a mile long dirt road from the Pembroke highway to the lot, must be carve out of the wooded area behind the land that will eventually end at the garage area of the coming building.

As part of the deal, Al offers to help Ted build a five bedroom Swiss style lodge on the site. They agree on the current hourly wage of .75 ¢ per hour. This is a greater pay rate than the average pro- baseball player receives ($1350.00 a year).

To keep the costs low, Alvan will work with Ted on Ted's days off.

Ted, in full uniform, shops for the building supplies at the local lumber and hardware stores. The showing of his uniform usually gets him a price discount.

Anne Nevins, still fulfilling Ted's occasional libido desires, works a labor agreement with her V.A. hospital interns and nurses, plus Ted's *hoi polloi* friends. For those that volunteer to donate their free labor to help build the lodge, each will get two weeks use of the finished chalet for free.

Builder/carpenter John MacDonald and his assistant, supervises six nurses and four interns that volunteer their labor two days a week. Some work in their hospital *scrubs,* others bring work clothes.

Occasionally, a nurse just before going on duty at the hospital, takes off her nurse uniform dress, and works in a girdle and bra. This pisses Teddy because it gets the males that are working that day, to want to work within sight of the scantily clad female and other parts of construction are neglected. Plus, when the rooms are sheet rocked, the door to that room might suddenly close, and female low moans/groans are heard before the door is re-opened. Can this be a possible indication that this location may become a *Sodom & Gomorrah?*

A dirt road is created from the mile away state highway to thirty foot wide concrete drive at the front of the lodge that is a paved parking area in front of the three car garage built under the lodge. A long pier, at the rear of the 15' foot by 30' screened in back porch, extends sixty feet out into the lake. There are two bathrooms set between two of the four 11X12 foot bedrooms. The 20'X20' maple paneled family/living room has a huge fireplace and a long cocktail bar.

An arched passage separates the 12'X16' kitchen from the 12'X16' dining area. Ted's 12' X 12' office faces the front porch and has a trap door under a huge desk that is on casters. Sliding the desk aside, he can lift a trap door and go down into a secret 12' X 12' vault type room next to the garage. The vault has no windows, and is built of bullet proof walls, all high security.

By any ones estimates, this makes a costly construction package.

Upon completion, Labor Day 1950, each of the Blue Haven Lodge working crew, as salary compensation, selects the couple of weeks that they wish the use of the lodge. One worker selects Thanksgiving for family and friends to enjoy. One selects Christmas to enjoy a winter *wonderland at the lake.* Interestingly, the others combine and share their time, giving them extra use, giving them more time to enjoy the summer or winter fun on the lake.

To celebrate the completion, Father Timothy Coughlin blesses the lodge and Ted baptizes the house with the official name of *Blue Haven Lodge,* also officially naming the mile long dirt entry *Blue Haven Lodge Road.* Kegs of beer and ales are donated by the Ballantine brewery and for a Baptism ceremony Ted has a *beer bust* for all the workers. The local *koshe*r deli supplies the food.

All guests are informed that the Lodge is not an open house for visits at any time. They are informed by a posted bulletin on the wall of the front and the back porch entry.

Guest will remember that visits to Blue Haven Lodge will be by invitation only– except on Saint Paddy's Day, Ted's birthday, Fourth of July, Labor Day and the period of Christmas through New Year's Day, at those times it will be open-house for friends. Please respect this notice.

This Labor Day weekend, a new juke box is pounding out jitter-bug as well as romantic melodies. The more imbibing, the more demand for cuddling slow-dance music. While the temperature on the outside is a pleasant seventy-two degrees, inside it is in the nineties from the roaring seven-foot fireplace that is ablaze for effect, not need.

For water skiing and trips to the landing, at the far end of the lake, where the local stores are located, Ted purchases a speed boat from Sears.

South West side of house

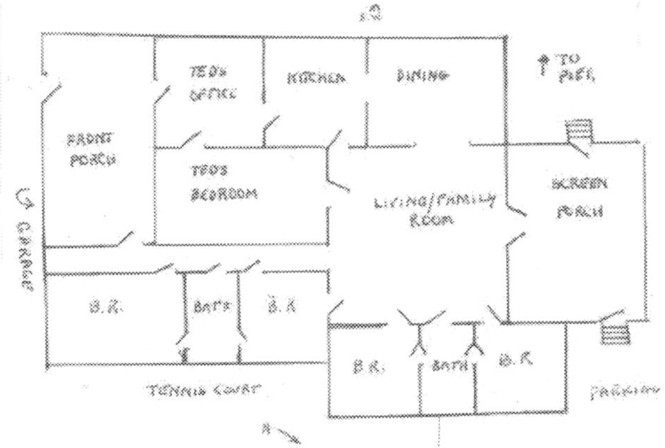

On Thursday September 7, 1950, the day Sears promises delivery, Ted drives to the Lodge. As the saying goes *Time is of the essence,* it could be noted also, *Timing is everything.* His heart increases its beat as he approaches the Lodge and sees Anne's 1950 Chrysler T & C coupe parked there.

In hurried anticipation of what he believes might be the raging estrogen of Anne Marie he rushes into the house. Not seeing her in the living room, following the fragrance of her perfume, he heads to the bedroom. With a heart aching pain in his chest he sees the naked Anne, in an obvious state of carnal oblivion, straddled atop a naked intern who has worked with her during the Lodge construction.

Seeing what he believes is as a violation of a commitment, the only fornicating that Anne would partake of at Blue Haven Lodge will be with Ted, irritates him. She is free to explore additional males at other locations. Ted believes Anne's venal extracurricular activities should be held elsewhere – what he does not know won't bother him. For all that matters, she is eligible to join P.U.M.A. After all she is known to be a perpetual party goer, hard drinking, and a conqueror of handsome men.

He returns to living room and flops on the sofa. Undeterred at the presence of Ted, Anne does not come out of the bedroom until her moans and groans indicate that she has enjoyed her orgasm. Donning a kimono, she strolls into the living room with the slightly open robe exposing her *pecker cavity,* to tantalize Teddy.

Then pretending to ignore him, she goes to the liquor bar, pours her a cognac over ice then sits next to him on the sofa. The fornicating intern, obviously nervous, does not come out of the room. It can only be a guess that he decides not want to confront Ted and exits via the bedroom window.

After a couple of sips, Anne rationalizes, "I never said that I was committed to you Teddy, or you to me. I make no apologies, when I am horny, I follow the theory of when I am not near the male that I want, I will settle for the male that is near."

"You and I had an understanding about sex at Blue Haven Lodge Anne. I knew you were no *vestal virgin,* but at the rate you are *turning tricks,* with your many liaisons, the title whore comes to mind. You are a typical *Tampa gal,* Anne."

Still pissed, he gets up from the sofa, pours a scotch, then goes out and sits on the double swing that hangs from the roof of the back porch. Since not another word is spoken, Anne dresses and leaves. Ted stays on the porch until he is suddenly alert to the arrival of a pickup truck hauling a new speed boat.

Pulling along side of the porch the driver leans out, "Say mister, are you Edward Sheerin?"

"Yeah, you've got the right address. Back your trailer up on the beach along the side of the pier. I'll help you get the boat into the water."

After a few muscle sweating movements, the boat is in the water. "Mr. Sheerin, my name is Fred Banks. Would you like me to give you a few pointers in operating this skiff?"

"I damned sure would Mr. Banks. I never operated an inboard motor this big."

After about thirty minutes of handling the boat at different speeds up and down the lake, Ted suggests, "Let's tie this rig up at the pier and go up on the porch and have a couple of cool beers."

Sitting comfortable while enjoying a cool lake breeze across the porch, Fred comments, "I noticed the flag flying off your porch. Sadly you don't see too many flags flying around here. I think it is a shame that the average American isn't interested in showing *The Colors."*

"You are right in that statement, but wrong in saying *average American.* They should not be called Americans because they just occupy a spot on the U.S. soil and could care less about this country or its future. Only a veteran is fully aware of loyalty to our flag and our country."

"Mr. Sheerin, you sound bitter."

"It's Ted to you, not mister. I am still pissed. I served overseas for a few dollars a month, while the draft dodgers and four F'ers made big dough at home. So fuck them all, I am going to make money anyway I want, be it legal or illegal."

"I am with you on that and I'm not looking for an argument, but I have more reason than that to be pissed. You didn't have to suffer the degrading segregation that I received when at eighteen years of age in 1944; I was drafted into the Navy."

"What do you mean Fred?"

"Since we are on a first name basis Ted, we are going to lose our new found friendship, as fellow veterans, if you try to bull-shit me, or patronize me. Tell it like it is and always be up front is what I say. You know from your experience that colored men like me were segregated, subjected to ethnic subjugation."

"Sorry Fred, I was trying to be diplomatic. That was stupid of me and I sincerely apologize. I must truly admit that I saw segregated black *Tuskegee Airmen* taking flying lessons when I was stationed at twin engine flight training at Freeman Field in Seymour Indiana. I also saw some other Tuskegee men training as for aircraft mechanics when I was stationed in Rantoul, Illinois."

"At Freeman the commissioned Tuskegee Army Air Force officers went on strike for equal access to the officers club. They won out, but some were falsely jailed. I could see from that incident that blacks were mistreated by the *red-neck* base Commander, Col. Robert E. Selway. He was relieved of his command soon after the unjust jailing."

"It is after flight training at Freeman Field that the Tuskegee went on to set all kinds of records. They sunk a Jap destroyer, the only naval vessel ever sunk by a fighter plane using only the planes machine guns. They were nicknamed the *Red tail Angels* because the tail of their P51 Mustang pursuit/fighter planes were painted red. With outside fuel tanks it had a range of 2080 miles at speeds up to 437 mph. Without the outside tanks it could carry two 1000 lb bombs."

"Only after such Tuskegee deeds did the Pentagon realize the importance of Blacks in the military," continues Ted. "Those Mustangs are great fighter planes. Chuck Yeager, flying such a Mustang, once downed 5 German fighters in one mission. The Tuskegee is the only fighter plane group that never lost an escorted bomber to the Luftwaffe during the E.T.O. area of war."

To further emphasis his point, Ted continues, "The first U.S.

bombers they were to protect and escort were the B-24 Liberators whose pilots initially thought they were being punished by having all black fighter escort plane. They soon changed their opinions and praised and saluted the Tuskegees. Even so, they were still segregated until after the war and then Truman banned segregation in the military."

"What about the expression that I am hearing from colored people – 'African/American' or black, Fred?"

"Well that is too encompassing. I am technically Brazilian. I can trace my family back over three hundred years in Brazil. They were educated teachers and literate people. As you can see, I am not black, just a light brown. So technically I'm neither Afro nor black, just a mellow middle."

"Yes, Fred, but you are very tall and so are the Watusi' in Africa. Maybe all eventually can be traced back to Africa."

"So can you be Ted. In Ethiopia they dug up the skeleton of the first female homo sapien and they named her Lucy. She is three million two hundred years old. All Homo sapiens are supposed to be traced back to her, colored or white. That includes you my friend. Doesn't that mean you are also an African/American?"

"You sound like an educated guy. How come you are a delivery-boy at Sears & Roebucks? Why don't you take advantage of the G.I. bill and get some college time in?"

"Ted, to be honest with you, I can say in the hereafter, there will be no *Stars in my crown,* and no Angel feet have trod with my soul. I served time in the brig and I was cashiered out of the Navy for beating up a white southern Navy Ensign. He was in charge of the ship kitchen and tried to tell me how to cook some ham and cabbage. I politely said, 'Sir, I am chief cook of this kitchen, you have no large scale cooking experience, so please sir, leave the cooking to me."

"He shoved me against the hot stove and yelled, 'Nigga, don't you ever sass me do you hear'?"

"My ass was burnt from the shove against the hot stove. I pushed him backwards so I could get away from the stove. He fell down from my push, then got up, says he is going to give a Nigga a lesson. When he swung at me I cold cocked him with one punch. You know the Navy, for that I did brig time. So with a *dishonorable* I am not eligible for the

G. I. Bill or any good paying job. Sears is pretty good, with my record; no one else will hire me."

"You sure have me thinking, Fred. Do you know anything about me?"

"More than you think I would know, Ted. I lived and worked in the grocery store at the corner of Center and Green Street just a block from the police station. I used to see you on the motorcycle and watch you when you were going into the bookie joint. I mean not insults but I wondered how you could be involved in so many illegal ventures, as they say."

"That kind of talk can cause you and me to have problems Freddy."

"That talk stays with me. Damit Ted you want me to be truthful with you and I am doing so. Do you want me to lie and say I don't know anything? Let's face it, you are implying that some work you do may not be not kosher. I just want you to know that I can keep my mouth shut. I was placing a bet in the bookie joint one day when you came in, with full uniform on, and they handed you an envelope. I just want you to know that I didn't give a rat's ass then and won't now. Keep in mind, later on, my knowledge of that territory may come in handy for you?"

"Touché Freddy, you are right, be truthful with me always. Okay smart arsse, if you know all of that, legal and illegal, do you want to supplement your income by working with me?"

"You damn right, I do. When do I start?"

"Freddy, you realize that working with me, as the saying goes, is *until death do us part?*"

"I understand thoroughly Ted. When do I start?"

"You are on my payroll as of this moment. Now don't strain my brain any further, let me fill your glass again," he teases as he pours for his new protégé. The rest of the afternoon is spent comparing war stories and they finished their third beer before parting.

Pilots of the 332nd Fighter Group, "Tuskegee Airmen," the elite, all-African American 332nd Fighter Group at Ramitelli, Italy., from left to right, Lt. Dempsey W. Morgran, Lt. Carroll S. Woods, Lt. Robert H. Nelron, Jr., Capt. Andrew D. Turner, and Lt. Clarence P. Lester. (U.S. Air Force photo)

P51 used by the Tuskegee

Chapter eight

U. S. Army First Lieutenant Stanley Sheerin is transferred from the Belfast Ireland Military hospital on Tuesday August 6, 1946 and sent to the Veterans Hospital in Boston for further physical and psychological treatments. There is a delay on the *first come first served* need and it is not until Monday July 21, 1947, before the surgeons begin the first of four major operations necessary for the reconstruction of Stanley's pelvic area.

By this time Stanley still in the V. A. Hospital, is so depressed that he refuses to see any visitor, not even his brother Teddy. Fortunately for Stanley, Anne Nevins is the head nurse in the same ward as Stan is a patient.

"My name is Anne Nevins; as head nurse, you are one of the patients under my care. Your name Sheerin is quite familiar to me, are you kin to a Teddy Sheerin?"

"Small world nurse Nevins. Ted happens to be my kid brother."

During the next two weeks, Anne and Stanley have many friendly conversations. Sometimes it is just tongue wagging palaver, other times, serious discussions. On occasions when Stan would grow silent, Anne would be in a monologue. In any event, these tension relieving dialogues bond nurse and patient, a medicinal aid for the patient.

It becomes most obvious when Stan is persuaded by Anne, to welcome a visit of his brother Ted. Moreover after his fourth pelvic operation on Thursday January 28, 1949, Anne takes the steps and phones Ted for a conference.

"Don't get your balls in a lather Teddy. This call is not about us,

I am asking you to come to this V. A. Hospital because your brother has agreed that he misses you. There will be no self pity on Stan's part to prevent a get-to-gether. As you can imagine, the hospital's biggest problem with Stanley, is psychological. Losing his genitalia at such a young age is something so devastating; he cannot handle it easily."

"He is in severe need of physical rehabilitation, and the painful operations he will have to endure will have been in vain if we cannot get him to exercise and strengthen the muscles of that area of his body. There is a slim possibility that with your encouragement, he will attend the physical therapy sessions."

"Anne, as you know, I have attempted to visit Stan on many occasions and he refuses to see me. I will do anything to help my big brother, just get me into see him."

"How about coming out right now Teddy?"

"You're on Anne. I'll head out right away."

Entering the ward where Stan is in the fifth bed on the right, Ted Approaches his sleeping brother, sits down on a chair beside the bed and waits. Anne comes along side the bed, nods at Teddy bares the upper arm of Stanley, and injects a shot, then turning to Ted, "Glad to see you here. The doctor thought that a small tranquilizer might calm your brother at this meeting."

The sharp sting of the injection wakes Stanley. He has been asleep on his left side with his back to Ted. He rolls onto his back looking up toward the ceiling, and then becomes alert to the fact that someonc is sitting on a chair near his bed.

Surprising to all the patients around him, as well as the staff, Stanley just turns toward Ted, "Hi kid, *conas ata tu*? Ta me go maith. What brings you here?"

Caught off guard by the greeting, Ted stammers, "*Ta me go maith*, big Bro, just doin' great."

(The following is spoken in Gaelic between the brothers because Ted does not want to embarrass Stanley with Anne and the doctors listening.) :

"Stanley we never bull shitted each other at any time in our life. Don't change our relationship by handing me bullshit. You know that I have been here a half dozen times and you refused to see me. It didn't take a call from Anne to get me here. Me –, not only am I your brother, but the best pal you

ever had. Therefore, I know that you have had your fuckin' life screwed up. I know that you have a right to have a chip, no – a log—on your shoulders, but play it straight with me. No bullshit – okay? You are pulling a fuckin' cop-out, no guts."

"Kid, you haven't change a goddamn bit. You still shoot straight from the shoulder, I love you for it, but remember it is a two way street. Play straight with me, and it will be like old times. Now let's start. I see that the doctor and a nurse came with you, which is unusual, so why are they here with you?"

"You're sharp, Bro, no bullshit from me. They are worried and upset at your lack of determination to get back on your feet. I want you well. You refuse therapy and without it your muscles are going to debilitate and you are going to end up a sickly 90 pound bed ridden weakling. They wanted me to try to persuade you to take therapy."

"Thanks for being up front, Teddy. I don't give a damn what they think. I don't want sympathy, nor pity, I have no desire to live the life of a crippled eunuch with a urinary bag attachment. Thus I have no desire to get well. Dad has been in here several times with the same old pitch as yours."

"Bullshit, I would be lying to you if I said that I understand because it is not me in that bed. I can only try to get you to be practical. Get real! Your life is not over; you're in a stage of self pity. You are being melancholic. The doctors say they can get you back on your feet, enjoying life without the sex part. Goddamn it Stanley, the only difference in your life is that you get rid of that tube and bag and you sit down to pee. So what if you can no longer play with your pecker. Eventually we all have our pecker change from a penetrating rod to a water spout, but we don't give up living. I know, yes I know, – it easy for me to say, but you aren't the only one giving up sex at your age. Other Grunts have had that area become non-workable. In addition, young priest give up sex for the privilege of following Jesus, which reminds me, take this crucifix that I have been wearing. When you want to understand pain, rub the face of the crucifix. You will feel the outline of the one that suffered great pain."

"That will remind you of how he suffered the horrible pain of spikes driven through his hands and feet. A deep wound in his side, and forced to wear a crown of long, piercing, pointed thorns. (Paliurus spina-christi). Imagine that scene of suffering and ask him to help you in your suffering."

Things grow quiet and oddly, both men reach for cigarettes, not for its pleasure alone, but to break the tension that has arisen. The arrival of the supper tray allows the subject to be temporarily dropped and small talk in English to begin while Stan picks at the evening meal. Finishing up, Stan lights the inevitable meal ending cigarette.

Oddly, Stanley only takes a couple of drags then snuffs out his cigarette, then in a somber pensive mood. "Teddy, you have always been the brains of the family. While this hospital is a good place for wounded vets, it is no Elysium. I will agree to take the therapy program starting next week, and I will take up your offer of staying with you after I get well."

"Well bro, we will then be able to do things like a hockey match, baseball game or just getting drunk together. I want you *slan abhale.*"

"Teddy if I am that well the first place of pleasure for me will be a visit to Scollay Square and the hurly, burly, Old Howard theatre. It may be the grimy grotto of the bump and grind and I want to watch those barely draped broads twirl their *titty* tassels. Plus see some of the burlesque comedians like Abbot and Costello, and the Marx Brothers, do their thing."

Highly elated, Ted bends over, and gives his Bro a very strong masculine embrace. With a parting, "*Slan agiv, and a slan go foil,*" he leaves. Stanley smiles, but Anne's curiosity gets the better of her. Now waiting at the exit, she pulls Teddy aside, "What was all that Gaelic gibberish about?"

"I was wishing him well and encouraging him to try the therapy," he lied.

Anne can't resist being her natural self. She reaches over and strokes Teddy at his crotch, "You can give Stanley all that bull-shit about no sex, but you know damned well, you'd rather die than to go without dipping your pecker Teddy boy."

After Ted leaves the ward, Stan holds the gold crucifix up in front of himself and gazes at the man on the cross, and then kisses it and silently places it under his pillow.

PM

Chapter nine

Friday September 8, 1950, Ted at home in Blue Haven, answers a telephone ring. "Ted, this is Alvan, I've got a business proposition for us. If after I explain it you are not interested, we will forget it."

"Well Al, if it doesn't take much cash, I'll listen. Remember, I just finished building this lake property and I am tight for cash."

Given the information Ted shows interest. "How about giving me directions and I'll head there at once and get the first hand details from you?"

Given directions, and about a half hour later, Ted and Fred are having a drink at Callahan's bar while Alvan explains the details. "This guy, a fella named Johnny Di Birtallo, owns a used car lot called Freeport Motors. It is in the 1200 block of Dorchester Avenue at the corner of Freeport Street. He has been drafted for the conflict in Korea, and needs to sell the place. His terms are good, five G's down, and five percent of the profit each month until when, and if, he comes back from the war. Then if you want he will buy it back. "

"Jesus Christ Al, I don't know shit about buying cars."

"But I do know something about buying them Teddy. You know that I have dabbled in buying and selling used cars for years. I will go to the new car dealers and bid on the cars they take in trade. They usually want to sell fast any car taken in trade that is over three or four years old. They make a package deal of four or five cars for any used car buyer to bid on. I even have the manager of Fuller's Packard dealership *in my wallet*. He will phone me when he has a bunch of used cars he wants to sell. In addition, other new car dealers will be calling us. I will see that we have more than enough cars to sell."

Freddy interrupts, "Ted, I know where Freeport Motors is on Dorchester Avenue. I can help you. For a while I worked in the car lot across the street from it, called Applebaum's Used Cars. I can train whoever runs your place, in the basics."

Ted becomes more interested. Getting to the car lot they are introduced to a long side-burned heavy set fellow about 5'9" of dark complexion, "Hi, I am Giovanni di Birtallo, but everybody calls me Johnny."

"Please to meet you, I am Edward Sheerin, but everyone calls me Teddy. This is my friend Fred Banks. Mind if we look at the equipment and cars on the lot?"

"Hell no, be my guest, I will wait for you in the office."

After about a thirty minute analysis Ted enters the office, "I've got a question for you Johnny. How come it is only five G's down and you have over thirty cars on the lot? Alvan estimates those cars at being worth fifteen to twenty-five big ones."

"Alvan is close, it is about twenty three thousand, and they are being floor planned. You would be buying the business, the land, and the buildings, not those cars."

"To a point we did understand that, but we thought that just included a few clunkers. However when we saw all those cars, we knew they could not be included. Will the floor planner go along with us taking over?"

"I have already spoken to the floor plan guy. When I told him who you were, he said he knew of you and yes he would floor plan for you also. He also suggested that in your case he would lower his interest rate on the floor plan down from eighteen percent to eight percent. I don't know why that fucka is so generous to you and not to me, other than you being a cop that may be an advantage to him later. However, being that you're a cop, this may be a problem in your buying this place."

"Why and who the hell is the floor planner that we are talking about Johnny?"

"We are talking about Thomas *Jazz* Kelley from Southie. Ever hear of him?"

"God damned right I have heard of Kelley. He's the Mik boss appointed by the Mafia Syndicate boss man Don Raymond, *Il Patrone Patriarca,* to run the greater Boston syndicate gambling area. Raymond has control of everything above the Connecticut River; this gives him the New England branch of the Mafia syndicate. He has 150 members and bout 200 associates at his command."

"I and also Johnny knows that the Italian branch of Patriarca's Boston visceral operations is being run haphazardly, mostly with emotion rather than logic. Since the Irish outnumber the Italians by three to one, Raymond decided to groom a Southie Irish *up and coming*, petty gangster to take over the greater Boston area. With Jazz brother John J. *J.J.* Kelley being a contract killer for Raymond, it is easy for Patriarca to make the decision to go with Thomas Jazz Kelley from South Boston and give birth to an Irish Mafia."

"Ted, also as part of the *Jazz* Kelley financial floor plan, I also run a profitable *banking* operation here for him. The local *nigga pool bookies* bring their cash here and we hold it for Kelley's runner to collect once a week. Before I give the cash to the Jazz runner I get to keep 10%."

(P.O.V.) In the1930's a Harlem negro group started a *penny ante* gambling racket. Bettors would put a nickel, dime or quarter on three to four numbers. There are 999 possible winning connections. The payoff is 600 to one. If their numbers won, the bettors would get from fifty dollars to six hundred depending how much they would initially bet. The winning numbers are selected, by the pool operators, from the 1st, 2nd, 3rd place winner payoff on the race track tote board. Later on to be politically correct the word *nigga* was dropped and *number pool* is currently used.

"You mean that you do not actually run a booking joint for the nigga pool here you just act as a bank?"

"Yes Ted, I don't have anything to do with the numbers running, but I do hold the collection money. Jazz needs a place for his *bookies* to put their cash collections every day. As far as the law goes there is no illegal activity going on here."

"That is bull-shit Johnny, while it is damned difficult to make a pinch because there are no actual collections from the individual bettor; it is still an illegal operation. However the police would have a hard time getting enough evidence to make an arrest. How does all this illegality fit with you Alvan?""

"As far as I am concerned it is okay with me as an additional source of revenue for Freeport Motors. How does it sit with you Teddy?"

Ted lights a Chesterfield then, after a couple of drags, pours out a cloud of smoke and ends his moments of silence. "If it meets with your approval Alvan, I will go along with it. After all, as partners, we want the business to make a profit for us, don't we?"

Alvan and Freddy put their heads together then turn to Ted. "Can 'Jazz' association with Freeport Motors be a problem for us Teddy?"

While Alvan may have less knowledge of all of Teddy's illegalities, surely Freddy is quite aware of Ted's past corruptions and is aware of what Ted's reply could be.

"Shit, no. This can be an asset to us. With Mister Kelley's connections, and protection, no police are going to bother the place and Kelley evidently knows me. So as long as we play square with him, he will love to do business with us. But if you have such a good deal Johnny, why do you want to sell this place?"

"Well Teddy, I have to sell this place because I have been drafted. I am damn sure I will be shipped to Korea as soon as I finish basic training."

"How can you be sure of that?" asks Ted.

"I can, because President Truman goofed. The past June 30, he sent only two divisions of green U.S. troops to fight seasoned *Commie troops.* He under estimated the North Koreans. By last month it was a full scale war with four thousand G.I.'s killed, fourteen thousand wounded. Therefore, they need new troop replacements and I will be one of those that are needed. I'll make a lousy soldier; I couldn't hit a bull in the ass with a banjo."

After a bit of minor questioning and then examining the ledgers, an agreement is signed by all three. With that Johnny pulls a bottle of Chianti from a cabinet, and pours three glasses, *"Buona fortuna."*

Ted raises his glass, "*Slainte.*" While not to be outdone, Alvan raises his glass to, "*Shalom.*" His response gets a chuckle from all.

Getting comfortable, small get acquainted talks begin. "I guess you two guys were in the last war?" questions Johnny. "Have you any advice to give this new recruit?"

"No one can give a recruit such advice, it is a must learn from the *experience only* school. Don't you think so Ted?"

"As we used to say in the service, *hubba, hubba big Al,* I damn sure do agree. There are okay times and there are scary times. I was most scared, no one could have advised me on what I should do, when the first time I faced a Jap's machine gun fire. I was scared shitless. I was near enough to a Jap Zero to see the eyes of the pilot. I often wonder why Kamikaze pilots bothered to wear a helmet. To this day I sometimes wake up in cold sweat when in nightmares I see that red meatball emblem that was painted on the side of those Jap Zeros."

Both men are now in a war-time reminiscence mode. "We all experienced that nervous feeling at some time. In '44 only my laundry man would be able to tell you how nervous I became. On Christmas Eve 1944 our infantry outfit was close to Bastogne. We had captured about four hundred and fifty German Wehrmacht soldiers and had limited ability to guard and feed them," Alvan explains.

"Our troops had been on canned rations and we suddenly came upon and abandoned farm with hundreds of chickens scrounging about. Two local Belgium women offered to cook a bunch of the chickens in exchange for us allowing them to take a dozen for themselves."

"The Christian soldiers felt this was a timely way to celebrate the feast of Jesus and to enjoy their religious Christmas Holiday. Their Chaplain set up an altar in the property's huge barn and said Mass. After Mass, cooked chickens, carrots, and potatoes were served to our men. The captured Germans were normally guarded by at least twelve of our soldiers but in order for all of the Christian G.I.'s to enjoy Mass and eat a Christmas Eve Dinner, I volunteered, with another Jewish soldier, to guard the prisoners," details Alvan.

"It was psychological warfare at its best, us two soldiers replacing twelve. It was announced to the German prisoners that two very nervous Jewish soldiers, with machine guns at ready, would be the prisoner guards. The highest ranking German prisoner there was a Captain Fritz Stauffenberg, a *yutz,* who came to our Colonel Plunkett to relay his fears of possible Jewish reprisal."

"Sir, *scuttle- butt* has it that you are planning to put my men in harm's way by having them guarded by machine gun armed Jews. How can you assure me that my troops will not be in danger of a Jewish retaliation?"

"That is a very interesting remark on your part Captain Stauffenberg. You say Jewish retaliation? Are you now admitting that the Jews have a good reason to retaliate with a bit of *quid pro quo,* against the German military? I can assure you Captain; my troops are not like your German soldiers, they do not indiscrimately kill. If they did want to retaliate, you would have to be concerned about all my troops, not just the Jews. Your men were participants in the murder of twenty thousand G.I. prisoners last month. Now get your Nazi lard-arsse out of here and sweat, while my troops enjoy a little Christmas time cheer." (19,000 Americans were killed in the six weeks *Battle of the Bulge at Bastogne.*)

"Shit, did anyone think that could have been risky for you and the other Jewish G.I.? It could have been a time that the Huns could have tried to overcome you Al?"

"I thought so at the time, Ted, and worried about it. In addition, I wanted to further tantalize them so I put a German gold *Star of David* amulet on my uniform so they could see it. However, it seems that the Nazi P.O.W.'s were glad they were out of the fighting and the camp treatment was better than facing a bullet. Moreover, the weather was sub-freezing, our winter uniforms had not reached us, and the *krauts* wore heavy winter gear. They were lucky we didn't take their protective winter overcoats from them to keep us warm."

"Guys, I was so damned scared I made a pledge to my *Goel.* If I came out of this alive, and also get the opportunity to visit Paris, I would follow kosher rule and become a strict *sabbatarian.* I never again would work, or smoke my daily cigar, on the Shabbat, and I began wearing a yarmulke under my helmet. After the war I became more Orthodox, even to living in a *diasporas* area, like Mattapan."

"I'll donate a bit of trivia to our conversation. Did you know that on our one dollar bill the thirteen colonies are shown as stars and in the shape of the *Star of David*? It was ordered there by George Washington, to honor a Philadelphia Jew name Hayim Solomon who saved the Continental Army by giving money to continue the fight against the Brits. He died a pauper as the results," continues Alvan.

"Since you are being historic, let me add to the trivia," comments Ted. "The year before that Christmas, while we are in battles that cost hundreds of Americans lives, John L. Lewis, the President of the United Mine Workers Union, pulls a strike of the coal miners from Friday May 1, 1943 to Nov. 1, 1943, for higher wages."

"This was at the time of the extreme need of coal for the war effort. His Union's idea was *Fuck the War Effort,* and the dying service men, which make only $30.00 a month; Lewis wants higher wages for the miners. They were making more wages in a week than most of the G.I.'s were making in two months. We felt he was a traitor."

Due to the fact that Alvan's Congregation frowns on their Rabbi being involved in owning a used car sales lot and because regulations forbid a Boston policeman to have a license to sell used cars, it is agreed that the City of Boston license to sell used cars will be issued in Eamon Sheerin's name. Having some experience at a used car lot, Fred Banks will help out at the car lot until Eamon and Alvan can become adjusted to their task.

Salesman Arnie, Rabbi Alvan Waterman, and Teddy Sheerin

Chapter ten

Stanley is released from the hospital on Tuesday August 8, 1950 and becomes a V.A. outpatient requiring physical therapy twice a week. He begins work repairing and maintaining the autos at Freeport Motors, while living with Ted.

The idiosyncrasy of wars – and its physiological temperamental peculiarities, challenges the credulity of many war veterans. It is further strained when they hear of Stanley's suffering and the *feather bed* manner of Johnny di Birtallo's enlistment.

Since Johnny is in the Army, veterans like Ted, Alvan, Stanley and Freddy now follow the news accounts of what is commonly referred to as the Korean War, it is never officially declared a war. The Koreans refer to it as *a Jogug* (Police Actions). The U.S. calls it the Korean Conflict.

Like every conflict, *goof-ups* occur. The latest occurs in September of 1950. Mortar crews have a habit of giving their mortars a pet name. In Korea the U.S. forces named theirs *Little tootsie roll and Big tootsie roll.* Running low on ammo for the mortars they send orders to Di Birtallo's Army ordnance warehouse in Japan to send ammo for *Little and Big Tootsie Roll.* The ammo came back – ten cases of Tootsie rolls.

Late October 1950, Mac Arthur has succeeded at invading far into North Korean. Then the *Chinks* swarm across their border into North Korea with 225,000 experienced army troops. Then in November they send two additional divisions, along with some Russian Military advisors, to help the North Koreans invade the South Korea held area, causing the U.S. / U.N. troops to retreat below the 38th parallel.

Draftee *Johnny di* wonders if Truman gives a damn about the loss of American lives. Mac Arthur asks President Truman to allow an atomic bomb attack on the area of North Korea that the Chinese are based. Cowardly, Truman refuses, if he just threatens to do such a bombing, China who has no such a weapon, will fear tremendous loss of Chinese troops, and thus withdraw their troops from Korea. That will save thousands of American lives. Because of Truman not using this potential threat North Korea will be a problem to the world for decades to come.

"During WW2 the U.S. was an ally of China Nationalist, but the commies beat them. So maybe the commie *Chinks* wanted to enter the fight against us? Why should there be any compassion for the Chinese that come to kill, capture, torture, and maim our soldiers? In addition, they send any captured G.I.'s to prisons in Russia, and three years ago the Ruskies were our allies."

"Well Teddy, Truman was part of the corruption following the *Teapot Dome* scandal. His election allowed four more years of inaction against the crime syndicates and the corruption in the I.R.S. You guys forget that the U.S. bleeding hearts would rather that our boys suffer and die than to threaten to use the atomic bomb to instantly end the conflict. With these thoughts in mind I can understand why Johnny decides he is going to take good care of himself and fuck America and its bleeding hearts," explains Freddy.

In the meantime, while most of the *Grunts* are enduring severe bone freezing cold, lack of, hot meals, clean clothes, supplies, insufficient ammo from the nonchalant American arms manufacturers, and atrocious mind damaging conflicts, Johnny finagles a soft, safe berth in a supply depot at the port city of Pusan far south of the conflict.

In less than three years, with the suave of a '*snake oil seller*', he bribes for himself the rank of Staff Sergeant. He is in charge of all military supplies from condoms to tanks, whiskeys to penicillin, aspirin to morphine, and Jeeps to boats.

Anything that any of the Military *Brass* wants *–or anyone* else with cash wants to purchase. Such material control makes him a most powerful G.I. in the U.S. Army. Any person's credulity is strained when they compare what happened to Stanley vs what happens in the life of Giovanni *Johnny* di Birtallo.

With the cessation of hostilities, the port of Pusan becomes the entry of hashish and scag into South Korea for distribution through-out that part of the world. Johnny has learned that money is his Aladdin's lamp when he makes these lucrative deals for contraband.

It is a sad thing when a man betrays his oath for monetary gain; moreover, all rules are eroded by filthy lucre

To quote from the bible: *A feast is made for laughter, and wine maketh merry: but money answerth all things.* Ecclesiastes 10:1

Chapter eleven

Shortly after midnight Thanksgiving November 23, 1950 Ted has finished his tour of police duty and upon entering his apartment he is greeted with the constant ring of his telephone. Figuring it might be the precinct wanting him to come back to the station for an emergency fill-in tour of duty, he lets it ring.

Normally the precinct does keep calling, but they will let it ring five times then hang up and redial every fifteen minutes. After five minutes more of the noisy ringing, he gives in. It might be Jazz trying to get a hold of him, so it becomes the moment to find out who the goddam hell is so persistent. His voice indicating that he is grudgingly giving in to the harassing ring of the telephone, and in almost a shout yells, "Yeah, who the hell is on this line?"

"I am so sorry Ted, I have no one to turn to, and I am hurt," comes Cathy's sobbing voice.

"Jesus Christ Cathy, I did not realize it was you on the phone. What happened? Is it Steve?"

"Yes Ted. I am just a block away from your apartment, I am cold and in pain. May I please come over to you?"

"Certainly, most certainly, come over. Do you want me to come and get you?"

"No, I have my car. I will be right over."

Ted is standing at his apartment open door as Cathy comes up the steps. She is disheveled, hair rumpled, blood on her blouse, red bruise marks on her face. With one hand at her breast level and the other lower down, she is modestly attempting to hold together her torn dress. Had

Ted not been alert, she would have crumbled at his feet, but wisely, he is prepared for such a happening and catches the fainting colleen before she hits the floor. He lifts the petite female, and carries her to the bed. While putting her down, the torn dress separates and a split bra exposes a small cut on her bare left breast. There is no underwear and there is an equal size bloody cut on the lowest part of her tummy close to the pubic hair line.

Removing the torn garments, he begins to attend to her deeply scratched thighs that are still bleeding. Areas of dried blood and semen require warm soap and water, then peroxide, mercurochrome and bandaging. While he is covering her with the bed sheet she awakes from her faint. Slowly she becomes aware of the bandaging and her nudity.

Taking Ted's hand she kisses it and brushes it across her cheek. "I am so embarrassed but you are so wonderful Teddy. I owe you so much."

"You owe me nothing Cathy; you know how I have always felt about you. Now tell me what happened between you two."

"Stephen had been to the Boston College football game with some of his drinking buddies, and they brought him home drunk. I asked them where his car was. They said he insisted on driving and they were following him home to be sure he got there safely. On the way he plowed into elevator train steel upright and totaled the car."

"Did the cops come?"

"Yes, but when they found out he was a Boston cop, they made a report that the car was a stolen vehicle and the culprit, that was driving it, got away."

"I began yelling at him about his drinking and his abuse, and he knocked me down onto the floor. I got up, grabbed a suitcase, and began packing. He grabbed the suitcase and swung it at me, and began yelling that I had nowhere to go except to Lawrence Cameron, my boss. He accused me of having sex with Mr. Cameron, honestly Ted that never happened. I have never had any man but Stephen."

"I believe you Cathy, Steve is a jerk; go on, what happened?"

"He then threw me down on the bed and grabbed a pair of scissors from the side table and cut and tore my dress from the bottom to the top. Then he cut my bra into pieces, and the scissors caused those cuts on me.

She then bursts into a cascade of tears. The tears eventually subsiding, she continues, “He then painfully scratched my thighs as he ripped my panties off and then it was not love making, it was, degrading animalistic sex.”

Cathy’s body begins shivering, not from the room temperature; it is an emotional reaction to the trauma. Ted reaches over to the dresser and removes a pair of pajamas. “These may be a little baggy but they will be warmer and more comfortable.”

Attempting to don the pajama bottoms, she slips down onto the floor. “Oh God, I sure am hurting. Please help me.”

It is paradoxical feeling for Ted. Removing her torn clothing, and for the first time, viewing her lethargic heavenly body, fascinated him, however, now he is viewing a full motion *Aphrodite*. In spite of Cathy’s unrealized tease, Teddy tries to maintain some phase of modesty for Cathy as he helps her put the pajama bottoms on. Resisting a desire to kiss her bare breasts, her further assists her donning the pajama top but he is noticeable slow with buttoning.

Cathy calms down a bit, “Teddy would you get me a couple of aspirin please?”

“I’ll do better than that, I’ll get the aspirins and Cognac and we then can change the subject to a calmer theme as we sip our drinks.”

After helping her to lie down, he retrieves Cognac and two aspirins.

“This might help you sleep. However, in the morning you will have to make some plans, because it is time that you realize that the romance is over. Try to face the reality that Steve is an alcoholic and his brutality is becoming dangerous to you. You need to face the fact that your destiny of heavenly stars is no longer a reality. Stop looking to the stars and look to yourself and your future.”

“Ted, please don’t misunderstand me. Right now I am torn between the thin line of love and hate. I am still hopeful that he will one day realize he is killing my love for him. I still remember our youth and what used to be our great passionate love for each other.”

“Cathy it is time that you examine the beginning, middle and the end, the whole truth. You are living in a dream world and it is now time for you to have a reality check. Steve has become a mean inconsiderate individual. He will not change back to the nice guy he once was.”

"I know you are right Ted, but it is my oxymoron. While I love and adore him, I am also scared to death of what Stephen will do if he finds me here with you."

"That will be solved in the morning. I am going to take you to my lodge in Pembroke. You will be safer there for sure. I have never mentioned this place to anyone at the precinct, so no one on the force knows about it, including Steve."

"That will be wonderful Teddy, but for now, please, sleep here with me; I don't want to be alone right now."

What a dilemma for Ted. He has never slept with a woman that he did not fuck. He is still in a stage of arousal from seeing her nudity. Will he be able to tell the devil to be gone? However, feeling a bit of empathy, he will respect her innocent naïve wishes.

In the morning, after a light breakfast, Ted asks, "Do you feel up to driving to Pembroke, it's about forty miles?"

"I may not feel like it, but I damn well know that I will feel safer there, so – the sooner the better."

On the drive down to the lake, while keeping his eye on his rear view mirror as Cathy follows, Ted is listening to the radio commentator Lowell Thomas in his weekly broadcast. Some of his statistics pertains to present company.

The information is interesting to Teddy as Lowell notes that the population of the United States is 150,697,361 and the annual income average is $3319. As far as divorces are concerned, Cathy will be one of 385,000 divorces this year. Comparing himself with Lowell's facts, far as Ted's annual income is concerned, at $.75 per hour, Ted is glad that he is not dependent on his annual income of $2224.00. Such a measly fund would surely cramp his life style.

Finally at, and settled in, at Blue Haven Lodge, Ted shows Cathy around the house, and the bedroom she will use. "I will have to get us some groceries. The stores are at the other end of the lake. It is a long way around by auto, so I use the boat. I'll be gone for about an hour, just make yourself at home."

"Oh, let me go with you, I'd love to feel the breeze of a boat ride."

"Are you sure you are up to it?"

"Yes, I do. Moreover I can't be wearing your shirts, underwear, and pants forever. I need to shop for some dresses, lingerie, and other female stuff. That is if you will cash one of my checks. I don't want to use a check at these stores, somehow Stephen could find out where I am."

"We'll use one of my checks and I will cash your check at my bank in Jamaica Plain. I don't give a damn if Steve finds out that I am in touch with you."

Returning from shopping Ted pours two Cognac and brings them to the bedroom where Cathy has shed the clothing that he loaned her and is preparing to don bra and panties. Ted a bit startled, "Jesus Cathy, I am sorry for barging in; I didn't realize that you would be putting on the new bought stuff right away. I'll put your drink on the dresser and leave."

"Teddy, don't make a hypocrite out of me. You have not only seen me nude, washed my body and I still can feel your warm hands that touched me. Ted, you have been wonderful. The only thing I can offer in payment is for you to come here and kiss me."

Ted has always wondered how it would feel to have her full warm lips against his lips or other parts of his body, and he embraces her nude frame excitedly. Is it her plan to further tantalize Ted, or is she not aware that she has become a tease?

His tight embrace alerts her to the fact that she has cruelly repaid this wonderful friend with a form of sexual torture in return for his tender care. Hesitatingly she gentle pushes him away. Having in the past seen Steve's irritation at her stimulation then *I've got a headache* mode, she realizes this was not fair on her part. After all she caused Teddy's arousal; she should be fair and follow it through. A clinical observation would conclude that a man is turned on by visual and woman by emotional, thus the pattern is set for a logical conclusion on the part of each.

As Ted turns away from her, she reaches out and takes his arm. Pulling him close she gently strokes the front of his pants. "It isn't fair that you were tantalized with my body while cleaning me. I know that you are a man that enjoys sex and your erection indicates you want it from me."

She slides his pants zipper down, drops his pants and boxer shots, falls to her knees and encompasses her warm moist lips with oral copulation until his extremity has experienced rapturous, ecstatic satisfaction. Typical female domination of the male species, yet if logic is to prevail, why would she want to have sex with another man after being raped by her husband. No man will ever understand only she knows exactly what she is doing. Was it a payment for what Ted had done for her or was it a combination of that and a feeling of revenge against Stephen? In any case the oxy-moronic self-contradicting female mind allows Cathy to give Ted a bit of oral sex and leaving him to wonder if she will allow him the pleasure of further sexual activity with her.

After he finishes his tour of duty at midnight Saturday he heads down to the lake. When he comes in the lodge, Cathy is sitting up in bed, reading a National Geographic. On the night stand is a bottle of *Grand Marnier*. With a smile she lifts her glass as though a salute to Ted. "I hope you don't mind, after all you did tell me to make myself at home."

"Not at all, I am sure glad to see your spirits are up and that I can see that lovely smile once more."

"Teddy, I am only strong when I am leaning on your shoulders."

"Cathy, you will always be able to come to me for support. I would love to take your hand and lead you to Paradise."

"For now, this is Paradise and reality. However, since we did not buy me a nightie when we went shopping, I am still using your pajamas, and I like it."

"I think you look cute in them. If you need there, are more pairs in the dresser. What have you been doing while I have been gone?"

"I phoned Mr. Cameron, explained what has happened and asked him to file divorce papers on Stephen. He told me to take a couple of weeks off and stay here so that Stephen will not be able to find me until after he is served the papers."

"Cameron sounds like an okay guy, you are lucky."

"He is a great guy, but don't misinterpret that. I never even kissed the man let alone have any form of sexual contact."

"Now hold on little one, I believed you the first time you said that. You do not have to explain anything to me."

"Maybe not Ted, but men seem to jump to conclusions that can be wrong, and I do respect your opinion. However, enough of that, would you like me to get you a sandwich or something?"

"No thanks I had a snack about eleven and I will just mix me a drink and relax."

"Put your jammys on and bring your drink in here and let's talk about any – this or that's."

She does most of the talking and finally gets sleepy. Ted decides to get off the bed and go to his bedroom. His movements cause Cathy to turn on her side, waking up she pulls Ted's arm close. "Stay with me, please. I want to feel your protection and strength beside me."

During the night, Cathy tosses and turns often. Occasional loud moans come from her as night mares of Steve's attacks reoccur. On one such turn, still sound asleep, she backs into Ted. As his erection indicates, he is only human, a nocturnal emission occurs. Ted jumps out of the bed, goes to the bathroom, showers, puts on clean pajamas, and then goes to his bedroom.

The next morning Cathy brings a cup of coffee to wake Ted. Sitting up to drink it, she climbs under the covers and snuggles up close to him. "Ted, I am embarrassed by my actions last night. I did not realize what happened until you went to the shower. I guess I am always explaining, but I am not a tease. I guess I just did in my sleep what I usually do when in bed with Stephen. It wasn't fair to you what happened."

"Well to be truthful, I did not plan that erection, it just happened. While I am a horny guy, I would never make the first move on you."

"Ted, I know you wouldn't, you're not the type to do something without the female indicating it was her desire also. After all I have had enough sex as a married woman, to be an expert at enjoying and bringing enjoyment to a man. Multiply fifty two weeks by three to four times a week in the first year of my marriage and it is well over several hundred times. That is enough of a sexual experience to understand what happened to you last night, and right now I am indicating my desire."

Taking Ted's coffee cup from his hand, she places it on the side table and embraces him with a long soulful kiss, then reaches down to his crotch. "That indicates to me that you are ready. While I thrilled you last night I want you to know, that I think you are a fantastic guy and I am yours for whatever you wish; but I want you to thrill me – so lead me to what will thrill us both."

It is no problem of heads up or heads down, now in full cooperation, Cathy stands up, her pajama bottoms drop. The uppers are unbuttoned. She undoes her braids and allows her long blonde mane to blanket her back from her head to her gluteal muscles. Relishing the revelation, Ted once more feasts on the nude frame from the firm round breasts to the mons venires. He slowly lowers her gently back onto the bed. Softly starting at her erect nipples he begins to kiss her body all the way down to thc bruises on her thighs.

Over whelmed, he can no longer hold off and thus makes an erect entrance to her anticipating receptacle and is rewarded in its magnificence, by her faint satisfying cry as her body gently quivers at his penetration.

The following day, Monday November 27, 1950, Ted is at his locker in the police station when Stephen comes over to him. "Teddy, you and I used to be close friends, now you are not even trying to keep our friendship. I have been trying to apologize to Cathy but I can't find out where she is. I know you and Cameron are the only one close to her and he won't talk to me. I firmly believe you must be hiding her from me. Be a friend; let me talk to her so I can say how sorry I am. Tell her I will take *the pledge* at church with her watching."

"Steve, you are assuming that I know where Cathy is, but even if I said I know where she is I would not allow you close enough to assault her again. Even right now I can smell the booze on your breath. You are a goddamned drunk, get yourself into rehab and then come and talk to me about her."

"Well fuck you both; I can handle the booze if I want to. I am not a drunk. I use occasional alcohol to give me escape. Lately I have been reliving my Iwo Jima nightmares and a little drink helps me to forget. You never were in hand-to-hand combat, so you don't know what those memories do to you when you dream. I haven't had a good night's sleep in months. Sometimes I want to escape them and kill myself. So don't judge me."

"Steve, I am sorry about your combat experiences, and no, I have never had hand to hand combat and no, I cannot understand them. I just know that after a few drinks your demeanor is anti-social and therefore you drive friends away. It makes you angry and you abuse Cathy."

"Okay preacher, enough of your sermons, I will find Cathy and explain it to her. She will understand because I have wakened her up many times at night because of my nightmares."

Reporting for duty the next evening, seeking information at roll-call formation, he asks Chuck if he has any information concerning death of Ryler. "Teddy, it was a fuckin' shame. While on duty last evening, Steve went to the Ballantine Brewery Pub Room. He drank too much he became sick, vomited, and choked to death on his own puke. The poor bastard was alone and he laid there for hours before we went looking for him when he did not report in at the end of his tour of duty."

Alas and alack – such self-destruction – such a waste of youth. Such obvious life time actions often lead a person to a sad demise. The funeral on Friday December 1st is a grand display of the Brotherhood of the Police. Bagpipes and kilts, flags and gun salutes prevail. With Cathy and Ted sitting in the first pew, Father Tim, in his eulogy, seems to be addressing Cathy.

"We often wonder why God allows such things as what occurred in the lives of Catherine and Stephen. Some things do not work out, as we believe they should, and we blame the Lord, when it is the human that erred. Jesus is not pentimental, he is not going to change his mind, what is to be is to be. Remember that death is two-fold in emotions. While it is bitter in the pain to friends and relations – it is sweet in the Salvation of his soul. Now let us pray a *Benddact Anim* for Stephen. Agnus Dei, (Lamb of God) who takes away the sins of the world, pray for us. May the soul of Stephen, and the souls of all the faithful departed, rest in peace. Amen."

Continuing, he offers a reminder, "What began as a heavenly happiness when I married them on Saturday June 15,1946 and ended tragically on November 27,1950 can never possibly be understood even by doing a post mortem critique of their life. Moreover, we are not here to review or sit in judgment. There will be no *mea culpa;* we are here to pray for Stephen's soul and Catherine's future without the man that she loved so dearly. So let us bid Stephen *Slan go foill (*Goodbye for a while*)* until our souls meet again in Heaven."

Chapter twelve

Tuesday Oct. 9, 1951. Sheerin and Neil McLaughlin stop their patrol car at the Egleston Square diner for an evening snack. Owner Anthony Pino greets them with his ever so false felicitations. His façade to customers is jovial, *hail fellow – well met,* however, his inner feelings for police, is contemptuous.

Tony's robust five by five foot frame makes him seem real friendly. In reality he is a well-known thief. He will take an order for any item, and then go *boost* it (steal) and sell it to the order giver. Any article, that the buyer wants, small or large. It is known that a friend of his wants a refrigerator. True to form, Tony takes a deposit, and then steals the refrigerator from the Sears Roebuck warehouse. The basement of his lunchroom diner has numerous, still packaged, new articles such as toasters, electric mixers and many small items the he *boosted* just to keep in practice.

Tony, no dunce, has a sharp analytical mind. As it turns out later, he is a leading planner for the Brink's money vault robbers. Tony busts into the American District Alarm building several times to steal blueprints of the alarm system, of the Brink's building.

These things are not known to Ted and Neil at this time. They just proceed to a booth and friendly Tony brings them fresh coffee. With a big grin, he asks, "How about a slab of pie a la mode, on me?"

After assuring him that the cups of Java are enough, Tony returns to the counter to tend to some incoming customers.

Teddy puts a 25-cent coin in the music box slot at their booth. Selecting the six tunes for a quarter, he picks *Bi mir bisch du—I'm in the mood for love—There's a small hotel—You may not be an Angel—Don't fence me in—Walking the floor over you.* Psychologists say that lyrics; of a song a person enjoys can indicate their sub-conscious thoughts. What do the selected songs indicate about Teddy's subconscious thinking?

Thoughts aside, he comments, "I find it strange we can listen to that character's bullshit and pretend we are interested in what he has to say. In reality, I believe every cop builds a shield around himself to keep from any close involvement with civilians. Remain immune to the emotions and feeling of those around him."

"If that's the case," questions Neil, "Why the fuck did Lloyd Shea blow his brains out with his own '38' last week? They found him on the other side of Jamaica Pond after he got off duty, in his own car, dead."

"That case is different. I happen to know more about that," responds Teddy. "A couple of summers ago I was on limited duty, recovering from broken ribs and knee injuries caused from *cracking-up* my motorcycle in a high speed chase. Because of my injuries, until I am fully recovered, I was assigned to limited duty walking the Franklin Park beat."

"I had just come from the Rose garden area onto circuit Drive. There parked under a street light was a disabled car. Standing at the rear of the car was a guy and two gals. They hadn't seen me yet so I stayed in the shadows and wondered why they are looking into the open trunk of the auto. When they went to the right side of the car and stood quietly staring at the front right wheel, I then noticed the tire was flat. I walked up to them. They were very pleasant and obviously glad to see a uniformed cop. The girls are good looking wenches. The fellow told me his problem was that he didn't have a wheel jack to enable him to put on the spare tire."

"I told him I was getting ready to check off for the night and would *hit* the call-box then head back to my car, pick up my buddy, then I'd come back to help them. He introduced himself as Paul Shore; he was with Tracy and Sheila. Tracy seemed to take a shine to me. No, I think it was the uniform I had on, she is one of those who can't resist a uniform. A typical broad that is always gushy and silly over any man in a uniform. Sheila seemed more level headed."

"I picked up Lloyd Shea and we came back to loan them a jack. That was the night that Lloyd and I were headed to my place on the lake. While Paul was changing the tire Lloyd and I were putting the *make* on the girls. I told them we were heading for my lakeside place and asked if they would like to join us for the week-end."

"Tracy had changed her interest from me to Floyd and was hanging onto his arm. Needless to say, he is tall blond and handsome. Sheila turned to Paul and asked him if he would mind if they left him after he changed the tire. Paul said no, he had to get home to his wife. He was only going to drop the girls off at their apartments after their late night office conference. It would save him time. He advised Sheila to keep her eye on Tracy."

"I tell you Neil, it was a hellava weekend. On our drive to the lake, Tracy was all snuggly and cozy in the back seat with Lloyd. At the lodge, after a couple of drinks, she and Lloyd went into the bedroom and hardly got out of the bed the entire weekend. She moaned and groaned and squealed. Either Lloyd was a great stud or Tracy just likes to fuck."

"Sheila and I spent time on the lake fishing and puttering around. Tracy made it tough on me because Sheila wouldn't fuck; she was too embarrassed by Tracy's noisy actions. She said she wasn't the same type of a one-nighter as Tracy and only let me in on some heavy petting. Then she slept in a bedroom, by herself, behind a locked door. I had guessed wrong, I thought that the fact they would go with us for the weekend, they were sure fucks. Sheila said it was only because we were cops that she agreed to come with us. Said she felt secure, they could have some fun, and no harm would befall them."

"She believed that a girl that would *put-out* on the first date was a slut. I agreed and said that I felt a girl that put out before the third or fourth date, would put out for any guy and that is no compliment to the guy. It was more of a compliment to a man's ego if he thought that he was someone special to the girl and that is why she eventually gave in to his advances. Maybe Floyd was so wonderful she couldn't resist him."

"You know Neil, it was only four months later that he married Tracy and the marriage was rocky from the start. He made her quit her job a year in the marriage. He didn't like her close relationship with her boss. She was always coming home with nice gifts, supposedly for her outstanding work."

"I occasionally dated Sheila, later she told me Tracy's employer was believed to be *banging* Tracy. I guess that is what Floyd believed. Since he couldn't afford to keep Tracy in expensive jewelry, theater tickets, etc., they constantly argued. Not only that, she ran him up to his arsse-hole in debt, charging fancy clothes and other stuff."

"In the three years they were married, being a good Catholic he wouldn't use any birth control, so they had two kids and a third one on the way when he did the un-Catholic act of committing the mortal sin of suicide. He must have over-looked the fact that he could not be buried in a Catholic Cemetery because of his sin."

"You know he must have had a lousy life, and wanted out of it very badly." Neil says.

"Yeah, I guess so. Anyhow it is time we got outta here and make another swing around the area, my long week-end leave time will begin in about an hour," suggests Teddy. Then adding," My motto is from the Latin *Nil Admirari* – to be surprised at nothing. You could come to me and say 'the Pope's mistress just had a baby' and I would only ask –is it a boy or a girl?"

Witnessing the great contradictions Teddy observes in the oxymoron conduct of so-called proper people, his cynicism is inevitable. The after dark conduct and/or supposedly secret nefarious actions, belie their decent citizen veneer. When he catches them in an illicit or illegal situation they won't face up to pay the consequences of their actions. Ted learns the culprit's attitude is that money is the way of buying out of their predicament. Who is to blame? The policeman who may have carried his society observations into his own home? The natural inclination for wanting his family to be different than the society that the cop witnesses? Maybe it is caused by the decline of the female morals that the stalwarts of society had depended upon in the past. Somehow no one wants to suffer the consequences and pay for their misdeeds. Just blame society or a poor upbringing and continue their misdeeds and let the weak or corrupt judges and the bleeding heart juries, slap the miscreant on the wrist.

Teddy's attitude became more anti-society when he chased a bum check writing artist, across the country costing a lot of time and money, and the judge ends up giving the felon a suspended six-month sentence. Don't pick on the judges alone – - the *bleeding heart* juror sometimes is worse! So Teddy says, "Fuck them all, the long the short and the tall, I'm going to play the game the way *they* do."

"He was a partner of Love, tenderness, and bliss'
Now joining the great maker. Did he die remiss?"

Chapter thirteen

Oddities of life sometime referred to as *it's a small world*, occurs on Sunday morning February 3, 1952, when two girls, from Teddy and Stanley's past, have their paths cross. Virginia has been to the eleven o'clock Mass, and is coming down the steps of the Holy Name Cathedral when she hears her name being called. "Virginia, Ginny, wait up."

Turning to the loud voice, "My God, Claudia Demarest, what a great surprise to see you. Are you home for keeps or just visiting the old home grounds?"

"I am back to start life over. Pushing twenty, I'm a little bit wiser than when I left here at seventeen, and a lot less naïve."

"Claudia, I wondered what happened to you. Your mother just said that you were living with her sister in New York and had a job there. Ted has asked me a dozen times, if I heard from you. He said your mother is upset at him and would give him no information about you."

"I am now living with mother. She gave me a job in the boutique shop she manages. If you've got time Ginny, we can get a cup of coffee, and I will bring you up to date."

"Better still Claudia, I am going to stop at the bakery and get some Danish coffee rolls, and we can go to my place and relax. I have all the time in the world to talk to you."

At Virginia's apartment, fresh brewed coffee is poured, juice and sweet rolls on the table, the girls feeling *Chick* comfortable, resume conversation. *Comme les leurs su mal,* the French have a word for it. (She is a *blossom that has gone bad).* Claudia tries to explain the change in her life style, -- no explain is not correct -- rationalize is more apropos.

As far as Ted is concerned, the female can be deadly specie. How much better off would men be if they could bond like women do? He is always aware that women warmly embrace each other to show their empathy and understanding, especially when their discussion pertains to a man. They pour their hearts out to each other to share their pleasures, passions or problems, a true case of psychology 101. Ted believes their common ground is to dominate men. In a non-sexual emotion, they cuddle and comfort in bed while the male almost becomes homophobic at the thought of another man in bed with him.

"Really, Ginny, the reason I left town is Teddy Sheerin. I was madly, passionately, in love with him and he was just using me to sate his passion."

"I always knew that Ted was cold calculating womanizer, or should I also say a young naïve girl user. I truly believe he is a damned misogynist. But tell me, what happened."

"It was Saturday July 15, 1950, three months short of my eighteenth birthday, and I had just graduated from high school. As a step to maturity I wanted to buy a used car. I went to the Freeport Motors on Dorchester Avenue because they advertised five dollars down buys a used car. I was meandering around the car lot and had stopped and opened the door of a car when this good looking man, about twenty-five years old, came over to greet me."

"He says that he is name is Ted and he'll put me in this car for just five down and five dollars each week and says for me to get in and see how it feels. With that he gently took my hand and led me to the driver door on the other side of the car, opened it and gestured with a wave of his hand."

"I was naïve, I never had such a smooth talking older man pay attention to me like this, and while I blushed, I felt like I was a grown woman who was being flattered by a *man of the world.*"

"Claudia, you are carrying me back to the days of my early youth. I've been there and experienced that sensation," offers Virginia.

"Teddy is a good salesman, he must have kissed the *Blarney Stone,* and he continued his spiel, and he suggests that I take this car for a spin-around-the block."

"I tell him that with gas costing 20 cents I can't afford to buy a car just yet, but most important that I don't know how to drive He went silent for a few moments, and then he says for me to get one of my parents to sign to purchase this car and he will let me gas up there for six months. As a plus he will teach me how to drive as part of the sale. I was thrilled at the idea, plus the attention I was getting, and with a big smile, I went with him to the office and got the needed paper work."

"It takes years and tears before a girl realizes life is no fairy tale, try as we may to have it be so. Remember, the guy with the white hat riding his white stallion, does not exist Claudia."

"My mother said the same thing Ginny. She sensed something was not kosher with this deal and she wanted to meet this Ted. The next day she escorted me to Freeport Motors. When we entered the office, Ted was sitting there in his police uniform. He was very gracious to mother."

"He went on to explain that he is Boston cop and that he, his Dad, and Rabbi Waterman, are the owners.

"Mother was pleased, and I think she was a little smitten with him, I think his uniform made an impression on her. She had not been dating lately and after all she is just ten years older than Ted and can pass for being much younger than she is, and Teddy is just eight years older than I am. "

"Turning on her female charms, mother said, 'I am Claudia's mother, and I do appreciate your cordiality Mister, or should I say, officer Sheerin'? "

"Please, no formalities, I am Ted to my friends and I'd like you as a friend."

"Mother selected a car and after signing the car purchase papers, Ted changed into his *civvies* and took mother, and I, for my first driving lesson. It lasted thirty-minutes, and when finished he took us to dinner. Three days later he took me alone for another lesson and it was a little different. I was wearing a short skirt and as I applied the foot-brake my skirt slid upward, exposing about eight or nine inches of my leg above my knee. I was wearing a pair of bobby-sox and my upper leg was bare. Ted, so gentlemanly, took the edge of my skirt and slid it back toward my knee. I wasn't wise those days. He pulled the skirt forward by placing his palm on my leg with his fingers sliding down my inner thigh, while apologizing."

"He apologized for pulling my skirt down, he said he was afraid my modesty might be a distraction and that I'd take my eyes off the road and we would have an accident. Foolishly I thanked him for being so considerate, but it thrilled me terribly. I had never felt the hand of even a boy friend, on my inner thigh. To have the touch of this very worldly man was exciting."

Claudia stopped talking and gazed out the kitchen window. The expression on her face seemed to indicate that she is in a mode of reminiscence.

Virginia takes out her cigarette case and offers a Lucky Strike to Claudia. It brings Claudia back to reality. "Thanks, I'd like a smoke. With these things going up to twenty-two cents a pack, I should give them up."

Lighting her own cigarette, Virginia extends the torch to Claudia's. The women take long drags on their *cancer sticks* to gain a physiological effect from the nicotine. Then, as though in meditation, they blow out large clouds of smoke toward the ceiling. In what seems to both as a long period of tranquility, but it is only a couple of minutes, Virginia asks, "Did he keep his word about the license?"

"Oh yes, on October 4, 1950 I got my driver's license. As a reward for getting my license, Ted phoned mother and said that he has a lodge on Pembroke Lake and he would love to have mother and I spend the coming weekend boating there. Mother very excitedly accepted."

"On Saturday October 7th, a warm day for October, we followed him to the lake. It is a five bedroom Swiss style lodge, with a large family room, and a screened in back porch that overlooks the lake. Sitting there you can watch the boaters, swimmers, and even fishermen."

"Mother at that time was a thirty-six year old widow with a magnificent figure that is sexually accented by her bathing suit. She had put on a bathing suit in the pretext of going for a swim, but never did swim. She dominated our time with Ted, and after many *Gin & Tonics*, I hear her giggly from Ted's bedroom. I was so mad at here for what I imagined went on in that room that night, that I would not speak to her for a month."

"That sounds like typical female jealousy, we are sometimes guilty of that," offers Virginia.

"Mother wanted to keep in the sexual good graces of Teddy and when he asked, she okayed for me to go by myself to spend the following weekend water skiing on the lake. Teddy was great at teaching me how to water ski. He powered his motor boat in a manner that showed kindness and prevention of injuries to this beginner."

"However, after an afternoon of skiing, I showered and when I stepped out of the shower dripping wet, Ted walked into the bathroom holding a huge beach towel. He hesitated and seemed to study my nudeness, from my nose to my toes. I wanted to cover up, yet wanted to flaunt my nude body for him to compare with my mother's. He wrapped the towel around me and squeezed me tightly, then apologizes, says it just occurred to him that there were no large towels in the shower area."

"He seemed to say it as though apologizing for the lack of towels rather than his voyeurism trip. I was torn between two emotions; I wanted to chastise him for coming into the bathroom, yet was thrilled when he put his hands on my buttocks and pulled my toweled body intimately close. So close that I could feel his erection. Dumb kid that I was, I was ecstatic to think that this handsome Adonis is *turned on* by seeing me nude. "

"He then lifts me bodily, carries me to the master bedroom and lays me down on the king size bed. Gently he spreads apart my towel, and softly strokes my stomach. I was so excited that I trembled. Using my trembling as an excuse, he lays beside me and pulls me close, supposedly to warm me, and then begins to stroke my pubic hair."

"He asks me if I am still a virgin and asked him how does he mean the word virgin to mean. He asks have I ever had an orgasm, – been fucked?"

"I explained I never have had a full intercourse, but I have had an orgasm several times when I made love orally on my boyfriend. With that, he kisses my pubic hairs then slowly slides his hand between my thighs and put his finger in me, I had a terrific orgasm. He does not remove his finger until I have several orgasms, then he gives me a very warm kiss and moves away from me. I pulled the towel back over me and began to cry."

"Gently he hugs me while explaining that I should not be crying, that to a young woman, sexual satisfaction is normal. He said he would go no further right now because of my trembling he believes this is a first time for me. However the next time will be because I indicate that

I want to go all the way. That will be the time to face reality of sexuality and we will stop using polite terms for sex acts. Use correct everyday lingo, not oral love. Fellatio should be called a blow-job or giving head. An orgasm is called cum and a fuck should be called a fuck. All these expressions are also stimulating for any partner to hear."

"Virginia, I confess, I enjoyed his hugging me. After I calmed down, I surprised him and myself by using the sex words that he said. I felt guilty that I had caused him to become aroused and I asked him if he wanted me to help him to cum. I even went so far as to say I would give him a blow-job."

"Get to the giant step; you have me horny just wondering what happened. Did you go back to the lake house?" Virginia asks.

"By this time I am madly in love with Teddy. I did go there on Sunday October 15 and I experienced a wonderful loss of my virginity, and at least once a week, for the next several months Teddy and I made love. However I think he was still doing Mom."

"That is so wonderful that you two were so in love Claudia."

"Not so fast Virginia, I realize that it was strictly one sided. I was romantically infatuated with the great Ted Sheerin, but he is only enamored with what is between my legs."

"You probably gave in too soon Claudia. Being easy, you are no bargain to them, no challenge, and men consider if you are quick to give sex, you as just a convenient *piece if ass* for them or any other guy. No romance, he could care less that you were in love. In fact he may not have realized that you were in love with him."

"Regardless. To quote Charles Dickens, '*Bah -- humbug,* He told me that he was going to be at Pembroke the week of April 17th, and was going to give the house a touch-up coat of paint to get it ready for the summer. It would be all work, no play. I knew that the 19th was his birthday, I wanted to give him a surprise P.O.P. birthday present so I packed a large picnic basket and on that date I headed to Pembroke."

"In the drive down to the lake, I imagined all wonderful things, even hoped he would propose. You can't be cynical or smart when you are in love. Pulling into the driveway, I saw no sign of Ted painting. Since his car and another car are there, I figured he was out in the boat going to the grocery store at the end of the lake. So-o-o, I went in, put my basket of picnic goodies on the kitchen table. Needing to pee, I heading to the powder room, I had to pass the master bedroom and to my utter horror there was he and Cathy Ryler."

Claudia stopped, tears flowing over the dam, she reaches for a tissue.

"Stop the tears; I am all excited, were they doing what I think they were doing?"

Wiping her eyes, Claudia stutters, "In the vernacular of Ted -- *he is fucking the arsse off her."*

"Oh my God, I am so sorry. This brings to mind another quote, *Life's a bitch and then you die,"* proffers Virginia.

"At that moment that is how I felt. On seeing me in the doorway to the room, Teddy jumps up, his erection goes down, and Cathy grabs the sheet to cover her nudeness."

"Claudia, what the fuck are you doing here? I told you there would be no play time. Why did you come here?"

"You ask why I came here Teddy; you evidently planned something other than work. You may call what you were doing work? I call it betrayal time. How could you do this to me? I thought you loved me and that I was all that you needed. Do we have a future, some permanence, or is my body something for you to just use?"

"Struggling to put his pants on, he stammers" 'I never told you that I loved you. We are in a relationship because we enjoy sex together. I never said we are committed. I never said you could not jump into bed with another man. Wake up girl, get real.' Then he goes back to Cathy."

"Ginny, I left there in a rush, bawling like a baby, I drove crazily back home. The next day I left Boston and went to live with my Aunt Beatrice in New York City. My life deteriorated there. Seeking admiration, still naïve, wondering if I was desirable to other men, I went *bar-hopping* while dressed in panty revealing short skirts and my breasts almost out of my blouse. I believed then that it pays to advertise *meat for sale.* I got more studs than I ever believed would be available."

"I thought I was irresistible Ginny. After all, what could be the *Big deal* of letting one more guy get a *hole in one*? It's like taking just one more slice off a loaf of bread. I bedded down a dozen different men sometimes two in one day; I'd still be dripping from one when I was in bed with another. I even had an abortion."

"A virgin's *nether region* is considered *terra incognita,* but after a half dozen guys it becomes well explored," adds Virginia." With that many men you become an expert on size and lengths and you begin to compare your men."

"I gave myself an A.K.A. of *Silver dollar.* Like the old song, *A silver dollar goes from hand to hand and a woman goes from man to man,* until last month. I then realized I was used goods and decided no more men for me."

"Aunt Bea tried to bring reality into my life. She told me that I may grow out of my first love but that I will never get over it and then handed me a letter for me to read not once, but every six months for life. She said that it was given to her when she was a teenager."

"It read:" *As we grow up, we learn that even the one person that wasn't supposed to ever let you down probably will.' You will have your heart broken probably more than once and it's harder every time. You'll break hearts too, so remember how it felt when yours was broken. You'll fight with your best friend. You'll blame a new love for things an old one did. You'll cry because life is passing too fast and you'll eventually lose someone you love. So take too many pictures, laugh too much, and love as if you've never been hurt because every second you spend upset is a minute of happiness you'll never get back. Don't be afraid that your life will end, be afraid that it will never begin'.*

"So here I am, back home for good, maybe a little wiser and more mature. I'm through swirling my skirts to attract men wanting me just for sex. I want a man that will want me for myself and sex is secondary. I found that females have something powerful that no man has and we should not just give it away."

"Claudia that type of man is as rare as the mythical Unicorn."

"Virginia, how do you happen to know Ted?"

"We were neighbors at 162 Cornell Street in Roslindale. His family lived on the first floor; mine lived on the second floor. Ted was my idol."

"I was constantly going down stairs to pretend that I needed to borrow something, when I knew Ted was alone in the house. On many occasions I would walk into his bathroom when he was peeing, and I would stand and watch. On one occasion, I took a hold of his penis and held it while he peed, and he got a *hard-on*. I got more curious about the male animal after getting excited while reading a pornographic book that a girl friend and I would read while we hid in the backyard big tree house that Ted and Stanley built as boys. The book would excite us and we would hug and kiss and touch each other."

"Ted knew that Wilhemina Bemis and I would carry on in the tree house. On Sunday, June 6, 1943 Ted is home on furlough from the Army Air Force and while his folks are at Sunday Mass, I walk in on Ted while he is in the bathtub. I brazenly stripped down and got into the tub with him."

"He got mad and he yelled, 'Jesus Christ Virginia, your cock-teasing is going to get us both in trouble. Get out of this fuckin' tub, and go play with Wilma, I didn't go."

"When I just lay there in the tub, he got out and while on my knees in the tub, he bent over to pull me out of the tub, I grabbed his erection and put it in my mouth like I had seen in pictures in the porno book."

"He then yelled, 'You want to lose your virginity then God Damn it you will' and he lifted me up and laid me down on the carpet and fucked me."

"How was it Virginia, how did you feel? Was it exciting?"

"It wasn't romantic, it hurt a little, but I did cum. Ted just got up, wiped his thing and got dressed. Never said a word just lit a cig and walked out of the room. It made me feel that men don't give a dam about romance like women do."

"Ted was not as exciting as his brother Stanley. Stan is six years older than I am. Ted had told his brother about us and Stan came to me. He lied and said that Ted had told him to have me show Stan my secret meeting place in the tree hut."

"Stan made me climb up the ladder to the hut first so he could look up my dress. When sitting on the floor of the tree house, he reached over and gently pushed me backwards onto the floor. I was scared, excited, and curious as to what he was going to do. He said nothing, slid my dress above my waist, and took my panties off me. He ran his left hand under my bra and fondled my breast, while his right hand took out his penis. He was in me in seconds."

"Did you scream? Did you hit him? What did you do Virginia?"

"Nothing, it became oxymoronic paradoxical. I knew I was being a bad girl, but it felt good. I knew from the start that I could have stopped it, but chose not to. It made me feel like I had grown-up, and I loved the idea of sex. It was rough, not gentle, like a woman would be."

"He got finished, wiped himself with my panties, and left. I never again had sex with either Ted or Stan, but we remained friends all these years. How do you feel about Ted since your New York sex experiences?"

"I have a better view of the difference of so called love sex and lust sex. Some where I read that a woman's emotional core lies in her reproductive organs. I have matured and understand that Teddy just wanted unemotional sex. He was not in love with me; I was his *bella ficca* (piece of arsse), as I was in New York for those guys for whom I spread my legs. I am now a stronger person Ginny; after all, Eleanor Roosevelt said it best when she said that women are like tea bags. They don't know how strong they are until they get into hot water."

"However Ginny, I thrilled with orgasms I had with Ted, not so with the men in New York. It never was as good with them as it was with Teddy. When it comes to sex, not love, a man's brain shrinks to the size of a humming bird's. He lets his six inch weapon do his thinking. However, I still care for him, but I won't go to bed with him again. I don't have any regrets, the memories are great, but I don't ever want to be his *piece* again. No hard feelings, friends yes, sex partners, no. If he wanted to dinner and dance me, I'd say yes for old time's sake. But what did you mean when you mentioned women were gentle."

"Claudia you are full of surprises, and maybe so am I. But for now I will only say that I have experienced sex with a female and it is a lot gentler and satisfying to me than with a man. That is all I will say for now. You have a car and a driver's license. I do not know whether or not you will ever visit me here again. If you do choose to visit, you will know how I feel about sex and if you are interested it will be your choice. That way I will know that I am not forcing you. You will be here of your own volition."

Chapter fourteen

Sunday January 7, 1952 General Eisenhower announces he is a candidate for the office of President of the U.S.A. and on Saturday March 29, due to the scandal of corruption in his staff, and his low popularity, Truman decides not to run for re-election.

While this is information on the national level, on the local level, Ted has begun to study for a promotion to be a Sergeant on the Boston Police Department. He takes the examination on Thursday November 19, 1953 and is notified on Thursday December 3, 1953 that he has won a promotion to Sergeant.

Wednesday December 9, 1953 Ted receives a phone call from Alvan, "Ted, I just made a sweet deal for you. Fuller's Packard Dealership's used car buyer just sold us a 1952 series 62 Caddy convertible coupe at a way below market value. It is a repo that is tangled up in law suits and they wanted it off their property in a hurry. It is the perfect car for you. You'll love it."

"What's it gonna cost me Al, I am strapped for cash right now?"

"Since Christmas is just a couple of weeks away, let's consider it your Freeport Motors *Yontef* gift and we just deduct the price from your share of end of the year profits?"

"*Shalom* partner, if everyone is that willing, you've got a deal Al. Leave the ignition key in it after you close, and I will pick the car up later tonight, I've got an early duty tomorrow."

The next morning Ted heads to the precinct in his Caddy convertible. At this time, Boston Police believe that all of the suspects to the Brinks vault holdup had met and planned this venture in a backroom of Joe McInnis' J&A Café and/or in the basement of Anthony Pino's Diner, in Egleston Square section of Police Division 13 Jamaica Plain.

This has been Edward Ted Sheerin patrol area over the past years and he is therefore familiar with all of the suspects. (Re: Doubleday book – The Great Brink's Holdup).

Wearing his recently earned Sergeant stripes, Sheerin reports for duty at 8 a.m. and receives written orders and a pair of handcuffs, (At this time Boston uniform cops do not have handcuffs, only detectives are issued handcuffs) for him, to bring Brink's holdup suspects Joseph McInnis and Anthony Pino to the Suffolk County District Attorney's Office for questioning. These two became prime suspects because they are known to have been the leaders in other local major crimes. They also fit the top of a profile most detectives rely on –the three A's, – Available – Ability – past Accomplishments.

The pick-up order is part of the usual harassment of suspected criminals, for obviously this being Christmas week end, any interrogations would be suspended until Monday December 28th. Therefore the men will remain in custody until questioning begins on Monday.

John *Fats* Buccelli a top man in dope dealings in Boston and New York is a greedy bastard. Two long shore men that work the Boston docks, Thomas Francis Richardson and James Ignatius Faherty are members of the Brink's gang. They are such close pals that they become known as the *God Dust Twins.* After the Brink's holdup, they are wanted for questioning by the B.P.D, as well as the F.B.I. Re: The Great Brink's Holdup by Doubleday.

In April of 1958 the duo pays Fats Buccelli to hide them in the B&

P Contracting Company at 617 Tremont Street, a building 'Fats' and Wimpy Bennett own.

Needing provisions, they pay Fats exorbitant amounts of their illegal holdup stash, for food and other necessities. Meanwhile, Buccelli is negotiating with the U.S. Air Force for a large parcel of land that he owns in Limerick Maine. The U. S. Air Force pays him one million dollars for the land. Check in hand, becomes money in his bank and he heads back to Boston.

The first thing he does is to confront Richardson and Faherty. "You guys have to leave this place immediately. I just got a bundle of legit dough and if you guys are caught in my building I could do time and not enjoy my money. So grab your duds and scram."

The inflated prices for their necessities was bad enough, but now he is putting them in jeopardy of getting caught by not giving them sufficient time to find a new hideout and demanding that they leave this building immediately. They have no choice – he is armed – they are not.

On June 4, shortly after the Twins leave the building the F. B. I. receives a tip and they raid the Tremont Street offices of the B. & P. Construction Company. The 'G' men find, hidden behind the wall, a small water cooler with $51,906 of which all but a few thousand dollars is part of the Brink's loot money that Faherty and Richardson had given to Fats.

Buccelli had the fairly new bills soaking in coffee water to age the bills appearance. When interrogated Buccelli gave the F.B.I. some phony names of people that he said he had rented the building to.

The Brink's robbery was at that time the greatest armed robbery. Over two million seven hundred thousand dollars was taken. It cost over twenty nine million dollars to convict the gang. Part of that high cost was caused my J. Edgar Hoover's ineptitude. His favorite past time was as a devotee to horse racing and he, and his constant companion and room-mate F.B.I. Agent Tolson, spent many hours betting at the race track. Hoover's friend Walter Winchell gave him many betting tips that were provided to Winchell by gangster Frank Costello a.k.a. Francesco Castiglia.

Thursday June 19, 1958, in a fall-out, Buccelli's partner Wimpy, in typical *hit-man* style, fires a 22 caliber bullet at an angle into the back of the skull of Buccelli. The small entry hole of the bullet is hidden under his hair therefore it conceals the fact of this style of gangland execution. It causes the bullet to spin around inside the skull and the .22 caliber plays pin-ball as it destroys the brain. The bullet entry hole remains concealed by the thick hair at the back of the skull. This method of execution is not easily detected.

Wimpy Bennett then put the deceased John Buccelli behind the wheel of an auto at the top of a hill. He let the car roll downhill and it crashes into a parked truck. The police list it as *death by auto accident.* However, sudden deaths in Massachusetts require an autopsy exam by a M.E. and in this case he soon discovers the bullet entry hole. The Medical Examiner renders his verdict as *Death by gunshot.*

Not so in Texas which has 254 counties and only four of these counties require an M.E. exam. The other 250 rely on a non-medical Justice of Peace to guess as to the cause of death. The city of Alice Texas is not one of the four requiring an M.E.

Border patrolman Edward Wheeler is investigating suspicious autos parked under a bridge near Lake Mathis in Alice, Texas. He apparently thought that the cars were involved in illegal alien smuggling and went to investigate. Instead these were *dope mules* that were transferring dope from a car from Mexico, into three other cars. One auto headed for Chicago, one to Houston and the other one to New York City.

The *dope mules* overpower Wheeler; put the 22 caliber to the back of his head, and fire. They proceed to put Wheeler behind the wheel of his automobile and drive into the steel girders of the bridge. When he is found at the so called *crash scene*, a local Texas J.P. declared 'death caused by auto accident'. When the details of the Buccelli death is published in the Massachusetts Police Association magazine the Chief of the U.S. Border Patrol reading about that case, requests that the Boston Police send a policeman familiar with the information to meet him in Alice. Superintendant Hanratty sends Sergeant Edward Sheerin.

After receiving the details from Sergeant Sheerin, the Border Patrol Chief orders Wheeler's body to be exhumed and a M.E. autopsy performed. Discovery of the bullet hole in his skull, leads to the fact Edward Wheeler was murdered.

John *Fats* Buccelli

Chapter fifteen

Decembers in Boston can be very cold and sometimes snowy. Used car sales are at a minimal because the *working class stiff* needs his cash for Christmas festivities, food, gifts, and partying.

Around Thanksgiving week, Ted and Alvan drive a large flat bed truck up to Maine and purchased bundles of Christmas Trees to retail from the car lot. It is a very profitable business because the car lot is in a heavily Catholic area, therefore a big demand for Christmas trees.

Boston's Sunday Blue Laws allow no selling on the Lord's Day. Businesses must close down, at midnight Saturday and not reopen until Monday. No one can even be in a retail building. Therefore Saturday's are the big sales days. Due to his religious vows (he swore to on the battle field), Alvan does not work on Saturdays, his Shabbat. Eamon Sheerin fills in for Al on Saturdays.

Saturday December 19, 1953, a heavy cold snow fall has Stan, Ted, and dad Eamon hovering around the office stove, trying to keep the chill off them at the car lot while handling last minute Christmas tree shoppers, when Claudia Demarest comes into the office.

At first Ted and Stan do not recognize her, she has aged, lost weight. Just twenty-one years old, looking fifty, a mere shell of the girl they once seduced. Now use to the fact that she has physically changed dramatically, and friends no longer recognize her she explains, "Teddy, I'm Claudia Demarest, I've been ill, thus the change in my appearance."

"I am so sorry to hear that, how can I help you Claudia?" He asks while offering her a chair.

"I'd like a small table top Christmas tree but it fatigues me to stand out in the cold air to try to select one."

Not hesitating, Stan goes and out then soon returns to the office with an excellent shaped table top Christmas tree. Then addressing Ted, "I locked the gate, closed the lot down for the night, now I think we need a bit of the hair of the dog," and removes a bottle of J.D. from the file cabinet.

Raising the bourbon bottle in a form of a salute, "Miss Claudia will you join us in a tad ova taste?"

"Just a small one will help warm me thank-you Stanley."

Raising their glasses, Stan shouts, "Slainte, Erin go bragh." (Salute, good health and Ireland forever). Eamon adds, "I'll drink to that."

While Ted and Claudia do a mild case of reminiscence, Stan, sits sipping additional Jack Daniels, while silently studying Claudia. Finally Ted could not stem his curiosity any longer. "Bluntly, I am asking, what illness caused this condition to affect you?"

"I have kidney failure. There are so very few dialysis machines in the greater Boston area, and therefore I can not get the number of appointments that I need to filter my blood of uremia toxic infection until I can get a kidney donation. Therefore my body began to debilitate to the weakened condition that I am in now."

"Can you get a dialysis machine of your own?"

"Yes, there is one for rent down on the Cape in West Barnstable, but I can not afford it."

"What's it cost Claudia?"

"They want me to put two thousand dollars down, and then I must agree to pay then one hundred dollars a week."

A case of love, loss and redemption, Ted says, "Well this can be my long overdue Christmas present for you, we will arrange for it next week."

Stan jumps, "Bullshit Ted, I know what pain she is going through, make a phone call and we will pick up the machine tonight."

Claudia is so stunned, she bursts into tears, doesn't know which of these shining knights to embrace first. However, getting the machine is but one tiny step, kidney donations are few and rare, – very rare.

After picking up the dialysis machine it is discovered that a 220 volt electric outlet is required. Claudia's household electric power is the normal 120 volts, so Stanley installs the machine in a separate office at the car lot. Ruth Demarest brings daughter Claudia to the car lot at three day intervals to spend four hours with her arm hooked-up for her dialysis blood filtering.

Over the next two months, Stanley has become a caring man with great empathy for the sickly Claudia. Having experienced much pain and suffering he understands what she is going through. He devotes many hours to her needs while she is having her treatments and this TLC obviously begins to show as her body's physical condition improves.

With the uremic poison being kept somewhat under control, she is able to eat and sleep better. She regains some of her weight and begins to look like the Claudia of old. However, the kidney will eventually fail completely. Death will then soon follow.

Sunday June 20, 1954 Stanley receives a phone call from Ruth Demarest, "Stan, they just rushed Claudia to the Mass General Hospital, her kidneys have failed. She asked me to phone and let you that she will not need dialysis treatments anymore."

"What a crying shame Ruth, I'll go right down there and see if I can do anything for her."

Arriving at the emergency room, he is met by the medic in charge. "Are you a relative of Miss Demarest, Mr. Sheerin?"

Knowing the consequence of a negative answer might mean a refusal by the hospital to allow him to see her, "Yes, I am her brother. Where is she?"

"I am very sorry to inform you sir; Miss Demarest has lapsed into a comma. Her kidneys have failed, and she is in the I. C. Unit on the third floor."

Arriving on the third floor, Stan is met by Dr. Edward George who details Claudia's present condition to him. After listening politely Stanley asks, "You've given me details of what has happened now please tell me what can you do for Claudia doctor?"

"Nothing, at this stage, other than a kidney donor and there is only a very slim chance of getting such a donation," explains the medic.

"Then take one of my kidneys. I've recently spent four years as a patient in the VA Hospital and I know that she and I are blood compatible. We are both type O blood."

The following morning Claudia awakes in a morphine haze. She is puzzled and tries to fight off her mental daze, she asks her mother. "What is Stanley doing in a bed next to mine? What are the tubes connecting us together? I guess I am dreaming," she moans and peacefully falls back to sleep. Many hours later she again wakens and now a little bit more alert, "Yes that is Stanley and he is in a bed next to mine. However we are not still connected." She mulls.

That evening Ruth explains the puzzle to the now more cognizant Claudia. Stanley has been moved to another room and Ted is visiting her. Ted goes into more of the details of what has occurred. Claudia, between outbursts of thankful tears, makes Ted promise to bring Stanley via wheel chair to visit her tomorrow.

Ted and Ruth's nightly vigil at Claudia's bedside has become more relaxed. They now feel that everything is going to be okay. At about 3 am, Ruth awakes from a doze in her chair and turns to Ted standing next to her. "I haven't bathed in a couple of days, I think I will jump into the shower here and clean up."

"I know how you feel, I feel the same way. When you get out of the shower, I will step in to it."

"We have not been close in a long time, how about this opportunity to get close Teddy?"

"I hope you mean what I think you mean Ruth. Make the first move to the shower and I will be nude beside you."

The hot shower feels great; their physical encounter gives complete satisfaction to both parties involved. The inner moisture as well as the showers outer moisture, gives Ruth's body lovely goose bumps, and pleasure through every pore. Nevertheless, after the duo's sexual shower the usual female P.O.P. materialization prevails. The hospital bill of $15.00 per day is due and Ted is elected to pay it.

Ready to be released from the hospital with her replacement kidney functioning well, they bring Claudia home to recoup. Stanley makes numerous visits to Claudia and on Friday July 30, 1954, the first time that she is strong enough to venture out of the house; Claudia has Ruth drive her to meet with Stanley at the car lot. She kisses and embraces him, "As you can see my hero, your kidney is doing miracles for my body. You know the Chinese say that if you save a person's life, they belong to you. Will you marry me Stanley?"

Tears begin to well up in the big tough guy's eyes, "God Almighty woman, you are out of your ever lovin' mind. You know I am a crippled eunuch, more than ten years older than you and your marriage to me would not be fair to you."

"You give excuses, but I notice you did not say you did not want to marry me. You fall back on why I should not marry you. I know what you are saying. I vow to you that sex is unimportant to me. You are a good man and good men are very hard to find."

To emphasize her words, she gently caresses Stanley's face with her two hands, "You are a very caring man, I love, you big lug," and she presses her caring lips upon his. It is not her imagination; she definitely feels a compassionate shudder from Stanley's embrace and she returns it with another very gentle kiss. Still holding her close, "Don't you want children what about when your estrogens are raging?"

"Let's face it Stan, you are not getting a prize package. You know about your brother Ted and me, and I am now going to tell you of what I did from seventeen to nearly my twentieth birthday while living in New York. If you will have me, after hearing the details, we will get married. As far as children, I will be truthful, yes, but there is always adoption so that is not the most important thing to me. You are the most important."

She begins to narrate the tales of her occasions of unemotional periods of acting like a whore with numerous men when Stanley gentle places his hand over her mouth.

"Give yourself a break Claudia. All of that is in the past. I do not want the details or the whys or wherefores of your past. You were not committed to me then. I only want you to know that it is not important to me, it will always be *Sinn Fein*."

"Then Stan, please believe me when I say that as far as male sex is concerned I mean what I said. I can take it or leave it; it is no longer of importance to me. Regarding babies, I never have been the motherly type and if I were, as I said, we could adopt. Now let's end this because we have had enough of these silly discussions."

Taking a calendar off the wall, Claudia turns the pages to December. "How about we have a small Chapel wedding on the anniversary date of your first kindness and empathy towards me? Saturday December 18, 1954 will be exactly one year."

Stanley does not verbalize, instead he embraces her tenderly.

With moist eyes, he kisses her left cheek, right cheek, then, gently encompasses her lips with his. Then softly, "Funny face I need you. Sweet enchantment, hold me tight, I love you deeply and my heart cries for you."

It is a small chapel wedding ceremony that binds Claudia with Stanley. She in a baby blue dress, trimmed with a white lace collar. He with his ill fitting brown suit, they lovingly embrace after each saying their *I do.*

Ted is attendance as best man, Cathy's sister Jeanne is Maid of Honor, Ruth Demarest mother of the bride, Art and Marie Brooks, Alvan and Phyllis Waterman, Ted and Stan's dad, Eamon Sheerin, and Ginny. Ted and Ruth set up a reception party of friends to enjoy food and drinks and extend wishes of longevity to the newly wedded couple.

Sitting at a long dining table each guest offers bits of humorous advice and Ted offers a wine glass salute to the couple. "Let me give a bit of trivia for you all to contemplate. In the old days, most people got married in June because they took their yearly after winter bath in May. They still smelled pretty good by June. However the females were starting to smell a bit, so as brides, they carried a bouquet of sweet scented flowers to hide their body odor. When Claudia throws her bouquet to you ladies, you must hastily remember where the tradition comes from and take the hint – if the *shoe fits.*"

Chapter sixteen

After graduating from Wellesley on Thursday May 4, 1954 Jeanne Marie Brooks (who was born on a Thursday) appears to follow the adage of *Thursday's child has far to go.* She is a stunning twenty-two year old beauty, recently hired by North East Airways as a stewardess on flights from Jeffry Field in East Boston. Thus her traveling begins.

On many occasions when the airline is very busy, the pilots and stewardess are berthed, at the company's expense, in the nearby East Boston hotel, so as to be ready on a short notice to fly an extra flight.

The owner of the Hotel Amicizia Italiano (Friendly Italian), Tito Mangino, has bribed the proper airline individuals to get this lucrative rental business. With the current hotel room rate averaging about $15.00 a night he gives the air lines a special rate of $10.00. Moreover, he treats such a guest with great care. Awaiting the guest, in the reserved room is a bottle of Chianti, a vase of flowers, a bowl of fruit, and a box of chocolates. Also available is companionship of the opposite sex, if requested.

The hotel's dining room walls have panorama murals of elaborate scenes of the Italian country side, rivers, and or religious personalities. Off the dining room is a vine arched terrace with a pathway, of elegant terrazzo, that leads to a small Italian style courtyard.

Placed appropriately apart in the courtyard are four tables, each covered in red checkered cloth. The tables are shaded by large umbrellas. It is in this area, away from scrutiny and eaves dropping, that Tito conducts his lucrative illicit enterprises.

Jeanne has become close to Patrick Eden, the pilot captain that flies most of the flights to which she is assigned. As a means to satisfy here estrogen drives and also to save money and cut her expenses, she shares quarters, meals, and bed time with Patrick. It is he that introduces her to smoking *Mary Jane*. He believes that inhaling the smoke causes male or female, to become sexually uninhibited. After a couple of joints, the female *Id*'s desire to be a dance hall stripper usually manifests it's self. An undraped moral leads to an undraped torso.

On the Fourth of July weekend in 1955 Jeanne is in a layover and staying at Hotel Amicizia. While having a late breakfast in the courtyard, Tito approaches her table, "Buon giorno signora Esposito, coma esta?"

"I am fine thank you."

"Tu capice Italiano?"

"Si, poco. Mio Madre di Firenze." (Yes a little. My Mother is from Florence Italy)

Passing a small white envelope to Jeanne, "Mio domestica found this in your room."

"Found it you say, I say bullshit! Your maid had to go through my underwear in my suitcase to find that envelope. So what?"

"It is obviously marijuana signora."

Again I say so what?"

"So what you say? The Jeffery Field airport is in a big publicity campaign to change its name next year to the General Lawrence Edward Logan Airport, after a Spanish American war hero from Southie. Therefore, if I contact your employers, they would be upset at the bad publicity of a dope smoking stewardess on their planes. Hearing that—it won't be a – so what. You will be lucky to get any other job even at the current minimum wage of a buck an hour."

Tito's obvious first stage of blackmail unnerves Jeanne so much that she drops her coffee cup and begins to visibly shiver.

"Why would you do that Tito? What have I ever done to you that would have you cause me to lose my job or get arrested?"

"Nothing at all Miss Jeanne, just that I have an advantage that I believe will gain me some cooperative privileges from you."

The usually loquacious Jeanne Brooks goes silent. His non-verbal cue of rubbing his groin, gains her response. "I get your message. Are you talking about a quick roll in the hay or am I going to be your steady piece of arsse. If it is the later then I will rather suffer penalties then to have your greasy body on top of me whenever you get horny."

"I'll tell you what little lady, let us go to your room right now, then after a little stimulation of your libido intimacy, we will discuss our future relationship. I promise you that I will not be the only one to financially gain after that."

In the room she lifts her skirt, sits on the edge of the chair and slowly removes her stockings, garter belt, and panties, then lies down on the bed.

"No hurry *Bella Donna mia.* First we shall cozy over here on the sofa and inhale some grass; I know that cannabis smoke will make things easier for you."

Finishing the rolled weeds, Tito taking her hand leads her from the sofa to the side of the bed. "I am not going to be abusive. I am not an animal, for the slim possibility that you might get some pleasure, before I *scopare*, I want you naked so that I may make love to your body. If I go at it like you are dressed, I would indicate you're a *puttana* and that I have no respect for you."

Tito stands Jeanne up and slowly removes her blouse, her skirt, then her bra, and then brings the nude nymph in front of the full length mirror. While there, with the aid of the reflection he gains the full stimulation being able to view Jeanne's body from the front and the back simultaneously.

With a sweeping flourish of his right hand towards this nude enticement, "I am going to enjoy that heavenly body tremendously; as any normal male would do if they were fortunate enough to sample such a *bella corpa* as this."

Gently he leads her back to the bed, and then lies down along side of her. Anticipating his next move, while he is sliding his right hand slowly up and down her inner thighs, she spreads her legs. His lips are softly tantalizing many areas of her most desirable body.

The effects of the marijuana have made it easier for Jeanne to cooperate. Her soft moan encourages Tito as his fingers penetrate her mons veneris area to stimulate an erection of her theoretical *man in a boat,* and her vaginal contractions begin. Still maintaining the attitude of a lover, not a rapist or abuser, he now uses his right knee to nudge her thighs further apart. In anticipation, she reaches down, takes his extension, and guides it to the thrilling consequences for their mutual satisfaction.

While Jeanne is in the shower, Tito stands outside the stall, "You sure jumped to a conclusion when you saw me rub my groin when I was seated at the table in the courtyard. I happened to need to scratch that area, and you interpreted my movement as sexual. I believe you thought that a coitus liaison would solve your problem. What I had in mind, that you misinterpreted, was to get you into a business deal with me. I was just lucky to get a fuck in the deal."

Soaking wet, the screaming Jeanne pushes open the shower door, "What the fuck are you talking about you miserable *dago* bastard?"

"Finish your shower, calm down, get dressed and we will talk."

Completely puzzled, the now dressed Jeanne, takes a pack of Lucky Strikes from her purse, pulls one out and in a highly emotional style, lights and inhales deeply. Her actions alert Tito that she is highly pissed as she faces her *partner in venery* as angrily she snaps back, "Spit it out —-what are you talking about?"

Tito now needs to try and calm a now possible damaging volatile encounter, peace by all means is vital. He realizes that his taking advantage of her sexual misunderstanding might cause him to lose a potential financial bonanza.

"Jeanne, per *favore.* Calm down and listen to what I have to say. By your cooperating response, our physical liaison was not such a terrible thing for you. After all, you certainly had a good orgasm, so you can't say that you did not enjoy it. I did not start the idea of sexual activity, you did. Surely you realize that your solution to any problem can be solved by sex indicates that you have had many penis insertions before me."

"Tu ingannare mio Tito."

"No, now be fair Jeanne, I did not trick you or deceive you in any manner. I just went along with what you thought I wanted to do at that time."

"But I would not have let you fuck me if I had known that is not what you had in mind when you hinted that you intended to blackmail me."

"Jeanne, you are typically female. You know, and you use, pussy-power when it becomes convenient to get your way through, what you perceive to be, a tough situation. That is exactly what you just did. I know that I intended to black mail you, and I still am. However, it will be financially great for you as well as for me."

"Are you suggesting that I become your puttana and you will be my pimp?"

"*Gesu Cristo y Madre di Dio*, you are one aggravating bitch. I am not a whoremaster. I know that you make the Newark flight once a week. All I want is for you to take a package to my cousin Sergio Canalejo at the Newark Airport each month. He will meet you there and swap packages with you. For that I will pay you a grand for each trip you make. Within a year you will make more money than President Truman makes a year."

"That's got to be bullshit, Tito."

"What is in the packages?"

"Don't ask questions, the less you know the better, obviously you know that it must be illegal or I would not pay you so much. In fact, because you think that I such a mean bastard, I could pay you not a god damned dime and cause you to lose your job if you refuse. Think of it, you will get a package that will fit into your stewardess valise and for that you will get almost the same amount of dinero that North East Airways pays you in six months."

Since Jeanne, like Johnny di, is a great believer that ready cash money is Aladdin's lamp, she agrees to become a carrier. Her first delivery trip is on Sunday August 7, 1955.

While the Newark airport debarking area is sparsely occupied and all seems pleasant and serene, she is still extremely nervous. Pilot Captain Patrick Eden walks with her from the plane to the concourse and before departing, asks, "How about dinner and a rendezvous later this evening?"

"Sounds good to me Pat, I'll see you then, I need to make a couple of phone calls, and I might as well do them here. You go ahead and I will meet you later."

Standing near the row of telephone booths are four different men. One is in a dark black suit, a black shirt, tie and fedora. With his a dark complexion and bushy black moustache he is sinister enough for anyone to assume he is a sinister criminal. A few booths further, a sweat shirted, dungaree wearing mid-twenties male whose appearance could hide him being a possible undercover badge wearer. The third is a clean shaven man in his mid-thirties, beige sport coat over dark brown pants. The fourth is a non-descript male in a business suit and is reading a newspaper.

Decision, decision, the logical man must be the one with the newspaper. As she approaches, he slowly lowers the newspaper and smiles at Jeanne. More decisions, judging by appearance alone, can be dangerous. This guy must not be Sergio; it must be the obvious black fedora dago, she ponders.

'I wonder if that greasy looking mustached dago wop speaks understandable English. I bet he hasn't had a bath in months. Oh, what the Hell, I don't even have to speak to him. All I have to do is to give him my package and take that package that he is holding.'

As she heads towards the phone booths, the sporty mid-thirties stud suddenly moves toward her and grabs her arm and kisses her on the cheek. "Great to see you Sis, did you have a nice flight? Let's head for the restaurant and have lunch?"

A startled Jeanne is confused. Should she break away and run? Is this guy a cop? She tries not to panic, looks back at the dark dago for help and his no longer there. Did he run and hide? It all comes to a head as the mid-thirties guy says, "Relax Jeanne Marie, I am Sergio Canalejo."

The relief from fear almost causes her to pass out. "My God you sure scared the Hell out of me; I thought you were a cop."

"I knew you were confused when you headed for that cop instead of me."

"What cop?"

"That guy with the black hat is Carmen *Bruto* Colizzi. He is a lieutenant in the New Jersey State police narcotics squad. He was waiting to meet someone coming in on your flight. I saw him look you over, up and down. I was at first afraid he was coming after you, but when he got up and walked toward another woman, I knew you were safe."

While in bed that evening with Patrick Eden, she would love to tell him about the excitement and her luncheon engagement with the handsome Italian stud Sergio, but it might cause a jealous reaction and ruin her evening. Plus, more important, he must not realize that she is a cocaine *mule.*

Tuesday April 17, 1956 Tito has an emergency shipment that must be delivered ASAP. "Jeanne, I need to send a large package to Sergio. He has to have it by Thursday the 19th. Since the package is larger and delivery is on a weekday, and therefore riskier, I will double your pay. "

Taking advantage of the urgency of this delivery she responds, "Double pay is bullshit. This trip can be riskier. Triple or no go."

Now over a barrel, Tito acquiesces. The extra money is inducement enough for Jeanne. Granted the crowds at the airport are greater on week days than on Sundays, she will take a chance. Arriving at Newark, *lady luck* is with her, most of the people in the concourse of the airport are spellbound watching the television showing a fairyland of an enchanting elaborate dream world. The viewers are enthralled witnessing a magic T.V. show of a real live beautiful Princess, marrying her hero Prince. It is the Philadelphia debutant angel Grace Kelley being married to Monaco Prince Rainier lll.

Jeanne wonders – but surely the Prince has heard rumors and is aware of the fact that Gary Cooper and Bing Crosby had already dipped their wicks in Grace?

All this euphoria is giving these viewers the rare opportunity of experiencing a truly childhood fairy tale. Even *Bruto,* supposedly on duty, seems mesmerized and oblivious to his surroundings. Sergio, also watching the T.V. is unaware of Jeanne's arrival until he is brutally alerted by her yanking his arm and pulling him away from the viewers.

"Dam you Sergio; you are getting careless, forcing me to have to come over to that crowd and Bruto, to get you."

Her fifth package toting flight to Newark is on Sunday March 8, 1956. The usual procedure of changing envelopes is at lunch or dinner at the airport restaurant, this time Sergio makes an exception. "Let us celebrate our successes by dining at Tio Luigi's restaurant, he makes excellent lasagna."

The atmosphere is most romantic, an Italian baritone singing *Arrivederci Roma.* Tart Chianti, and palate pleasing food, it is body, soul and a heart pleasing meal. At the end of the meal, Uncle Tio brings a small gift wrapped package on a silver tray and passes it to Jeanne, "This is for you, Saluto, Bella Jeanne."

"What is the occasion?"

"Shush, just open the package."

A quiet yelp comes out as Jeanne removes from the purple velvet case, a diamond tennis bracelet. "Oh my God Sergio, what gives?"

"We believe that you have been loyal, trustworthy and a great asset to us. This is our way of saying thanks. Wear it in good health and think of me when you take it off or put it on." Then he assists her in placing it on her right wrist.

Every woman has her little cue that she gives to a man when she is ready to spread her thighs for him. It can be via her eyes, a spoken double entendre, a certain smile, or maybe a touch. She sends three signals to the unsuspecting male. First – she is approachable, – second, she is available and finally – she is agreeable. In this case Jeanne reaches over and slowly rubs her right palm gently on the back of Sergio's hand. Testing the cue, he embraces her cheeks between his two palms and gently kisses her.

Bingo! He read the correct cue and they head upstairs to the private rooms of Uncle Tio. After all, such an expensive gift must be rewarded with a *grazie* by whatever means a female has, but Hell, she has been ready months ago. The bracelet just gives her a stab at respectability, so he will think well of her after she seduces him. The usual female comment after her first sexual encounter with a new lover, "Do you still respect me?"

Chapter seventeen

Sergio and Jeanne cook up their own chicanery. Each month, before they exchange their packages, they remove, from Sergio's package, a small amount of the heroin. The laws prosecute dope peddlers, yet the contribution *to the American Corruption* begins with those that seem to feel that a little nice people party should have a little powder sniffing. If no purchases, picayune, or massive, are made, this innocently inspired corruption would cease to exist. It is time to arrest the users as well as those that are aware of such use or purchases. Such criminality is bad behavior - to ignore bad behavior is tolerate it. To tolerate it is to accept it, and to encourage it is to promote it.

After many trips, they have skimmed a half a kilo that Jeanne sells to sponsors of society parties. By the time the next Newark trip is due, *Jeanne* has accumulated eighty-nine thousand from her chicanery and Newark deliveries. Sergio obviously has accumulated a heavy amount of dinero, but never reveals to Jeanne how much he has.

On the Sunday May 6, 1956 Newark delivery, they spot *Bruto* Colizzi at the airport and carelessly assume that it is just another coincident that he happens to be there at the same time as they are. Unbeknown to the couple, *Bruto* has been at the airport on three previous months to note their modus operandi. He has determined the exchange is being made in the hotel room and he is at the airport to be sure that Jeanne has made the flight. Confirming this he sets in motion the sting.

The fact that Jeanne sees Sergio waiting at the airport for her, falsely assures her that everything is quite normal. She greets him with a kiss and gets a passionate hug indicating he has more in mind than just business. Laughingly she gently pushes him back. "Sergio, most of your brains as well as your thinking, and *vita strada,* comes from below your waist. Relax baby, I promise I will be ready by the time we hit the bed at the hotel."

Sergio smiles, takes her arm, "I can't help it. Ringlets of testosterones are trickling down my leg."

Like all romantics, there mind becomes set on the anticipated fun sex, so they jubilantly head to the hotel. True to her promise, no sooner in the room, Jeanne begins to leave a trail of her clothes on the floor ending up at bedside stripped down to her panties. Turning to face Sergio, "Evidently you are not as anxious as you were at the airport; you are damn slow at getting your clothes off."

"Not so *Bambina*, I am thrilled and fascinated, watching you shed your clothes. You may never understand how exciting it is for a man to watch a woman disrobe even though he knows she is going to spread her legs as soon as she hits the bed. Each time that we have shared our bodies, you have become less sexually inhibited than the previous time. This time is ecstatic; you have not a bit of an inhibition. I love it, and that is why I am slow in undressing."

Finally nude, he reaches over and removes her last piece of clothing, then says, "Take a look at this piece of my manhood and decide if I am ready."

"Hush, *mio amare.* Let me hold and caress it with my lips before I enjoy its penetration."

However, it is not to be. Sergio, as with most other criminals, becomes careless and doing so he fails to put the deadbolt safety lock on the door. With a pass key, Colizzi, and six uniform cops barge into the room. The shock has Jeanne grabbing a sheet to cover her nudeness, Sergio's manhood becomes limp, and he slumps into a nearby chair. In a matter of minutes *Bruto* locates the contraband package. Jeanne and Sergio are booked at the Newark Police H.Q. Almost as soon as they are booked the mob Consigliere is there to post the low $20,000 bail that he arranges through the corrupt courts.

Their cover blown and facing hard prison time, the couple decides to jump bail and head for heroin heaven, Naples, Italy and the family homestead of Sergio Canalejas grandparents. Presenting themselves as married, Jeanne is reluctantly accepted into the family. However the subtle undertones are painful to her. She is given the nickname of *the slut in stiletto heels.*

Although they are all Italians, ancient feudalism still remains. Amongst Italians, a person of Florentine (Florence Italy) ancestry is considered of a higher class than those from other parts of Italy. The Napolitano or Neapolitan (Naples) group are considered as lower class criminals, and those south of the Holy City of Rome are considered peasants. Jeanne, being of Florentine ancestry, treats Sergio's Napolitano family as a lower class of people being far beneath her.

In the narrow streets of Naples, laundry clothe lines are strung from second, third and fourth floors of one side of the street to the buildings on the other side of the street. While wet laundry is hung out to dry, it also absorbs the smoke and smells of the street below giving the locals a traffic odor. Being typical American, Jeanne is compelled to tolerate this miserable scene of blatant peasantry that is not duplicated anywhere in Tuscany.

To get away from this hostile element, she spends her days touring the many magnificent historical parts of Italy. It takes her on many visits to Rome to even absorb a small part of its antique beauty and history. The same applies to her parents Tuscany area and its main city of Firenze (Florence), and then southward to the ancient ruins of Pompeii and the underground tombs of the early Christians.

Venice and its canals, when not flooded, a visit is a must. Near Naples are the Isle of Capri, its blue grotto, and Funicular trolleys. Sorrento, the city made famous in song is close to Naples and daily visits can be made there. Moreover the sights, sounds, and history of Italy would take a person a decade to visit all parts of the country. Jeanne is doing her best to enjoy it and also to escape from the unfriendly, bigoted Canalejas family.

Since the people Sergio was working for in the States, receive their merchandise through Lucky Luciano, it is no problem for Sergio to get a job working for Luciano's Neapolitan *Camorra* (Mafia run mob). However, it puts him in a close proximate to the many prostitutes in Luciano's stable.

Luciano is a big time Mafia criminal in N.Y.C. from 1931 until April of 1936 when he is tried by District Attorney Thomas Dewey and sentenced to Dannemora for 30 to 50 years. Released and deported to

Naples he takes over the *Camorra*. During the war Lucky works with the U.S. Military in Sicily and also prevents war-time sabotage on N.Y.C. water front.

Some of the *puttana* are young and beautiful and Sergio cannot resist the free *meat* that is so tempting. Like most stupid young males, he makes the error when on several occasions he brings one of these girls home to dine with his family.

In a screaming match with Sergio, Jeanne vents her feelings. "You are fucking those whores, and then come home to me. I won't have it that way. You put your pecker where dozens of men have put theirs before you and you expect me to accommodate you. No way! Mr. *Wallyo. No* way. From now on your pecker is in isolation as far as I am concerned. You will sleep on the couch and not in my bed from now on."

Moreover, she does, but it gets her more ostracizing from the family.

"A husband has the right to have other women if he is not satisfied with his wife," declares Nonna Canalejas. "You think because you are a Florentine that he is beneath you. You are not a good wife to him, go back to America. For Sergio, you are zero between your loins."

What Jeanne has yet to learn from Nana is that in the U. S. or Italy, or for that matter, anywhere in the world that there are females, the worst enemy that any woman has is – just any other woman. The fact that she had dyed her hair red and dressed provocatively does not gain her any female friends.

After witnessing the tirade between Jeanne and Sergio, one of the visiting whores tells Lucky of Sergio's wife trouble and the Canalejas family's desire to get rid of Jeanne. On Wednesday November 14, 1956 the now fifty-nine year old Luciano has Sergio bring Jeanne to his office.

"*Rosso testa,* I understand that you are familiar with Tito Mangino in Boston, is that correct?"

Not sure of what Lucky is alluding to Jeanne hesitates to answer.

"Relax Senora, relax. Sergio tells me that you were a *mule*' for Tito. Is this correct?"

"Yes Don Luciano, yes, that is correct. I was working for him when I was busted in Newark."

"How would you like to return to Boston?"

"That is not possible, I jumped bail. They would nab me the second they read my passport."

"Nothing is impossible; I will get you a new passport under a different name. You can make a new start in America. Are you interested?"

"Yes, I certainly am interested. But why would you do this for me?"

"Don't get me wrong, I am not being generous, this is strictly business. I need to get some kilos to Tito Mangino and you would be the most experienced carrier that is available here in Napoli."

"Will I get some money also? I will be flat broke going to America."

"You will receive ten *Gs* from Tito and two from me before you leave here."

"That does not seem to be a lot of money. I should get some new clothes to wear home."

"Don't fuck with my plans. You are going as a middle class Irisher not a dressy Florentine. What I am offering is a lot of cash. Back in the States the minimum wage is now one dollar. Forget the idea of buying new clothes. With my experience at smuggling, and my *ricatta* connections, you will be okay, something that you alone could never be."

"What about Sergio Don Luciano?"

"He is not included and so tell him nothing. Tomorrow morning get up and come to my office. Here you will be cleverly disguised. We will form a soft plastic shell that will resemble the outline of a woman six months pregnant. It will be firmly taped to your body. Between the shell and your stomach we will tape packets. You will wear no facial makeup, a plain hair arrangement, and low cost maternity dress. The only jewelry you will wear is a gold wedding ring, no signs of wealth."

"You will appear to be just a plain middle class Irish housewife that is pregnant with her second or third child. Your new name will be Bridget Ahearn. You will be carrying an Irish passport and you will go from Naples to London, and there to Boston to supposedly visit your aunt. With your Boston accent you can pass for Irish easily. Now do you want to return home my way or just sit on your *culo* in Naples?"

"I am nervous, but I will try it. I can't get much more jail time if I am caught at this than what I will get for having jumped bail. The plan sounds good, after all an Irish lass coming from London to the very Irish City of Boston, will be so logical that it should not draw undo speculation or scrutiny."

On the first leg of the journey, the Italian authorities, being family orientated, treat this obviously highly pregnant mother with special care in her trip from Naples.

Chapter eighteen

On Friday February 4, 1957 the a.k.a. Bridget Ahearn is sitting in Heathrow Airport waiting her flight to Boston. London is different than Italy; here there is still an anti-Irish immigrant attitude by those in authority. A British immigration agent notices that when he announces to a group of women sitting waiting passport examination, "Bridget Ahearn next." Jeanne made no move to answer to that name. The second time he yelled a little louder, "Bridget Ahearn next." A women sitting next to Jeanne nudges her and says, "Are you Bridget Ahearn?"

Jeanne jumps up, breaks out in a heavy sweat, and walks to the Agents post.

"Well young lady, did you forget your name?"

"No, no, me mind was fa' away. I was thinking how nice t'will be to be visiting me aunt in Boston over Saint Valentine's Day."

"Well little lady, outside this terminal is a cold wind blowing and a few snowflakes falling and you are sweating heavily. Are you not feeling well? Do you need me to call for our nurse to examine you to be sure you are well enough to travel today?"

Not waiting for an answer, the agent picks up his phone. "This is Hightower at the passport desk I have what seems to be a very pregnant *Mik* who is sweating heavily. Maybe a nurse should exam her to see if she can go aboard the plane to Boston. We do not want to chance her becoming ill half way across the Atlantic."

Turning back to Jeanne, "Please take a seat, and a nurse will be right out Mrs. Ahearn."

"Please, sir. I could use a glassa wata'."

The agent goes to the water fountain, using his coffee cup, brings her a drink of water. With bated breath, Jeanne slips a Librium pill into her mouth and drinks the water. Thankfully for Jeanne, the usual delay for service at airports gives the tranquilizer fifteen minutes to do its job before a male nurse comes to the agent's booth.

"Agent Hightower, you do realize that I am not allowed to physically exam a female patient without a female nurse in attendance, and no such a female nurse is available today. All I can do is check her pulse, blood pressure, and such to see if there are any obvious danger signs that would preclude her flying out of here today."

"Well, dam it, that red headed *mackerel snapper* (Catholic) is acting suspicious. She is sweating and it so cold in here that I have on this heavy jacket. I don't know if it is just that she is so far along in her pregnancy that she is nervous about flying or what. After your cursory exam, just tell me what you suggest."

After a hasty exterior examination of Jeanne, the male nurse reports to the agent. "As far as I can see, her blood pressure is a little high, but she says that is because she is nervous about flying. She is not sweating anymore than any person, male or female, that is carrying extra weight like a pregnant woman does and it is obvious, from her physical appearance, she is a little over six months pregnant."

"I gave her a tranquilizer. She will be okay to fly and be more relaxed after the pill takes effect. I'd suggest that you get her to hell on her flight to Boston so that she can fall asleep in her seat."

Taking the male nurse advice, the Agent signals for an Aer Lingus attendant to come and escort Mrs. Bridget Ahearn aboard the flight that just came in from Shannon, and heading to Boston.

The Librium and nurse's tranquilizer soon sedate Jeanne into a deep sleep that ends twenty minutes before landing at Logan Airport. More problems await Jeanne at the terminal, it is snowing heavenly and she tries to get a taxi, but none is available. She goes to a booth and phones Tito, "There are no taxis available because of the heavy snow Tito. I can't sit in the airport lobby for any length of time, I might be recognized."

"You worry too much Jeanne."

"Worry my arsse Tito, one of my former fellow employee who knows me best, Captain Patrick Eden passed by me and because of my disguise he didn't give me a second look, but some of the stewardess might."

"Okay. Jeanne, okay. It will take me a little while but I will get *Big Tony's* tow truck and pick you up at 5:30. So that we won't miss connecting, say that I pick you up in the area that the taxis usually stand. Okay?"

"Thanks. Set your watch. It is now 4:00 o'clock; I will find a secluded spot for that hour and a half."

What better hideaway could she pick other than a stall in the ladies room behind a locked door? At 5:20 she goes out to the front door of the terminal. Seeing Tito pull into the taxi stand area, she bends to pick up her suitcase when a Statsie on duty there, reaches over and picks up the suitcase.

"Let me help you little Mama," the Commonwealth Trooper says as he uses his other arm to take her by her elbow and escort her to Tito's truck. There he gently assists her into the vehicle and with a wave, shuts the truck door and returns to the terminal.

Finally in the sanctity of her room she orders Tito, "Get me a tall gin and tonic, all that tension has given me internal shakes. In all, from the trip between Naples and here I must have sweat off a good ten pounds."

Waiting her drink she sheds the maternity clothes, takes off the cavernous fake maternity shell, and lays out the plastic wrapped heroin packs onto the dresser. Still a little bit woozy and now down to her panties and bra she lies down on the bed.

Tito returns to the room with her drink. He gently assists her to sit upright on the bed to consume her gin and tonic. In the assist, he bends and softly places his lips on her semi-exposed right breast.

"Down boy, down. Do not waste your time salivating over my tits. If I have a mind to, later on I will check my hormones and if you are lucky, I may let you climb into the rack. In the meantime – business first – I don't want your erect six inches. I want what you owe me, ten big green ones. I want them now. Go get it while I take a much needed shower."

Anticipating Jeanne's arrival, Tito has the money in his safe downstairs, so he retrieves it and is back up in Jeanne's room before she is out of the shower. Stepping out of the shower, she looks for the towel that she had lain out on the bed and sees that Tito is standing by holding the towel in a gesture that indicates he wants to dry her off.

To Jeanne the path of least resistance is to let him get his *kicks'* wiping her dry. Tito is gentle in the toweling; it is obvious that he spends more time drying Jeanne from the belly button down than from the belly button up. He then gently sits her on the bed and reaches for an envelope on the dresser. He hands her the envelope, knowing that she will open and count the contents and this will allow him more time to lasciviously stare at her nakedness.

"Tito, you are only torturing yourself staring at my body. I am in no mood to satisfy you or anyone else. So go into the bathroom and *beat your meat,* I don't want to watch you get rid of your load," as she dons a bathrobe.

During the next thirty minutes Tito has brought her three double strength Gin and tonics, believing that giving her one more drink, and she will soon be under him.

"Jeanne, you will notice that there is an extra thousand bucks in that envelope. You have a choice, give it back to me or lie flat on that bed with your legs apart and let me drain my overloaded balls."

"You bastard, a girl can put out for a dinner or a dollar and you men think of us as puttana. If I take that money you will consider me an expensive puttana."

Then roughly shedding her robe, she says, "Oh, hell I don't care what you consider me, a *grand* sure makes me high priced, so climb on."

Staying at Tito's motel, by the end of March, Jeanne is drinking too much; she is in constant fear of being recognized by one of the flight crews that lay over at Tito's hotel between their flights. In addition, she is in no mood for Tito's constant horny harassments.

In turn, he is tired of her constant rejection, her moodiness, and her drinking. Through his source of supply, he arranges a two kilo package that needs to go to Victoria in the British Columbia. There she will be given the opportunity to work for the Canadian mob and with her Irish passport and new name – and in Canada; there will be less chance of the U.S. Narcs finding her.

However, nothing ever seems to work out to Jeanne's advantage. Arriving at the airport in B.C. on Tuesday April 16, 1957 she is supposed to be met and escorted to a sanctuary by members of the local Mafia. Instead she is met by an undercover member of the R.C.M.P.

On a tip, she is body searched and her eleven thousand in U.S. currency and the cocaine is found on her. The cash is considered to be illicit money and also seized. After finger printing and checking with the F.B.I. her true identity is made. Under Canadian/British law at a court trial she is guilty and must prove her innocence. This is the reverse of U.S. Bill of Rights, wherein you are not guilty until a prosecutor proves you guilty by trial.

On Friday June 7, 1957 unable to prove her innocence of the crime of having two kilo of coke, and eleven thousand in cash, she is sentenced to three to five years.

Chapter nineteen

Monday August 6, 1956. It is quite a surprise to Ted when at breakfast coffee he reads the Boston Globe headlines, *Brink's robbers rounded-up.* Listed in the Globe, as one of the leaders of the gang, is the Egleston Square Diner owner the five-by-five *booster,* Anthony *Fat Tony* Pino.

At this time Teddy wonders how many in law enforcement remember the asinine statement made in January of 1950, by J. Edgar Hoover: *"This armed robbery of the Brink's money vault could not have been made by local Boston petty thugs, so we will look to Chicago and New York to find the gangster culprits."*

Hoover spends many thousands of dollars sending his agents to other cities, hastily over-looking Boston thugs. As it turns out, all the gang members are from the greater Boston area; three own and operate business in the Egleston Square area that Ted patrolled. Tony and his brother –in-law Vinnie Costa are like ham and eggs while owning and operating the Egleston Square Diner. The gang member who turns witness for the Commonwealth, the 48 year old Joseph Specs *O'Keefe,* is their close buddy.

Diagonally across the square from the diner is the J&A Café and night club, owned and operated by the Brink's gang co-leader – the known felon – Joseph, *Canvas back* McInnis. At least six of the eleven gang members are well known to Sheerin. Putting the newspaper down to answer the ringing phone Ted is pleasantly surprised to hear Cathy's voice. "Ted, I have great news, may I come by your place?"

"Cathy, as close as we have been you insult me by even asking that question. You know that you are welcome anytime, day, or night, just ring my doorbell."

"Is tonight open, do you have a first half or second half duty?"

"I am on the second half tonight. I am free until eleven p.m. Tomorrow is out, then I am off Friday, Saturday and Sunday this week. Pick your time sweetheart."

"How about Friday around seven Ted?"

"I'll be anxiously waiting. Don't eat; I will prepare an evening fireside meal like old times."

Friday evening a few minutes before seven, Cathy is at the door. Opening it, Ted is met with a beautiful vision in a light tan flowered dress. A black knit shawl is draped over her left shoulder with her long blonde tresses in a double braid on each side of her shoulders.

Taking her extended hand, he gently snuggles her close and softly kisses her warm anticipating lips. Having enjoyed their scintillating embrace in the doorway, they adjourn to sofa in front of the flaming fireplace. The fireplace takes the evening chill away, moreover it enhances and adds to a romantic aura that encases the room.

The undulating flames flicker in rhythmic waves synchronizing with soft stereo music. Timely enough, the *4 Aces* singing *Love is a many splendored thing,* begins to play.

At the time that Ted purchased the recording, he had bought it to enjoy the flip side, however this night, when he turned it over and it played *Love is a many splendored thing,* it caught the interest of Cathy and Ted. Especially so when the song refers to *true love* that they especially believe they posses.

All this is accented with sips of a light Zinfandel wine. The romantic part is soon shattered for Ted. Cathy puts her wine glass down, "I have decided to get married Ted, and I want you to be at the wedding. It will be on Saturday October 6."

"Jesus Christ Cathy, you sure picked one hellava way to end a romantic evening. You bed me down, and then you floor me with the fact that you are going to marry someone else."

"I am sorry Teddy. While this may not have been the best time to tell you, I had to tell you before I leave you tonight."

"Let me guess. You are marrying Lawrence Cameron?"

"How did you know?"

"A couple of logical things come to mind. First, he is the only man that I know of that you work close to. Second, you always spoke highly of him. In the newspaper accounts, showing him running for Suffolk County District Attorney, the photos always show you standing close to him. In the third place, I know that you have not been with any man other than me."

"And Lawrence knows that also, he is not stupid Teddy. Remember he is the one who advised me to stay with you in Pembroke until he served Stephen with the divorce papers. He most obviously knows that I have spent a great deal of time with you. He surely knows that you are a testosterone male and that I am a widow."

"Which brings the question of how does this affect our relationship?"

Taking his left hand she squeezes his ring finger. Lifting the hand she kisses the back of it two or three times. "Ted, you know that you have always been my oracle, however, this finger does not have a wedding band. I would rather be marrying you. You have been so good to me, and I do love you, but such a marriage, to you, would fail. I would be nagging you to change your life style. No woman, no matter how much she loves you, can survive the apprehension of danger and possible death that you daily expose yourself to."

Continuing, "Larry is a safe, secure, non-violent life style and mature gentleman. While I love you, with him I have a chance of a great, fairly normal, future. I can enjoy a comfortable life as his politically perfect token wife. But if it is okay with you I will still be yours whenever either one of us wants the other."

"Token wife be damned. You mean all of it will be a political image not a true relationship. You still are going to have to let him fuck you."

"Don't be mean and crude, Teddy. That is all you know. Larry happens to have a low sex drive and is only interested in how I can help him as a political asset. He is not horny and loving as you always are. In fact, when we became engaged, like most intended, I would be available if he insists. I would have been logical to have sex with him before we married because he knows that I am not a virgin. We have had no sex yet, and he never hints or tries to seduce me. I don't care that he doesn't try, because you turn me on, he doesn't. Furthermore Teddy, I have learned, from being with Lawrence that he wants his image more powerful than he or any other politician can ever be. He believes that I will enhance this image."

"Don't be so sure that he might not change his *stripes*. Harry Truman once said that his choices in life were either being a piano player in a whore house or a politician. And he said if we were to tell the truth – there's hardly any difference. So beware, down the line, regarding your so pure Lawrence Cameron."

With that, feeling sorry to have said all this, Cathy softly places both of her hands on Ted's face, pulls him close, and gives him a long warm kiss. Interpreting her cue, he leans her back on the sofa and passionately kisses her. A deep shudder encompasses her body as she pulls him closer. Her response proves her point.

With shaky hands, he unbuttons her dress, removes her black laced red trimmed bra, and puts his hot lips on her now erect nipple. Intimately placing his hand between her thighs, he inserts his finger. After a few quivers Cathy says, "Your love muscle can finish what your finger has started. I want you in me." Then she unzips his pants.

In a few moments passionate, low moans and a shuddering sigh flow from their blended bodies. After a relaxing composure gaining spell, Cathy lies on her back and silently stares at the ceiling.

"This could be ours forever Cathy if you would reconsider marrying me instead."

"Our moments like this are so great because we are in love, but be honest Teddy, you know living with you every day could give any woman a great deal of stress. I wouldn't know, from one moment to another, what was happening or even going to happen."

Rolling over on top of Ted, she gives him a loving kiss. "Is there any better way of proving that I love you other than what just occurred?"

Slowly getting up from the bed she begins to dress. While putting the finishing touches to her disheveled hair, Ted hands her another glass of wine. Her hands still with an after sex quiver cause her to spill the wine on her dress.

With the pleasant thought of another interlude being possible, Ted suggests, "This is no problem my love. Why don't you rinse out your dress and undies and put on my robe while I prepare a meal."

Mealtime is always a good reminiscence time. Even going back to the time that they took rides on the Swan boat in the Boston Public Gardens. They reminisce the past and the present and touch on prognostication possibilities.

Boston Public Gardens Swan boat rides.
(The only boat, of this type, in the world)

Finishing the meal and leaving the dishes on the table, Ted asks, "Do you have to report to anyone?"

"Since you sarcastically mean Larry, no, he never asks me where I have been, or what I have been doing. I guess he figures that he needs me more than I need him. Therefore, I take advantage of that. I can't allow myself to ever be subjugated by masculine superiority, as you would do. If I am to remain independent as I am, then I will always be a free woman."

"It is late and you are still in my robe," Ted gently removes her robe, "let's go back to the bed."

"I'd like that. Maybe you can lend me another pair of your jammys."

"Forget the jammys Cathy, I want you nude."

Without exchanging another word they position themselves on the bed in anticipation of each pleasing the other and do so until Morpheus coaxes them into sweet dreamland. After a morning session of additional romance, Cathy says, "I have never had so much love making in my life. I have just had over fourteen hours of great love, which is more than I ever have had even in any full week's time. Including our past romances."

Saturday Oct.6, 1956, St. Columba Church is awash with politicians of all ilk. Democrats, Republicans, Libertarians, and Independents. All *stripes,* from the lowly *Ward Heeler* to elected politicians, Judges and even Cardinal Cruikshank. Each person is attempting to ride on the coat tails of Lawrence Joseph Cameron, who is running as a Democrat for the powerful office of Suffolk County District Attorney.

They are anxious to be noted, as being at his Wedding Mass and Reception. They want it to be known that they witnessed marriage to Catherine Brooks Ryler, so later on, when asking for favors they can imply they are personal friends because they attended his wedding.

A great deal of the conversations among the guest is today's news reports that are about the Brink's gang being found guilty this day. While the gang had six years and eight months of free time before their apprehension, their day finally arrived. Three days later Judge Felix Forte sentences all of the gang, Pino and McInnis are sentenced to life in prison. Forte gives the rest of the culprits varying sentences ranging from six to 12 years. O 'Keefe is given probation and put in the witness protection program and sent to California to be a chauffeur for Cary Grant (a.k.a. Archibald Leach).

While Ted is also corrupt, he passes judgment on others so criminally inclined and is pleased that Pino and McInnis are going to jail.

Fr. Tim begins the Wedding ceremony with a jesting greeting. "All you righteous politicians and followers in attendance, don't you fear that observers might realize that your appearance here means that the government does run quite well without you?"

Ted sits in the organ loft and after the formal ceremony he joins the line of good wishers where Cathy introduces him to Lawrence.

"Cathy, I know Sergeant Sheerin, he and I, have met several times on police business. He has been a great help in the Brinks case. Sarge, you have been a friend to my Catherine, I hope you will become a friend to me also."

At the wedding reception, Cathy and Ted, for obvious reasons, do not take any opportunity for private conversation. Tuesday November 6, 1956, the Republicans make a clean sweep riding on the re-election of Ike Eisenhower's Republican ticket and the Democratic candidate Lawrence J. Cameron is defeated by a large margin in his run for District Attorney.

The following week Cathy phones Ted, "I can only get away for a couple of hours this coming Friday afternoon. I'd like to come over, is that okay with you?"

Using her full name whenever he wishes to stress a point, "Catherine Jane Cameron, whatever will it take for you to finally realize that I mean it? You never have to ask that. You are a very important part of me. My life and my home are yours any time that you wish. I'll be anxiously awaiting your visit."

"Edward Sheerin, this is serious; I need advice from my oracle. Please, think with your top head, not your bottom one." A bit puzzled, Ted responds, "I will agree with you as long as you promise you will come here with nothing on under your dress."

"God, sometimes I think you are hopeless my love, but I will abide by your wishes if you will hold off your sex drive until I explain my problem."

Friday November 23, 1956, Ted greets her with a hug. He places a friendly kiss on her check, while gently sliding his hand up and down her rear cheeks to see if he can detect a panty line.

Quite aware of Ted's action, "Satisfied my love? No panties, but you must wait until we talk."

Smiling at her observation of his derriere exploration and noting no panty ridge, and due to her somber attitude he leads her to the sofa. Her first comment is a request "Have you any more of that Zinfandel wine, I could use a drink."

Pouring two glasses, Ted sits along side of Cathy on the fireplace warmed sofa. The heat from the fire takes away her chill of the cold November evening as well as her inner nervousness of what she is about to reveal to him. After a few sips, "Ted, I do not know what to do. I am pregnant. I have not told Larry. What should I do?"

Ted, unprepared for such a climatic statement from Cathy, hesitates to answer. Pondering possible solutions then his suggestions, "Cathy, you can get a divorce and I will marry you or you can get an abortion. But I suggest that you go full term and have Larry believe that he is responsible. I am sure he would be pleased at thinking he is to become a father. That is an asset to a young aspiring politician. Have you been having a normal sexual relation as a loving wife?"

"Our sex life, compared with that of a young newly wedded couple, is not normal. We usually have sex only once a week and on those occasions I try to imagine that it is you on top of me. It makes it more tolerable when I do imagine that is you. Abortion is out of the question, and the idea of marrying you is a dream that can never come true. I have told you why that is a no-no, in our past conversations. Like most women, I need security, and again I say that I do not want the stress that comes with your life style."

"Then you must tell Larry that you are pregnant and he is going to be a new father. No one else knows that it is not his sperm that made the baby."

Cathy accepts the decision of her oracle and has another glass of wine. Finishing the wine, Ted takes Cathy by the hand, "Since you did abide by my request of you coming panty-less let us validate that reason."

He assists her from the sofa to the bedroom. True lovers cannot resist any opportunity, and Cathy does not hesitate. The bed waits to become their co-conspirator.

After enjoying her dramatic strip-*tease* of her shedding her clothes, Ted kneels down on the floor and kisses her slightly rounded tummy. (Men seem love a slight tummy on a woman; to them it seems to imply sexuality). With a likeable male awkwardness, he lifts her into his muscular arms and carries her, and very tenderly and gently, lowers her on to the linen sheeted bed. At times like these she is so glad that she is a female who can enjoy her male. Instinctively Cathy anxiously spreads her loins for her true love to impact a sealing flow of his sperm. Such an embrace brings a temporary, stolen, Elysium.

Chapter twenty

Freeport Motors has become quite profitable for Ted and his three partners. Holding the daily cash deposits of Jazz's bookies has made the company big time from the growth of the operations. Ted's dad is in charge of daily operations, and is a full time salesman. Alvan is a salesman and the used car buyer. Stanley is the full time mechanic and part time salesman. The trio make a great team.

When buying a used trade-in car from new car dealers, Alvan figures in the cost of making a car profitable and salable this will include any needed mechanical repairs by Stanley. He will then set the retail price. His purchases are profitable and in one case, very profitable. Jack Carroll the used car manager of South Boston Ford dealership, phoned. "Al, I owe Teddy Sheerin a favor for that fantastic weekend that my wife and kids spent last month at Blue Haven Lodge. I just took in trade from a driving school, six 1952 Nash Ambassadors, the ones that look like an upside down bathtub."

"Yeah Jack, I know those tubs. No one wants them because the fenders on the front wheels are so big and deep that it prevents the driver from taking wide turns. They are also old and they won't sell."

"Listen to me Al. I never steered you wrong, and I am not going to cheat you. I still want another invite, to Blue Haven for my family. I swear to you in your own language let me tell you this is a hellava kosher deal I am going to offer you. I want to get these cars out of my building before my boss sees them. I will give you all six for $350.00 cash, plus $50.00 for me. You can sell them for $350.00 each with your policy of $5.00 down and a weekly payment. Stanley will have damn little work to do on these cars. They all are ready to sell, except one. Stan can use that one for parts."

"I don't think I can get that much for each sale Jack."

"Are you kidding? Have you seen the cost of the new cars coming out next year? It won't be long before $5000.00 will only buy a used one."

1952 Nash Ambassador

It is very profitable and Al closes the deal that day after assuring Jack that Ted will be told of what a good deal it is.

Meanwhile, Claudia and Virginia continue their friendship and often spend time together at lunch or just occasional visits to one or the others home. On her Sunday December 22, 1956 visit to Ginny Bushnell, Claudia is seeking advice from her confidante

"Ginny, the first time that I saw you, after I returned from New York, you were coming from Sunday Mass. Do you remember that long conversation that we had about our love-life?"

"I surely do. I meant every word of it."

"Then if I may get personal, I need some advice that relates to that conversation and I have a few questions."

"Claudia, we are close enough that you may ask me any question that crosses your mind. What is it?"

"I have been married to Stanley for over a year, and I am having a problem with the no sex part. I know that I pledged that I would not have an affair with any man, but God Almighty I have been so passionate at times that I am in danger of violating that promise. I am no longer satisfied by the vibrator nor the dildos, since they no longer do their job. I almost want to accept a hint from Ted."

"From Ted, it's no hint, it is a fact; he has no conception of integrity, or morals. He will fuck any female that is ready, including his brother's wife."

"Yes, I know that. He told me that things do not always work out as they are planned. He said that I am a wild bird that should not be put in a cage without sex. I told him that I was not looking for his stud service, and I lied and said that Stanley is taking care of my passions."

"Stanley isn't?"

"No, both you and Ted know that Stanley can't have sex. But he is so good and I love him, however, my hormones do rave. I constantly dream about having sex and you said that you had been without a man for a long, long time. How do you do without? Don't you ever get passionate?"

"I guess the old adage of confession is good for the soul would be apropos at this time. Present day morality be damned. However, I want your promise that what I tell you will never be violated, understand?"

"My God Virginia, you know all about my trashy times that no one else knows. You have known me long enough that you should not even suggest that I would say anything."

"Well if you remember, I said that I had been without a man, I did not say I have been without sexual satisfaction. I am a bi-sexual lesbian."

"I don't understand."

"You don't understand what?"

"What is a lesbian?"

"My God, Claudia, I did not realize that you are so naïve. A tribade – lesbian – queer, a sapphist or whatever name you have heard a homosexual woman called. We believe that men should not have the only right to a woman. "

"Virginia doesn't the Bible say that homosexuality is a bad sin."

"Well we Catholics are prohibited to read the Bible, so I will not argue the Bible point with you. I will only say that this form of sexuality satisfies me more than a dildo or a penis."

(Editorial note: While the Church of Rome did not change the centuries old Canon Law that forbids Catholics reading the scriptures by themselves, in recent years it did not enforce penalties for doing so. In fact, that edict remained until Pope Benedict the 16th who on Sunday October 6, 2008 ordered that the Bible will begin to be broadcast in Rome, from the start to the finish. He then encouraged all Catholics to read the bible.)

"Claudia, if a mechanical penis device no longer satisfies you, it may be because you are not emotionally fulfilled from this method. Could lesbianism be an option for you and bring you emotional satisfaction?"

A bit startled at Virginia's revelation, Claudia pushes back against her chair.

"Virginia, is it the thought of a physical female contact that makes me apprehensive? No, we have, in the past, embraced, kissed, and touched in a non-sexual action. Moreover, it is logical that masturbation may be a physical necessity but not emotionally satisfaction anymore than a cold dildo."

Realizing that she is not intimidated by these thoughts, Claudia is suddenly aware that a long disquieted period of silence has occurred and apologizes. Virginia remains silent; it is obvious by her Mona Lisa smile, that she expects Claudia to react, and also that their long relationship can handle it. She is correct.

"I certainly understand your feelings. No apology is warranted for your normal reaction Claudia. However I want you to know that I am not making a sexual hit on you that could endanger our friendship. Not that I would not desire such a relationship, you do have a beautiful body, but that decision must be yours."

"Virginia, while I have had close feelings for you, I have never felt it to be sexual so it will take time for me to morph that in to my lexicon."

"Claudia, please let us put all this aside and remain the friends that we have always been. If your thoughts change, we can always discuss it further, later on. In the meantime forget guys like Teddy. Sexual relations should mean something. A real woman would never cheat and thus degrade herself. If she is going to *soil her oats* she should break the relationship. Women, who have been tricked centuries ago, by the apple, are now being tricked by adultery/sex. It is still a man's world and such female so called misdeeds, will dearly cost her later on. "

That evening, Claudia put out feelers as to Stan's opinion pertaining to lesbianism.

"To tell you the truth Claudia, most men feel as I do. We think woman to woman thing is okay. They can sleep together, men will not. Females kiss and hug each other, while men abhor the thought of such action with another man. Most men do not frown on lesbianism, but they do get their hackles up at the thought of man to man. After all we men believe that a man's penis is a revolting thing and to have another man's pecker against his body, or in his woman, is disgusting torture. So what brought this subject up?"

"I visited Virginia today and when I was leaving, she gave me an embrace that was warm and comfortable. It makes me wonder how you would react when I tell you this."

"Sweetheart, is it the same feeling as when I embrace you?"

"Oh! Heavens to Betsy, no! You are my alpha omega man. Your embrace reflects a deep masculine love. No other can make me feel that kind of a love like yours does. I guess it is a physical, as well as an emotional satisfying feeling."

"Well, I would not be jealous of her embracing you, that is a different feeling and it is a feeling that can be shared with her and not affect our love for each other."

Claudia is confused by Stanley's explanation. However, it is consistent with his wish to understand and fulfill his desire for her happiness. She will let the situation remain status quo for the time being.

Chapter twenty-one

Friday, April 19, 1957 is Ted's 33rd birthday and Fred Banks believes that it will be great to hold a week-end party with Ted's inner circle of friends to celebrate all the good times that Ted has shown them at Blue Haven Lodge.

Fred brings Jacquelyn *Jackie* Coleman, a light caramel colored mulatto that could pass as a coquettish white female with a light sun tan. Long flowing, shiny black hair streams down her back. She is a tranquil sloe-eyed, Junoesque beauty.

Jack Carroll brings his wife Bernice *Bunny*, a blonde, blue eyed, five foot five inch female that is well shaped in her one hundred thirty-five pound frame. With her are their children, Brenda eight, and Jamison now two years old and also Noreen Jean Keenan.

Noreen Jean is so dramatically different than *Bunny*. Slightly taller with a stunning contrasting alabaster white skin, black bobbed hair that makes her beautiful facial lines seem ornamental, cold, and chiseled. The only similarity of the two is their bodies that oozed and delighted the male senses.

Not wanting to close down Freeport Motors, Eamon and Alvan elect to stay at Freeport Motors. However, Alvan does send his wife Phyllis. Most of the old gang are in attendance.

Father Tim arrives with cute auburn haired Irish lass, 18 year old, Mary Margaret Mitchell, on his arm. Both have obviously been imbibing long before their entrance to Blue Haven. Ted's life style has cynically hardened him and thus he is not easily shocked by the actions of others, but he is a little disturbed when Mary Margaret impatiently decides not to wait for privacy before changing into her bathing suit.

Ordering Tim to get her vanity case from the car, she then disrobes on the back veranda and dons her swim suit. Ted looks at Tim and then shakes his head. "Whatsa matter Ted? You don't think I have seen a naked female before?"

"Timmy, your broad should stand naked for you and no one else. Something is not copacetic. It is none of my business, but for what it is worth, I believe that you should go a little easy on the booze intake. It seems to interfere with your common sense. Maybe you should wear your Rosary around your neck so that it will remind you that you have vows and they were not made by Bacchus. However, take my advice and do as you please."

"Teddy, I came to know Mary Margaret when she became the Altar flower arranger. As you are aware, the only female allowed to be on the Altar at any time, is the flower arranger. Therefore as we worked together we became friends. She is so refreshingly young and uninhibited. I have become enchanted with her lilting Irish accent."

"Enchanted be damned Tim, you are interested in moistening her loins. She has no social or moral constraints. Her colorful hair, blue eyes, and alluring figure can corrupt you and dangerously cause you to forget your vow of celibacy. This can add up to your imagining sonnets of love and the companionship of the flesh."

"I may be a priest, but I am also a male human. I would leave the priesthood to marry her if she asked me. She has qualities that delight the senses. She is a shade of winsomeness."

"Shit, Timmy, you are in dangerous territory. Get rid of her. When you go to confession what absolution do you get from the priest?"

"The same as I give to sinners that come to my confessional – go and sin no more."

"Timmy, face it, that is corruption on the part of the Church. It should not allow you to continue committing a mortal sin as a priest. But hell, the Church is not going to change; corruption is never going to be resolved. It still continues with the pedophiles not being punished. Church corruption goes back centuries to the time Giordano Bruno, a Dominican friar was burned at the stake when he argued with Pope Leo about corruption in the church."

"Ted, for the first time in my life I feel like a normal male, capable of loving a woman. I am certainly enjoying her smile, her touch, and yes, her body next to mine and if the Church was not so stubborn, priest could get married."

This is too much for Ted, "You will never wear a purple or a red biretta thinking like that. Like I said before – take my advice Tim and then do as you please. This is over my head. Get yourself a drink while I mix with the others here."

Anne Nevins makes a grand entrance by having her date, Seamus McMann, a former Marine, a former middle weight professional boxer; carry her, with her skirt above her thighs, up to the back veranda. When he puts her down, she removes his shirt and dramatically strokes his bulging muscles. "Mine, all mine," she belts out.

Booze is in abundance, the party is humming, some dancing, others frolicking in the chilly lake, or playing tennis. Couples pairing off include Ginny Bushnell and Claudia. They decide that they have imbibed in too much food and alcohol and that a private nap, behind a locked bedroom door, is desired.

Intoxication may be a factor in a frightful water skiing incident. Fred Banks is at the controls of Ted's motor boat towing the water skiing Jacquelyn. Several times he maneuvers the boat close so that it allows her to slide up the ski ramp to soar in space for a few fleeting seconds before slamming back down on to the lake surface. Each time she almost crash lands in the water, only to quickly regain her balance and continue the thrilling embrace into the head winds.

On the third attempt, to give her a chance to slide up the ski ramp and again soar for a few seconds, Fred misjudges his closeness to the ramp. Instead of swerving along the side of the ramp, the right side of the boat goes up onto and over the ramp. It comes to an abrupt halt upside down in the water. The trailing skier, Jacquelyn, is unable to change directions, crashes on top of the upside down boat. Unconscious, she sinks down in the water.

Passengers, Timothy and Mary Margaret are thrown a short distance from the boat and are slightly bruised. Seeing the unconscious Jacquelyn head first in the water and one ski still attached, Tim swims to her aid.

Struggling to remove the hanging ski while trying to keep Jackie's head above the water, he slowly drags her to safety on the ski ramp. Seeing that Mary Margaret is safely swimming towards the ramp, Tim dives back into the water to find the missing Fred.

Swimming beneath the surface he finally sees Fred semi-conscious in an air space. His legs are dangling beneath the overturned boat. One of his legs has an odd bend to it, that, plus a bloody area around it indicates a compound fracture. Going beneath the overturned vessel and into the air pocket, he asks, "Can you swim, Freddy?"

A dazed reply, "I don't know. I think my right arm is broke and I can't feel anything in one of my legs."

"Use your left arm and grab my bathing suit. I will get you out from under here and on to the ski-ramp."

There is no need to attempt a swim to the ramp; the area has become alive with helpful fellow boaters. Coming out from under the overturned craft, Tim has the much needed assistance of several men.

Returning from the hospital, where Jackie and Fred are being treated, Ted comes up the stairs of the lodge long porch and is met by Bunny. After inquiring about the hospitalized friends, she says, "Teddy, Jack is drinking far too much. Please speak to him. He gets foolish when he drinks too much, and I don't want our kids to see this."

"You may not know what I mean Bunny, but, right now I am wondering WHAT NEXT?"

However, he still goes to the imbiber, "Jack, Bunny is a little pissed at you for your boozing. Try letting up a little. As you can see, I have enough problems I don't need an irate wife adding to the problems. Let's keep it a nice party."

"Relax Ted. I've had enough to drink. Any more booze and I won't be able to get it up, and up I want it. Up and in! Cover for me while I get a piece of that ass over there."

"Bunny said you get foolish when you booze up. Who the hell have you got in mind Jack?"

"The other gal I brought besides Bunny."

"Do you mean you're going to bang that aphrodisiacal looking Noreen Jean Keenan?"

"That's the one. Take a good look, Teddy boy, and get envious. Just the way she walks, dresses, will give a man a *bone*."

"How do you know she will go for it?"

"I've been there before. All it requires is a half dozen gin and tonics and she will spread her legs. After I get my piece of her ass, she will take you on next, just say so."

"No thanks, I don't go for sloppy seconds. That would make me feel like a homo, dipping my wick in a hole that you had just dumped your sperm into."

Shortly after Jack leaves the room, a thoroughly *pissed* Bunny comes to Ted. "I know where Jack went. Why he would want a bimbo tramp like that, I will never understand."

"Bunny, the old saying still is applicable. Beauty is seen in the eyes of the *alcohol guzzler*. What booze he has already consumed will give him a hellava hangover. In the morning he will be suffering the wrath of grapes."

The now obviously highly irate Bunny responds, "I guess you are right. I can see that you're talking to him was a waste of time. Is the boat operable?"

"Yeah, they got it back to the pier, it has minimal damage."

"Would you mind taking me in the boat me down to the shopping center. I need some hygiene napkins in a hurry."

"If you don't think the boat is jinxed, let's get going, I am always ready to help a lady in distress."

They are far out into the middle of the lake when Bunny reaches over and cut the motors power. Then she begins stripping down. First, her tan blouse, then pale blue bra, followed by her pleated dark brown skirt, half slip, then her stockings and finally, her pale pink panties.

To say that Ted is in shock from the sudden rise in his blood pressure is an understatement. Granted that her doing a striptease causes his erection, he is still utterly confused.

"Close your gaping mouth, Teddy. You said you are always ready to help a lady in distress. As you can see, I do not need any napkins. Come and feel, other than a little arousal moisture, I am ready to give you your thirty-third birthday present."

"God dam it Bunny, what the fuck are you doing?"

"That's the name for it Teddy, I want you to fuck me," as she unzips his pants and inserts her now shaky hand. Upon her retrieving, "Well look what I have found and it indicates that you are ready. I am very nervous but determined. Jack is in the back of our station wagon on top of Noreen Jean, I want revenge against him with you or someone else on top of me. I would prefer that it be you."

"God almighty Bunny, I sure would love to slice you, but what if Jack finds out?"

"I have no intention of him finding out, I just want the personal and cold satisfaction of knowing that I got even. It is quid pro quo! Now please, get your pants off and climb on me, because I have never done this before and I do not want to lose my nerve and change my mind."

"There is nothing I would like better, but I don't want you to have regrets later and blame me for taking advantage of you. Maybe you should think this over for a minute. You may regret this later. Sit down and think a minute, cause once I am in you it is history. You will never be able to forget and possibly may regret doing this."

"I am determined Teddy. For your part I may not be the best piece you ever had so just consider it lust, and see if you can make me cum."

Bunny tries her best to enjoy the copulation but fails. While the ideas of *tit for tat* to get even with Jack and Noreen Jean seemed logical, she had no past experiences with men other than her husband. Everything is against her revenge trip. The weather turns overcast, and sudden winds cause waves to rock the boat and to whip up cold mists to spray her bare loins. Her conscience begins to bother her even though Teddy's erection is now loaded and ready to fire. But damit, it must be full speed ahead if she wants her revenge. Sub-consciously she views Ted's penis as to big and too ugly when compared to Jack's. Her clitoris never attains an erection, but damit—*in for a penny or in for a dollar* – she will play the game. Just lay back and get it over with.

Ted – typical male, has no problem. Lying before him is a 37 year old now nude body that could pass as a twenty year old. It is obvious that she is chilled from the cold breeze and doesn't fully co-operate. For a mini-second, his upper head has a momentary guilt of conscience. However, his lower head anticipates physical pleasure so it is slam bang, thank you Mam! While she is correct in saying it might not be the best piece he ever had – pussy is pussy.

However, Bunny feels, by her actions with Ted, she has now paid a heavy moral price, but somehow she will make Jack pay double. Plus she will never speak to Jack about it; by her actions he will soon know that she is well aware of his illicit affair as she exiles him to the living room couch.

It is a surprise to Jack when, after a long dry spell, that on the Fourth of July Bunny has a romantic, candle light dinner ready for him when he comes home from work. While wearing a thin silk robe, she greets him with a kiss and a warm embrace.

As he holds her close, it becomes obvious to him that her sheer robe reveals that she is wearing no underclothing beneath this silken covering. After an elegant meal, with romantic records playing in the background and many glasses of red wine, Bunny begins, "While I don't forgive you for your affair with Noreen Jean, I believe I have had you *on ice* long enough. Now let's start over and after our meal, we will bond again with your body into mine."

It is still puzzling to Jack. Since he had fired Noreen Jean Keenan, he has been without. While Noreen Jean is an exciting misadventure, Bunny is always terrific at maneuvering her beautiful body for the greatest of copulating satisfaction to him. Moreover, Jack is in no mood to question her change of heart, just get on with her awaiting gift for him. However, he notices, but does not question her, that her tummy seems to have expanded a bit.

At the annual Labor Day Celebration at Blue Haven Lodge, the accidental pregnancy of Bunny is being discussed and Jack seeks Ted's advice. "Ted, as is obvious to everyone here, Bunny is many months into a pregnancy. While she will not talk about it I know it can't be mine because after she found out about me and Noreen Jean, she cut me off and isolates me to sleep on the couch until the Fourth of July."

"As near as I can figure it must have happened the Thursday after your Friday birthday party, so I figure she got it on with some guy over that week-end. I am stumped as to whom the hell it can be? I don't know of any guy that she is close enough too, that she would sleep with him. She is not that type of a girl. Surely she wouldn't take just any guy to lay her. You're the *shamus,* got any ideas."

"If I had any ideas, I would not tell you. All that will do is to create a greater problem, so forget that, and wake up to the fact that your gene pool could use a batch of chlorine. Moreover, men want to think women don't cheat and women want to continue that illusion, they want men to think they do not cheat."

"Teddy, in a few months she is going to have that baby and to have that child around is going to be a daily reminder that she fucked another guy. That will be too much for me to handle but what the hell can I do?"

"Jack, life is tough. It's even tougher when you are stupid. You made your bed and some guy took advantage of the opportunity to help Bunny get even. I doubt that she wanted a pregnancy to come from her *roll in the hay.* In any event, the consequences of you both being so foolish it is going to cause you two to break up unless you plan to do something about it now."

"I know that Ted, but I love her and I am my wits end. I will daily wonder to what guy Bernice spread her thighs. That is why I am looking for ideas from you."

"Jack, living with that child in your home won't work for you; did you ever think that the pregnancy, from her illicit affair, might be regretted by Bunny? Maybe she does not want the child around to daily remind her of paying the consequence for her hasty infidelity. You have been cuckold, and now you must be a *wittol* or a *libertine.* Face it Jack, now is a time for a reality check. It is now too late for an abortion, and it is fast time for a discussion with Bunny to find out just how she feels about this pregnancy. Are you both forgetting about what your animosity will do to the child? You are discussing what this will do to you, never what it will do to the innocent off shoot? The only alternative, that I see, is to find a good home for the baby and put it up for adoption. So take my advice and do as you please."

"Oh bullshit, Teddy, who can we get that will be good parents and love someone else's baby?"

"Off hand Jack I can think of one couple that would fit that bill and that is my brother Stanley, and Claudia."

However the accident of a pregnancy is not the only non-thinking accident. Freddy at Blue Haven for the Labor Day week-end repeats his accident proneness. Although requiring a cane to manipulate the stairs from the porch to the pier he still refuses Jackie's assistance. Successfully getting down to the pier, he waves his cane in the air, "I told you I didn't need your help to get down to the boat Jackie."

Persistent Jackie yells back, "Do be careful Freddy, wait until I can get to you to help you into the boat."

Male ego inevitably is every man's down fall. Freddy does not notice that the boat is not tied to the pier fore and aft. The only tie-down rope is the one at the front of the boat. Ready to board, Freddy puts one foot on the edge of the boat the other still on the pier; he does a movie style split. While the scene is comical, it becomes no laughing matter because the drop into the water came at a sharp angle, Fred's head hits the edge of the pier and he is knocked unconscious.

Pier side the water is only three feet deep and Jackie comes screaming, jumps into the shallow water and lifts the unconscious male onto the pier. Others hearing her scream come to her aid. They carry Fred into the house and after a few minutes on the couch, the now embarrassed egotist wakes. Maintaining the male egotism, Freddy's first remarks, "You know Jackie if the boat had been tied down properly, the accident would not have happened."

The ever forgiving Jackie's reply, "Sure rationalize, blame someone else for your problems, but because God made you mine, I will always be around when you need me darling."

New Years Day Monday 1958, Bunny gives birth to a six pound angel, and three days later adoption papers are signed and Claudia and Stanley have a new daughter whom the birth mother has named, Edwina.

Chapter twenty-two

Sunday August 11, 1957 Teddy receives a phone call from his Dad, "Conas at tu, Laddie."

"Ta me go athair."

"I need you for a delivery tomorrow."

"Hell Da, why do you need me? You guys are doing a great job handling Freeport Motors without me. Why is there a sudden need of my presence?"

"Well son, we sold three cars to a taxi company in Brockton. Alvan will drive one, I will also drive one, and we need you to drive the third."

"Hell's bells, Da, get Freddy to drive the third car."

"Teddy, he will be driving the fourth car that will bring us back to the car lot. I haven't given you all the details. The cars are to go to Lexington Street in Brockton. That is the heart of the local Mafia crime area, so we need you in full uniform to cover our arsses."

"Why the hell did you sell to anyone from that area?"

"That is the kicker. The deal was too damned profitable to pass up. Never the less, will you be able to make it?"

"I won't need my uniform. Brockton is the Mafia Don Ray Patriarca's territory. I'll ask Jazz to speak to the Don. I'm sure he has in the past done a couple of favors for him. I will phone him and let him know we are coming on car business only. I will still go with you, just in case. You know that I will not let you come to any harm if I can help you."

"Thanks son. By the way Teddy, I was up to Seabrook Beach in New

Hampshire a week ago yesterday and I came home with a bride. You will meet your new step-mother when you get here tomorrow."

"That is great news Da, you have been living alone long enough. Congratulations. See ya tomorrow."

The next day's experience may cause him to one day wish this day never happened. Arriving at the car lot he notes the presence of Alvan, Ruth Demarest, and his Dad who gives him the usual embrace, and then turns and gestures, "You know this lovely lady Ruth, the new Mrs. Eamon Sheerin. How about giving a little hug to your new step-mother?"

Utter befuddlement races through Ted's thoughts at this bit of information. Surely his father must realize this means of introducing his new bride would be a shock. Ted's mind races, how to react is confusing. Out of respect for his father he will not plant a long sexy kiss to the lips of Ruth while clasping her firm arsse in his two hands, as he has on past occasions. A handshake would be a cold way of rejection. He will settle with giving her a gentle embrace and a half hearted, "Congratulations step-mother." As he whispers in her ear, "We will talk about this later."

"Dad, I'd love to hear all about your trip to the altar. How about Ruth or shall I say, step-mother, bringing me up to date while riding in the car that I am driving to Brockton?"

In the car with Ted, Ruth remains silent. She has no idea as to how much Eamon knows about her relationship with Ted that might give him ideas that would arouse jealousy. She knows she must face a show down with Teddy, so let it be now and get it over.

The first question on the drive to Brockton comes almost the moment the auto is put in to gear. "How long have you been using your *pussy power* on my Dad?"

"I haven't been using *pussy power* on your father. We got to know each other when I used to bring Claudia to the car lot for her dialysis treatments. We dated occasional at dinners or movies. He is always very nice; he is so different than you."

"Knowing you Teddy and anticipating your next question, did I sleep with him, did I make out with him. The answer is no, not until we got married last week. While I may not have correct morals in your mind, he is morally better than you and I. He did not try to seduce me and I did not attempt to entice him."

"Forget all the euphemisms, is he a better fuck than I am?"

"You are a *zipper fuck,* no emotion. Your father is a compassionate lover. Need I say more?"

Teddy reaches over with his right hand, slides her dress up, and runs his palm between her fleshy thighs. "Does this bring back any memories? How about meeting me later on?"

In the word's of poet Matt Trusskey,

Ashes to ashes, dust to dust
You'll know the man if you know what he
Lusts!

Without showing any reaction, "That may arouse you Teddy, but it does nothing for me. Just because you have been there before, doesn't mean you will get there again. Moreover if you continue to act like this, and do not remove your hand, I will tell your father. I will not allow you to use our past to blackmail me. If you want showdown, pull this car over and I will get into his car and tell him all the past details. It may hurt him but I will not live in fear of any so-called blackmailing exposure from you."

With his ego shot to hell, Teddy removes his hand and in a sarcastic dramatic gesture, shoves her dress hem back down below her knees. It is silence for the balance of the trip to Brockton and minimum conversation on the return back to Dorchester when all pile in to one of the cars and are transported back to Freeport Motors.

Off duty until Tuesday evening, Ted heads to Blue Haven Lodge and pulling into the parking area he is puzzled by a strange car parked there. Getting out of his Caddy and going up the steps to the back porch, he is startled by the sight of Mary Margaret Mitchell; while facing him, she is hesitatingly pulling up her bathing suit from her ankles to cover the rest of her nudity.

His puzzled mind tries to analyze the situation. 'Surely she heard his car, thus had time enough to cover her nudity. Is she being a *cockteaser?* Moreover what is she doing here?' Nevertheless, dam it, he has to take a long hard look at this magnificent now nude frame, it is perfect regardless of the angle of his view. From her mons veneris to her gluteal muscles she is a tantalizer.

"Hi there Mary Margaret. Is Tim coming down here?"

"No. He is making a Novena for something. He said it was okay for me to come down here for a swim any time. Don't just stand there Teddy, come help me to pull up my bathing suit."

"You do realize that visits here are by invitation only as that bulletin over by the door states?" He teases.

With a demur smile, "Tim said you would not mind if I told you that he said it was okay for me to come down here for a swim. If there is any question, he said that he would explain my visit when he sees you. In the meantime I will not be a bother; I promise you will not be unhappy that I am here."

With a passive gloating curiosity he wonders what she might be saying or hinting, "Tim is right," but his only response is by way of a smile.

"I just didn't get a chance to get my suit completely on before you came up the steps." She grinned, however her actions indicate that what a girl puts out is what she will get back. After all it pays to advertise. The display of her *goods* performed, she finishes donning her bathing suit without Ted's assistance.

With her nude image still in his mind, he decides to press his luck. "Let's go inside and I'll pour us a couple?"

"That will be nice. If I have a choice of drinks, how about you making me a Grand Marnier over ice?"

"Your slightest wish is my command," he teases. "One French drink coming up." Coincidentally, the radio begins to play the beautiful, romantic La *Vie En Rose* being wonderfully sung by the lamentable melancholic Edith Piaf.

With his firm belief that this gal is capable of looking out for herself and that the majority of females do have *round heels,* he's not missing the opportunity of putting out a sex inclination feeler, Ted adds, "French liquor, French love song, French songstress, maybe it is time for a French kiss? Tell me the truth, was it your own idea, or did Tim make the suggestion of you visiting Blue Haven by yourself?"

It becomes obvious he did not have to press his luck, as is typical; the female is in complete control. "Confession is good for the soul; I confess it was my own idea, and French love making appeals to me Ted."

No– *que sera sera what will the future bring* – is heeded – let the action begin now. Ted gets up from his overstuffed Morris chair, removes the drink from her hand, pulls her close, and peels her bathing suit from her body. Stepping back he further teases by placing his hands as though to view the enchantress through a camera.

"Do you like what you see?" She asks.

"I sure do and I can better understand how Timmy must feel after seeing this enchanting body of seductiveness."

"Well Teddy, Tim handles it with appreciation; do you think you can handle it?"

"We are going to find out right now. Let the French love game begin."

Funny, how a couple of *Miks* can enjoy playing French love games. Moreover, Teddy must have enjoyed Mary Margaret. After their sex binge, is it sarcasm? "Thanks for the opportunity to penetrate your magnificence?"

Yet as insurance for a further romp, he adds, "Let me show you where I hide a key so that you will have more privacy and comfort while waiting for me your next time."

However, the fun games are furthest from Tim's mind when he meets Ted at Blue Haven Lodge on Labor Day September 2, 1957. "Teddy, I need a place to stay, any chance I can bunk down at Blue Haven for a while?"

"What the fuck has happened Timmy, did they kick you out of the Columba Rectory for debauchery?" Ted teases.

"No, I am serious. I just made a Novena to St. Jude for guidance, and I am leaving the priesthood to marry Mary Margaret."

"In the name of the Holy Mother of Jesus, are you off your fuckin' rocker Timmy? The kid is sixteen years younger than you. Moreover, you don't know shit about her. You are thinking like a teenage school boy, you're just using the head between your legs. Play it smart, take a sick leave from the priesthood, and give it a year to straighten out this new found world of yours. Get to know Mary Margaret better before you make a big mistake."

"How could it be a mistake? I love her and she loves me. We are made for each other, I could write sonnets about our love. She is my darling of a lifetime and while it is not the kind of love my mother and daddy had, I realize life is made up of harsh reality. The hands of fate can be cruel Teddy."

"You are still thinking like a sixteen year old boy that just discovered pussy. How are you going to support her? You have no work experience, what are you going to do, the Catholic Church has halted the practice of *simony*?"

"Be serious Teddy."

"Okay maybe that statement is facetious, but be more pragmatic. You are so damned naïve that she will end up breaking your heart. You will be left with very sad memories. Did she ever say 'I love you', or are you assuming it?"

"Mary Margaret does not have to say those words, I can feel it. If it turns out the way you think it will, I will have many happy memories to sustain me."

"Jesus H Christ Tim, think positive for a change, right now you need a *shrink*. Meantime you are welcome to the bedroom that leads off the front porch. That will give you a private entrance to your room and you can come and go as you please. Maybe it will give me time to get you a reality check. Hopefully I can get you to grow up and know the difference of a piece of arsse and a lover."

"*Kyrie eleison*, my good friend Teddy, I don't know what I would do without your friendship. However, just remember – the Lord is in his heaven and all is well."

"Let's face it Timmy, I may be cynical, but you surely must admit that while *He* may be in his heaven, from what I see around me, sometimes Heaven must be asleep. Regardless of what name they call *Him*, all religions believe in God and what they are doing in *His* name, is a shame."

Is it cynical hypocrisy that Father Timothy sets up a small altar in his room and a free standing crucifix next to the altar? The ever lit red vigil light to symbolize the presence of the Holy Sacraments should cause him thought. He goes so far as to hold Sunday Mass for those who wish to attend. A good example of a man thinking with the wrong one of his two heads. Being a priest does not change the fact that first, he is a male animal.

Chapter twenty-three

Still believing that he is a servant of Christ, thus his new found sexual experiences and acknowledged moral weakness, may make him better qualified to console sinners, Timothy Coughlin now rationalizes that he has a *calling* to spread the words of a *forgiving* Christ.

Realizing that he is not emotionally or experienced enough to live and work in the *secular* world, he seeks ways, even though venal, of continuing a religious calling and yet be married. Since that must be outside of the Roman Catholic faith he has a major problem. It is partially resolved when Reverend Paul Perkins, of the local Episcopal Church, extends an invitation to join his pastorate.

"Timothy, I have known you for some years. You are a good priest. Although considered a sinner by your Church, to me, your sins are not as lamentable as the sins of some priest, even Bishops. They are violating the rules of the bible with men. However, as you know, our priests are not required to be celibate and can marry. Because of this celibacy rule, you now must leave your Church if you plan to marry. However in our church, the only thing about being married, you cannot become a Bishop. The fact you are an ordained Roman Catholic priest, the tenets of both churches are similar. I can get you in a three month seminary course to qualify you to join our Church as a married priest."

Monday March 3, 1958. Jubilantly, Tim explains the details to Ted, "I have been enrolled in the Saturday April 19, 1958 Episcopal Church Seminary class. I don't like leaving Mary Margaret alone for the three months; she might become lonesome without me with her."

"Tim, relax, in a couple of weeks, I am taking our annual I.R.A.

Saint Patrick's Day collection for the *troubles* fighters to use against the anti-Catholic Ian Paisley's U.U.D.A., and the B.S.A. (British Security Authority) in Ulster territory of Ireland. After I give the money to the I.R.A. leaders, I'm going to make a hasty retreat and head south."

"I plan to visit Blarney Castle to kiss the stone. I'll take Mary Margaret to Galway so she can visit her kin for a while. We will be over there for about a month, and she will be ready for you when we get back."

"Bless you; I have saved part of my salary. I can afford to pay all her expenses."

"If it is okay with you Tim, I will pay for the trip. To keep expenses down; I will have her stay in rooms with me. That way she will not be lonesome and I can watch over her."

It is impossible to understand how Tim can be so naïve in giving agape love that asks for nothing. He is so trusting, not only of Mary Margaret, but also of Ted. *Love is so blind.* The ocean cabin is *Sodom and Gomorrah* for the couple. Soon it is too much of what begins as a good thing for Ted.

On his visits to Belfast it is always a rush to complete his dangerous I.R.A. business. It has to be a get in, and get out, of Northern Ireland with his phony passport. After landing in Belfast on Monday March 17, then completing his business and successfully avoiding curious military Orangemen, and or U.U.D.A. spies, Ted is loaned an I.R.A. car and driver to head south to the Republic. The first stop in the Republic is to drop Mary Margaret off at her Aunt Birdie Quinn's in Connemara.

True to her colors, after being left at Aunties, the little nymph quickly abandons Aunt Birdie and seeks out her ex-boyfriend in Limerick. Gavin Johnachie, (Celtic for Shaughnessy) is much younger than Ted, and seems to bear up well spending the next many days bedding Mary Margaret. However, Ted figures she can do as she wishes; it is now time for him to take care of his trip plans until it is time to pick her up and return to the States.

With so much to see, he first heads to the Waterford Crystal manufacturing company. Like most visitors, he is fascinated watching their famous glass blowers turning melted glass into fine pieces of art. While there, he purchases a twelve inch crystal cross for his bedroom wall and a crystal chalice for Tim.

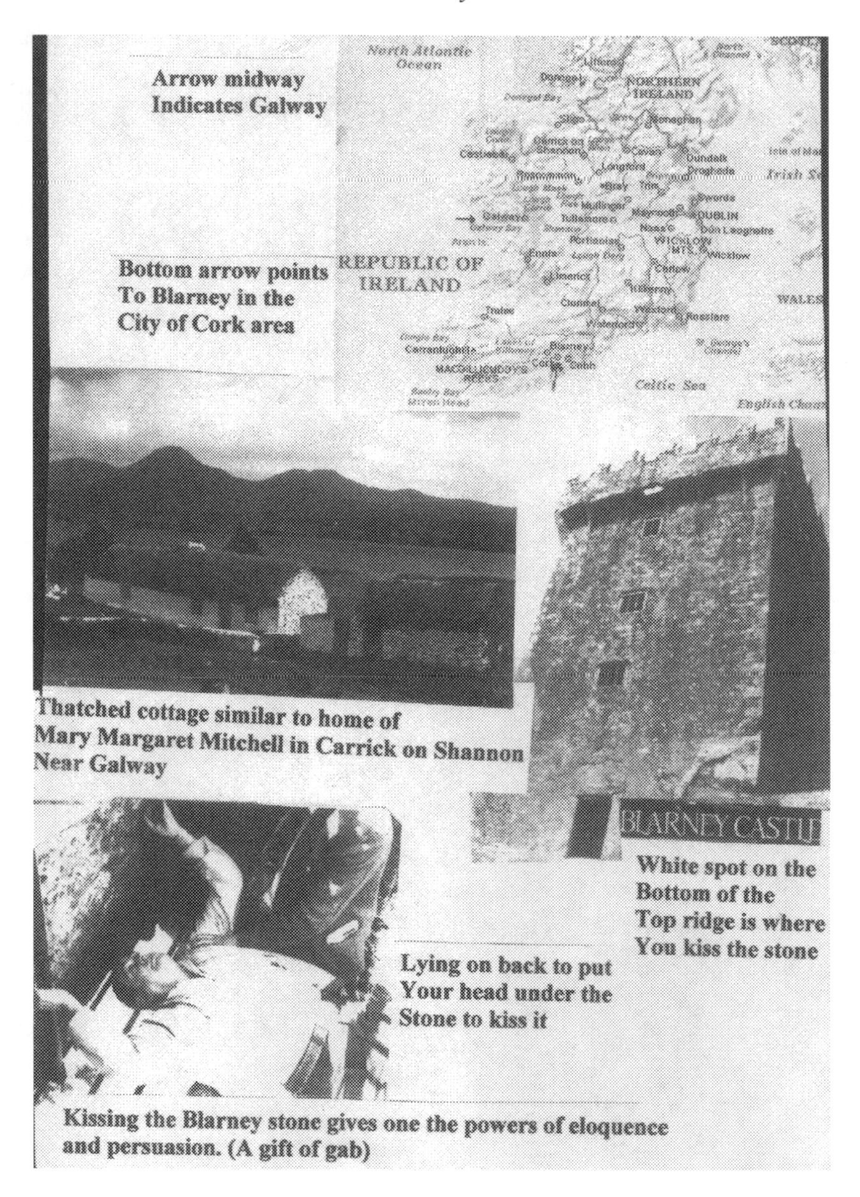

From Waterford, he heads south to the City of Cork, there to kiss the Blarney stone at that famous ancient castle. By such actions it is claimed that one gains the mythical power of the bestowed gift of charming loquaciousness and charisma.

At the end of the two weeks of sauntering, his testicles are reminding him that it is time for a return to the states to resume another ship orgy with Mary Margaret.

Chapter twenty four

Sunday, July 13, 1958, Timothy is ceremoniously inducted into the Episcopalian Ministries and assigned to St. Elizabeth's parish in St. Albans, Vermont. By now Ted is bothered by his inability to bring Tim into the reality of what is a love farce on the part of Mary Margaret. As almost the last straw, he wants to use this time as possibly his last chance to convince Tim of his, according to Ted, lack of good sense.

After the ordination, picking Timothy up at the Episcopalian Seminary, and heading to Pembroke he lets loose. "Timmy, I need to save you some embarrassment in front of your friends when we get to Blue Haven and meet with Mary Margaret. I hate to be the one to inform you of her new condition."

"Is there something ailing her? Is she all right? What is wrong, Teddy?"

"I'll spit it out; she got knocked up by her old boyfriend while in Galway. Now I am sorry to be so blunt, but dam it I tried to warn you about your little darlin'." (Or was it from Ted's sperm?)

"I don't care what you say; we can marry, have the baby, then take up my ministry in St. Albans. I can get a sick leave until the baby comes."

"Jesus H Christ Timmy, you are one fuckin horse's arsse. Why can't you see that she's no good; she will let a snake fuck her if one is available. She has no morals, she is a slut, and she is what I call a *TAMPA.* If she agrees to marry you it will only be to make her bastard baby legitimate."

"Ted, you are heartless, no compassion, you are exaggerating this situation. If you love God you must have empathy. You should never forget what is worth remembering; moreover you should never remember what is best forgotten. Have you ever done things that fit that statement? If so – did you forget what is best forgotten? Do you believe that you never have done anything bad? I will still marry her; I truly love her and can forgive a few mistakes. She is my *honky tonk angel.*"

"Mistakes, God dam it Timmy, I have been fucking her for months. On the boat trip to Ireland we did it at least twice a day. No woman can fuck another guy if she truly loves the one she is supposedly committed too. She has held the peckers and fucked close to a dozen others. Is that loyalty and love in your mind? You're the supposedly religious one, not I, and you are supposed to set the moral standards of a good Christian, not I. She is gonna have to spend a hellava long time in Purgatory because, I'll wager even Jesus will have a hard time forgiving her."

"Kyrie eleison, Teddy. Omar Khayyam, an ancient Persian philosopher, once said, '*One who threatens he will toss to hell – the luckless pots he marred in his making. Pish! He's a good fellow, and t'will all be well'.* I believe Omar is correct Teddy. It is a loving God and while he did make her in his image, He will not blame her for her transgressions. Jesus is merciful and will forgive the sinner that you say she may be, therefore who am I that cannot also forgive? Moreover, if you are my friend you will help me in my time of my loving too much instead of trying to bring a tear to my eye."

At the lodge, Tim is welcomed by all gathered there to celebrate his Episcopal ordination. Mary Margaret is the first to greet him, and she warmly embraces him, "Timothy, I missed you. Let's get alone so that I can show you how much I truly missed you."

Finally alone in the bedroom, Tim asks, "Mary Margaret, Ted has been telling me tales about you. Did you really love and truly miss me?"

Using P.O.P. "Let me show you how much I missed you," and she rapidly sheds her clothing. A little excited by her swift venture to nudity, but cleric as he is, "Please do wrap a sheet around you as we kneel and thank the Lord for our love."

Prayers over, emotions stimulated, their bodies enmesh. Thumping and bumping can be heard throughout the house. With exhausted Timothy, falling back on to his side of the bed, the pragmatic Mary

Margaret lays alongside him. "Timmy, let's get married right away, before my stomach gets bigger?"

"I'm all for that, how about the first week of September my darling?"

"I'll need some money for the bridal outfit and some new clothes for our honeymoon, my love."

"I'll give you a check for all of that in the morning."

Tuesday July 22, 1958, Mary Margaret gets Ted aside. "If you don't want a very dramatic scene, listen to me and say nothing to anyone, including Timothy."

"I'm listening."

"I don't want to further torture Timothy by his wondering where I disappear too, so I am telling you one story, and him a different story. I needed some money so I told him that I am flying to Ireland for one more trip to explain my marriage and all that to my Aunt Birdie. I said I was going to tell her that the baby is his."

"I am leaving today and I told him that I will be gone about a week. I know that you will be god damned glad to hear that I am going back to marry Gavin Johnachie. He wants his baby and me. To cover your arsse, I will phone you from Ireland supposedly to tell you the news that I married Gavin. Then you can tell Timothy and he will never know you knew of my plans."

Some broken hearts never mend, after Teddy has informed Tim about Mary Margaret's betrayal, a few weeks later he now must say good bye to a most melancholic Father Timothy Coughlin who is in the final stages of getting ready to leave Pembroke for St. Albans, Vermont.

"Timmy, there is no language that has the words to offer hope when a person says good bye; it is never pleasant or joyful. All I can truthfully say is I am available if you ever need me, May God bless you Timmy."

Somber, and pensive in what appears to be deep contemplation, the inconsolable Episcopalian Father Timothy Coughlin, hugs the visiting Cathy and then shakes Ted's hand.

"You have been great friends. I have one consolation to sustain me, just remember, I gathered orchids for a short time in life. You two should gather them more often, because like me, there will come a time when you will only be able to gather weeds. *Slan agus beannacht libh* *go leir. (*Good bye and God bless you all my friends), I will keep you in my prayers forever."

All kinds of thoughts are crowding Teddy's brain, but the only thing he can think to say, "Timothy my dear friend, go with God and may the Angels protect you always."

One most outstanding point of Timothy's life – if it weren't for bad luck Timmy would have no luck at all. This would make a great *Country/Western,* song of woe. What better example of the so called *Luck of the Irish?**

However, it is the scene of a man with an emotional masochistic desire to be punished.

As much as he overlooks the transgressions of Mary Margaret, he is haunted by memories. They have a way of inviting themselves in to his mind, whether asked or not, they are filling his head with images that cannot be removed. Moreover, Fr. Tim never arrives at St. Albans, and he has not been seen or heard of to this date.

The souls of the just remain in the hands of the Lord!

* "Luck of the Irish" is a misnomer. It is an ethnic slur from the days when Irish immigrants were pouring into the U.S. A. The belief of the bigoted anti-Irish was that any Irish man who made good must be lucky rather than smart, hard working or talented.

A *Paddy* is a drunken Irishman, thus the use of Paddy Wagon; is an insult to the Irish. It implies that the Patrol wagon was initially used only to pick up and arrest Irishmen because they were all drunkards.

Chapter twenty-five

Stanley Sheerin's visits to Veteran's Hospital are now down to quarterly check-ups. On his second quarter of the 1958 checkups, Friday June 27, a bleak damp cloudy day, that could morph the healthiest person into despair; Stan is sweating-out an extensive examination that could depress the healthiest person. His despair is exacerbated by the report that the doctors note a presence of abnormal proteins in his blood. He is re-scheduled to return on Wednesday July 2, 1958.

Bad *karma* is the destiny of Wednesday's child Stanley. At the scheduled meeting, Doctor Edward George meets with Stan and Claudia, "It is with heart felt pain that I must tell a war hero like yourself, but it must be said, and the task has become mine. You have a cancer called multiple myeloma."

"Jesus Christ, what the fuck did I ever do to deserve all this? All your prayers and rosaries Claudia, didn't amount to shit. Why me? Haven't I suffered enough? Where was the Virgin when you lit candles to her?"

Dr. George, a devout Catholic, remains silent, feeling if the tables are turned; he might disparage the Deity as Stanley is doing. However, more anguish is to follow.

Stanley's hands are shaking so severely that he is unable to torch the hastily drawn cigarette, Claudia, takes the lighter from his hand, and ignites the cigarette. Slowly regaining a little composure the inevitable questions follow. "What the hell is multiple myeloma?"

"It is a bone disease, caused when the myeloma forms malignant plasma cells in the bone marrow. These myeloma cells make osteoclasts that speed up the dissolving of bone resulting in the bone breaking very easily."

"Blood cells that develop in the bone marrow are called stem cells. Marrow is the soft material in the center of bones. Myeloma begins when these cells become abnormal by forming cancer cells that eat away the marrow in the bones. The heavy bones, like those in your arms and legs, become a paper thin shell. The shell can then crumble if bumped and lead to painful fractures of the arms or legs. If this occurs it will leave an arm or a leg limp, unable to give physical support."

"No bull-shit doctor, lay it all out, how much time do I have?"

"That is difficult to say. At the stage yours is, I would estimate three to twelve months. Hopefully you have months before the disease progresses to that stage."

"I am an auto mechanic. What if I bang an arm or leg in my work and the thin shell of a bone crumbles?"

" Each bone marrow debilitation is different. Some damaging marrow is less active to some degree than the marrow in other bones. In the event that such as this occurs, I can remove the damaged bone and insert a stainless steel rod to replace the damaged bone. Our Supervisor nurse Anne Nevins will give you literature explaining the details."

Given a few tranquilizer pills, Stan and Claudia, leave the V. A. Hospital. He spends the next few days trying to formulate some plans. Most important, with his love for Claudia and Edwina he must see to protect and provide for their future. Meeting with Ted, dad Eamon, and Alvan, Stanley explains the financial needs of Claudia.

Dad is the first suggester. "We must set up funds for them Stanley. We can give you a lump sum to buy you out or a monthly payment."

"Dad, forget the buyout idea. Claudia and baby Edwina need money for years to come. A monthly check and cost of living increase is the best way," offers Teddy.

Alvan is most practical, "She should continue to get Stan's monthly check plus any wage increases and profit sharing that we get. After all, he is kin; he is one of the Freeport Motors partners and has been instrumental in our growth and our profits."

With Claudia's future care intact and trying to make the best of the worst of times, Stanley decides to visit old memory spots before the debilitation sets in. Grandma Ruth takes care of Edwina as they couple spend two weeks in July near his former Army base in Belfast Ireland. While the base still exists it is now under control of the notorious anti-Catholic Presbyterian Ulster Police, who make it obvious, veteran or not, Catholics are *persona non- gratis.*

As far as how Stanley physically feels there are no obvious signs of the disease. The cancer is deceptive, he physically does not notice any change in his appearance. However the tumors are multiplying in his bone marrow.

Their August reception in Palermo, Sicily, visiting the Palermo Hospital that first treated his war wounds, is vastly different then his Ulster experience. Here Stanley is given a copy of the x-rays taken at the time of his pelvic area injuries and friendly advice given.

Palermo Mafioso, Don Vito Ferro, who in 1943 was appointed Mayor of Villalba by the U.S. Military, happens to be visiting kin in the hospital. Hearing that Stan was one of the G.I's that freed Palermo in '43, and feeling generous, he invites the couple to his home for an ostentatious, extravagant dinner.

"You are one of the great warriors that drove the Germans out of Palermo. You soldiers saved my family. God bless you and your fellow soldiers." With that the Don holding a velvet jewel case, turns to Claudia, "My wife, with your permission, would like to place these pearls around your lovely neck."

Upon returning to their hotel room, Stanley suffers the first pains of the many soon to follow. Awakening after his nap, the pain is so severe that he needs Claudia's assistance to get him up from the bed.

Returning to the Palermo hospital, he is held for three days. Diagnosed as first stages of progressive multiple myeloma then released. To ease his pain, he is given enough pain pills to cover his boat trip home.

Thursday September 18, 1958, back at home in the States, the pain wracked Stanley, on this morning he is unable to get out of bed. The ambulance attendants, one male, and one female, are unable to lift him onto a gurney. A phone call to the local fire station for assistance brings a fire engine to the scene and with Stanley screaming in pain, the firemen lift him on to a gurney for the one way trip to Veteran's hospital.

During the stay at the hospital, Claudia rents a nearby room and visits Stan each day and evening, until his last day when on Wednesday

October 8, 1958 Stanley's body surrenders. He is buried with a military ceremony in Mount Calvary Cemetery in Roxbury. The traditional military funeral, with flags and *taps*, played by a bugler from his American Legion Post, in death, salute the fallen hero.

Benddact anim Stanley

Reacting to the obituary in the Boston Globe, Jack Carroll visits Claudia on Sunday November 9th with an offer. Since she is a widow, she and Edwina may now have financial problems. He has divorced Bunny and married Noreen Jean Keenan and because she is infertile, he and his new wife would like to adopt Edwina.

Claudia's only response is to show him the door.

Chapter twenty-six

The final death and burial of the patient does not become an initial great shock to the survivor. The reality of the death and loss begins to set in, to the survivor, on the first sign of the painful debilitation. Thus it was that Claudia's loss, and her reality of his death, begins to register almost nine months before Stanley's death.

In an attempt to get away from the bad memories of the nine months of watching Stanley slowly die, Claudia wants a change of scenery. On Friday December 19, 1958 she and eleven month old Edwina, go to live with Aunt Philomena Buchannan in Hingham. It is about a forty minute drive from Boston and Claudia's new Buick makes it a pleasant ride.

As times may become a little better for Claudia, Jeanne Marie Brooks' troubled life continues. On Sunday December 21, 1958, she is released from the British Columbia prison and extradited to the New Jersey authorities to stand trial for being a coke mule. Tuesday, December 23, as is typical of elderly aunts, Aunt Phil, noting Claudia's periods of depression, decides to bring a new interest into her life. "I need to buy a typewriter ribbon, mine is all frayed. Bring Edwina along and we'll go to a friend of mine who owns an office supply store in Newton."

At Ferber's Office Supply store, Aunty is met by the owner, a tall fellow who resembles a polo player rather than a shop keeper. He embraces Aunt Phil in a big warm hug.

"Claudia this is Matthew Ferber, Mathew, I want you to meet my niece Claudia Sheerin and her daughter Edwina."

Shaking hands with Claudia, "my pleasure Miss Claudia," then turns his attention to Edwina held in her mother's arms.

"What a beautiful child, may I hold her?"

"I don't know if she will let you, she is rather shy around strangers."

"Aunt Phil knows how I love children."

As Matthew extends his hands; little Edwina turns and outstretches her arms wanting to be held by Matthew. Both Claudia and Aunt Phil are amused at Edwina taking a fancy to Matthew, but his only reaction, "I love children, I want to one day to marry and have a dozen or so kids, like this baby, surrounding me."

"That sounds like a lot of children. Your future wife may not agree to that count," responds Claudia.

"Oh, I am exaggerating a little bit. It would be up to the woman I love and marry, to determine how many. I am thirty-four now so just as long as I have several before I am too old, I will be happy."

"By the way Matty, what are your plans for Christmas? A bachelor like you should be sitting down at a Christmas dinner with friends. I betcha you are going to be alone. How about sharing Christmas Day with us?"

Glancing toward Claudia, "I sure would love that Aunt Phil, I sure would. What time?"

"How about eight in the morning, that way you can watch Edwina enjoy some gifts and the sparkle of Christmas ornaments on the tree?"

On the way back to Aunt Phil's house, Claudia inquires, "I did not know that you had a nephew Aunt Phil. How is he related to our family?"

"He is not related to us, Claudia. When he was about twelve, his mother, a friend of mine, became quite ill and I took her and Matthew to live with me. Since he wasn't to call me Philomena or Miss Buchannan, we suggested that he refer to me as Aunt Phil. When his mother gained her health she remained with me as my housekeeper and friend until she passed away a few years later."

Continuing, "Matthew won a business scholarship to Boston University while working at an office supply store. After getting his degree, he wanted to open his own shop. He had saved a bit of money but needed to borrow a little more. I co-signed a loan for him and he has been very close to me ever since. He says if it weren't for me he would never have the Ferber's store he has now."

Christmas Day, a prompt arriver, Matthew is so loaded down with so many gifts that he has to use his elbow to ring the door bell. Not forgetting anyone, he brings a portable typewriter for Aunt Philomena, a phonograph record player for Claudia. Plus a little doll, a Teddy bear, and a small red cart for Edwina. All this brings a lump in Claudia's throat as she remembers her last Christmas she and Edwina shared with Stanley.

Sundays, begin as Matthew brings Aunt Phil to Mass, then returns to have lunch with her and Claudia. Edwina always welcomes him with a big hug. On Sunday February 8, 1959, at lunch with Aunt Phil, Claudia and Edwina, he makes a subtle proposal that might bring him closer to Claudia, "I am planning on having a Valentine's three day sale. I will need additional sales help, would you be interested in working those days Claudia?"

"I would Matthew but I can't. I must take care of Edwina."

"No you don't," injects aunty, "I will take care of her."

It is a new experience for Claudia, and a welcome change. She enjoys the work very much. Sensing her availability, Matthew suggests she become a full time employee. With Aunt Phil's urging, it does not take much persuasion for Claudia to agree to work permanently at Ferber's Office Supply.

Life is an oxymoronic bitch. Claudia's future looks bright, while for Jeanne Marie Brooks it is anything but bright. On Monday March 8, 1959 Jeanne is sentenced, by the New Jersey court, to six to eight years for being a *coke mule* plus jumping bail. Cathy and Ted are at the court hearing and make subsequent visits the following years. Jeanne's only consolation is that it is easier for her sister Cathy to occasionally visit her in New Jersey than it would be if she were in a Canadian British Columbia prison.

Matthew uses many occasions to act as a family by taking Aunt Phil to picnic lunches, visits to Franklin Park and even to Fenway Park to watch her favorite Red Sox. However, he coincidentally makes such invitation only when Claudia and Edwina are present, knowing that Aunt Phil, *the matchmaker,* will always say, "I'd love to go if Claudia and Edwina will join us."

Sunday August 9, 1959, they spend the day at Norumbega Park in Auburndale. Edwina, Claudia, and even Aunt Phil, love the rides, like the huge Ferris wheel, on the midway. The day is climaxed at Norumbega when Matthew takes them on a canoe ride on the Charles River. This the same ancient river that the Scandinavian Norsemen, known as Vikings, sailed their long boats up and down and explored it around the year 1000 AD.

The ride back to Aunt Phil's is typical of those who are tired, but happy from a pleasant day together. Matthew has been quiet, ostensible concentrating on his driving. The ladies are dominating the conversation. Taking advantage of a momentary lull in conversations, Matthew calmly notes out loud, "Our family get-to-gether today was a great example of what could continue forever."

Claudia remains silent but continuing to be a match maker, Aunt Phil responds, "Yes Matthew that sure would be so nice, and maybe someday it could occur for Claudia and Edwina."

This prompts a response, "Aunt Phil and you too Matthew, I am not ready to give up my independence, so cease and desist, please."

However, her oxymoronic thinking allows her to enjoy Matthews' companionship as they date a couple of times a month.

The Ferber Office Supply store is open for business five and a half days a week. Saturday noon May 21, 1960 Matthew Ferber closes and locks the store. "Claudia please sit-down." Then, gently taking her hand, he kneels in front of her. "I have something to talk over with you Claudia."

"You sound very serious Matty, what is the matter?"

"Not knowing how you feel about me it has stressed me out rehearsing what I am about to say to you Claudia. Please listen and please do not interrupt me."

Matthew's approach makes Claudia nervous. It is obvious, to her, that Matthew's intentions are romantic. She is unsure of what her decision will be.

"Claudia, we have gone to movies, plays, dinner, and dancing. By now, you must know that I love you and Edwina. I want us to become a family. I want you to become my wife."

While it is no shock to hear Matthew, Claudia is still unprepared to answer immediately. Silently, she reaches over and removes a pack of Chesterfields from Matthew's shirt pocket. Takes a cigarette lighter from the desk, lights and inhales deeply.

It is amazing how the brain works. What would seem like a long time, in her two to three minutes silence, she weighs some pros and cons, noting mostly the cons are in his favor. Matthew is definitely a good stable future, and he is a kind, and a very considerate person. Her life in Hingham has been good. He being a pious church goer could be a problem for she no longer feels the need of Sunday Mass.

However, her analysis continues. While dating, he never made a sexual pass at her; does that indicate he has a sex problem? Going without sexual satisfaction while married to Stanley was a problem, would this occur with Matthew? He loves Edwina and wants to adopt her. That is in his favor. "BUT – I do not love him. "

However, she still has a moderate monthly income from Freeport Motors, but she is depending on the undependable Ted Sheerin for it to last forever. Moreover, with Matthew, there will be no more lonely Thanksgivings or Christmas' for her. She would gain a father figure for Edwina, and he would be there to share her as the child goes through her various changes in growth. "BUT – I do not love him."

A bit worried at Claudia's hesitating to answer, "I know this is a big decision for you, but be realistic and think of Edwina's future, as well as your own. You have seen enough illness to realize it can happen to you. What then for her future? I have a nice home that would be yours and Edwina's. I can provide her with a great education. I promise to not interfere with your need to be independent. I will do everything to keep you happy and not pressure you."

"I need to give this further thought, Matthew. After you go to Mass tomorrow, come by the house and I will give you my answer then."

"Claudia, while at Mass I will say a Rosary to the Blessed Mother Mary asking her to persuade you to make my life complete by marrying me."

A sleepless night of tossing and turning, and only slightly nearer making a decision, Claudia piles out of bed at six in the morning. Still in her nightie, she pours herself a cup of black coffee, lights the inevitable *fag*, and sits fretting at the kitchen table.

At one o'clock Matthew is at the door, holding a large container of geraniums. With a smile, "It's a lovely day. The birds are singing and there is only one lonely powder puff cloud in a beautiful azure blue sky. This day can go down in my life as the worst of times or the best of times. My fate lies in your gentle hands, and if you reject me, my heart will break. Do you bring me thoughts of exuberance or despondency?"

At the sound of his voice, the now two and a half year old Edwina comes running into the living room. Extending her pudgy little arms she yells out to Matthew "up, up, me up."

He picks up the child, as he hugs her she wraps her arms around his neck and kisses his cheek. It is no longer a difficult decision for Claudia; her daughter's love of Matthew makes the pros in favor – out weighs the cons.

"Matthew, my heart knows what it is like to lose, however, while I do care for you, I must be truthful and up front. I do not have a deep passionate love for you. You sure have a great ally in Edwina and it is obvious that she is all for my marrying you. If you will accept my feelings and agree to my independence, then let's set a date."

"I thank God for your decision. Claudia, I love you and our marriage may have a long way to go before experiencing an afterglow, but since God has answered my prayers to make you mine, I will love you forever."

The elated match-maker is so pleased, "He will make you a good husband Claudia, and a great father for Edwina."

The first person Claudia phones is her beloved brother-in-law. "Teddy, I have a question for you. I want to know if it will upset you if I get married so soon after Stanley's terrible death."

"God love you Claudia, you were a wonderful loyal wife to Stanley. You went through Hell tending him while he was ill. Life must go on for you and Edwina, and after all, it has been over two years. That is not what I would call as too soon. Is it that guy the Matthew that I met?"

"Yes Teddy, it is Matthew Ferber and while I do not love him as I did Stanley, he is a great considerate guy and Edwina loves him. Will you be able to give the bride away?"

"Claudia, nothing could ever prevent me from that honor. Would you like the ceremony to be at Holy Cross Cathedral?"

"Oh Teddy is that possible?"

"Claudia, I won't promise, but I do have a few connections with

Cardinal Cruikshank, I'll see what I can do. In the meantime tell your guy that I said he is one lucky fellow. There must be a hell of a lot of shamrocks in his clover patch for him to have such good luck in getting a wife like you."

The proper Irish connections and corrupt gratuities enable Ted to arrange for the wedding at Holy Cross Cathedral on Saturday June 25, 1960. The Cardinal knowing Ted, and his strong Irish ethnicity, arranges to have, a fresh from Ireland priest who has a great resemblance to *Friar Tuck, tie the bonds of matrimony* for the couple. The robust charming Father Liam O'Hagan realizes that these people are ethnic Irish when Ted, detecting an Irish accent from the priest, greets the Friar in Gaelic, *Conas ata tu Athair. Is mise Eamon Sheerin. (*How are you Father? I am Edward Sheerin).

So pleased at hearing the tongue of his homeland, the priest responds in Gaelic, "*Failte romahabn go leir a chairde go dti ard eaglias naomin Padraiig.* (Welcome friends to Saint Patrick Cathedral). He then begins the wedding with a Gaelic greeting, "*Failte caras.* (Welcome friend). We are gathered in this sanctuary to join Claudia Sheerin and Matthew Ferber in the holy ceremony of matrimony." With three year old Edwina as the ring bearer, the betrothed are wedded.

For his wedding gift to Claudia, Ted gives his former sister-in-law a Celtic gold cross with colorful enamel inlay and a slim gold chain, and an invitation at any time to make summer visits to the lake at Blue Haven.

Matthew adopts Edwina an ads his mother Frances' name as her middle name. She is now Edwina Frances Ferber. Thursday August 10, 1961 the Ferber's have a new addition, a healthy baby boy that Claudia names John Fitzgerald Ferber after President JFK. She selects Ted Sheehan and Virginia Bushnell as God Parents in the baptizing of the baby. After the baptism, they all join a few friends and relatives at a small reception at Blue Haven Lodge.

Chapter twenty-seven

Thursday June 12, 1958, Catherine brings three year old Lawrence Edward to visit his father. "Lawrence, say hello to your Uncle Teddy."

The normally unemotional Ted has tears in the corner of his hazel eyes as he hugs his son. "I am so glad to meet you Lawrence Edward." Then turns to Cathy, kissing and embracing her, "Cathy, you will never know how much I appreciate you bringing him here. Maybe I should not have kissed you in front of the boy. What if he tells Larry that he saw Mommy kissing a man?"

"I sincerely don't care Teddy. If he is to not know that you are his father, I will see to it that Little Lawrence knows his Uncle Teddy. I want you in his life. Larry may believe you are the boy's father, but he is so involved in campaigning for the election of Senator Kennedy for President; he pays no attention to what I do. You don't seem to believe me when I remind you that my marriage is strictly a professional relationship. He has me as his *token beauty* to accompany him across the U.S. in rallies for Kennedy."

"Does that relationship include sex?"

"Teddy I could almost have predicted that you would ask that question, and damn it, while it is minimal, it does include some sex. You will never stop asking the same old questions. It is time that you become aware that you must face your demons as well as I must face mine."

"Larry has a new assistant, Raylene Redmond, and they are campaigning for J.F.K. across the country. I believe she is taking care of all his needs. Larry and I have not even slept in the same bed but two or three times for over the past year let alone to have sex. And since Kennedy has become president, I am seeing Lawrence even less times."

"Cathy I am glad you told me that, with your ever loving cooperation, we will take care of the sex with our own little peccadillo after you put our son down for a nap. Okay?"

"Okay you ask. I am brazen enough to say I would be heartbroken if you had not wanted to bed me down. But first, please put our song on."

Realizing the significance of *Love is a many splendored thing* in their romance, Teddy doesn't hesitate. And so it is – until Saturday June 17, 1961, when he receives a phone call, "Teddy, I am sorry for the short notice but I have just been told that Lawrence and I have a meeting with President Kennedy on Tuesday so we will be flying to Washington tonight at seven. "

"What is that all about Cathy?"

"The President is appointing Lawrence to be a legal adviser for the Ambassador to Ireland."

"Cathy, for a guy that received less than one percent of the popular vote to beat Nixon, Kennedy sure isn't wasting anytime. He appointed Bobby Kennedy as the 64th U.S. Attorney General and had him confirmed by Congress on January 1st this year."

"Teddy, he seems to not worry about having a little nepotism. We think he may reward Lawrence also. I guess political quid pro quo is a necessary repayment for loyalty." Changing the subject of conversation, "Teddy, tomorrow is little Larry's fifth birthday, I would like to celebrate it with you today. Can you meet me this afternoon?"

"I sure can Cathy, where do you want to meet?"

"How about meeting at the Parker House?"

"Did you pick that hotel so that you can get some of their famous rolls?" he teases.

"The only rolls I want at the Parker House are with you in a bed. Does that shock you my lover?"

"Hell no darling, it excites me. In making our room reservations, let's not sleep in the same room that John Wilkes Booth used a few days before he shot Abraham Lincoln. Maybe pick the room that Charles Dickens slept in there on the night that he made his first reading of his *A Christmas Carol,*" he continues his teasing. "In any event, the anticipation makes everything most exciting."

Blissfully – they rendezvous to celebrate little Larry's birthday, the only thing missing at the birthday party is their son.

Sunday August 6, 1961 while dipping his doughnut into his cup of hot coffee and reading the Boston Globe, he is a little shocked at the headlines, ***Marilyn Monroe commits suicide.*** Before he can read the details the phone rings, "Teddy, Cathy here. We returned from D.C. yesterday and I am now at Logan Airport."

"J.F.K. has rewarded Lawrence for having resigned from his D.A. seat to help Kennedy's campaign to be President. Larry is to be a legal adviser to Matthew H. McCloskey the new U.S. Ambassador to Ireland. We are headed for Dublin and it looks like we will be in Ireland for a while, but I promise to write. Darling of my heart, I love you baby. I won't say for you to behave, but please just take care."

"Before you go let me tell you how much I love you my love, it is limitless. Now go, enjoy the ocean trip. I know that you will love Ireland Cathy, please do keep in touch."

There are strong rumors that Edward Ted Sheerin was seen in Dublin on several occasions over the Christmas holiday of 1961. Since no one has viewed his passport, nothing can be confirmed.

CHAPTER TWENTY-EIGHT

ON WEDNESDAY FEB 15, 1961 the FDA approves a contraceptive pill that Catholic, Protestant, Jewish, and Mormon religious groups, become irate over its availability. At the beginning the regulations of the pill allows only married women to legally go to their doctors and obtain a prescription for family growth control only.

"This pill will eventually ruin the morals of the nation. Giving the pill to unmarried women will cause them to forget their virtuous morals and become as promiscuous and immoral as men."– Quotes a religious quorum. Moreover, it shall be noted that any religious zealot is automatically a hypocrite, for it is impossible for anyone to strictly adhere to the tenet of any belief.

The religious group's advertisements scream, *No longer will virginity be cherished. No longer will the respect for the virtue of a woman be assumed by men. By its use, men will rationalize that women will lower their sexual moral concepts to the lowly level of the men's.*

"Prepare for the abuse of a pill that will lead to universal female moral decay," is the cry from the pulpits. The religious groups go so far as to erect billboards with a quote from the Jewish Bible that they thought will be most apropos.

Who can find a virtuous woman? For her price is far above rubies.
Hebrew Proverb 31.10

"Like the camel with his nose in the tent," it is contended, "the Torah's moral laws will be eroded, and ignored, one by one, until it no longer is a guide for those who try to maintain a moral standard for them, and their children, regardless of any religious dogma."

At this time, abstinence on the part of females is acrimoniously believed to be their chaste morals. The ambiguity remains. Is she chaste because of the parables of religion, or is it because she can't trust the lust of the male to protect her from an unwanted pregnancy? Having a bastard child is disgraceful.

However, since the only animals that have sex for fun, are dolphins and humans, the pill will remove any fear of such a pregnancy that might deter the female from fun sex. Chastity and morality be damned, no more romantic tomfoolery, lustful fun is now a female bonanza, let the promiscuity and indiscriminate fucking begin.

Some folks wonder if the 1960's is the *end,* for the last generation of moral standing, innocent females. *Only time will tell!* Woman – get the hell down off the pedestal. Forget the idea of a long spell of old fashion love, fuck them and leave them is the new liberated female cry.

The demand for the contraceptive pill becomes so great that the doctors can't get enough of them to fulfill their patient's desire for fun sex. Like the era of prohibition, or rationing, a highly profitable *black market* opportunity arises.

Pharmacia supplies warehouses become Teddy Sheerin's targets. A three month packet of these pills cost the doctor $2.50 when bought legitimately. Since there is a scarcity from Teddy's raids on the warehouses, the demand is high. Ted offers the packets for $20.00 each to any buyer, married or single. This is at a time that gasoline is 31 cents, a McDonald hamburger 15 cents. A man's average salary is $4961.00, while a new Chevy is $2529.00. Corruption prevails; there is a ready market of contraceptive pill buyers.

In most states, the limitation of the pills availability to unmarried females lasts until 1965, at which time the pill then legally becomes available to unwed females. In Massachusetts (A hypocritical phony puritanical Commonwealth) not until years later, and it is not until 1972 that it becomes legally available to unmarried females in all the U.S. states. Thus Teddy's corrupt income lasts until then.

With the male population it becomes an opportunity of low investment available *pussy.* No need to waste money at courting a female with hopes of being laid. It is no longer the doubt, "Does she?" It is now, "Your bed or mine?"

Dump the load and leave! No longer is it the male that should use birth control methods, with the advent of the pill it is entirely up to the female to have a built in protection against an unwanted pregnancy. If she fails to protect her body, tough luck, she wants liberation – that goes all the way!

Chapter twenty-nine

Things are going great for Teddy Sheerin. Some cash comes from annual funds received from the New England *Capo Bastone* Mafia boss D'Honore Raymond Patriarca, for his use of the lodge to be a safe haven, if needed, for him or any member of his organizations.

In 1954 he moved his New England syndicate operations to Pawtucket, R.I. (to get away from the Boston F.B.I. corruption and shake downs). Moreover Blue Haven Lodge becomes a transferring point for inter-state contraband when Patriarca's Boston base of operations is under scrutiny.

Thomas *Jazz* Kelley, now smoothly operating his territory, feels it is time to begin opening new territories and thus the need for new leaders. With permission from Kelley, Ted is given a gambling territory in greater Boston as his own domain. Here, Ted sees to it that the pay-off cash that he receives from Kelley is properly dispersed to those who are on *the take.* In typical style of *American Corruption* he sees to it that the graft goes to legislators, to law enforcement and to local judges. Since the average citizen participates in traffic violations, gambling, dope, bribery and prostitution, the public can't complain. If John Q. Public violates even the pettiest law, he participates in the corruption of America. Therefore he can't complain and must suffer the *consequences* of his actions. Moral decay is prevalent and it begins at home.

Tuesday May 9, 1961 Blue Haven Lodge receives a phone call from the Ireland born Jazz Kelley. His strong Irish brogue requires concentration on the part of the listener in order to completely understand what is being said.

With the usual dropping of the letter *r* and *g*, "Teddy, I am goin' to expand me bookie operations a little fatha' noth. I am settin' up a Gloucesta' *Portugee* (Portuguese) named Joaquim *Jockey* Ayaho. He'll be makin' book in a territory comprised of noth of Revea', south of highway 101 in Manchesta' New Hampsha', and west to Lowell. Wouldya be interested in overseein' this territorial expansion?"

"Do you think that I should become more involved in your organization Jazz?"

"Teddy, it is like sayin' a woman is slightly pregnant. You are already makin' money from my organization so, a little or a lot, you are already into the syndicate's business. Rememba' the three pledges of the syndicate that we all try to adhere to –Hona' – Loyalty – Obedience. It fits you to a *T*. All I am offerin' is an opportunity to financially expanding ya' interests. Take over that territory and see to it that you and Ayaho each receive 40% of the net profits, and I get 20%."

"You make a good point Thomas. How about letting me go up to Gloucester and see if I can handle it from here. I will analyze the potentials, and then give you my answer."

"Sounds good to me Teddy."

Monday May 15, Ted and Seamus *Jimmy* Mc Mann head north. Seamus drives up to the front door of a restaurant with a sign over the doorway, **Gloucester *Haddock & Cod*.** Underneath this in a much smaller print, – ***Port Anne's gifts from God.***

Upon entering the building gives the patron the sensation of being inside a three master schooner. The walls curve in style emulating the interior of a sailing ship. On the starboard side is a green light. On the port side is a red light. Rope scaling ladders go up the walls to the 14 foot ceiling where a crow's nest accents the superstructure. Port holes, anchors and other ambience add to the nautical atmosphere.

At the entry they are greeted by a cute petite dark complexioned nymphet. She couldn't be more than seventeen. "Would you gentlemen like a table for two for dinner?"

"Yes, please."

Handing them a menu, she goes to a nearby counter and in a couple of minutes returns with two glasses of water. Teddy on many occasions seems to draw female attention, but in this case, the female is drawing his attention. As she bends over the table placing the glasses of water, her low slung blouse gives a full exposure. In stereo view are two symmetrically perfect orbs. In one case even a pink nipple appears to be extending an invitation for male lips. She is a sexual memory maker for sure.

While the menu offers many choices of fish dinners, the all American choice of hamburgers are available at twenty-five cents each and a twelve ounce Coke for fifteen cents.

With a smile that indicates his full knowledge of what this gamine is portraying, Ted asks, "Will you please tell Joaquim that a representative for Mr. Jazz Kelley wishes to visit with him?"

With the mention of Joaquim, she becomes most demure and appears nervous. To put her at ease, Ted takes her hand and kisses the back of it, with a relaxed smile, "I am Teddy Sheerin. What's your name pretty one?"

"Donna Louise Broes."

"Well relax Donna Louise, I think you are beautiful and since I am staying overnight, would you be so kind as to join me later for a nightcap?"

"Mr. Ayaho might object if I were to meet you."

"I promise that he will offer no objections and he will say it is okay."

"Mr. Sheerin, please wait and then talk to me after you have finished meeting with Mr. Ayaho."

After leaving the restaurant area, she returns a few minutes later with Ayaho. Unable to curb a nervous hand shake, it is obvious that he is well aware of the importance of Teddy. So tense that in this nervous greeting, Ayaho all but bows. At any moment, Donna Louise gleefully believes Joaquim might even genuflect or kiss the ring of this important visitor.

Ayaho's *nome de plume of Jockey* is a wide stretch of the imagination. This individual is about five foot six and one hundred and eighty pounds. A dark skin, paunchy individual, with his ominous foreboding eyes, he could readily haunt a house.

After minor discussions and a hearty meal of baked haddock, fully decorated baked potato and a dago salad, they adjourn to a private office at the nearby motel.

Trying to put up a brazen front, Ayaho says, "I own this motel and

I operate out of my office in the back. I have police protection and also enforcers from my money lending enterprises. I have a very healthy organization; I don't need any help from Jazz Kelley."

"That is a matter of opinion on your part Mr. Ayaho. To stay alive and healthy your opinion does not count. If it comes to a show-down, the fact that you have some so-called enforcers in your cadre will not matter to me one bit. Mr. Kelley has decided that he is expanding his territory and it includes Gloucester. Do you wish me to go back to Mr. Kelley and say that you decline to cooperate?"

Visibly shaking, and in a cold sweat he asks," Please, Mr. Sheerin, how do I benefit from all this?"

"I am not here to give you S & H Green stamps or have a hula hoop contest. I am here to expand your present picayune territory. We will expand your territory and under my supervision you will still have control over it and enjoy a very substantial increase in your income. You will report to me and you will donate 40% of your profits after costs of operation. You have no options, take it or leave it or I will become an albatross around your neck."

Having previous knowledge of Kelley's operation and of what might happen, Ayaho decides it is going to be healthier to accede to the program laid out by Teddy. To save face and contrive a form of apology he says, "With Mr. Kelley's Irish accent and my Portuguese accent, maybe I did not understand the value of joining up with Mr. Kelley's program."

"That could have been a problem that I understand. I sometimes have that same situation with Mr. Kelley. Since you have no problem understanding me, and we understand each other, we shall proceed with the plans for your future. However, in case you change your mind, as a bit of security for me, I have drawn up a note for you to sign. This document states that you have deeded your businesses to me. I will hold this deed as my insurance that you will stick to our agreement. If you default, I will legally take over your operations. You have nothing to fear if you give me no problems, do you understand Mr. Ayaho?"

"Yes Mr. Sheerin, yes indeed I do understand you, even if have no choice in the matter, I will go along with your offer."

Contemptuous of the faltering Jockey, yet there is no need to aggravate the situation at this time. "You are a wise man Mr. Ayaho.

The alternatives could be fatal for you. Now that we have come to an agreement, I will be spending a few days looking over your operation. Shall I go elsewhere or do you have quarters for Seamus McMann and me to stay for a few days?"

"By all means you should stay here. I have a large suite for you to stay in, and another room for Mr. McMann."

"Thank you, and do you mind having Donna Louise take care of my needs Mr. Ayaho?"

Like a pimp his reply is, "No not at all, I will send her right over."

Enjoying an elaborate most comfortable suite, with a heart shaped bed; Teddy is preparing a gin and tonic from the bar in the room, for him and Seamus when there is a gentle tapping on his door. Putting his drink down, and opening the door he is greeted by Donna Louise, "I believe that you were expecting me Mr. Sheerin."

"By all means come in Donna Louise."

Taking a hint, even before a hint is made, Seamus touches his forehead with the edge of the tall glass as a salute and a see ya later.

Teddy's stay in Gloucester is for four nights, each night this exquisite nymphet sleeping partner keeps him from being lonely. In addition to many forms of sexual satisfaction Donna Louise gives him wonderful nightly massages; this combination allows Ted to have the most relaxing sleep he has ever experienced before.

Returning from Gloucester Ted phones Jazz, "Thomas, I do believe that the Ayaho acquisition can be very profitable and easy for me to oversee and expand. It is too small for my full time attention, but with your permission I have a young guy named Fred Banks who under my supervision can do a good job handling it. He could spend a couple of days every three months, going over the operation and report back to me. I will see that your share of the profits is discretely sent to your bank."

"That is fine by me Teddy. I shall turn that territory over to you immediately."

After a few months Ted feels that he does not need to make the quarterly visits to Gloucester, just twice a year is going to be enough. This could be opportunity to see if Freddy Banks can take on more serious duties. After all he has the makings of the organizations description of a *Made-Man* by the holy three requirements: Trustworthy – Clever – Secretive.

"Freddy, I want you to take over the servicing of Jockey Ayaho's operation in Gloucester next week. He is a conniver so be firm but not unfair in handling him. You will need to spend a couple of days every three months to go over his books. There will be accommodations of a room and meals for you there. You can you can take Jacquelyn along with you if you wish. "

"I won't bring Jackie every visit to Gloucester. I can find a perfunctory diversion there. It is time I had a change of diet in my females Teddy."

"That's a sure thing Freddy. When you get in Gloucester, go the restaurant first and tell Donna Louise that I would like her to spend a couple a days a month at Blue Haven. See to it that she has transportation."

"I shall, and thanks Teddy, for the promotion and the fringe benefits. I'll see you when I get back from Gloucester next month."

Donna Louise knows that her association with this powerful man will be rewarding. And so it is for her each of Ted's visits to *Jockey's* operation and, in turn, Donna Louise visits to Blue Haven Lodge. She enjoys Ted's companionship and his generous gifts.

In September Jackie insists that Freddy begin to take her on his business trips to Gloucester. A smart chick, she sizes up the chumminess of the heart shaped bed in the room that Freddy sleeps on, and what the likely ultimatum follows.

Feeling that the trips to Gloucester might encourage Freddy to *graze in greener pastures* and to settle Freddy down, on Friday September 22, 1961, Jacquelyn Coleman becomes Mrs. Fred Banks in Judge Casey's office, and Teddy is the best man and Anne Nevins the maid of honor.

Chapter thirty

On Monday May 15, 1961 Ted receives an official notification that he has passed the Police exams and receives his Lieutenant's bars Thursday May 18, 1961 at a H.Q. ceremony.

Friday May 26, 1961, *Jazz* phones, "Teddy, I have neva' seen ya place on Pembroke Lake, but Seamus McMann tells me that it is beautiful. I need a quiet area to have a little R&R. Now wouldya' be interested in selling me a piece of the watta' front?"

A bit startled – and analyzing the ramifications of having the big boss of the crime syndicate as a neighbor, Ted is slow at answering.

"Taking advantage of the fact of our being partners in the legitimate business of Freeport Motors that put us on a first name basis Thomas. I will be up front with you. I won't sell it to you; instead I will give you a good size lot. Since all of our business has always been over the phone it never gave us the opportunity to meet in person, I suggest that at your convenience you come and see the lot, and we can get to know each other a little better. However, there will be strings attached."

"I think I may thank you. That is afta' I know the strings attached."

"Blue Haven is an excellent location for truly beneficial R & R Thomas. Therefore I would like to keep it as a sanctuary for you and me. So the lot is yours if you will agree that you will not operate your enterprises from here."

A bit startled by the audacity of Teddy to set the rules for the Irish Mafia boss, Kelley's response is cordial. "Teddy, I agree ha'tily. I will build a nice house and garage for me to use occasionally. In the meantime, if t'is okay with you, afta' the house is built I shall have Sean McLaughlin and his wife, reside theya' and maintain it for me visits."

"That sounds great to me Thomas. Let me know when it will be convenient for your visit."

The following day, a dark eye-browed, ruddy complexioned over weight *muscle hit-man* and obviously an *Old Sod Mik,* comes calling on Ted.

Playing on their Irish ethnicity, "*Conas ata tu,* Mr. Sheehan, I am Sean Mc Laughlan, Mr. Thomas Kelley of South Boston sends his thanks and gratitude for your kindness in giftin' him a piece of land he'ah, and wants me to introduce meself as ya' new neighba'."

"*Ta me go maith. You're* sounding like an emissary visiting the White House. What happened to the names *Jazz* Kelley and *Johnny Three strikes* Mc Laughlan, and *Teddy the Fuzz* Sheehan? Let's not have all this bullshit. If we are to be neighbors, let's not put up a false front, okay?"

(Mc Laughlan is a Mafia *Piciotto.* He would approach a victim and say *you're out* as he shot them, thus got the nickname of Johnny three strikes)

"You are sh'uah outspoken. You are at a different level in the association with Mr. Kelley, than meself. I di'na know what Mr. Kelley will say to that."

"I don't give a fuck, that's how I am, that's how my friends find me to be. I'm not a hypocrite that pussy-foots around. If you, or *Jazz,* are going to be neighbors of mine you will have to accept me as I am. I will only refer to your formal names when I am around others. In the meantime *Johnny Three strikes,* I welcome you, and extend a welcome to *Jazz*. Now go back to Mr. Kelley and tell him that I will seal the deal with a *slainte* over a Hennessey when he comes here."

"Mr. Kelley di'na says nothin' about him comin' over he'ah in person."

"Maybe not, to you, but he and I have agreed to a long overdue personal meeting and I will expect a handshake to seal the deal. Now go back and return only after the lot belongs to the Jazz."

Not used to being ordered around, other than by *Jazz.* Mc Laughlan, steps back a few steps and turns away. He then turns back again and slightly moves toward Ted. Noting the movement, Teddy pats his concealed pistol in a gesture of "looks what's here."

"Something you forgot Mr. Mc Laughlan?"

Not saying another word, *Three strikes* turns away and leaves the room.

Sunday May 28, *Jazz* Kelley's Cadillac limo, at a pre-arrange meeting time, pulls into the Blue Haven parking area. Kelley and two bodyguards get out of the vehicle. In an ostentatious pompous- ass stride, the 42 year old *Jazz,* heads up the path to the front porch stairs as though he is marching to the tune of the Vienna Philharmonic Orchestra playing the General Radizy March. Two body guards fall in step behind him. All three are meticulously attired in the latest Hart, Shaffner and Marx suits and top coats.

Common sense forces Ted to not push his luck. After all, Kelley is one powerful man and has a temper. So Ted, in deference, is at the front door to greet the Irish Mafia Don. Extending his hand, "*Failte*, Thomas, *Ta me* Teddy Sheerin." While enjoying their Italian Mafia titles, when together, they flaunt their Gaelic language.

Getting his message across implies recognition of equality of power in some form, thus not demean the power of the Don, "Nice to finally meet you. I am glad that you could arrange our get together. Please come in and have a bit of the *hair of the dog*."

"Teddy, I don't believe that you have met me brotha'J.J. or me man Seamus McMann."

"No Thomas, I have not."

The six foot 165lb Seamus makes no move or motion other than nodding his head in acknowledgement of the introduction.

"Seamus is me trusted aide. He's a foma' middle weight champ and Marine Gunny's Sergeant who at times is very efficient on my beha'f. During the war he killed many enemies of the United States and now is available to do likewise to me enemies. As he says, 'an enemy is an enemy and must be dealt with as such'. I like his philosophy."

With that Seamus goes out and sits near the doorway on the front porch. *J.J.* stands close to his brother. At that moment, Anne enters from the kitchen area, "Tom and *J.J.* this is my guest Anne Nevins."

Kelley stands up, "Me pleas'ah, Miss Nevins."

"Thank you Mr. Kelley. May I get you gentlemen a drink from the bar?"

"That would be nice Anne; I would appreciate a scotch and soda. How about you Thomas?"

"T'is fine with me Ted," while his brother shakes his head negatively.

Bringing back the drinks and a coke for herself, she passes them their libations. Holding up his drink, Tom says, "*Slainte, Erin go bragh* Lieutenant."

Ted raises his glass to acknowledge Tom's salute. "Slan *agiv Thomas."*

After a few drinks, Ted brings *Jazz* out and around the lot of land that he is about to donate to the Kelley holdings. "Do I have boat pe'awh usage?"

"You certainly do. The right side of the boat house and the right side of the pier will be yours to use as you wish. I will keep the left side and its beach for my boat and my guests."

Quite pleased with all that he has surveyed, Kelley flaunts his political influence, "I am indebted for yu'awh gift and considerations and I never allow a good thing to go unrewa'ded Teddy. You've handled ou'wah Gloucester territory in an excellent man'awh. It is time you influence grew mo'awh. I have been thinking of what I can do and I have come to the conclusion that you may like yo'awh title of Lieutenant."

"Howeva' I believe Lieutenant is an impotent position of pow'ah. I shall see to it that yo-awh title will be an assistant to Superintendent Frank Hanratty of the Boston Police Depa'tment before the Fou'th of July. That will give you a great deal of influence and pow'ah. I always say, that to me, pow'ah's an aph'owdisiac. This position will give you more free time to roam the city and conduct our mutual interests," continues Kelley.

Stunned for the moment, mentally translating Kelly's brogue into English, Teddy regains his composure, in deference, he raises his glass, "Thomas Kelley, may God bring good health to your enemies' enemies. Slainte."

As unabated crime grows, corruption flows!!!

Ever observant of male idiosyncrasies, Anne in attempt to *butter up* to *Jazz,* "Mr. Kelley, I notice that you are wearing a unique ring."

"Very observant Miss Nevins, but please if I may, I'll call you Anne if you will address me as Thomas. As to the ring, it comes from

Claddagh near Galway not fa'h from wa'ya I went to school in I'eland. The two loving hands are holding a haw't. That is a way of wa'hin' the ring to indicate that they are lovingly givin' their haw't."

Extending his hand for her to hold and examine the ring, "Wa'hin this on me left ring finga' and pointing inw'ood it becomes a weddin' ring. If it is pointed outw'ood it will indicate that I am unmarried. My Irish wife makes shoe'ah that it is pointed in," he kids.

Anne pours Coco Cola into her glass and begins to take a sip of the freshly poured Coco Cola. The fizz tickles her nose. Quickly wiping her nose, she apologizes, "The fizzing is irritating."

"While a little fizzin' is irritatin', think of a lot of fizzin'. It is a great to'wtue tool. '*Tip toe*' Ferrara, an enfos'ah for loan shark *Baldie* Jason, will take a bawh'til of Coke, shake it up, then while holdin' a victim down, the sadistic one will shove the fizzin' soda up a victims nose. It becomes one of most gruesome infliction of pain that the human head can experience. The victims head feels like it is going to explode. It is more painful than being hit on the head with a hamm'a," Tom details.

Quickly changing the subject he goes on. "While at Mass this mawnin' Ted, I told Cardinal Cruikshank of my buildin' a retreat next to yo-awh Blue Haven Lodge. He said he would bless the house when it is built, and that he would like to occasionally relax near the watt'a in such a lovely location."

"The Cardinal is familiar with this area; he also blessed this house for me, Tom."

Kelley's house is finished by November 15, and he has a house warming for friends. Cardinal Cruikshank, as one of notable guests, blesses the house and it is given the name Hibernia. "Let this be a home for many Irish celebrations. May all who enter here enjoy Jesus' blessing."

Knowing he is with Mafia mobsters, the Cardinal must be experiencing a severe case of *amblyiopia as* to those presently around him!

At this Ted makes the sign of the cross on his chest, as others do also. He wonders, 'Will Jesus really bless the likes of these people? Especially the hit-man Sean '*Johnny Three strikes*' Mc Laughlan, who will now live here, within 200 feet of Blue Haven Lodge, as he and wife Norma's year around home?

After all the guests leave Hibernia house, and the McLaughlins about to be entrenched there, the main bedroom is indoctrinated sodomy style by Anne and Mr. Kelley.

Having McLaughlin as a neighbor has its good points, after all, when Ted needs extra strong-arm muscle, McLaughlin and McMann, and John Kelley will hire out to Ted for a fee, and on many occasions it does happen. Plus to cover his own ass, Sean is a watch dog over the area.

But Hibernia house problems occur from a direction Teddy never would imagine. The following July according to Norma, Anne has become too friendly with Sean, and resents their water skiing rendezvous. Sean rationalizes to Norma, "You are afraid of the water and the skiing, and since it takes at least two persons, don't begrudge me a water skiing partner."

"I don't trust you with that Scandinavian bitch Anne Nevins. Remember it was she who left her panties on our bed the day she screwed Mr. Kelley. I wouldn't be upset with you two if I could see you and hear the boat motor noise, but you disappear at the far end of the lake and so does the motor sound."

One who is not jealous is not in love.

"We sometimes stop at the shops at the far end of the lake for a snack or a drink, or stop along shore to fix a rope or a ski. That's why we stop the motor. For your peace of mind, in the future I will try to stay at this end of the lake," Sean lamely alibis in an attempt to appease Norma.

Ted's only thoughts are that maybe, to be more convincing, Sean should also get rid of the air mattress and blanket folded up inside the boat hatch.

Claudia Anne Norma

Chapter thirty-one

With Cathy in Ireland, Teddy has been making frequent visits to Gloucester to luxuriate at the marvelous full body massages offered by Donna Louise. On several occasions she spends a few days at Blue Haven before returning to Gloucester.

Friday November 22, 1963, the tragic assassination of President John Fitzgerald Kennedy by Lee Harvey Oswald dominates the world news. Teddy, like most, is glued to the T.V. coverage of this heinous tragedy.

Other than post cards and letters, there has been no communication from Cathy until this evening when the telephone rings, "Teddy, just a quick phone call. Due to the untimely death of wonderful J.F.K., we will be leaving Ireland tomorrow. We will be back in D.C. and I will phone you at the first chance that I can talk freely."

"God, I missed you Cathy. I figured you two would be coming home after hearing this ungodly news. I will be waiting for your phone call. Please make it as soon as possible. I miss you."

"I miss you too Teddy; I will never let us be apart for such a long period, ever again. I love you darling."

Ted's first sighting of Cathy, back in the States, is in the funeral procession of the late President. The television news-camera's close-ups of the procession show Cathy and Larry riding in the limousine of Ambassador Matthew H. McCloskey.

Ted does not hear a further word or note, from Cathy, until Sunday December 22, 1963. "Teddy we have just returned from the funeral in D.C. and are now back home in Boston. How have you been while I have been away? Did you miss me? Please tell me that you want to see me? Oh I guess I best shut-up and let you talk, but I am so glad to be home again, and do so want to be with you as soon as possible."

"Well as usual, my lovely gabby one, I missed you, and yes, I want to do more than just see you, so stop the idle chatter and get down to facts. I want to see you, and more so, to *do you,* my sensuous sweet."

"When is best for you Teddy?"

"I have taken off the next two weeks as vacation time, take your pick."

"Take my pick be darn, I want little Larry and I to spend Christmas with you at Blue Haven Lodge."

"How can you get away and stay with me over Christmas? What the hell are you going to tell Lawrence?"

"While in Ireland, Larry hired a new secretary, Maev Bridget O'Toole an Irish lass. I walked into his outer office one day in Ireland, and since the secretary was not at her desk to announce me, I walked into his inner office unannounced. Lying on the plush carpet was Maev, with her dress up around her neck and Larry on top of her, banging away."

"That must have been a *kick in the teeth* for you Cathy?"

"Well I have to admit that my, and Larry's, sex life hasn't been the best, however it was a blow to my vanity."

"Maybe now that you are back in the States, you can once again renew your wifely relationship with Lawrence?"

"Fat chance Teddy. By paying bribes, Larry was able to smuggle Maev and her brother Gaelach, from Ireland. Gaelach is a wanted criminal in Ireland and they are to live here now. Moreover, at my age, my sex drive is not as intense as it was. I would be satisfied with just occasional nights spent with you, that is, if this old woman can still satisfy you."

"Jesus Christ Cathy, you're only thirty-six and have always been an enthralling exciting lover. I will always be yours whenever you wish it to be. You know that I would have married you anytime. It was you that chose to wed Larry and not marry me."

"Teddy, I told you my reasons. I am still afraid of your life style. Maybe I am wrong. However, my life with Larry has not been all bad.

There have been many good times with occasional not so good. I will discreetly have to adjust to this Maev intrusion."

"How's that Cathy?"

"While in Ireland, Larry negotiated a partnership with the Boston law firm of Edelstein, Bracken, and Morse. J.F.K. used his influence to get Larry appointed as a Suffolk County Assistant District Attorney. He will use this as a stepping stone to run for a political office again. Maev will be his private secretary/mistress. Gaelach is now Larry's chauffeur and gopher. However, that is enough of my B.S. I know I am acting like a brazen *hussy* but I want to feel your warm body on top of mine. I want to again experience my body tremble from the sensational thrill that comes to me when you flow into my body. Is tomorrow night about seven convenient?"

"Convenient be damned, Cathy. You have got me horny already so as far as I am concerned darling, the sooner, the better. See you tomorrow night my love."

Until a lover has experienced a long gap in romancing a soul mate, a sensuous satisfying lover, they will never understand Ted's anticipation of a coming wonderful evening with Cathy. Like *make-up* sex after a bitter quarrel, the anticipation adds thrills to the event. His multitude of sex partners has led him to believe that there is man's lust, in which romance never occurs. Then there is true love that brings an exhilarating tingle of goose bumps from his nose to his toes that lust alone can never give such a fulfillment.

Cathy is the only female that he has ever had a deep feeling for as a sex partner, thus this must be truly love and romance that exists between Cathy and Ted. On her arrival, Ted begins the evening with cocktails, grilled steaks, candles, flowers, and their song. Little Larry is put to bed.

"Sure missed you while you were Ireland. Did you see all the important sights?"

"For sure, I was the typical American tourist, camera and all," and she proves her point by producing ample photos. "I was mostly surprised in my visits to England; did you know that the state of Florida is bigger than England?"

"No I didn't. But carry that thought a little further, that is such a small country yet at one time it powerfully dominated or controlled a huge part of the world. However, what did you miss the most of America?"

"Driving on the right side of the road, beef steaks like you cooked tonight and a warm water swim. The lakes and streams in Ireland are too cold to swim in, very frigid, but those cold streams produce the best salmon. The restaurants offer dinners of many different salmon dishes with fish that has been caught just a few hours before cooking. Those are the best salmon meals ever."

Ted gently places his hand on her mouth. "Cathy we have given our son enough time to fall asleep, who the hell are we fooling with all this idle chatter. You know godamned well that you are as horny as I am at this moment."

Gently lifting her from the chair he carries her to his bedroom, then standing her next to the bed, he slowly, gently, and romantically begins to disrobe her. She in turn affectionately places her two hands softly on his cheeks and her trembling lips embrace his.

Hastily he sheds his own clothing to embrace her warm body and then gently leans her back on to the white linen sheets. As many times that he has viewed this prone, nude, magnificent obsession, this exotic breath taking creature, it still thrills Ted. Fondly perusing her nudity he softly expresses himself to Cathy. "This is image is more beautiful than Goya's painting of his nude – and this nude is mine, all mine."

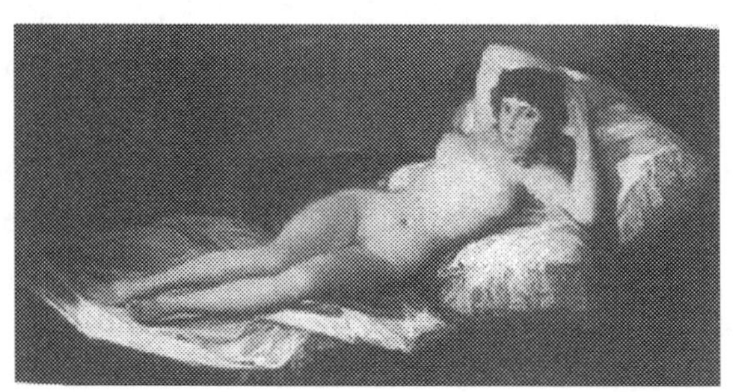

In 1815, the Spanish Inquisition summoned Goya to reveal who commissioned him to create the "obscene" *La maja desnuda*, and she was consequently stripped of his position as the Spanish court painter. If Goya gave an explanation of the painting's origin to the Inquisition, that account has never surfaced. Two sets of stamps depicting *La maja desnuda* in commemoration of Goya's work were privately produced in 1930, and later approved by the Spanish Postal Authority. That same year, the United States government barred and returned any mail bearing the stamps.

Chapter thirty-two

Close to midnight Tuesday, December 24, 1963. Claudia and Matthew have just finished wrapping gifts for Edwina, and little John, when Matthew emotionally involved in the Spirit of Christmas suggests," Darling why don't you get ready for bed and put on a robe and we will sit by the fire and reminisce over a couple of cool Zinfandels?"

Claudia snuggles close to Matthew on the sofa, and slouches down to place her head on his lap. Pensively reflecting of Christmas' past and how pleasant this Christmas brings euphoria. Her marriage to Matthew has blessed her with two great children Edwina and John Fitzgerald. Romantically, and gently, she pats Matthew's thigh.

Matthew, deeply in love, and believing that this woman is his dream come true, responds as any man will do. He slowly lowers the zipper on her robe, exposing two beautifully formed breasts, and in a gentle loving gesture he fondles each breast. Claudia responds by slowly sitting up and further lowering the zipper, then very gently she brings Matthew's face between her beautiful orbs. As he suckles her left nipple then to the right nipple, Claudia lets out a sound of pain and pushes Matthew away.

"My God sweetheart, what is wrong?"

"I don't know, I don't know, that gave me a sharp pain."

"Have you bruised that breast recently, baby?"

"Not that I can recall, I do know when I showered earlier, I felt a little ache when I washed that area."

In January she is diagnosed as having breast cancer and is operated on by the renowned Dr. John Waterman the son of Alvan and Phyllis.

After performing a radical mastectomy at Brigham's Women's Hospital, Dr. John has a conference with Claudia and Matthew.

"Claudia, I'd like to be a bearer of good news at this time, but I must be realistic. Rhetoric is sometimes okay, but reality is in the facts. The operation that I performed was successful as far as it goes, but I cannot be sure that we removed all of the malignant cells. We can only hope and pray that the cells do not metastasis to other parts or the body and that we have succeeded at removing all of the malignancy. Only time will tell. I will keep you on medication and monthly exams and hope for the best."

Patriot's Day, Sunday April 19, 1964, is celebrated in the Commonwealth of Massachusetts to commemorate the first battle of the American War of Independence. It was at Concord and Lexington that the first fight against the British occupation began. The annual Patriots Day twenty-one mile Marathon is preparing to begin. However, this is also the date Claudia's fruitless battle against cancer is now over.

At 6 a.m. with her mother Ruth, step-father Eamon, and Matthew, at her bedside, she succumbs to the dread disease. Being over eight months pregnant, the doctors remove the live fetus and incubate a six pound boy. After three weeks incubation the baby boy is released to Matthew.

Shakespeare, as usual, had expressions for any situation, in Matthew's case: *Grief's of mine own lie heavy on my breast.*

To constantly remind him of his love for Claudia, he names the new born son *Claude Shane Ferber.* He selects the name *Shane* because Claudia upon her pregnancy selected it after seeing the movie with Alan Ladd. She admired that strong character.

However, since Matthew is raising Edwina and John Fitzgerald, it is obvious that he cannot properly take care of a new born Claude Shane. For the beginning, Grandmother Ruth will take on the duties of raising the baby.

July of 1964, Matthew hires a Marion Frazier to work in Claudia's place at his store. She is a good worker and is excellent at customer relations. On several occasions, over the next several months, she takes Edwina, along with her two boys, to Nantasket beach, Franklin Park Zoo, and movies.

Matthew has no physical or emotional interest in Marion. She is so different from Claudia in all ways. Physically, she is shorter, darker and indelicate at times, so much so to it borders on crudeness. He is naïve and is unaware of the wiles of female stratagem that first rears its head Labor Day.

"Matthew, since we are going to be closed for the holiday, how about you, Edwina and John Fitz, go with me and my boys to spend that weekend at Paragon Park in Nantasket Beach? We can ride the roller coaster and the carousel. Have a fun weekend."

"Why don't you just take Edwina, I can use that time to take inventory?"

"Matthew, you are just stalling, you don't need to take inventory right now. It is time that you adjust to the fact that the woman that you loved is in heaven. It is time that a reality checkup is needed for you. My boys could use your masculine influence. They are missing, and need, the paternal part of their lives. Your children will experience the maternal needs of youngsters."

The weekend is spent in separate rooms at the Nantasket Hotel. Matthew has to admit it is a pleasant occasion, and Edwina and John Fitz also enjoy it. The next few months have a few family style visits to restaurants, and movies. It is at the Ferber Office Christmas party that Marion makes her strategic move.

Acting as the hostess for the staff of six employees and families, she makes sure that Matthew is kept well supplied with vodka splits. At the close of the party, and everyone has left, she locks the store and goes partially behind the door of Matthew's office; supposedly she is modestly shielding herself from scrutiny. She removes her skirt and says, so that he can hear her. "Matthew I am sweaty and I need to remove my panty hose, you don't mind do you?"

"No, not at all, get comfortable."

Removing her red Christmas blouse, reveals naked breasts, then in total nudity from her nose to her toes, she approaches Matthew. "I am comfortable, now do you think you can handle this?"

"Jesus Christ Marion, get dressed."

She reaches down, unzips his pants, reaches in, and removes an erection. "What are you going to do about this rod? Don't waste it, I'll put it where it will do us both, the most good, in the place it belongs." She then she leans back onto the desk and pulls him on top of her.

As the saying goes, *it has been a long time between drinks,* while it is strictly lustful satisfaction and not great, as his love sex with Claudia, it feels good. However, Matthew avoids any further sexual encounters with Marion. It has been a pleasant moment; however future repetitions could lead to problems. Never the less, the wiles of Marion proceed further.

On St. Paddy's Day 1965 she goes into Matthew's office, closes the door behind her, and sits on the corner of his desk. "We have a situation that must be resolved Matthew. Since I am not on the pill and you did not use a condom when you seduced me at the Christmas party, I am now three months pregnant."

"What the hell do you mean I seduced you? You came at me, as any piece of arsse would do. You acted like a whore."

"Let's be realistic Matthew, I can claim rape. I can say you sexually harassed me and forced me to *put- out* or lose my job. I can say you took advantage of me because you were my boss. Now before you say any more nasty things, let us talk. This can be a good thing for you, Edwina, and John, as well as Randolph and Frank. We also can bring Claude Shane to live with us."

"I know that you can never love any woman other than Claudia, but you can make life a little better for you and your children by marrying me. Your kids need a female adult and mine need a male influence for them to grow up with stability."

Realizing that he is damned if he does or damned if he doesn't wed Marion, and that he is trapped, he rationalizes to himself, 'After all she has been a good worker, a good mother for Edwina and John, this could be a good thing for his children. They will have the companionship of Randolph and Mark plus a maternal influence in their upbringing.' Moreover, the memory of her Christmas time seduction has him experiencing re-occurring nocturnal emissions.

Thursday, April 1, 1965, Judge Casey marries Matthew Ferber to Marion Frazier. Could this April Fool's Day predict the future of this marriage?

Tuesday, September 21, 1965, Marion gives birth to five pound six ounce little angel that Marion names Beatrice Elizabeth after her deceased grandmother.

Chapter thirty-three

On Saturday April 18, 1964 to celebrate Ted's 40th birthday, he reserves an elegant suite at the Ritz Carleton. It has a splendid view overlooking the beautifully manicured Boston Public Gardens and the Swan boats on the pond below their suite. A romantic at heart, when it comes to Cathy, Ted orders a table be set in upscale style with cut flowers, Zinfandel wine, candles and soft music in the background.

"Teddy, I do believe that you have out-done yourself this time. This will be a most memorable occasion."

Slowly helping her to remove the coat from her shoulders and dropping it onto the floor, Ted responds, "Any time that you are mine alone, is always memorable to me. I have reservation for us to have a late dinner and dancing in the roof garden to add to our romantic day."

Smothering her lips with passionate kisses, he begins unbuttoning the front of her dress. "Teddy, let's not rush this, I want you as much as you want me, but we can look forward to doing this after the dinner and dancing."

Not persuaded in the least while taking her hand, he leads her to the bedroom. "Cathy, let's be romantic and do it now as well as later. This is going to be an all day, all evening rendezvous. So let us enjoy now and repeat after the dance." And slowly disrobes her. There is no further resistant on Cathy's part.

In the evening, they adjourn to the Ritz roof garden to dance to the fabulous music of Vaughn Monroe and yes Vaughn is requested and plays Love *is a many splendored thing.* Holding Cathy ever so lovingly close, Ted whispers softly, "Taim i' ngra leat cushla ma cree."

"Teddy, my ever loving darling, I am always so happy when I am in your arms."

It is a story book romantic evening. A warm breeze flows over them as they waltz across the open dance floor. The scent of Ted's Stetson cologne blends with Cathy's Chanel and joins the aroma of her white corsage that accents vividly the contrast of the lovely red evening gown Ted has bought Cathy.

Many dances later, they hear the orchestra playing *auld lang syne*, indicating the orchestra will no longer contribute to their romance. Returning to the suite, she helps Ted remove her red gown, her matching black lace trimmed red panties, and finally her bra, for the exotic mesmerizing morphing of their bodies and souls.

The next morning's parting is painful, but communication is maintained by Cathy phoning Ted at least twice a week. For obvious reasons, Ted cannot phone Cathy and it is 8 p.m. Thursday June 18, 1964 when they meet again, this time, to celebrate little Larry's 7th birthday at Blue Haven Lodge.

About 9 p.m. Ted questions, "Last Christmas you said you missed two things while you were in Ireland. One was my bar-b-que steaks; the other was to swim in warm water. I gave you the steaks last Christmas and the warm water now awaits you. How about fulfilling the second missing thing and go skinny dip in the lake right now?"

"I'd love it." She excitedly grabs Ted's hand and heads to the back porch then down the steps to the pier. Not embarrassed, completely uninhibited, upon arriving at the beginning of the pier she begins a slow trot while she sheds her blouse, then skirt, and finally her panties and bra. Ted following close behind, and in *horny* anticipation, has stripped before she even gets to the bra stage of her undressing.

Diving off the end of the pier, Cathy swims out to the raft and is on deck before Ted. However, she does not sit there; she stands up giving him a nude full frontal then dives back into the water and swims back to the pier. Instead of climbing up onto the pier she lays on the sand along side. The still warm sand is comforting as she lay looking up at the bright stars flooding the skies. Her view of the stars is suddenly blocked by Ted as he stands looking down at her sandy nudeness.

With this masculine hulk standing so erect and a matching erectness below his waist line, a smile encases her beautiful face. Arms extended, she beckons him to come down on top of her. Their smoldering subliminal passion exceeds the famous sandy beach erotic scene of Deborah Kerr and Burt Reynolds in the film *From here to Eternity* and moreover, lasts just as long. The next morning, they do a bed enactment of last night's beach scene, before breakfast, then sad goodbyes.

Tuesday August 4, 1964, Ted receives a panicky phone call from Cathy, "Teddy, as usual, I turn to you when I have a problem. This time I am petrified. "

"Jesus H. Christ Cathy, what's the matter?"

"Teddy, Gaelach the typical Irisher, could not help bar hoping and getting stupidly drunk. This time he was in the North End at a dago bar called Vincenzo's di Pranzo and *shot his mouth off* about the fact that Lawrence bribed an Irish official and a U.S. Customs agent to illegally give him and Maev entry into America."

"The owner of the North End restaurant *Sonny* Paraviccino gave Gaelach a bundle of money and a plane ticket back to Ireland, to kidnap little Larry. Now Sonny is holding little Larry for a ransom of a half a mil from us. Do you know him Teddy?"

"I sure do. That is Vincenzo *Sonny* Paraviccino. He owns a joint called Vincenzo's Luogo, a hang-out for the *malta vita*. He is the gangster mob boss of the dago held North End area of Boston. He runs his rackets from his office in the back of the restaurant."

"Have you gone to the cops or the F.B.I. about this Cathy?"

"No, because Sonny has papers Gaelach gave him, detailing all of Lawrence's nefarious immigration misdeeds and that would cause Lawrence to go to prison. Lawrence asked me to go to you for help, hinting that maybe he knows that little Larry is very close to you."

"Does he know that I am the boy's father?"

"He is not sure, but as the boy grows, he begins to resemble you more and more each day."

Ted phones East Boston Division 4 police station. "This is Sheerin; let me talk to Captain Lombardo."

After a few minutes a voice came on the phone, "This is Captain Lombardo, what do you want with me Sheerin."

"What can you tell me about Sonny Paraviccino's bistro?"

"Why do you want to know about Vincenzo's place? Is it something that concerns my division?"

"No, it is a personal matter Captain. Now how do I get in touch with him?"

"Personal matter be god damned sir, Sonny is a personal friend of mine, and I know your reputation."

"I'll skip that remark Captain. However, like it or not you know my connections. Don't tangle with me or I will have your arsse and have you cashiered on one charge or another. Do I make myself clear Captain?"

Silence for a moment.

"So let us start over Captain."

"Sonny's private telephone number is East-2811."

"Thanks Captain, maybe I can do you a favor sometime."

"I doubt that sir, I would never want to be beholden to you."

Telephoning Vincenzo, "Sonny, this is Licutcnat Sheerin of Deputy Superintendent Hanratty's office. I understand that you are holding my son for ransom from Lawrence Cameron."

"I know nothing about your son. What goes on between Cameron and me is my business. I know who the fuck you are, you don't scare me a bit. You interfere in my business and you will be biting off more than you can handle. When I hang-up I'm phoning Captain Lombardo to tell him to keep you outta East Boston."

"You call anyone you want Dago, if you really know me, you know you need to worry because I will reduce you from a *Greaser* to becoming just a grease spot."

"Well puttano, I'll give my answer later, you will learn what a tough wop is."

Phoning Captain Lombardo was of no help, his only answer, "Sonny, my advice to you is – don't fuck with Sheerin."

"He don't scare me Carmen, I will show him that we Italiano's are not to be fucked with."

"Sonny, what kind of flowers do you want for your funeral?"

Chapter thirty-four

At about 7 p.m. Wednesday, August 5, 1964, Alvan Waterman phones Sheerin. "I've got some bad news Teddy; however, please listen before you get your testicles in an uproar."

"Well I will decide the heat of my balls if you get to the point Al."

"I am at the E.R. room of BCH your dad and I got a going over by Sonny Paraviccino's enforcers. The doctors here say that while I am badly bruised, I am okay. Not so for Eamon, he is unconscious."

"Say no more, I will be there in about thirty minutes or less, I am coming to the hospital as fast as I can."

Pulling to the front door of the hospital emergency room, Ted hurriedly exits his car and heads for the entry. A young rookie Boston cop grabs Ted by the arm and yells, "Who do you think you are? Get that car into the parking lot where it belongs."

A bit startled, Ted shoves the cop away and pulls his badge, "Listen to me rookie, you are grass, and I am the fucking lawn mower. Take these keys and YOU park the fuckin' car or my lawn mower will begin in seconds."

Shocked and scared of unknown possible consequences, the young policeman stammers an apology, salutes and heads to park the auto. Teddy is met at the nurse's desk by Alvan who goes into a hasty explanation. "Teddy, it looks serious. Doctor Rothstein will give us the details in about thirty minutes."

"What the hell happened to him Al? "

"Your dad and I were sitting in the office when three pug-uglies came in. The leader, holding a menacing *lupara,* says that he is here from Sonny Paraviccino's office and Sonny believes that Lieutenant Sheerin needs to learn about *Dago power* and they have come to Freeport Motors to deliver Sonny's message. It was obvious to your dad what they meant. Your dad told them to fuck off, that his son Lieutenant Sheerin will show what Irish power is all about. With that your Dad slugs him one."

"Pissed off to a fare-de-well, the guy called Gussy gets up from the floor and tells a King Kong size of a brute to show this Irish bastard what Sonny thinks Teddy Sheerin's protection is worth. With that they beat your Dad and me on the head with *slap-sticks.* Your Dad puts up a hellava fight, but the *slap-sticks* were too much for him. He fell down, cut, all bloodied, and unconscious and Gussy says for me to tell you that Sonny sends his message."

"Sonny will pay, so help me Christ, he will pay, and so will his thugs."

"Teddy, to be honest with you, they are fearless. They said Sonny said he doesn't give a fuck for Sheerin and Kelley. They say Sonny will now take over this territory and let you see just who is the toughest. They will be back next Friday afternoon to prove their point and to collect a ransom for your son."

"You won't be alone Alvan. I promise you I will be there and I will teach them what Lieutenant Sheerin's protection is about. Plus Sonny will then realize that he is not dealing with a pussy wimp Irish male."

Sipping on coffee offered by the nurse, Ted and Al are met by Dr. Rothstein.

"When can I see my Dad, Doctor?"

"He is being brought up from surgery very soon. You can go in his room after the nurses get him settled. However he has received severe damage to his brain, and he may not recognize you. From the head wounds he possibly has lost a great deal of memory. His *cerebral cortex* and *hippocampus* are affected. Both of which store memories and we can't be sure what is remaining. With prayers and a recovering brain, his neurological processes may begin and in a few days some of his recognition and interpretations may be restored. However, if it does not, it will take more time for him to remember how to walk, speak, recognize, and so forth."

Alone in the private room at the bedside of his father, Ted experiences an eerie silence that prevails from being alone along the bedsides of his coma stricken father. Although he still is wearing a top coat and a soft felt fedora, a cold shiver encompasses his body. This hospital room of stark white, walls, ceilings, sheets, and blankets, gives Ted the feeling of sitting in a mausoleum crypt. Turning as Alvan enters the room, "I swear to you, I am so pissed that I can hardly wait to get those sons-o-bitches that did this."

"Ted, Jazz sent Jimmy McMann over. He is out in the waiting room, says he needs to talk to you."

Confronting Jimmy, "What the fuck has got into Jazz's mind that he will allow Sonny to start a territorial confrontation with me? Sonny should come after me, not my family."

"You got it all wrong Ted. When Mr. Kelley heard about Sonny's goons beatin' your father, he sent me to meet Sonny. That dago has gone berserk. Says he is breakin' away from Jazz and is going to take over all the territory. I am to stay with you as your back-up until this is resolved. I'll eat, sleep, and stay with you at Blue Haven or elsewhere. Also, *three-fingers* is yours if you need him."

"I appreciate that Jimbo, but I think I can handle Sonny."

Looking over Ted's shoulder, Jimmy spots two men, obviously detectives, approaching Ted. "I think you've got company. I'll get us a couple cups of coffee and be right back."

"Are you Teddy Sheerin mister?"

"Yes, why do you ask?"

Flashing detective badges the Peter Falk looking cop says, "Captain Lombardo says to stay away from Sonny Paraviccino and out of East Boston."

Grabbing the detective by his coat lapels, Ted yanks him forward, "Detective, when you address a senior officer you say Sir. Now let me hear you say Sir – loud and strong."

With that the other detective pulls his gun and shoves it into Teddy's back. Jimmy rapidly approaching the trio quickly reacts to the conflict by throwing the hot coffee into the face of that detective. In a synchronous move, pulls his own weapon, and jabs the still armed detective in the back. For a moment it is a Mexican Stand-off. However, the aggressive armed one raises his weapon above his head reaching high in a surrender, "Hold it, and hold it, Sir. I didn't bargain for this. We'll get the hell out of here Sir."

Ted takes out his .38 police special and whacks the culprit across the nose. "Show that bloody nose to Captain Lombardo and tell him that the next time I will kill any bastard he sends. If he interferes with me he will be raw meat. Better still, you warn any of Division 4 that I will attack their wives and children if there is any interference from them."

Even though they are in the hospital and first aid is available in the nearby emergency room, the bloodied detective and his coffee burned partner decide it is in their best interest to get the fuck away from Teddy

The next morning, phoning Lombardo. "Captain this is Sheerin. I want to scc you in my officc at H.Q. in one hour."

On Lombardo's arrival he is keep waiting in Teddy's outer office for over an hour. Finally being admitted Ted orders the Captain to sit down and shut-up.

"You had the fuckin' audacity to send two detectives to the hospital while I am sweating out my Dad's condition. You give them orders for me to stay out of East Boston. You know that by your meddling you have gone too far when it comes to me getting my son back from his being kidnapped by Sonny Paraviccino. Lombardo you have become a pain in my arsse for too bloody long. I know that you are getting bribe money from one of Jazz's bookies and you shall be disciplined for such corruption."

"Sheerin you seem to forget that I can prove that you saw to the delivery of that money to me. Your deportment seems to be that you have forgotten that you are a Lieutenant and beneath my rank of Captain."

"Lombardo if anyone has forgotten anything, you seem to forget that it isn't the title that is important, it is the power of the individual and you best recognize that fact. That is why you showed up here on my orders. Remember that Hitler and Napoleon were mere corporals. Have you forgotten that I am attached to Superintendant Hanratty's office?"

"Since we are alone in this office, I will be blunt with you Lieutenant Sheerin. I think Sonny is wrong when it comes to your kid. However it is obvious you know that I am getting a monthly envelope from Jazz that is delivered to me by Fred Banks. You know because you are one of Jazz Kelley's flunkies."

"Well, Lombardo, I'll be just as blunt. You did not do a damned thing to help me about Sonny and my boy. I will not stay out of *Easta Bos* but YOU will be out of East Boston permanently. I want your letter of retirement before you leave this building. If I don't get it, I will have the bookie that you are protecting, testify against you and Superintendent Hanratty's office will put you under arrest for taking bribes. You best think of your family and your future, retire with a full pension or go to jail."

Absolute corruption – absolutely, totally corrupts.

Thursday August 6, Captain Carmen Lombardo is hastily feted at Vincenzo's bistro with an extravagant retirement party, booze, broads, thugs and cops, all mingled together for a grand farewell. It is Lombardo's *Il punto di fuga.*

Chapter thirty-five

Friday, August 7, 1964. Ted is at the car lot office early. At any sign of activity, he hides in the storage closet. It is nearly eight p.m. and getting dark, when a deep navy blue Lincoln limo pulls into the lot. Needing to be sure of the identities, he listens as two thugs get out of the car and come in the office.

"Remember me my friend Alvan, and truly Sonny wants us to be friends, he says to me, 'Gussy, be nice to those guys at Freeport Motors'. However, your cop buddy Sheerin needs a lesson friend Alvan. Now do you have the money?"

"I don't know about any money."

"Must I have to convince you guys that you need Sonny's protection," as he brushes imaginary dust from Al's gray suit coat?

"I remember your ugly face Gussy. I see that you brought your not so friendly gorilla Herman, and left the baggy suited other guy in your car."

At the hint of baggy suits, Gussy re-adjusts his double breasted Hart Shaffner Marx blue serge suit coat, and Herman unbuttons his camel hair sport coat to reveal his custom made shirt and tie.

"If you want to remain healthy, I suggest you get your garlic breath dago ass out of here."

"You never learn do you Jew boy?"

Gussy gives Alvan a hard, open hand, slap across his face. "Your smart mouth will get your kin to gather together ten Jews to hold your *minyan*. Just to teach you a lesson I outta re-sculpt your face." Then he turns pale as Ted, shotgun in hand, steps out of the storage closet.

"The ransom money is here at the end of this shotgun barrel. You Wops are so long with one side you forget those on the other side can show you that you are fuckin' with the wrong guy. Make a move and I will blast your face off your head. Al, frisk them for weapons."

The gorilla, has an imported Brazilian .45 automatic and a Smith & Wesson .38 revolver. Gussy has a sleeve derringer, a Colt .38 revolver and a .45 Beretta semiautomatic pistol.

Attempting bravado Gussy jabbers, "You are flirting with severe trouble mister. We are just here to pick up the money so that nothing happens to your kid. Sonny says that you need to know that anyone who fucks with Sonny will pay a heavy price."

"Well Gussy, I am Lieutenant Sheerin, the insurance man, and you are going to be sorry for the beating that you inflicted on my dad."

Panicky sweat pouring from his forehead, Gussy stammers, and lies, "On my sainted mother's grave, that was a big mistake, I didn't know that guy was your father. I just thought he was a troublesome nobody that needed a lesson. No shit about it, ask Herman he will tell you that if he knew he would never have laid a hand on your father. Would you Herman?"

"Nah, nah, we better leave."

"Gussy, your mother was no saint; she was a puttana that gave birth to an amoral guinea bastard, a depraved reprobate. It is too late for your penitence or *mea culpas.* I am going to give you my interpretations of the Sacrament of Extreme Unction then send you to a fiery eternity in Hell."

"Lord help me Jesus," Gussy hollers.

'Lord help you my arsse Gussy. If you think that the man from Galilee may help you I will expedite your trip to meet him so that you may seek his help in person. There will be no *Missa pro defunctis for you Gussy.*"

Ted turning to Alvan, "Al, I know this is against your religious beliefs, so get the hell out of here. Go say a *Kaddish* for these arsse-holes."

Alvan hesitates, shakes his head negatively, he is torn between his beliefs and yet his empathy and understanding of Ted's reasoning. Moreover these thugs are truly *yutz kelevras. (*Stupid mad dogs). The old testament of the *Torah,* does say *an eye for an eye* thus, he rationalizes that their imminent death is not *terefah* (forbidden). However he chooses to take Ted's advice.

It is amazing how much abuse the human body can sustain. The duo remain conscious even after the close contact of Ted's shotgun, exposes their intestines. To add to their torture Ted stands over the dying men, "I promise that you will not be buried in sacred ground. No Rosary, no burial Mass, nothing. You better start saying your *Act of Contrition* now. I'll start you off, *Oh my God! I am heartily sorry ––*. Now you take it from there 'cause, I am going to take your carcasses out in the bay and gut you so that your body will sink and never float up. With no last *rites* or forgiveness, you will skip purgatory and end up in Hell."

The third man does not get out of the car. Waiting a few seconds after hearing the shotgun firing and seeing Ted standing in the office doorway, the *Terzo Italiano,* burns rubber in his hasty retreat from Freeport Motors.

Backing a half-ton pickup to the car lot office door, Ted begins the arduous task of loading the now very limp bloody bodies into the truck. However, it is strenuous but violent temper seems to give added adrenaline for greater physical strength and he completes the physical nightmare.

Parking the truck in the three car garage under Blue Haven Lodge, he locks the doors and goes upstairs to the living room. Still shaking from a combination of an adrenalin surge, anger, revenge, and sheer after effects of his killing the two scum-bums, he pours a stiff Johnny Walker Black Label and stretches out on the sofa. Even the toughest of men, sometimes have a tinge of conscience, and so with Teddy. Omar Khayyam had a paragraph that at this moment might be apropos for Ted and other sinners.

"Dear my God, you are merciful, and mercy is pity. Why has the greatest sinner been shut off from paradise? If you only pardon me because I have obeyed you, what mercy is that? It would be merciful to forgive me, sinner that I am."

The following morning, and off duty, Ted cooks himself a breakfast of crisp bacon, eggs sunny side up. It is finished off with heavily buttered grilled split Danish buns and coffee. He is casually sipping his second cuppa when *Three strikes* come up the back stairs and knocks on the porch entry door.

Answering it Ted says, "Maidin mhaith Sean. How about a cuppa and a Danish roll?"

"Thanks Teddy, coffee will take the mornin' chill off me." In typical *shange tighe (shanty)* Irish style, they sit at the kitchen table to talk.

"What brings this early morning visit Sean?"

"Well Teddy, I wondered, do you still need protection at Freeport Motors in Dorchester?"

"Yes, I do and as a matter of fact, I am wondering what your interest in Freeport Motors is?"

"Well, Mr. Kelley was askin', says he will send a watch-dog to protect the bookie money for you."

"I appreciate that Sean. I may have bit off more than I can chew. Meanwhile I have something to show you."

Gesturing directions, the two proceed down to the garage. Getting to the back of the Ford pick-up, Ted says, "This would be a bit unnerving to the ordinary joker, but you have seen plenty like this," as he lifts the tarp.

After an impassive and stoical view of the bodies, showing no reaction other than a darkening brow, *Three strikes* asks, "What the fuck kind of a cannon did you use to blow that big of hole in them?"

"I used a twelve gauge shotgun held close to their belly. That way they live for a few moments to suffer the same as my Dad. I told them I was going to put a hole big enough to hold a watermelon."

"Well you held it too close. That hole would only fit a grapefruit, but it would cause them longer time to be sorry for their actions before they died. However, at the moment, I have no ox to grind with you, but if you and I get into some act, think twice – who gets it first – you or me?"

Continuing, "Mr. K has no dog in this hunt and he has informed me that it was a huge mistake made by Sonny's lieutenants. Mr. Kelley says you are important to him. Besides that he never allows attacks against cops or their families. The repercussion can be costly. The only time he feels different is if the cop does something wrong and not in their line of duty. Then it is just he and the cop, not the cop's family, and Sonny knows Mr. Kelley's rules."

"Mr. K. figures something had happened to these two moronic retards when they did not come by his office for a group meeting with

Sonny last night. At that time he was told by the third guy, Alphonse, that they had visited Freeport Motors."

"The third guy that you say is Alphonse, where is he?"

"Mr. Kelley says he will send Alphonse' body in crate to you, or if you will take his word, he will dispose of Alphonse for you Teddy. Mr. Kelley does not want this to become a major migraine for him. He says that you realize this could not be an attack condoned by him. Instead he will give Sonny a couple of big migraines for violating rules. After all, those were a couple of lousy *guineas*, and we Miks should remember Sinn Fein."

"Sinn Fein be damned Johnny, I don't trust you for a goddamn minute. What's to stop you from ambushing me anytime? After all, when I come home here at night, how do I know that a slug might greet me with a good-night kiss from your .45?"

"Now cut out the bullshit Teddy. You have known me for years; my modus operandi is to erase guys that have fucked-up against Mr. Kelley. You haven't, Herman, Gussy, and Alphonse did. By erasing them you just did my job for me. They fucked-up big time and Mr. Kelley would have had me terminate them. We are trying to tell you we are apologizing; no problems should exist between Mr. K and you. Also Teddy, with your permission, Mr. Kelley would like to have your dad transferred to the Huntington Therapy Clinic. The best care available in this country is at Huntington, and Mr. Kelley will pay all costs, and care, to get your dad back to health."

The following day at 2 a.m., Teddy hooks up the motor boat trailer to the rear of his Caddy, puts the two bodies in the back section of the boat, and covers them with a canvas boat covering tarp. Then placing the fishing locker, bait pails, rods, etc. on top, he is ready to complete his plan of revenge. At midnight, he gets in the car and heads out highway 123 to Scituate.

While passing through Rockland, he picks up a tail. A Massachusetts state trooper begins to follow Ted for about three miles until the Statsie decides to check out the rig. Hearing the siren, Ted begins to sweat a little. Should he make a run for it, shit, no, not while pulling this rig, might it best be to try to bluff it out? He pulls the rig over to the side of the road and the trooper walks up to the window. "May I have some identification sir?"

"Certainly, will this due," as he shows his Lieutenant's gold police badge?

"Well Lieutenant, I am merely a sergeant, I'm Sergeant Chuck Crowley," he kids. "The reason I stopped you, is that we don't see many boat rigs being pulled by a Cadillac convertible. It is usually being towed by a Texas Cadillac (pick-up truck). In the summer we see many fishermen on this road at night but it is usually no earlier than four or five o'clock in the morning. That way they do not have to wait too long for daylight to launch their boats. It sure is going to be chilly fishing in those waters at this time of the year, plus you are going to have to sit in Situate for a couple of hours before a daylight launching."

"I planned this early trip because I just got off duty and wasn't too sure that this load would be too heavy for the Cady. I planned a few days of R&R fishing. Plus, I need a bit of sleep time so I thought if I get to the docks without any problems I could then take a little nap before daylight."

"Good thinking Lieutenant. Hope the fish are hungry. Have a safe trip. See ya at another time," as he turns to leave. Then, "I see a corner of your tarp is loose, let me tie it down for you."

Ted becomes very nervous, if that trooper lifts the tarp before tying it down and sees the bodies, 'I am going to have to kill him', and he unholsters his weapon. However, for some reason, Lady Luck is with him, the trooper ties the tarp to a hook, then," Good luck in your fishing."

"Sergeant, here is my business card. If I can ever be of any assistance to you in the Boston area, just give me a call."

"Thanks, I just might do that Lieutenant. See ya later."

Getting to the Situate docks, Ted does not wait for sunup. He unloads the boat from the trailer, into the water, and heads out to sea. The water is slightly turbulent but not serious. A little over ten miles out into the Atlantic, he stops the boat, removes the tarp covering the corpses. He then hurriedly ties two cinder blocks to each victim's legs, and then guts each body, to remove the intestines and entrails. This way the bodies will not bloat and float to the surface later on. At the same time he removes the victim's thumbs.

Before tossing the two corpses over board, he mumbles, "I wish you guys all the pains of hell," knowing they cannot hear him but it gives him a bit of gratification. To adequately appease his sating of this illustrious occasion, he trolls for hours while sipping on a bottle of Irish cream before heading home.

Getting back to Blue Haven Lodge, he wraps the thumbs of the two deceased into a fillet of Cod and mails them to Sonny with a note; *You are not secure from me as these two were also not secure.*

On Thursday August 13, 1964 Teddy receives a phone call, "Teddy, Tom Kelley he'ah. I be needin' yo-awh cooperation. I met with Sonny Paraviccino and told him that this vendetta has gone fa'h enu'f. I ordered Sonny to bring the boy to me office. I will see that he is safely returned to his mothah. Howeva' Teddy, you will not go into East Bahston without getting me permission. While I tolerate a limited independence, don't push yah luck Teddy."

"Tommy, I have no reason or desire to buck you in any manner. I sincerely appreciate your getting my boy back. I enjoy our relationship and, as usual, I will contact you if I feel a problem exists."

"Teddy me friend, Sonny violated me rules. He shoulda not have ha'med family. He sends you a gift of solid ivo-ey statutes and extends an apology and rationalizes that he did not know that the boy is yo-awh son."

"Again Capo Crimini Don Kelley, I thank you for your intervention in this dispute," as a wise Teddy Sheerin accedes to the powerful head of the Boston Irish Mafia. Respect shown – gains him some *brownie points.*

However – the Thursday, August 13, 1964 headlines in the Boston Globe – *Arson suspected in the total loss of Vincenzo's Night Club.*

Each piece of the hand carved ivory figurines is two feet tall. The dragon is 18 inches tall and it now guards the front doorway of Blue Haven.

Chapter Thirty-Six

Eamon is hospitalized until Thursday October 8, 1964, at his release his physical condition is unstable and to stabilize his balance he requires the use of two canes in his walking. This along with a slur in his speech causes him to become irritable at times. Having his own room at Blue Haven Lodge allows him to retreat to his quarters when he does not want to be around others. For the next two weeks Donna Louise tends to him.

Thursday morning December 24, 1964 Cathy Cameron brings seven year old Lawrence Edward to spend the Christmas weekend at Blue Haven Lodge. Ted has erected a nine foot tall Christmas tree in the family room. The three spend the day decorating the tree with many multi-colored bulbs, tinsel, and strings of colorful electric bulbs. Eamon reclines in his rocker proffering decorating instructions between sipping hot coffee laced with Bailey's Irish Cream. A delightful Christmas spirit prevails.

Ted has wrapped, in fancy Christmas paper and beautiful ribbons, many gifts for Cathy and their son. These are scattered at the foot of the tree awaiting the thrill of opening them in the morning.

After Lawrence Edward has been put to bed, Ted breaks out a set of Lionel Electric trains and he and grandpa Eamon set it up on tracks that circle the tree. Cathy's response is a typical mother's logic. "Don't you think that is a waste of money? After all Eddy is too young to appreciate such a gift."

"Don't you believe that for a minute Cathy? I got my first train engine at seven. It did not have all its wheels and the tin was rusted, but it was mine. I realize he will not fully appreciate them until he gets a little older. However, he will get a thrill out of playing with them now. Something else Cathy, you just referred to him as Eddy, when did that come about?"

"After Mr. Kelley brought the boy home from Sonny's kidnapping, Lawrence said, 'Here is your bastard son.' So it now out in the open that Eddy is yours and mine, and that gives Larry a reason to be cruel and nasty. It has become so bad that I had to lock Eddy and me in the bedroom many a night in fear of Larry."

"But Cathy, addressing him as Eddy it must aggravate the hell out of Lawrence, so you are partly to blame for exacerbating the situation by calling him that. You are flaunting the fact that you gave him the middle name of Edward, the same name as mine."

With this, Eamon interrupts, "You two are going into a discussion that is private. I am going to bed and I'll see you after Santa Claus pays us a visit in the morning," he teases.

With Eamon in his room, Cathy continues the discussion. "It is the only way that I can get back at him for what he says and does to me. I haven't told you because I know your temper and you would beat, even kill him. I don't want that on my conscience."

"Did he beat you?"

"Not really. If I was near him he would give me a shove. It is mostly mental abuse. He details his love making with Maeve O'Toole and saying that she is by far a better lover than I am. He said that I am a slut and a whore. Any sex that he has with me would be sloppy seconds after your dumpings. He says that he doesn't have to worry about you dumping your sperm into Maeve's body. When he would see me applying lipstick because my lips were dry, he would reach over and smear the lipstick saying, 'Look in the mirror that is how your lips probable looks after you go down on the Shanty Mik.' He is so mean that I began to call Lawrence Edward, Eddy to get revenge."

June of 1965, Lawrence and Maeve Bridget return to Ireland to spend a couple of months with Maeve's parents. Returning to the U.S. in November, Lawrence again becomes abusive to Cathy.

Monday November 22, 1965, Ted, Alvan, Eamon, Fred, James, Sean, Anne, Jackie, Virginia, Ruth, Phyllis, and Norma are all gathered at Blue Haven Lodge to watch the heavy weight championship fight between Floyd Patterson and Cassius Clay on the TV.

Clay has recently converted to Islam and joining the notorious *Black Muslims* changes his name to Muhammad Ali, but Ted still refers to him as Cassius Marcellus Clay because, to him, that is a more prestigious moniker then the Muslim *nom di plume*. But most important to Ted is the fact that Clay has Irish blood from his grandfather an Irishman who immigrated to the U.S. from Ennis, County Clare, Ireland.

Like most military veterans, Ted is disappointed when Clay refuses to be drafted and submit to induction into the Army. How convenient that as a Muslim, he can in a bloody battle, beat an opponent to a pulp, while enjoying the title of conscientious objector. His reasoning does not hold water. Let others in the military guarantee his right of religious freedom.

Still remembering his years in the military, Ted feels Clay is no Elvis Pressley, who served after being drafted, nor is he like movie star Lew Ayers who in 1918 was a true conscientious objector. He refused to carry a weapon, yet served in the U.S. Army on the war front in a non-combative job as an ambulance driver.

Other than Clay's Irish ethnicity, the most important reason to watch the fight on TV is that he has covered some very large bets on Clay retaining his title. Therefore, Ted is rooting for Cassius to win and save Ted from a financial calamity.

It is a close fight; the 23 year old Ali is declared the winner in the twelfth round by a T.K.O. of Patterson. Thus, this saves Teddy a bundle as well as Ali retains the title of heavy weight boxing champion. The elated Ted busts out bottles of champagne to celebrate and enjoy the camaraderie and rapport of being with friends. All agree to meet again each New Year's Eve at Blue Haven Lodge.

The news about Clay is replaced on January 2, 1965 when the N.Y. Jets sign Alabama quarterback Joe Namath. Later to be known as *Panty-hose* Joe, to a $427,000.00 contract.

All are a bit surprised when the front door opens and Cathy and little Eddy struggle through the door dragging two suitcases. After getting settled down, Ted and Cathy go into a bedroom for a private conversation.

"Lawrence filed for a divorce, says he is going to marry Maeve. He said for me to be satisfied with two suitcases of stuff and my auto. He will keep the house and everything in it. I will get no money, nothing. If I do not accept all this, he will drag me into court and gain permanent custody of Lawrence Edward. He says he will drag my gangster sex partner into court as a *prejudiced witness* and openly question you about how many times I've had sex with you. He says that he will prove to the court that I am a slut and an unfit mother for my son. With that he took the door key from me and kicked me out of the house. I have no place to go but to here."

Holding her close, Ted irately says, "Goddammit Cathy, you know that I love you. What the hell do you mean that you had no place to go? You try my patience because I have told you many times that my home, my money, anything I've got, is yours any time you wish. Damit woman, I would marry you in a minute if you weren't so against my life style."

"Teddy, you know I am not a slut. Since Stephen died, I have had no man but Lawrence and you. You best not say you would marry me because I might call your bluff."

"That's no bluff, call my bluff, but when you do you better set the date for our wedding."

"Well my darling, with your connections, you could have my marriage to Lawrence annulled even though Larry divorced me. Then we could have us a church wedding on the first Saturday after the annulment, my darling?"

"Jesus H. Christ Cathy, don't tease me sweetheart. That is cruel."

"I said – how about the first Saturday you thick Mik?"

Annulment obtained, the soonest that Holy Cross Cathedral can schedule Cardinal Richard Cruikshank to perform the holy matrimonial wedding is Saturday May 14, 1966. Such love and commitment brings a sharing of each other's flesh that *until death do us part* brings the ultimate achievement of happiness. Nine year old Lawrence Edward is the ring bearer.

Chapter thirty-seven

After serving seven years of a six to eight year sentence, on Friday May 20, 1966, Jeanne Marie Brooks is out of the New Jersey prison. Cathy has great compassion for her sibling and has Jeanne move in with her and Ted. Other than gaining about five pounds, which seem to add more curves and boldness to her breasts, this unscrupulous female has amazingly endured years in prison and yet has not lost a bit of her beauty.

Meantime Eamon's health has worsened and his ability to get around without assistance has confined him to his bed or his rocker at Blue Haven Lodge. Needing full time care, he decides to move to a clinic in Galway that is owned by cousin Malachy *Mickey* Fallon. At Teddy's request, Donna Louise Broes spends a week at the Lodge helping to get Eamon ready for his trip to Ireland, and also nightly, satisfy Teddy's needs.

Eamon is not too feeble to understand the dangerous predicament that little Claude Shane is in. Realizing that Mathew is unaware of Ruth's gadabouts and the baby boy is being neglected, because she is leaving the child in the care of a fourteen year old female school drop-out, he tells Teddy to contact Matthew. Within hours of getting this information, Matthew picks up Claude Shane for he and Marion to take care of him.

On Saturday May 28, 1966 Teddy is at the airport to see Cathy and Donna Louise accompany sixty-one year old Eamon on the Aer Lingus flight to be sure he safely arrives in Erin. After he is settled there, the women return to Boston.

No one is surprised that Ruth is not there to at least see her husband off. Her well known philosophy is: *The only way to get over one man – is to get under another man.* As though to substantiate that fact, she is with Sean *Three strikes* on his latest *hit* assignment. They have gone to Hamtramck, Detroit to attend a Polish wedding.

Sean has been hired by the bride's father to *rub-out* the groom as he comes down the wedding aisle of the church. Due to the fact that the groom-to-be is in cocaine sales, Sean assures the father of the bride-to-be that he will make it look like a gang-land hit. To establish an alibi Sean has rented a suite at the Niagara Falls hotel and he and Ruth plan to return to the *Falls* after the hit.

Norma Jean McLaughlin is in the last days of her pregnancy for her first born; it arrives at midnight that May 28th Saturday. The only one at her side in the hospital is her mother Eileen Palmer. Before Sean returns from Detroit, Eileen has taken her daughter, and her new grandson Andrew Palmer McLaughlin, to live with her in Seabrook, New Hampshire.

Norma having left the McLaughlin lakeside house, her husband Sean makes no attempt to go after her and so Ruth moves in with Sean. The only problem for Ruth is the jealousy about this affair on the part of Anne. She has been Sean's water skiing companion and interlude assignation partner. Since she has been staying next door at the Blue Haven Lodge she is daily aware, and resents, Ruth's liaison with Sean so much so, that she plans to try to physically eliminate her.

On Sunday June 12, 1966 Ruth decides to go water skiing and Anne takes this opportunity for her revenge attempt. As Sean tows Ruth at a high speed across the lake, Ruth is enjoying the strong breeze and the thrill of skiing over the waves. Her mind is obviously on her present need to be alert to being towed; therefore she is oblivious of a potentially great danger about to be attempted upon her.

Anne has taken Ted's speed boat and is bearing down on the fast skiing Ruth. She misses her first pass at colliding with Ruth, but Anne's boat waves, on the second pass, toss Ruth off her skis and she flounders in the lake. Swirling around for another attempt on the near to drowning victim, Anne again begins to bear down on her target. Sean hearing Ruth's screams, and seeing her fall into the lake water, hastily does a ninety degree turn and heads to ward off Anne's high speed approach. Ignoring the oncoming Sean, Anne continues her attack and this time comes close and she barely misses hitting the partially submerged intended victim. This is too much for Sean, and he begins to fire his .45 pistol at, and hits the stern of Anne's borrowed boat.

This is enough for Anne, now fearing for her own life, she gives up the assault attempts and heads back to the dock. Sean gives up the chase and returns to rescue Ruth, giving Anne ample time to get ashore. Wasting no time to change from her bathing suit, she grabs a few clothes, her purse, and then jumps into her car and races to Boston.

The only enemy any female has – is any other female!!

Chapter Thirty-Eight

As with most working families, there are moments when children are left unsupervised, and problems occur. Such is the case on Friday August 26, 1966, the Nanny that Matthew and Marion hire leaves early and when the couple comes home from the store they find Edwina has locked herself in her room. She refuses to come out. At the request of Matthew she opens the door of her room that he might enter.

He closes the bedroom door behind him and goes to the bed where Edwina has taken refuge. Laying in a fetal position, clothed in only her bathrobe, she is trembling. He gently put his hand on her shoulder, "What is it my baby? What is wrong?"

She slowly sits up and grips Matthew closely, lays her head against his chest and hysterically cries out, "Daddy Matthew I have been a bad girl."

"Now, now my little one, this cannot be as bad as all this. What happened?"

"I can't tell you, I am bad and I won't go to heaven Daddy Matthew."

"Well my little angel, nothing is that bad. Let's wipe the tears and you let Daddy Matthew decide."

She slowly opens her robe and says, "Randolph put all this sticky stuff on my stomach as he played with his thing."

Startled at the sight, confused as to what he should say, unsure of what happened, he rubs his fingers in the sticky fluid. It becomes obvious that Randolph had masturbated on Edwina's tummy. Matthew tries to stay under control and not rush out to beat the shit out of Randolph, instead presses for details.

"You need to tell me what happened, Edwina dear. How did this all start, tell me dear did you ask him to come into your room?"

"I had been playing outside and became sweaty so I came in and took a bath. I put on my bathrobe and walked to my bedroom. I took off my robe to put on clean clothes. I was getting ready to put on my panties when Randolph came into the room and he dropped his pants and undies. He pushed me backwards on to the bed and got on top of me. He tried to make me spread my legs, but I fought hard to stop him. He then kept running his boy thing on my tummy and all that stuff came all over me."

Trying to remain under control, "Edwina baby, go bathe again and get dressed, I will see to it that you are all right. You've had an upsetting experience from a bad boy. You are not to blame, so do not think that this will stop you from going to heaven."

Hardly able to remain cohesive, "Marion, you have a problem with your son. He must learn that attempted rape is a crime."

"What the hell are you talking about; Randolph wouldn't do such a thing."

"Either you talk to him or I will, for both your sakes it best be you Marion."

Returning after talking with Randolph, Marion confronts Matthew. "What you are making a big magilla, is typical of boys and girls. Randolph says that he was going to his room when Edwina came out of the bathroom. She went into her room and yelled out to Matthew to come see her naked. Typical boy or man, he wanted to see a nude female. Typical female, she was the subtle aggressor. He said that she lay back on the bed and told him that he now had seen *her's;* he should show her his thing. He said that with her encouragement he got up on the bed and he couldn't help it, he got so excited that his *thing* sent out all this sticky stuff that went on to her tummy. Matthew, think back, when did you first tell a girl 'show me yours and I will show you mine' it's normal for God's sake."

"Goddammit Marion, you are not facing reality. Yes, all boys and girls go through that exchange pattern, but you are overlooking the big problem that does not occur normally. He left bruise marks on her inner thighs as he tried to force her legs apart to rape her. If things occurred as you too politely pretend, I would agree that it was nothing but a sex education. However, attempted rape is not normal; after all she is only eight years old. Put a harness on his testicular drive, have him direct it to himself, and masturbate in private, until he gets older and has a willing female."

It seems that harmony has finally returned to the family that is until on Saturday March 16, 1968, fourteen year old Randolph rapes ten year old Edwina. The family notifies juvenile authorities and takes Edwina to the hospital E R room for confirmation of the attack. The medical report notes rupture of the hymen, and red irritations, plus traces of semen in her vagina. Randolph is taken to Juvenile Detention to await a hearing.

Wednesday September 4, 1968, Juvenile Court Judge Patrick Hurley, sentences Randolph to juvenile incarceration until his 21st birthday.

On Monday October 7, 1968 Matthew and Marion are in the divorce court. Her lawyer Frederick Goldsmith addresses the court. "Your honor, we request alimony of $300.00 per month and custody of the juvenile girl Edwina Ferber."

Matthew jumps up and yells, "No way, no way, that is my step-daughter, Marion doesn't love the child, she just wants revenge."

"Mr. Childress, restrain your client, I will have order in my court."

"Yes your honor, but in defense of my client, I can hardly blame him for this outburst. I am startled by this desire of custody. Especially judge, since it is her son that raped Edwina."

"Mrs. Ferber, why are you making this request?"

"Your honor, on Friday August 26, 1966, Matthew made a big deal about my son Randolph and Edwina doing a bit of kids play. Matthew used his hands to check the inner thighs of the little girl, for bruises. I believe he has touched her inner thighs often and because of his touching, Edwina became curious about sex. She then seduced Randolph – he did not rape her. I believe that Child Protective Services should check this out before you allow a sex fiend to raise a little girl."

Childress hastily responds, "Your honor, I sincerely request a recess till C.P.S. can determine the facts. The ladies remarks are lies, and they damage the reputation of a good honest businessman."

"Mr. Childress, we shall adjourn until October 21st. In the meantime I shall have C.P.S. investigate, and if what she says is true it will add a significant bit of action on my part. However, Mrs. Ferber, if you are lying, thus doing tremendous damage to Matthew Ferber, I will find you have perjured yourself and I will see to it that you pay for the consequences of your statements."

It is one hellasious following week for Matthew. The agents from C.P.S. spend a whole day interrogating Matthew and take Edwina to the Agency for her side of the story.

On Monday October 21, 1968, at 10 a.m. Judge Hurley begins a new hearing. Addressing the two agents from C.P.S. that are in court, "Have you investigated this case thoroughly?"

Agent Agnes Flavin passing a written folio to the bailiff, "Yes your honor, we have. Here is a full report of our findings."

Reading the report, the Judge responds, "Mrs. Matthews, I warned you, yet you stuck to your story. As the results of this report I find you are to be incarcerated without bail until I set a trial date for you to answer to the charges of perjury. Bailiff, take Mrs. Ferber into custody."

Marion lets out a scream and drops to the floor sobbing. Goldsmith is stunned; he stands transfixed to the scene, unable to speak.

"Miss Flavin where is Edwina now?"

"We have her in your outside chamber your honor. I did not feel that she should be in this court room until you had made a decision."

"That is fine Miss Flavin, you have shown good judgment."

Goldsmith finally gathers his composure, "Judge Hurley, may it please the court, I would like a ten minute recess to talk with my client."

"Court adjourned for ten minutes," is the response.

Returning to court, Goldsmith begins, "May it please the court, my client Mrs. Marion Ferber pleads for the mercy of the court. Your honor, this poor woman's son Randolph is in Juvenile detention until he is twenty-one. She admits that she was wrongly blaming Mr. Ferber for the boy being in custody. She believes that she was blinded by the love for her son that possessed her to lie to seek revenge. She now realizes the seriousness of the charges she made, and she wishes to apologize. We request your piety for a mother whose love of her son has temporarily blinded her."

"I hereby grant Matthew Ferber a divorce, without paying alimony, and sole custody of Edwina Ferber, Claude Shane Ferber, and John Fitzgerald Ferber. Beatrice Elizabeth Ferber will stay with her mother Marion Ferber. On the charge of perjury, I fine Marion Ferber one thousand dollars and five years in state prison. I will suspend the sentence, and the fine, and put Marion Ferber on probation for fifteen years. If she contests this court's decision at any time, the probation will be canceled and she will pay the fine and serve the suspended sentence."

Chapter thirty-nine

Monday May 12, 1969 Teddy receives a visit from Jazz. "Teddy, me accountant has been goin' ova' the books of Freddy's Gloucester collectin'. The accountant fig'ers Freddy has skimmed over one hundred G's from me. Since Freddy has been a close associate of youse, I am comin' to you first."

"I appreciate that Thomas, how do I fit in on your plans for Freddy."

"I need you to see that Sean McLaughlin will handle it, but I want to know how this will affect ou'ah relations."

"Thomas, Freddy Banks knows the rules. Steal from the syndicate earns a painful death, so others will know it isn't wise to steal from us. Since Freddy is my protégé, I'd like to be the one to handle this situation. If I fail, I only ask that you order *Three strikes* not to torture Freddy. Just confront Fred and tell him why, then a quick shot to the heart so as not to mar up his face. I want to have an open casket funeral for Freddy; he has been a friend that just fucked up. "

Wednesday May 14, Teddy, to gain proof of Freddy's skimming, heads to Gloucester. After a full body massage visit with Donna Louise, he heads to Jockey's office. With lengthy discussions and examination of the books with Jockey, he concludes money due to the organization is missing. While it is obvious that funds have been altered and Freddy would be aware of it, Jockey probably did some of his own bit of larceny. With a warning to Jockey that from now on the accounts will be checked by him and thievery will be dealt with, Teddy leaves.

The last time that Ted's inner circle of friends met was on Sunday

January 15, 1967 to watch the TV game of the first AFL-NFL World Championship game, formerly known as Super Bowl. He wins his wager when the NFL Green bay Packers beat the AFL Kansas Chiefs.

On Monday May 8, 1967 Ted's favorite boxing wagering is temporarily halted when the Federal Government indicts Muhammad Ali for draft evasion. On June 27, 1967 Ali is stripped of his title and banned from pro boxing for three and a half years.

So it is a bit of a surprise to some, when on Memorial Day weekend Friday May 30, 1969 Teddy arranges an inner circle poker night at Blue Haven Lodge for Fred, Seamus McMann, Sean McLaughlin, and himself. At 2 a.m., just a few minutes after the game breaks-up, Ted slips Freddy a *Mickey Finn*. After he is unconscious, McMann, McLaughlin and Teddy, carry the limp Freddy down to the pier. Without a trace of regret, they strip him and shove him into the water and hold him under. Although unconscious, nature still causes the body to resist and its entire frame goes into huge spasms until he finally drowns.

Leaving the victim in the water, gases begin to form in the body and like a balloon filled with gas, the body eventually floats to the surface and the current swirls him out further in the lake. Four days later a local fisherman pulls the bloated dead man onto his boat and notifies the police. The medical examiner declares death caused by accidental drowning due to intoxication.

Friday June 6, 1969 an elaborate military funeral is held for Navy Veteran Frederic Xavier Banks a sailor that survived the invasion of Normandy on Jun 6, 1944, twenty-five years ago to the day, but couldn't survive the laws of the underworld.

Tuesday August 26, 1969, still in his pajamas, Teddy is having breakfast on the back porch and he notices two pug-uglies, getting into his speed boat at the dock. Grabbing his shotgun, he runs down the back porch stairs to the pier. Threatening them with his shotgun, he yells, "Get the fuck out of that boat and on your bellies on the pier or I swear I'll blow you into the lake."

One joker reaches inside his jacket, the other guy grabs the joker's arm and yells, "Jesus Christ Joey, he's got the drop on us. One shot from that shotgun will kill us both."

Disturb at the movement of Joey, Ted fires a round over the heads of the two. At the sound of the shotgun going off, Sean McLaughlin comes running out of his house weapon in hand and heads to the pier. Seeing Teddy, he holsters his weapon and yells, "Hold it Teddy, hold it. I will explain."

Turning to the two in the boat, "Joey, Gaeta, what the fuck are you guys doin'? Get the fuck outta that boat, it belongs to Teddy here."

"You tell that cocksucker to cock that gun. When I get out of this boat I am gonna cream him."

"Gaeta, tell your fuckin' brother to shut –up, he doesn't know who he is fooling with. More lip and he will not live to comb gray hair. You'll be meals for the fishes in minutes and I won't help you."

"Since you know these bastards Johnny, I want their weapons placed on the pier."

"Okay Teddy – okay. I will explain all this if you will please back off for a minute."

The two thugs are completely puzzled by the capitulation of tough Johnny *three strikes* to this pajama clad guy. Realizing that their situation at the moment is precarious to say the least, they lay their weapons on the pier and noting gestures of Johnny, they head to the McLaughlin house.

Johnny escorts them into the house then explains just who Teddy is and how close they came to meeting Saint Peter, they settle down. Johnny then heads to the back porch of the Lodge. Entering he finds Teddy finishing his breakfast with strong coffee.

The now calmer Teddy, "Pour yourself a *cuppa,* and have *a seat* Johnny."

"Thanks, Teddy. Those guys came in late last night and I was waiting for you to begin stirring this morning to come and tell you about them. They are the Petrocci brothers, petty mob loan sharks that operate Vic Damone Pizza Company in Chicago. They needed a temporary hideout and Jazz okayed my place and relied on me to explain it to you."

"The singer Vic Damone is wanted for questioning about his association with reputed Chicago loan racket terrorist Mafia mob boss Frank Buccieri. Evidently Damone forgot that he needed to make money, not bad headlines."

"The Las Vegas Sheriff's office wants to know Vic's relation with Bucci since Bucci spent a week as a guest in one of five rooms reserved by Damone at the Frontier Hotel. These two guys are associated with

Damone," he continues. "They thought the boat was mine and were going to take it for a spin. I explained everything. Gaeta is the oldest, and is more level headed. Joey is the typical non-thinking arsse-hole hot head."

"Do I need to be nervous about that little bastard doing something stupid Johnny?"

"No, Ted, I don't think so; he has been warned by Joey and me that if he fucks with you he will pay the consequences when he loses. I will let you know what day they are going back so you can be on your guard until that time. Joey might feel he can show you how tough he is and try to shoot you in the back and run to safety in Chicago. That gun he pointed at you is only a design accessory; if it came to a contest he can't hit the barn door. He surely is a neadrathal. No common sense prevails in his block head."

Chapter forty

Jackie knew Fred was playing poker with Ted, Sean, and Seamus, the night he supposedly accidentally drowns. She knows it is not logical that at 2 a.m. he would go for a swim. He was not that enthused about swimming, nor was he ever a heavy imbiber. She believes that Freddy was murdered. Playing a trope on a passage from the Book of Genesis: "The voice was the voice of Jazz Kelley but the hand was the hand of Teddy Sheerin."

Reasons forgotten, on Thursday June 12, 1969 she formulates a plan to revenge Freddy and Teddy Sheerin will pay dearly. For appearance sake, and throw him of guard, she waits until Friday August 29, to phone Ted Sheerin.

"Ted, this is Jackie. How are you?"

"I'm fine Jackie, how about you?"

"Not to good, Ted. Freddy and I had dreams of a wonderful future, but dreams don't last. To me these dreams are not forgotten. Since he drowned, everything that was warm is cold now, and I am back to reality. I was wondering if you would mind if I spend Labor Day weekend at Blue Haven Lodge. I miss Freddy and I thought it might be a cathartic experience if I could spend a couple of days swimming and reminiscing at the place where Freddy spent his last days."

"By all means Jackie, come down to the Lodge, stay as long as you like. Maybe you and I can reminisce about the many nice times spent with Freddy."

Cathy meanwhile has taken 12 year old Lawrence Edward to Disney Land to spend a week before he has to go back to school.

With Sean McLaughlin at the boat controls, Jackie spends Saturday water skiing enjoying the refreshing stimulus of a refreshing breeze as she skims across the lake. Sunday morning she joins Teddy at the breakfast table wearing a heavy, white terrycloth robe.

"Might I ask what you have on under that robe?"

"If my answer is nothing, you might get horny Teddy and that could be a problem for both of us."

"The thought of such beautiful woman as you, having only a piece of cloth between me and a nude eroticism, yes it will make me horny Jackie."

"Well cool down hopeful viewer, there is no nudity," as she sheds the robe and reveals a tight fitting swim suit.

"Jackie, you damned well realize that bathing suit leaves nothing to my imagination. You form fit it magnificently, from your full breasts down to the top of a pair of long lean aphrodisiac legs."

"Down boy, down, it is too early in the day for you to imagine what it might be like to spread these legs," as she dramatically demonstrates by gently sliding her open palms down her inner thighs. Then grabbing a mug of coffee and a bun, she goes out the back porch and down to the pier.

Teddy yells, "I'll join you in a minute, maybe the lake water will cool me down. If not, then as a favor to you, I will hop into a cool shower."

After her coffee and bun, Jackie swims to the ski ramp raft, getting on; she stretches out on her back to feel the warm sun on her body. Teddy changes to swim trunks and swims out to the raft to enjoy the view of this walnut toned enticement lying prone. The female mind is devious, with a slight spread of her limbs, she is poised in a puritanical sex position, is this to tantalize Teddy?

Desiring this elegant product of nature yet not wanting to push his luck by being hasty, he lays down beside Jackie. After ten minutes of the hot sun, Jackie slides off the raft and ducks under the water, coming up, she puts her back to the side of the raft while resting her elbows on the edge.

Ted gets up, then after a full stretch of masculine narcissism muscle exhibition, he dives into the water. Trying to show nonchalance he swims three times around the raft then comes up to the front of Jackie. Testing, testing, testing, it is time to make a move!

He puts a hand on the raft at each side of Jackie and presses his body against her now encompassed form. Gently he forces his right knee between her thighs, and as though on cue, she further spreads her legs. He interprets her lack of resistance as a possible message of cooperation and permission to go ahead, (No wonder the male animal has a hard time understanding female messages) and he gives her a full kiss.

Her response to the passionate kiss is an almost an un-discernible low sigh. This is more encouragement for Ted. He presses his bathing trunk covered erection firmly against her groin. Men are such fools when erections occur. Had he known that this is part of her well thought out plan of revenge for Freddy's murder, there would never have been an erection.

"Teddy, I am not one for showing such emotions out where everyone can see me. Let's head back to the house." Parallel swimming – the supposedly amorous two - head for the house. Once inside the living room, Jackie excuses herself, "A quick shower then I will join you Teddy."

He in turn, sheds his wet trunks and dons a robe. Pouring himself a drink, he turns on romantic music and sits on the bedroom sofa to await the implied seduction. Returning from her shower, she pours a Grand Marnier over ice and sits besides Ted.

"I doubt if you have cooled down, Teddy, but first things first. I have only been with one man in my life. I need you to understand this and act accordingly. While I think that you are quite a man, I am not like most of your female friends."

"Since we have come to an understanding of what is to follow, let's finish our drinks and reveal to each other what is under our robes," he teases. It doesn't take long before Teddy is at bedside and dropping his robe, the nude Ted is stupidly off guard as Jackie requests. "Lay on your back on the bed Teddy, I want to control things by being on top."

Jackie, still robed, kneels astride the prone Ted. Slowly she opens her robe and lets it slide off her shoulders. The sight of this fine chiseled light tan beauty straddling him, now about to become his conquest, has numbed his logic. Only when she disengages her right hand from the falling robe and produces a Colt .38 does he have but a fraction of seconds to realize this is no game, this could be fatal, she is not kidding. He rapidly turns sideways, and attempting to shove her away, slings her off the bed just as she fires the weapon. The slug hits his spinal column.

As Jackie is catapulted off Teddy, she loses her grip on the gun and it flies away to ricochets off the wall and skid under the bed. Momentarily stunned when her head hit the wall, she is slow in getting up to retrieve the revolver. There is no further movement by Ted, he is now just semi-conscious from the bullet entry.

Sean *three strikes* McLaughlin next door in the process of *pumping iron* hears the shot. Dropping the iron weights he runs to the Lodge. Jackie by now has gotten up, got around to the other side of the bed and crawls under it attempting to retrieve the weapon. As she is backing out from under the bed, with the recovered weapon, McLaughlin enters the room.

He is confused by what confronts his arrival. Teddy in obvious agony is moaning in pain, blood oozing from his back and an exposed caramel skinned female's arsse is halfway out from under the bed. Seeing Jackie come out with a weapon in her hand he kicks the weapon from her. Grabbing her and slamming her down in a chair he yells, "Teddy, what the good fuckin' Jesus happened here?"

Hardly able to be heard the semi-conscious Teddy responds weakly, "The bitch shot me."

Outside of Blue Haven Lodge, Mother Nature does not to reflect such an atrocious and dismal turmoil as is going on inside. Nature is at her most harmonious beauty with the colorful splash of fall foliages of yellows, reds, browns and greens it is accompanied by a slight wafting breeze. In the trickling creek stream that is rhythmically rippling over the rocks, a raccoon and her brood are enjoying a fresh drink. Tranquility reigns outdoors, pandemonium indoors.

Because a policeman is involved, the police investigation report, in typical cover-up, lists this as an accidental shooting. Jackie is taken by Sean and held prisoner in the secret underground chamber in Ted's office.

After the now permanently disabled 45 year old Teddy, is finally wheel chair released from the Boston City Hospital on Monday October 13, 1969, his first orders to Seamus are, "I want you to take a hot soldering iron and burn the word Ted on her chest to ever reminder of me. Then 'cause I didn't get to fuck her I will give hundreds of Columbian men that opportunity. Her new address is to be a Bogota bordello."

In most cases of murder attempts, women use poison as their weapon. Maybe Jackie should have stuck to the norm for women instead of using a gun.

Chapter forty-one

Jeanne Marie a partaker of the 1970's sexual revolution, and prison time lesbianism, comes into Ted's bedroom. Having just stepped out of the shower and only donning a robe, she opens the robe and says, "Ted, what do you think of this body?"

"God dam it, Jeanne Marie; get the fuck back to your bedroom."

"I asked you a question Teddy; I want a truthful opinion from you. What do you think of my body?"

"Jeanne Marie, be fair. You have a hellava beautiful body, now get the fuck outta here."

"You be fair Teddy. Other than a couple of pecker-less lesbian affairs I have had no real lovin' since Valentine's Day in 1957. You know you can't go a couple of days without a woman, why should I go over nine years without a man?"

"Jeanne Marie, I told you to get the fuck outta here, now go."

"Teddy you've got the fuckin' part correct." Dropping her robe and standing full length nude, she continues, "Either you are going to fuck me right now or I am going to tell Cathy that you attempted to fuck me and I refused you. Who is she going to believe, you or me, Teddy boy?"

When it comes to a beautiful female body, Teddy rarely needs much persuasion and now it is a win, win solution. His *equipment* still working well, with her help he is out of his clothes and on top of Jeanne Marie in less than two minutes. His roughness, lack of gentleness, is an awkward adverse to the gentleness of her lesbian partners. Shortly after, Jeanne leaves Blue Haven and joins Ginny now in New York City.

Meanwhile, Cathy has suffered in silence at Teddy's previous sexual peccadilloes but hearing of this latest incident, with her sister, is too much to bear. The females that he had sex with before their marriage were his business, after their marriage she believes in fidelity. She is mostly hurt with her sister's betrayal as with Teddy's.

After all she has proven to Teddy that no woman can satisfy her man better than she can, why is he straying? Their vows are *love, honor and – til death do us part* – so hands off the other women. But still he cheats with her sister Jeanne and continues with Donna Louise, and he is paying a severe physical price for his desire to penetrate Jackie.

Lovers are meant to cry when their love is betrayed. She is hesitant at going through a divorce that might cause Ted to take revenge upon her. Temporarily, she takes their son and goes to live with her parents. On Friday June 2, 1972 she enrolls young Eddy in Phillips Exeter Academy in New Hampshire. However, the female need of survival prevails, on Friday September 8, 1972, she contacts Lawrence Cameron.

"Larry, I haven't heard from you in ages, how have you been?"

"Cathy, let's not try to bull-shit a bull-shitter. You have a reason for phoning me other than to ask about my welfare."

"Larry, please don't be mean to me. Yes, I do have a reason for calling you. I have left Teddy and I am living with my parents. I have enrolled Eddy in Phillips Andover and I do not have enough money to keep him there. Since the law recognizes that he is your son, he bears the Cameron name, I wonder if you would help me?"

"Cathy, you once told me that your Teddy was the *salt of the earth.*"

"I know that I did say that, but now I am on a salt free diet."

Taking a softer tone, "Cathy, I will help you on one condition. Maev and her brother Gaelach were picked up by U.S. Customs and sent back to Ireland. I am alone now, so if you want anything from me then you must come and live with me. I also expect that you will divorce Ted if you really mean what you say. After all, your actions will speak louder than your words."

Female need for security and survival, while Cathy accepts the offer and moves in with Lawrence, she is nervous about what Teddy's reaction might be to her getting a divorce. What once is his, never changes. While he might tolerate her moving in with Lawrence, she is still his and should be available when he so desires.

Her survival attitude requires that she change her feelings towards Teddy, from soft rose petals to course sandpaper, and within a month more sandpaper for him. With his political connections, Cameron succeeds in getting Cathy a hasty divorce. Hearing of the divorce Teddy has his own plans.

He phones McLaughlin in Gloucester, "Sean, I need an outta town guy for a couple of months. Can you get in touch with that Vic Damone's guy Gaeta Petrocci and see if he is available?"

"Yeah, he hires out. For the right price I know that he is always available Teddy."

Thursday December 28, 1972, a light flaky snow is falling as a long sleek Lincoln town car pulls up in the Blue Haven driveway. Gaeta Petrocci gets out and comes up the front stairs to Teddy's office.

Donna Louise answers the door and Gaeta is escorted into Teddy's office. Then she goes to the large family room where Teddy is sitting in his mobile chair enjoying the sensuous tranquility of the warm fireplace, after a relaxing back massage from the strong hands of Donna. He has allowed his mind to peacefully wander as he watches the snowflakes gather on the pine trees outside the window and he compares the scene with the nostalgic winter sketch on his wall.

Advised that Gaeta is in the office, Teddy wheels his chair into that area. By the startled expression on Gaeta's face, Ted becomes aware that Gaeta did not know how seriously injured Teddy has become. Not knowing whether to reach over and handshake or just what to do at the moment, Gaeta becomes more at ease by the arm motion of Teddy indicating for him to take a seat.

Donna Louise takes Gaeta's topcoat, hat and gloves putting them into the closet and goes to the bar. "What is your pleasure Mr. Petrocci?"

Noting a Tom cat feline like look on the countenance of Gaeta, Teddy interjects, "Don't bother to say it Gaeta, she means drinks only."

"Scotch will be fine."

Drinks in hand, Ted gets right to the point, "I will need you for a couple of months. What is your fee?"

"That depends on what you want from me Teddy."

"I want you to harass the wife of the Assistant D.A."

"Harass is a pretty broad statement. Harass to be a nuisance, or harass to death, my fee is proportionate."

"I want you to worry and torment her. Slash her car tire when she is out shopping. Leave threatening notes in the windshield. Show up anytime she is about to get in to her car. Don't do anything if her 15 year old son is with her and don't harm her physically, just put her in fear as to what could happen. Do whatever it takes to scare her; I want her life to become miserable."

"Assistant D.A. is dangerous territory, baring anything unusual happening, my fee is ten grand a month – in advance!"

Chapter forty-two

Meanwhile Rabbi Alvan, who has been missing from his usual places and a long time since at Blue Haven Lodge, is at the Hebrew Union College on Saturday June 3, 1972 to witness the ordination of the first female American Rabbi, twenty-five year old Sally J. Priesand.

This day is great news to many, with the headlines of the newspapers blazoned, ***'YANKS BEAT WHITE SOX FOR THE 13TH TIME',*** and Teddy has again made the correct wager, and he is also not going to be defeated easily at Cathy's leaving. His reality check causes him to now analyze his physical handicapped situation. It is time for him to recapitulate and adjust to reality. He takes a disability retirement from the police department. To allow him to leave Blue Haven he has his limousine equipped with a swing out hoist that picks him up, while in his motorized wheelchair, and places him in the back of the newly outfitted limo.

Knowing that his enemies and some associates are going to test him, Ted decides that he now needs a strong *right-hand man* and he persuades Jazz to release Seamus McMann to permanently be on *Teddy's team.*

Tuesday December 9, after a few visits by Donna Louise to Blue Haven Lodge, and giving Ted a bit of bad information pertaining to Jockey's activities, he decides a visit to the Jock is expedient. Seamus McMann accompanies Teddy as he heads to Gloucester.

Ayaho is alone at his desk when Teddy, instead of using crutches, drives his fancy motorized wheel chair into Jockey's office. For some reason the sight of a person on crutches seems to yell *handicapped,* but in a mobile chair the person appears to be seated at ease and does not seem to denote handicapped.

Seamus takes a security position standing near the entry door with his back against the wall. With a press of a button on Jockey's desk, in seconds, an ugly looking, shotgun wielding pug, comes from the inner room and stands directly behind Ayaho's chair.

Ignoring the new arriver, "Jockey, you have not sent me any money since last August. Are you under the impression that because I am wheel chair bound that our deal no longer stands?"

"Teddy, I am tired of cutting you in on my operations, I don't need you. As you can see I have enough muscle to take care of myself," and gestures toward the shotgun wielding thug.

With that the *hit-man,* raises his shotgun and aims it toward Teddy. Seamus, no slouch in reaction time, fires his .45 automatic. The bullet goes through Ayaho, and the office chair, into the gut of the gunman before the punk can pull the shotgun trigger.

Ayaho is dead but his henchman lies moaning in excruciating pain from a torn gut. Wasting no time, Seamus annihilates the wounded man with another slug to the head. The noise of the gun firing draws no immediate attention, so Seamus puts the bodies into the trunk of the limo and they head back to Blue Haven. To confuse the authorities, on the way, he stops and drops the bodies off in a swamp in Natick.

Wednesday December 17, 1972 Teddy calls the newly paired couple of Sean McLaughlin and mother-in-law Ruth Demarest Sheerin to his office. "You two have been muddying up the waters with your hanky-panky actions. I am going to do us both a favor. I want you out of this area, but don't panic. I am not punishing you, nor am I rewarding you. I am just doing what is best for me."

"Tomorrow we are going to Gloucester to enforce a deed I hold on Jockey Ayaho's restaurant. It is closed for the time being but you two are going to re-open and operate the motel, restaurant and bookie operations. Donna Louise formerly worked there so she will go with you to brief you with her knowledge of the previous operation."

"If you do a good job you will get forty percent of the net profits. If I find you skimming you will need to go to church and light a bunch of candles to atone for your sins before I come to meter out a Freddy Bank's style of punishment."

With this financial arrangement Edward *Teddy* Sheerin adds to his annual income.

It is less than a week when on Tuesday the 23rd; Ruth pulls in the driveway at Blue Haven. She and Donna Louise Broes come into the house. Teddy, able to use crutches and leg braces, meets them in the living room.

"Teddy, I need peace of mind. What chance do I have at fifty-eight years to compete with the enticing body of this twenty-eight year old *femme fatale?* Lately my Sean has been extra horny around the house. Every time he sees Donna in some skimpy attire he is aroused. The only thing that keeps him in harness is that he is afraid of what you might do if he makes a pass at her. It won't be long before he sees her bend over wearing a short skirt, he will get a piece of her or rape her and we will be in deep do-do. How about if the little lady comes here to live? You can use a full time companion to run your house and your bed."

"Ruth, I doubt seriously that she is any sexual competition to you. From my experiences with your body, Sean knows he would be foolish to take a chance with Donna in fear of losing the good piece of arsse that you have proven to be."

"Have a heart Teddy; every time he imagines her sans clothes, he wants to climb on me. I don't mind a man's normal sex drive, but she is causing him to be much more demanding of bedtime with me."

"I have no objections Ruth. In fact, I'm damn glad that she is here now. I thought that she would rather choose Gloucester over Blue Haven, because all her friends and relatives live in Gloucester."

With that Donna pipes up, "Teddy, I would rather live here. You just had to ask me."

Since the only part of his body that does not perform are his lower legs!!

It's not love but—it's not bad!

Chapter forty-three

In 1964 the head agent, of the Boston F.B.I. (the most corrupt F.B.I. agent in history), Supervisor Agent Harold Paul Rico, J. Edgar Hoover's second favorite Agent, gives tips to the Mafia that lead to the death of Boston thug Ron Dermody. In 1965, further tips from Rico lead to the gangland demise of *Punchy* McLaughlin brother of Sean, *Three strikes,* McLaughlin. Sean tries to get Teddy to use his influence and connections to avenge his brother's murder.

"Sean, I have enough problems with the way things are getting without my tangling arsseholes with Hoover and his F.umbling, B.umbling, I.diots without trying to open a *Pandora's box* for you."

Hit man Stephen, *The Rifleman,* Flemmi on Wednesday March 10, 1965 obtains Patriarca's permission to whack Edward *Teddy* Deegan in a dispute over gambling money. Joseph *The Animal* Barboza, a Portuguese/ American hit man for Patriarca (26 kills), joins Flemmi in the murder of Deegan. Barboza, then turns government witness and Rico puts him in the not too safe (too many failures) *Witness protection program* under the alias of J.J. Barone. However, Patriarca, using corrupt officials, traces Barone (Barboza) supposedly hiding in the witness protection plan, to San Francisco and sends Joe Russo to kill him.

With Mafia Don, Raymond Patriarca now dead, his son Ray gets out of the Mafia rackets. He is an active business man who forms a group of citizens to change the formal title *Rhode Island and Providence Plantations*, to just – Rhode Island.

Contributing to the *American Corruption*, and for his CYA protection, F.B.I. Agent Rico, falsely arrests four Italian Americans.

Knowing Joseph Salvati, Peter Limone, Henry Tameleo and Louis Greco, are innocent and the law enforcers are the law breakers and indict them for the murder of *Teddy* Deegan, a crime for which Rico gave the actual killer Barboza *witness protection*.

Although they are innocent, the four are sentenced to die on Massachusetts *olde sparky* and F.B.I. Director J. Edgar Hoover, knowing the four are innocent of the charges, still allows them to be tried then sent to death row. However, and through no fault of Hoover, they are spared execution when the Commonwealth of Massachusetts Governor Weld abolishes the death penalty and commutes their death sentences to life in prison.

Greco and Tamelo die in prison. Salvati does 30 years then 3 years on parole. Limone does 30 years in prison. President George Bush and Attorney General John Ashcroft conspire and block a *congressional subpoena exploring the abuses in the Boston FBI offices.*

On Thursday January 19, 1967 Flemmi executes Edward *Wimpy* Bennett. (Chapter 13)

July 1972 a new group emerges from the underworld *wannabees.* Some South Boston second generation Irish come together for the best – or for the worst of things. The *Southie Irishers* headed by 42 year old James Joseph *Whitey* Bulger (9/3/1929. 5'7"—150 lbs.), form the Southies, and Stephen *Rifleman* Flemmi becomes his partner in crime.

Truly an anathema, Joseph Bulger on many occasions is protected by his younger brother William *Big Bill* Bulger, (2/2/1934) the former President of the Massachusetts House of Representatives, now Massachusetts State Senator for the 1st Suffolk District. The *Southies* become a deadly group, committing crimes of prostitution, gambling, extortion, usury, murder, dope distribution and anything else illegal. Their tax free income is 45K a day.

Little brother Joseph escapes criminal persecution on many occasions, not only by the help of big brother but also from his crime companions, the Boston F.B.I. Agent Supervisors John Morris, Harold Paul Rico, and Chief agent John *Zip* Connolly, who is brought up in the same crime-breeding city housing projects as Whitey and Flemmi.

Arch criminals aren't born that way; they grow up in an indifferent lackadaisical society. Like a wart they are ignored until it is too late. They emerge ugly and become a gruesome sore in society while throbbing with their self importance. Like many that grow up in the *Depression era* the Bulger brothers believe the survival of the fittest is only gained by a policy of grab while you can. Jazz Kelley, and Teddy, soon becomes aware of their nefarious ambitions.

Whitey has as his hit-man John Martorono, who murders over a dozen people, on Whitey's payroll exclusively. Those he kills, include Whitey's girl friend Debra Davis because Whitey feels that she knows too much about his crime activities.

However Whitey is no slouch at executing his enemies, (at least 18), ten of those he murders are while he is an informer for the F.B.I. While Martorono's hits are logical, clean and unemotional, Whitey's are cruel and sadistic such as pulling all of Bucky Barrett's teeth before he kills him. He epitomizes the fact that mankind is kept alive by bestial acts and he is the personification of the 666.Under orders from Whitey, Hobart Willis begins to sell *nose candy.* Something Jazz would never allow.

State Senator William Bulger holds a gathering of friends, and henchmen, each Saint Patrick's Day at the South Boston Bayside Club. Brother Whitey and his goons are in control there and elsewhere for his brother. In turn, with the Senator's assistance, he expands the Southie gang's empire.

It is imperative to them that they must eliminate all competition, so on Friday March 17, 1972 Whitey sends Jazz Kelley an invitation to the William Bulger St. Patrick's gathering. Hoping to maintain the peace, Jazz attends. Sadly he is informed that day: –"Turn over your entire operation to the *Southies* and get out of town – *or else.*"

Since Jazz does not accede to their demands, on Labor Day, Monday September 4, 1972, an attempt is made on Kelley's life. It matters not to them that Jazz is a product of the same era as the Southies, *there is no honor among thieves,* and trust is a liability in their business. They were all educated in the same Catholic schools, brought up in the same housing projects, and of the same Irish ethnicity.

However these are *half arsse* Irish/Americans who do not speak or understand Gaelic or understand Irish bonding. Their ethnicity does not matter. Even Jazz's trusted boy-hood chum Danny McGinnis is used as a ruse to entice Kelley to meet on the pretext that Danny has a tip about the Southies that will benefit Jazz. Danny is waiting, out in the open, on the steps of the scheduled Scollay Square building at the agreed meeting hour of 9 p.m.

Uncertainty, survival instinct, or sixth sense, whatever, causes Kelley to be most cautious in agreeing to this meet therefore he is using his trusted aide Seamus McMann as his wheel-man. This proves a most wise decision; Seamus has an eye for a quick analysis of situations.

As they approach the Scollay Square meeting place, McGinnis comes down the steps to the curb and is waving Jazz to pull close. The headlights of a suddenly passing auto silhouettes a vehicle parked on each side of the road with at least two men in each car. The windows of these autos are down and the occupants have some object leaning out the windows.

On seeing this and surmising an ambush, Seamus guns the limo, goes up the sidewalk slamming McGinnis through the air and fatally back onto the concrete steps. Then he swings the limo into high speed and is out of range of the machine gun bullets before the potential assassins can get their breath.

Trigger-man Florenze *Jim* Beam and his hired assassin crew flee back to New York rather than face the wrath of the Southies for botching the hit on Jazz.

From all this, it now becomes obvious to Kelley – his life is in extreme danger – he decides it is time to adjust to the changes. While the choice of location could be elsewhere in the east, he moves his operation to an area, which at this time, has the most *American Corruption* in the United States – Las Vegas, Nevada.

The elected Nevada officials, the law enforcement, and the general public continually ignore the famous proverb of Edmund Burke: "***The only thing necessary for evil to triumph is for good men to do nothing.***"

The Mafia mobs rule the police, judges and legislators in Las Vegas Nevada. Monday December 15, 1972 the Jazz arrives. With the proper pay-offs he operates here with immunity, his money laundering, usury rate loans and leg breaking delinquents.

Moreover, not only he, but all of his associates in the Boston area – minor or major –, need to change their style of life. By Christmas of 1972 the *Southies* are in full control of all of New England. With

Eamon gone to Erin, Teddy crippled, Kelley moving to Las Vegas, Alvan decides to close down Freeport Motors.

However, life goes on, with more financial hard luck for Teddy. On Saturday March 31, 1973 with the fight being at the Houston Astrodome, he bets heavily on Mohammad Ali beating Ken Norton, but Norton wins the NABF title from Ali. In a rematch on Monday September 10, he bets on Norton and looses a bundle again. Clay regains the NABF title by beating Norton.

Chapter forty-four

Matthew Ferber has decided that Edwina, now fifteen, should begin to learn the Office supply business so that when she graduates from college with a business degree she can take over operation of Ferber's. Her initial introduction in to the business commences Monday June 4, 1973. School closed for the summer, her store duties will continue on all non-school days.

After graduating from high school eighteen year old Jamison Carroll has trained to become a repair man for Burroughs I.B.M. Electric Typewriter Company. After an apprentice period his assignment is to make monthly calls on local business to maintain and or repair their electric office equipment. Most repairs are completed on the premises of the business, major repairs he brings to the Burroughs repair shop.

It is on his Tuesday July 10, 1973 service call to Ferber's Office Supply store that he meets Edwina who has evolved into a stunning five foot seven long haired beauty. Her looks belie her age at being just 15, definitely passing for 18. Jamison is attracted to her and while he gives some thought to this young beauty, she in turn, is enthralled at the sight of this slender six foot Adonis. It is a mix of pleasure and problems for him when she often stands along side of him while he repairs a typewriter. Good business relations prevail as Jamison explains his job duties to her. In her naiveté he is a man about the world who is giving her a great deal of attention.

Unaware of the existence of Bernice Carroll and only knowing Ted Sheerin as her uncle, Edwina never is aware that Bernice is her mother, nor who her father is. She only knows that her parents are Claudia and Stanley.

Living with those parents and then her upbringing by Matthew Ferber and Marion, all contribute to the confusion. Their lack of emotional or physical affection produces a young girl hungry for a loving attachment and therefore she is always seeking the unavailable *Bluebird of happiness.*

Could this be what she seeks from Jamison, whose father Jack Carroll, a notorious womanizer's advice to his son does not seem to be aimed at improving society morals. Jack always advises Jamison, "Son, to fully enjoy your manhood you must always keep your pecker armed and vertical."

However Jack Carroll's advice does coincide with the ignoble morals of present day society. World-wide treachery prevails when on Saturday October 6, 1973, Yom Kippur, the Jewish Day of Atonement; the Arab nations of Egypt and Syria take advantage of the Jewish Holiest day and attack Israel in what has become known as the Six Day War.

Unprepared for such a sneaky ambush, the Israelis put up a terrific fight. Severely out-manned, and under equipped for any such military confrontation, it is a David vs Goliath, Kokhba vs Romans, win for them. The Syrians and Egyptians sustain a humiliating defeat and great suffering and losses in man and machinery. However, the Israel cost of damage to property and people in defeating the intruders, is tremendous. Their need for finances to rebuild Israel is answered by the U.S. Government and its people.

Realizing that the average member of Israeli Kibbutznik is not a high caliber soldier, Israel sends out a call for ex-military men to come and train them. Those of good standing, such as Rabbi Alvan and Phyllis, offer their service to the Israeli Government. He, as a military experienced person, and with the added fact that as a Rabbi, he can fill duel positions to aid Israel. Phyllis, although a Catholic in her beliefs, volunteers to be a much needed English teacher.

To prepare for the trip to Israel, Alvan a true *sabbatarian*, laces on his arm and forehead, *phylactery*, dons his *kippah* and prays for the *tsuris* and *kelevras* of the world.

Society's morals are aided a wee bit at the death on October 5, 1973 of the mobster Anthony *Tony* Pino, who has been out on bail since Friday July 16, 1971. (Re: Chapter 12).

Meantime, like most young immature young people who live in their own little cocoon, and whose petty problems are more important to them, the drama of life goes on. For a little while, discretion and logic prevail with Jamison realizing that getting involved with Edwina to rapidly may draw the attention of her guardian Matthew Ferber. Jamison is going slowly, no rapid moves.

However, Edwina, this hungry for affection nymphet, is an instigator with different ideas. Too young for a driver's license, to be near him, she prevails on Jamison in his monthly business call, to drive her to the mall, and other places.

In the August of 1974 she persuades him to take her to Uncle Teddy's Blue Haven Lodge to swim in the lake. Swimming in itself is the last thing she has on her mind. She basically wants to get Jamison's reaction on seeing a full view of her bikini draped body.

It never dawns on Teddy, who Jamison is, or ties him with Bunny Carroll. At no time does he hear Jamison's full name of Carroll mentioned. Nor is he ever in a close relationship with any of Bunny's other children.

Accompanying the two, on the trip to the lodge, is her thirteen year old step-brother John Fitzgerald who tells Uncle Teddy, "Edwina is being a hussy wearing such a skinny bathing suit."

"Fitzy, when you are about five years older, you will understand a little bit, but son, no male animal ever gets old enough or mature enough to understand the female mind. Try to remember the saying that men are from Mars and women are from Venus, thus neither one will ever be able to fully understand the other."

Although extremely young, Fitzy is already applying society's double standards of female vs male. It never occurs to him that the extremely skimpy swim trunks that he is wearing, provides less body coverage than the bikini Edwina has donned.

On Friday June 6, 1975 she persuades Jamison to be her escort to her high school graduation prom. Most of the dance numbers are fast and noisy, but a couple of the numbers are slow and she makes sure that he holds her very close." It is a time where she consoles her thoughts with:

A little word in kindness spoken, a movement or a tear, has often healed the heart that's broken, and made a friend sincere.

While Matthew is aware of their dating, he assumes it to be casual and non-sexual. For the fourth of July Holiday Edwina persuades Matthew to allow her to go - with a few girl friends - on a trip to the *Big Apple* and to tread *Broadway.* But the girl friends alibi be damned, on the sly, she has persuaded Jamison to take her to Gotham City.

Still living at home, Jamison realizes that he cannot tell his mother Bernice that he bedded down this girl over the Fourth. Not that she would care if he got *laid* in New York. After all he is a male animal, but figures that later on when she will finally meet this girl friend and knew this is the girl that went with him to New York; she would classify the girl as a tramp. Instead he tells her that he and a couple of guys from work are going to New York City.

"Jamison, please be alert and careful in that big city. Try not to get involved with any of the girls there. You know what I mean."

"No problem mother, it will be just us guys."

On Friday July fourth, Jamison pays for a room at the Times Square Marriott. Presuming that Edwina wants to remain a virgin, he is on his best behavior. He sleeps on a couch and she on the bed. The next day, wearing casual clothes, they join the Holiday visitors to tour the Metropolis and take the ferry to explore the Statue of Liberty. While on the ferry to the island, they receive a brochure with information pertaining to the Statue:

The statue of Liberty was given to Americans by France. It is to honor slain President Abraham Lincoln. The sculptor Frederic Bartholdi chose the goddess of Liberty as his model. The tablet in her arms is of the Ten Commandments. The message is 'Freedom comes with law.'

They spend the balance of the day riding the double-decker buses, walking Fifth Avenue, and at Edwina's suggestion, go so far as to do the Stations of the Cross at St. Patrick's Cathedral.

(Maybe this church visit is to atone in advance for what this precocious one has in mind for later on that evening).

At seven p.m. Edwina dons a cleavage revealing gown that accents her lithe body. This is a problem for other females whose male partners can't help eye-balling this vivacious Aphrodite as she romantically glides the dance floor to the tune of a slow waltz.

Spend the evening at the Marriot Club, for dinner and dancing to romantic music is also stimulating Jamison's testosterone. Returning to their room, he has enough of the tantalizing, "Goddammit Edwina. This bullshit has to stop. How long do you think that I can keep on being the nice guy with you teasing the *beJesus* out of me? I have almost reached a stage of wanting to rape you."

Evidently believing that virginity is a farce, not a virtue, she stuns Jamison with her response, "So rape me, I'll help you." Simultaneously to back-up her words with deeds, she drops her evening gown and exposes a beautiful, young, and very tantalizing nude body. Mind preset, she reaches for Jamison's pants zipper.

The first thrust of his vertical prong causes her to emit a low moan from the ecstatic muscle activity in her pelvic area. Though this is her first intercourse, natural instincts prevail and the next three times this evening, youthful instincts, natural hormones, and testosterone, bring a bliss that only youth can experience. Moreover Jameson can add to his life experiences, --

A majority of females– have round heels!

Chapter forty-five

Bernice wonders about the girl Edwina that Jamison often mentions and the telephone calls that he receives from this young lady. Her curiosity gets the best of her and she suggests that he bring her to dinner on Sunday October 26, 1975.

During the meal, Bernice does not want to hear the wrong answers yet feels the need to ask Edwina questions. Trying to be tactful, while hoping for non-problematic answers, she asks, "Edwina is the female version of the male Edwin or Edward, how did your mother select that name."

"I really don't know Mrs. Carroll, you see I was adopted and never knew my birth mother."

Not noticed by Jamison or Edwina, Bernice almost drops her coffee cup at that answer, but now she must push further. "Oh that must be Mr. and Mrs. Ferber that adopted you."

"Yes and no Mrs. Carroll. You see I was adopted twice. First by Claudia and Stanley Sheerin and when they died, I was adopted by my present step-father Matthew Ferber."

Trying to hide the shock that she experiences from this bit of information, Bernice makes a hasty retreat to the bathroom and attempts to silently cover the sound of her vomiting. Unsure of how to further handle this terrible moment, she returns to the dining area.

Trying to direct her questioning to obtain more information but not arouse curiosity, "Edwina, from what I understand, Mr. Ferber has had his hands full with all his children and problems with his late wife."

"Yes he has, however I will no longer be a dependent of daddy

Ferber, since Jamison and I came here today to let you know that we are going to married next week and you are going to be a grandmother in six months."

To the inexperienced person Bernice appears to have run out of conversation; however an experienced eye would have detected a physical reaction to an emotional mental blow that stuns Bernice. A ghostly white sickly pallor has encased her face, her hands are trembling.

Jamison becomes aware that his mother is not acting as her normal self, "Mother, are you alright? You look a little pale."

"I am fine son, I'm having a little reaction from a vitamin shot that the doctor gave me," she lies, then adds, "You kids need time for yourself. I will clean up the table and do the dishes, you go into the living room and watch some TV and leave me to my household duties."

With the kids outside of earshot, Bernice, hastens to the medicine cabinet to swallow a couple of Librium tablets. Very agitated and excitable, to a point that she is not completely coherent on the phone to Teddy, not wasting any time she blurts, "Teddy, Jamison and Edwina are going to have a baby."

"Jesus Christ Bernice, are you drunk? What the fuck are you babbling about?"

Regaining her composure a bit, she goes into the details. Ted's reply is not exactly the response that Bernice wants to hear.

"God damn that Jamison, he should have his pecker in his pants. I ought a whip his horny arsse and teach him a lesson."

Defensive motherly reaction from Bernice follows as she chides Ted. "She's your daughter and like her horny father she has your genes. Did it ever dawn on you that she had to first spread her thighs before my son could fuck her? Attaching blame to one or the other does not solve a thing; both kids are equally at fault. Even Matthew can share the blame. Why didn't he have her on the pill?"

"Acrimony on our part is not solving the problem. I will contact Matthew and set up a meeting for all of us Bernice."

While a brisk wind cools this sunny October day it is a paradox to the melancholic disheartened souls now present at Matthew's house. Matthew, Edwina, Jamison, Bernice and Ted can't decide who should start the discussion and it gets off to a bad start when in a typical pious religious hyperbole, Teddy and Bernice begin the meeting by reminding the kids that fornication is a venial sin. This sanctimonious approach angers Matthew and he interrupts the diatribe, "Ted tell us just how are you rationalizing the fact that this all began with the mortal sin of adultery on the part of you and Bernice. If you want to go into the details of your affair so be it. But I suggest that the kids forgive you for that event and you begin forgiving them for their situation."

Turning to Edwina sitting in a nearby chair, "As for your remark about the pill, Edwina has always been a very precocious headstrong girl and very difficult for me to handle. As a female adult it might have occurred to you that such a discussion might be needed. However as a male adult, I did not have any idea as to when, what, and if I should discuss such a subject with an adolescent female."

Matthew continues, "I do feel that somehow I have not done a good enough job of raising her. Trying to rationalize my thinking, I guess that I must have devoted too much of my time to my other children and not enough time with Edwina. So let's come down to earth and decide what is now best for these kids."

A tearful Edwina jumps up and hugs Matthew, "Oh Daddy Matthew, I love you, I am so sorry of what I have done; please try to forgive me."

"My precious one, I love you and you will always be my darling," responds Matthew.

The ever so pragmatic Teddy counters, "This pregnancy scandal is going to be very embarrassing to Edwina so I suggest that she get away from where she is known and have her pregnancy and birth elsewhere. I shall contact my cousin Mickey Fallon in Ireland and have him make arrangements for Edwina to spend her pregnancy there at the convent of Saint Therese of the Little Flower. The Sisters have their own hospital and discreetly handle unwed mothers and their bastard off springs."

"It does not seem fair to me that Edwina suffer all of their consequences and Jamison typical male goes on with his life," Matthew injects into the conversation.

"I feel awful about what I have done, I will be punished by my thoughts forever. I never knew that Edwina was my half-sister; I loved her and still do. I am not going to stay around here any longer; there are too many memories here. I am enlisting in the army tomorrow, so no one need make plans for my future, I will do it myself," explains Jamison.

By now tears are flowing from the eyes of Bernice, Jamison, and Edwina. Matthew and Teddy are trying unsuccessfully to stem their own tears.

For the first time in her life, Edwina will not sit down at the American holiday of Thanksgiving as the now five months pregnant female enters the Saint Theresa Convent on November 23, 1975. March of 1976, she gives birth to a six pound seven ounce boy who is shortly adopted by a loving Irish couple. As for Edwina, she decides to become a novitiate in the Catholic Order of the Nuns of Saint Theresa of the Little Flower.

Is it solely her choice, or do the circumstances cause her to believe that she must atone for her sins – or is it a means of not facing the hypocritical realities of the real world? Let's not be cynical, she could sincerely believe that her only spouse should now be the *Divine Spouse – Christ.*

In any event, with the Mother Superior's encouragement, Edwina takes her final vows, dons the habit of a Nun and on his feast date of September 21, 1976, takes the name of Saint Matthew *The Evangelist*, to honor her guardian Matthew Ferber. On hand to view the holy blessings are Matthew, Bernice and Teddy.

Chapter forty-six

The oxymoronic experience of joyfully witnessing the beautiful ordination ceremony in Ireland, then sadly saying good-bye to the newly ordained Sister Mathew, is an unforgettable experience for Matthew and Bernice. This religious experience is the main topic of their discussions on the long plane trip back from Ireland and it will be a bond between them forever. Moreover, seated together in mid-cabin area gives Matthew and Bernice time to discuss and reflect on their own lives.

"Matthew, my kids have grown and left my nest, but you still have two young ones at home, how do you handle that by yourself?"

"To be truthful Bernice, they have now grown into the ugly *teen age rebel* period. I must admit it is difficult, and after what occurred with Edwina, I am worried about what the next half dozen years will bring with the other kids. With my office business growing, I wonder how I will be able to handle it all."

"All parents go through the *terrible teens* and my parental experiencing was no exception. My Jimmy and Brenda gave me all kinds of aggravating problems. The only thing that saved my sanity was my love for them and their love for me that prevailed."

"Bernice, I truly understand because Johnny, now fifteen, and Claude twelve, are not bad kids, just normal kids, but I am sweating out the next few years. They do show love to me, and too each other – when they are not fighting. However, right now Johnny has hooked-up with a promiscuous fifteen year old imp that has him enchanted and I am having a hard time handling that."

"Both Jimmy and Brenda went through that era of passion inquisitiveness successfully Mathew, and yours can also."

"Bernice, please do not misunderstand me when I propose something, but you have the experience of running your house and kids and I need help in that vein. I would like to request that you help me with my boys by moving in with us. We sure would love to have a mother image in our home."

"So that I don't misunderstand you Matthew, what does that entail?"

"Oh, I mean on your terms entirely. You would live with us and have no expenses. It would be an opportunity to provide for your future by selling your home and investing the money. You would have no expenses at our house."

"Matthew, spit it out! What do you mean by living in your house? Do you mean as man and wife, lovers, a servant, or what?"

"I mean whatever rules you set down. I don't know how to better explain myself then that. Whatever comes by your choosing, I will accept."

"Matthew, I just became forty-nine. I have only been married to one man and had a one nighter with Teddy, but that is enough experience for me to understand the male animal. How can I be sure that if I sell my house and move in with you that your sexual desires and/ or male ego might manifest and cause me to have to move out?"

"Let's face facts Bernice, I need you. You do not need me. I have gone without a woman in my bed since Claudia's passing and if necessary I can go longer to be sure my boys have your guidance."

"I tell you what Matthew, I'll give it try. If it appears to work out to all our benefit I will then sell my house and stay with you until we decide – time enough."

Friday January 12, 1977 Bernice moves in to her separate comfortable quarters. The king size bed has no bedspread. The bureau, side tables, even window curtains all reflect typical masculine negligence, but it doesn't take but a few days, using Mathews money, for her to bring the room up to date in true femininity.

After a couple of weeks their daily lives form a comfortable, compatible routine. Her congenial manner and interest in the boys elates Matthew. Simple motherly /wifely actions has changed Mathew's house into home, a hominess that has been missing since Claudia's passing.

Rain, snow or hail, the two boys have to walk two miles to school every school day. Bernice wins them over when she begins driving them to school and picking them up after school. Matthew is so pleased when she brings him lunch each day. If he is in need of temporary assistance, she assists at the store. Each day they become more and more a family. As the weeks go by, it becomes more obvious.

Ferber Office Supply store hours on Saturday are eight to noon. At noon on Saturday June 18, 1977, Matthew's birthday, Bernice, John *Fitzy* and Claude show up at the store carrying a birthday cake and bringing a hired accordion player. An emotional man, tears well up on Mathew's face as he hugs his boys. Turning toward her, "This is so thoughtful of you Bernice. Thank you so much," and innocently kisses Bernice on the cheek.

Tuesday July 12, 1977, kisses are an important subject on the west coast and the east coast. Frank Sinatra in the marriage ceremony, is kissing his bride Barbara Marx (the ex-wife of *Zeppo* Marx). At the same time Bernice is helping out at Ferber's Store's after the *Fourth of July* sale.

At the close of the day, Matthew embraces her in a gentle hug. "You were wonderful, you helped to make this day one of my most profitable sales days," and he gently kisses her cheek.

Typically, the female must make the first move to indicate what is to follow, "That is the second time in the past month that you missed my mouth by a couple of inches, Matthew. Why don't you try that again and aim better?"

Having stuck to his agreement, even though many times he wanted to embrace her, he now is released from that promise. Very affectionately, he embraces Bernice in a warm hug and doesn't miss as he places his warm lips on hers.

"My God Bernice, I have wanted to do this for months. Will you marry me?"

A bit surprised at that question, she hesitates for a second, and then embraces Matthew, "I thought you would never ask me. Matthew I love you and I am tired of sleeping alone on my king size bed. Yes, I will marry you."

The day that they take their vows, Saturday October 15, 1977, the Boston Globe has a small back-page society column note of the wedding of Bernice and Matthew. Front page announces: **Harry Lillis Bing Crosby, 73, a '2' handicap golfer, dies after playing 18 holes at a country club golf course near Madrid Spain.**

At the reception following the ceremony, *Fitzy* and Claude pull their Dad aside. As the eldest *Fitzy* asks, "Daddy instead of always calling her Aunt Bernice, would she mind if we now call her Mother Bernice?"

"Since she is now your Step-Mother, I think that would be very appropriate and I also believe that she will love for you to address her simply as Mom."

On June 11, 1979 Bernice, while having a last cup of coffee at breakfast, she is reading the Boston Globe, "Matthew life is so final for even the great ones. It says here that, *Duke* Marion Mitchell Morrison, alias John Wayne, has died. Just a short while ago I was reading about him saying that he was dying from cancer after smoking up to six packs a day. Now he is dead and that is sad. I guess his initials of three M's like the candy '3M's could indicate that he had some sweetness to his life and cancer brought some sourness. Death is so final. It is the end of that person."

"Bunny, since you and I don't smoke, maybe we will be lucky and our kids won't want to smoke. You know the axiom, *monkey see, monkey do.* We must also be reminded by his death, a man who had everything to live for, that we should always live each day to its fullness. We never will know when death will hit us or our family. So forget that and put down that newspaper and come and give me a kiss," is Matthew's reply.

At this time, they can never realize that in a little over a week the Grim Reaper will send an agent bearing news of a great tragedy of death that will hit home so soon. It brings that experience of finalism to a part of Bernice's life. All this pain comes about on June 19, 1979 when the doorbell rings. Partly opening the door foreboding and dreading the reason that a U.S. Army Lieutenant in full formal dress is in front of her she panics. With a scream she yells, "Mathew, my God! Mathew come here," and passes out at the now half opened front door.

Mathew races to the door and his heart drops at the sight of the uniformed man at the door. The officer says nothing but pushes the door fully open and assists Mathew in carrying Bernice to the bedroom. Mathew sitting on the side of the bed, gently stroking Bernice's forehead and the officer standing at the foot of the bed are both speechless until a few minutes when Bernice attempts to sit up.

"I am sorry Lieutenant for my shocked reaction at seeing you at the door, but was my reaction logical for assuming why you are here?"

"I am Lieutenant Roger Freed and I am sorry to have to confirm what you must have assumed at the sight of me at your door. I am here to offer condolence for the sad demise of your son Jamison Carroll. Sergeant Carroll was with an outfit serving as military observers in the Nicaragua Civil War. His outfit is there to protect the Ambassador's office, not to participate in the turbulence. Jamison was mortally wounded by the combatant's cross fire."

Chapter forty-seven

In an attempt to shut down Teddy Sheerin's vice operations, Assistant D.A. Lawrence Edward Cameron on Friday January 11, 1980 orders Massachusetts State Troopers to raid Teddy's Gloucester vice operations and arrest Sean McLaughlin and Ruth Sheerin and charge them with "*Operating an illegal gambling operations.*"

Cameron is not plying his occupation for the good of the people of his district; his motives are strictly for revenge.

In the Gloucester jail awaiting trial they are interrogated separately and/or together, on three different days, by Al Brown an investigator from the D. A.'s office. He is sent by Cameron to attempt to get solid information to try Teddy Sheerin with the most criminal charges that Cameron can file, to be sure that he will be able to send Sheerin away on a long stiff sentence.

On the fourth day of interrogation of the duo, who are now facing many legal, as well as trumpeted-up charges, that the District Attorney's office threatens to charge them, Ruth blurts out hastily, "The charges that you are accusing Teddy of is petty compared with what we know."

"I think we have enough information to severely prosecute Mr. Sheerin," responds Brown.

"How about murder," adds Sean?

"What the hell do you mean by murder," asks Brown.

'You think you're so fuckin' smart you dumb bastard. How about using the plural and say murders," Sean continues

"What murders are you talking about?"

"We are through with talking to *scutter* like you. You tell Cameron that the only time we will continue to talk again is with him only."

Leaving the interrogation room Brown heads for a telephone, "Mr. D. A., sir. This is investigator Alvin Brown. I am in Gloucester and have been interrogating the couple that you sent me here for. They have said that they know something about murders by Sheerin and they refuse to say anything more to anyone but you."

"Brown, you did say plural didn't you?"

"Yes sir I did."

"Transfer them from there to the Suffolk County Jail immediately," Cameron orders.

At the first meeting with Ruth and Sean, Cameron is challenged by an arrogant Sean, "Mr. Cameron I realize that you very badly want our information about Teddy Sheerin murders and before I tell you a God damned thing I want a guarantee that all charges against Ruth and I will be dropped and that we will not be prosecuted for this, or any other criminal comprised violations we may or may not have committed up to today."

"There is no way I will guarantee that."

"Well kiss my ass Mr. D. A. we having nothing else to say," injects to the conversation from the up to now silent Ruth.

Testing their bluff, Cameron leaves the interrogation room, goes for a cup of coffee, and then telephones his step-dad, now District Judge, Lawrence Cameron. Explaining the situation he then seeks a judicious decision then asks, "What do you think dad?"

"Eddy, you have nothing to lose and a hellava lot politically to gain if you can hang Sheerin on multiple murder charges. Be sure to apprise them of their *Miranda's*, then I say go for it."

Returning to the interrogation room, "Okay Sean, if you two agree to give evidence and to testify against Teddy Sheerin, here is my offer. To cover my ass, I will try you on a misdemeanor charge of being found in a building that numbers gaming occurred. I will drop all other charges for any crimes past or present, except, if I find that you yourself, murdered, no deal. There is no impunity, or '*statute of limitation*', to the charge of murder."

Wasting no time to *Pin Teddy Sheerin's ass against the wall,* twenty-two year old Suffolk County Assistant District Attorney Edward

Cameron, whose Christian name was given to him by his mother to honor his father Edward '*Teddy*' Sheerin, is determined to avenge Teddy on behalf of the heartaches, imagined or real, that Teddy caused Edward's mother Catherine to suffer. At times Cameron goes so far as fabricating evidence and crossing legal ethics parameters.

Monday February 4, 1980, in the midst of a very heavy *nor'easter* snow storm, and because of the six inches of snow already on the ground, the bull-headed Cameron is barely able to walk the short distance to his office. Assistant D. A. Cameron at 11.00 a.m. finally executes a felony warrant for the arrest of Edward Sheerin a k a Teddy Sheerin. The warrant is passed to the State Police office in the same Suffolk County Courthouse. At 1:30 p.m. uniformed troopers 'Candy' Cundiff and 'Mik' McDougal are ordered to serve the warrant and arrest Edward 'Teddy' Sheerin residing at the Blue Haven Lodge in Pembroke – ASAP.

However, by this time of day, the rapidly piling snow makes it a most difficult problem for the State police car, even with snow chains on the rear wheels. The thirty mile trip from the court house to Pembroke has taken two hours just to get to the center of the town. It is still a fifteen minute's drive on the state highway to get to the entrance of the private one lane Blue Haven Lodge road.

The snow has formed a blanket of from a six inch level to three foot high mounds that camouflage the roads path. Just forty yards on the path, their greatest problem manifests itself, the cruiser stalls in the high snow drifts. It is now nearing 4:00 p.m. and soon will be dark. The conditions are becoming life threatening for the two *Statsies.* Walking back to the state highway would not be wise; no vehicles have been traveling there for hours. Staying with the motor running could be fatal when the snow piled up over the tailpipe they will be overcome.

"We are going to become ice carvings if we sit here Candy, we got to haul ass."

"You're godamned right Mik, but I am not sure we can go anyplace except to Sheerin's place and that is a fuckin' mile ahead of us. Get on the *horn* and let HQ know our plans." That done, they haul ass, and try for the lodge.

Trudging through the snow on the road path, that is from six inches to three feet in depth, and occasional four or five foot drifts, is torture.

The only way they can be sure that they are even on the road path is that each side of the road is lined with bare trees indicating a possible corridor.

Meanwhile, because of the snow, although alone, Teddy is comfortable in believing that he is embedded in an impenetrable igloo. Seamus left last night to negotiate the selling of the restaurant Ted still owns in Gloucester.

It is a little past 5:00 P.M. sitting at his desk sipping a large cup of hot cocoa, when his tranquility is shattered and fear grips his heart at the sight two uniformed troopers coming through the haze of falling snow. With a surge in his blood pressure and a now racing heart rate, he breaks out in a hot body sweat.

Teddy realizes down deep that he no longer is the self assured, infallible icon, he once was. He is no match for those two husky men. Wiping his brow with a damp cloth, and hastily mulling his next ass saving action, he uses his crutches to walk to the front door.

Hoping they will not notice the insecure tremor in his voice, he brazenly says, "Well you guys look exhausted. Trudging over a mile in my snow covered road would be tough on those in the best physical condition, which by your bellies, indicates you two do not fit that description."

Teddy now is at a stage of near panic at the thought of his possible future ending in the electric chair; he tries to get his thinking process under control. Can he outsmart these cops? *Best to play it as it comes, one step at a time.* Why one so evil should be so lucky, no one later on will understand. Surely Michael the Archangel is not looking over Teddy. If there is a devil, is the Great Lucifer guiding him? Who so-ever is his mentor; they finally gave him the moment.

In his office, while standing with the aid of his crutches, Ted is frisked. Finding no weapons on Ted, trooper Cundiff breaks out the handcuffs, "Extend your hands."

Using counter strategy, and wanting to be in his mobile chair, Teddy says, "If you cuff me I will not be able to use my crutches. You gentlemen will then have to carry me and put me into my mobile chair. Not only that, realize you are going to be here for a couple of hours or more, until a road is cleared of snow for a patrol car to come here. While on my crutches I can see to it that you have warm coffee and sandwiches."

For some unknown reason Cundiff decides not to cuff Ted, "Enough of your godamned bull-shit Sheerin, where is the fuckin' mobile chair?"

"It is in the family room by the fireplace to being kept warm for me."

Not saying a word, just a glance at each other the troopers lift Ted and carry him to the battery operated mobile chair. Removing the blanket that covers the seat, they put Ted down and cover his knees with the blanket. Assuming Ted will be harmless in the mobile, carelessly no cuffs are applied. – Their extreme lack of thought to potential danger is a fatal mistake.

After he is seated Ted reaches under the seat cushion and withdraws a Beretta .9 mill pistol, puts it between his legs under the blanket. Timing now is of the essence to Teddy. For his plan to work, it is imperative that both troopers be in range.

It is now 7:35 P.M. Cundiff is in the kitchen, McDougall, is in the office, on phone, explaining the present situation to the state police HQ. Getting off the phone, he yells to Cundiff who is in the kitchen."Hey Candy, HQ says now that the snow has stopped, they will mobilize some plows and dig us out of here but it will take about four or five hours."

Cundiff is coming back, from the kitchen to the family room, with three cups of steaming hot coffee, sandwiches and soups. Is he showing compassion for Teddy? Could this be the *Stockholm syndrome* in reverse?

As Cundiff comes in to an easy range, Teddy fires his pistol at him. Dishes and food fly throw the air as Cundiff drops with a loud thud, into a heap on the floor. The returning McDougall pulls his weapon and fires at Teddy. The poorly aimed bullet only grazes Teddy's left shoulder, and Teddy returns fire to the now fully exposed McDougall. He empties his pistol to climax McDougall's existence.

While the grazing bullet damage is slight, the shoulder bleeds and requires attention. The so-called tough guy Sheerin, lets out a yelp when he applies iodine to his wound. He winces at what he imagines is pain. Bandaging and taping the area, he is ready to flee. It is now close to nine. The night is extremely cold the thermometer on the porch indicates sixteen degrees.

Taking three or four *belts* of Johnny Walker Black label, adds to Teddy's courage. The green fir trees are so snow laden that the large branches are touching the ground. The snow fall has stopped and the air is temporarily still. It is so silent that Teddy now can hear distant snow plows attempting to clear a passage to possibly allow police cars to follow the foot path made by the two troopers.

Teddy decides on a dangerous strategic escape plan. While the snow fall has ceased, what follows was unpredictable, for in this case, very heavy northeast winds begin to sweep the frozen lake clear of most of the snow, blowing it up to and past the lodge to further pile higher on the back roadway. Mother Nature has cleared the area from the back porch to the frozen lake side. Once again one can ponder Teddy's luck. Is this the cooperative actions of the Archangel, or maybe Lucifer, to aid Teddy in his plight?

The clearance of snow, off of the lake, reaches to a point that the lake now resembles a huge ice skating rink. It also has blown so strongly of the lake and up to the house that there is little snow at the pier side of the lodge. Moreover it has aided Teddy by blowing the snow into huge impassable drifts on the entrance road at the back of the building, impeding any snow plow movement. .

It is now 9:13 p.m. Bundling up warmly, taking a thermos of the hot coffee, laced with Johnny Walker Black Label, and strapping himself into the battery operated mobile chair Teddy is ready to put his mad plan into action. He guides this vehicle down the back porch ramp and onto the frozen lake. His plan is to head for the strip shopping mall on the far end of the lake. There he can hope to obtain an auto and escape imminet custody.

While the ice is thick, the lake is so large that the surface of the ice undulates like hidden waves might be under the ice sheet. Such motion, and Ted's anxiousness, plus the alcohol, many times causes his coordination to go off base. His hastily over-compensating maneuvers cause the chair to skid dangerously on the ice. The trip now becomes very arduous.

To maintain emotional control he stops for a moment to take a swig of the hot coffee from the thermos. The temporary warmth of the drink reassures him and he resorts to talking to himself in the third person, he mutters, "Mr. Sheerin, calm down, use your head."

This seems to psychologically work. It has taken him an hour, but he is now out into the middle of the frozen lake. It is still slow going, many wind gusts, cause his vehicle to swerve and sometimes push the chair backwards. However he struggles onward and is finally successful in traveling to within about one hundred feet from his goal of the mall landing pier.

Hypothermia has now befuddled his brain, he is carelessly beginning to feel safe – Without the help of his mentors, and nature throws him a deadly curve.

While he and others are aware of the huge warm water fish hatchery next to the mall, most are unaware of the fish tank water exchange. Once a week, after business hours, the hatchery pumps in water from the lake into its tanks while at the same time draining out the old water from the tanks. Sadly for Teddy, tonight is that night.

Approximately thirty minutes earlier, the hatchery sucked in lake water, it is warmed and pumped into the huge retaining pools and in turn the overflow goes out of the tanks through different pipes as it returns to the lake. The process of the warm water transfer, from the huge fish tanks to the lake, produces a water temperature at the lake edge to maintain an approximate of about thirty-three or thirty-four degrees causing the ice of this area to be thinner than the rest of the frozen lake.

Unaware of this freak of thinner ice, and within about fifty feet of the shore line, Teddy and his mobile suddenly crash through the thin ice and slowly begin to sink in the ten foot depth of the lake water. In panic, he is unable to unhook his now frozen safety belt. Even if he does release himself, because of the danger to others, there is no way that any attempts to rescue him will be made and if an attempt at this time were to be tried it would not be successful.

As he sinks deeper he screams for help, but he might have spent his waning seconds saying an *Act of Contrition* for an *Indulgence,* plus a few *maxi-culpas*, to atone for his life of sin. However, it is now time for those famous conceptions that when approaching death, *your life begins to flash before you.* His screaming is a waste of his energy; the inclement weather has forced everyone inside of the buildings for warmth.

Teddy's screams go unnoticed because the only ones that hear his wailing is weather hardy, drunk couple, who had stepped outside the bar for her to use his peeing pecker to trace her initials in yellow on the snow pile. They excitedly return to the bar and swore, to any one that would listen to their drunken babbling, that they heard the winds howl and scream like the legendary *Miria*. The only responses that he got from their buddies, "Yeah, you guys need another drink."

Alas and alack, it is six months later that a recreational swimmer happens to be diving in that area and is shocked at the sighting, of the unrealistic gruesome view, of a body sitting in a mobile chair at the bottom of the lake.

When the recovery of Teddy's body is finally made, the fishes have eaten away at the exposed parts of Teddy's carcass. If it hadn't been for the fact that when found, he is still strapped into the chair, no one would be sure that this was the infamous Edward *Teddy* Sheerin. There are no eulogies, and no Angelus ever sung at vespers.

Glossary

(I) Italian (F) French (G) Gaelic (L) Latin (S) Spanish (Y) Yiddish if

Ablation	The removal of the heart from the body to operate on and correct its operation
A.K.A.	Also known as
Aer Lingus (G)	Irish Air Lines
Agape	Love that is spiritual, not sexual
Agnus Dei	Lamb of God
Alas and alack	expressing sorrow
Alpha man	Beautiful body
Amblyiopia	Dimness of eye sight
Anathema	Devoted to evil, accursed
Ath cliath Erin (G)	Dublin Ireland
Bacchus (L)	Mythical God of wine & alcohol. Drunkenness.
Bella Ficca (It)	Piece of arsse
Benddact anim (L)	A blessing on the soul of ---
Biretta	Square cap worn by Catholic clergy. Black for a priest, purple for Bishop. Red for a Cardinal.
Boston Brahmins	Pompous, self important, elites. Boston Social upper class

B.C.H.	Boston City Hospital
Cad e mar ata tu (G)	How are you
Capo Bastone (It)	Mafia 2nd in command
Capo Crimini (It)	Mafia Super boss
Cara (G)	Friend
Carabiniere (It)	Italian police
Cead mille failte (G)	A million good wishes
Censer	Charcoal burning incense vessel whose smoke rises. Prayers up to heaven. Also a cleansing aspect.
Claddagh ring	A heart being clasped in 2 hands, with a crown on top
Cock-a-hoop	State of boastful exultation, rejoicing
Coitus interruptus (L)	Sexual intercourse interrupted by Withdrawal of the penis prior to ejaculation.
Columba	Irish Saint
Conas ata tu (G)	How are you
Culo (It)	Arsse, behind
Cupla focal (G)	A few words
Cuppa	Irish slang for a cup of coffee
Cushla ma cree (G)	Darling of my heart
CYA	Cover your ass –protect yourself.
Diaspora (Y)	Any Jewish community outside of Israel.
Dia duit (G)	Hello
Dildo	Artificial penis of wood or plastic
Dodrhan (G)	Goat skin drums
e.g. (exempli gratia) (L)	For example, such as
Elysium	A condition of ideal happiness
Erin goes Bragh (G)	Ireland forever
Eucharist	Sacrament instituted at *Last Supper,* in which bread & wine are consecrated

Euphemism	Substitute mild term for harsh or blunter
E.T.O.	WW2 acronym for European Theatre of war
Extreme Unction (L)	The Sacrament of E.U. prepares one for their death
Failte (G)	Welcome
52/20 club	20$ per week for 52 weeks
Gamine	Girl with saucy charm.
Giovane D'Honore (It)	Non-Italian Mafia member
Gluteal muscles	Buttocks, arsse
Goel (H)	Savioı
Grunts	Army slang name for a soldier
Hackney	Taxi Cab
Hashish	Marijuana, pot, grass
Hibernia	Roman for Ireland (Hibernus, wintry)
Horse	Heroin
Hoi polloi	Common people
Houris	Voluptuous woman
Id (L)	Dominated by pleasure principles to obtain immediate gratification of desires
IL punto di fuga (L)	Point of vanishing
Indulgence	Catholic method of a sinner to be absolved of any punishment in heaven for having committed sin. (Also see simony)
Ingannare (It)	Deceive
Inishmore	The largest of the Aran Islands, five miles of the western coast of Ireland, at Galway

I.R.A.	Irish Republican Army, an underground patriotic group fighting the U.D.L. & Britain to change Ulster to be part of the Republic of Ireland.
Is mise (G)	I am
Junoesque	Stately bearing & imposing beauty
Kamikaze pilots	Japanese suicide pilots
Kelevra (H)	Mad dog
Kippah (H)	Head covering Jewish men wear as recognition that God is above them
Kyrie eleison	Lord have mercy. A brief petition to Jesus
Liaison	Adulterous relationship
Libertine	Bachelor, free lover
Lobaircin / Leprechauns	Gaelic (small-bodied fellow). Cranky cobbler that repair shoes of other fairies.
Lolar (G)	Eagle
Lucy	3.2 million year old adult female whose skeleton was found in Ethiopia and is the first homo sapiens that all humans may have evolved from.
Lupara (It)	Double barrel shotgun w/a retractable stock that Folds like a jackknife &carried on hook under a coat
Maidin mhaith (G)	Good morning
Malleus	Maleficarum 1468 book by Dominican Monks, confirming that witches exist. Any girl that practices witchcraft on her boyfriend, or his wife, after she has been sexually intimate with him and he now rejects her.
Mass	Catholic religious ritual in celebration of the Holy Eucharist
M.E.	Medical examiner

Mea culpa (L)	I am culpable (deserving blame)
Mea maxima culpa (L)	My most grievous fault
Mik or Mickey	Slang sometimes derogatory name for Irish person
Mickey Finn	Sleep inducing drug chloral hydrate
Minyan (Y)	Memorial group of ten Jewish men praying for a deceased member of the congregation.
Mio amare (It)	My lover
Mishnah (H)	First section of Talmud's five books.
Missa pro defunctis (L)	Mass for the deceased
Modus operandi (L)	Method of operating
Modus Vivendi (L)	Style or way of one's life
Mons veneris (L)	Female pubic mound of hair.
Mule	Slang for a drug courier
Multiple myeloma	A malignant proliferation of plasma cells in the bone marrow causing numerous tumors.
Nether area	Located beneath or below
Non-com	Non-commissioned officer, i.e. Sergeant, Corporal
N.I.N.A.	No Irish Need Apply
Nonna (It)	Grandmother
Novena	Recitation of prayers for a special purpose said during 9 consecutive days
Nymphet	Pubescent girl regarded as sexually desirable
Oiche maith (G)	Good night
Old Sod	Sentimental name for Ireland used by Irish Americans
Omadhaun (G)	Fool
Omniscient	Knows everything, has total knowledge e.g. Omniscient Deity

Orange man	Protestant Ulster men determined to stop the I.R.A.
Paddy wagon	An insult to the Irish in a description of a patrol wagon
Peccadillo	Indiscretion
Pentimental	Change mind
Per favore (It)	Please (As a favor)
Phylactery (H)	Small leather box containing quotes from scriptures. It is strapped to the head and left arm of Jewish men during prayers.
Piciotto (It)	Mafia enforcer – button man
Poly-	Many
P.O.P.	Female power of pussy. Manner a female obtains favors from a man.
POV	Point of view
Pranzo (It)	Dining area
Proinsias (G)	Francis
Prostituire	To prostitute oneself
P.U.M.A.	Prostitutes Union of Massachusetts
Puttana (It) (S)	Whore
QED (L)	Quod erat demonstrandum. Undeniable, without a doubt.
Quid pro quo (L)	An equal exchange. Reciprocation To be proved
Que sera sera (L)	Whatever might happen in the future. Take no chances, let the fun begin.
Queen Elizabeth I	Decreed that all Irish Artist & Pipers be arrested & hung on the spot
Qui tacet consentire videtur (L)	Who ever remains silent assumes to agree
Recuer di me mi amor (S)	Remember me my love

Ricatto (It)	Extortion, blackmail
Sabbatarian (Y)	Religious Jew who is in strict observance of the Sabbath
Saint Jude (Thaddeus)	One of 12 Apostles the devout pray too when a situation seems hopeless. John 14:12
Scag	Heroin
Scopare (It)	To fuck
Scotoma	The human mind only sees what it wants to see
Scutter (G)	Feces
Seamroy (sham-roy) (G)	Shamrock
Seamus (shamus) (G)	James
Sean (she-on) (G)	John
Shalom (Y)	Semite greeting
Shamus	Slang word for police officer or detective
Shanekee (G)	Story teller
Shange tighe (G)	Shanty as in *Shanty Irish,* not *lace curtain* upper class Irish as the Kennedy clan
Simony	Selling spiritual items, such as relics, and/or, indulgences.
Signora (It)	Lady
Sinead (G)	Jane
Sinn Fein (G)	Ourselves, together
Slan (G)	So long
Slan abhaile (G)	Home safely
Slan agiv (G)	Health be with you
Slan go foil (G)	Goodbye for a while
Slan leat (G)	Goodbye
Slainte (G)	Salute – good luck
Statsie	State trooper
Taim i' ngra leat (G)	I love you

Ta me (G)	I am
Ta me go maith (G)	I am well
TAMPA gal	Takes Any Man's Pecker Anytime T – A – M – P – A –
Taspy (G)	Passion
Terzo (It)	Third
Terra incognita	Unexplored region
Thurible	See Censer
Trope	Word used in a figurative sense
Tsuris (H)	Troubles
Tuskegee Airmen	World War 2 all black Army Air Corps Airmen that were great combat pilots and crewmen.
Urbi et Orbi (L)	To the city and to the world
U.U.D.A.	Ulster Unionist defense alliance.
Valhalla	Place where those who die in battle spend their eternity in paradise.
Venal	Corrupt
Visceral	Emotional rather than intellectual
Vita strada (It)	Way of life
Viz (videlicet) (L)	That is to say, namely
Weal & woe	Prosperity & happiness
Wittol	A man who knows off & tolerates his wife's infidelity
Yarmulke	A brimless skullcap worn by religious men as a sign of submission to God. Jews wear this or a *kippah.* Priest wear a *zucchetto,* Buddhists don a *bao-tzu,* Muslims, a *kufi.*
Yontef (Y)	Holiday
Yutz (Y)	A stupid person
Zipper fucks	Unemotional, lust only, intercourse

Birthdays as of June 1, 1968

Eamon Sheerin	Sun. 3/4/05	63	
Edw. 'Teddy' Sheerin	Sat. 4/19/24	44	
Stanley 'Stan' Sheerin	Thu. 1/4/23	45	Died Wed. 10/8/58
Claudia Theresa Demarest	Wed. 10/5/32	35	Died Sun. 4/19/64
Ruth Demarest Sheerin	Mon. 10/5/14	53	
Lawrence Cameron	Wed. 8/12/16	51	
Lawrence Edward Cameron	Tue. 6/18/57	10	Son of Teddy and Cathy
Cathy Brooks Cameron Sheerin	Fri. 9/19/27	40	
Stephen 'Steve' Ryler	Wed. 6/10/25	42	Died Mon. 11/27/50
Jeanne Marie Brooks	Wed.5/5/32	36	
Anne Nevins	Fri. 5/12/22	46	Died Thur. 11/25/76
Seamus 'Jimmy' McMann	Fri. 2/10/22	46	
Alvan Waterman	Sat. 3/3/23	45	
Phyllis Waterman	Sun. 4/12/25	43	
Virginia Jane 'Ginny' Bushnell	Tue. 7/16/29	38	

Fr. Timothy 'Tim' Coughlin	Mon. 5/1/22	46	
Mary Margaret Mitchell	Sun. 4/23/39	29	
Sean 'Johnny 3 strikes' McLaughlin	Sat.9/19/36	31	
Norma Palmer McLaughlin	Mon. 5/29/1933	35	
Andrew Palmer McLaughlin	Sat. 5/28/66	2	Norma & Sean's son
Fred Banks	Mon. 3/6/33	35	Killed fri.5/30/69
Jacquelyn 'Jackie' Coleman	Wed. 11/1/33	34	
John 'Jack' Carroll	Fri. 8/10/17	50	
Bernice 'Bunny' Carroll	Fri. 11/11/27	40	
Jamison 'Jimmy' Carroll	Thu. 4/19/55	13	Died 6/19/79
Brenda Carroll	Tue. 5/11/48	20	
Noreen Jean Keenan	Mon. 8/8/38	29	
Thomas 'Jazz' Kelley	Thu. 10/9/19	48	
Matthew 'Matty' Ferber	Mon. 6/18/23	44	
Edwina Carroll Ferber	Mon. 1/1/58	10	Ted & Bernice's daughter
John "Fitzy' Fitzgerald Ferber	Thu. 8/10/61	6	Claudia & Matthew's son
Claude Shane Ferber	Sun. 4/19/64	4	Claudia & Matthew's son
Marion Frazier Ferber	Mon. 5/14/28	40	
Mark Frazier	Fri. 8/8/54	13	Marion's son
Randolph Frazier	Tue. 3/23/54	14	Marion's son
Beatrice Elizabeth Ferber	Tue. 9/21/65	2	Marion & Matthew's daughter.
Joseph 'Whitey' Bulger	Tues. 9/3/29	38	
William 'Big Bill' Bulger	Wed. 5/6/14	54	
Maev Bridget O'Toole	Thu. 7/13/33	34	

Gaelach ‘Gale’ O’Toole	Mon. 2/10/30	38
Giovanni ‘Johnny’ di Birtallo	Thu. 10/17/29	38
Donna Louise Broes	Fri.10/24/44	23
Sergio ‘Bello’ Canalejas	Thu. 5/7/36	32

Calendar of Events

Mon. Jan. 26, 1942 Stanley Sheerin's outfit lands in Belfast Ireland.

Fri. May 1, 1943 United Mine Workers Union President John L. Lewis
Orders a strike for higher wages for the coal miners, damaging the coal output needed for the war effort, U.S. military needs be damned.

Sun. June 6, 1943 Virginia 'Ginny' Bushnell loses her virginity to Ted.

Tue. June 8, 1943 Virginia raped by Stanley Sheerin

Thu. Sep. 9, 1943 Catherine *Cathy* Brooks loses her virginity to Ryler

Fri. Feb. 4, 1944 Stanley steps on a land mine in the Ploiesti oil fields.

Mon. Feb. 19, 1945 Edward *Ted, Teddy* Sheerin, and Stephen *Steve* Ryler's paths cross on Iwo Jima.

Sat. June 15, 1946 Catherine Jane Brooks marries Stephen Ryler.

Tues. Aug. 6, 1946.Stanley transferred to Boston V. A. Hospital

Thu. Sept. 12, 1946 Ted and Rabbi Alvan Waterman meet.

Fri. Sept. 13, 1946 Ted and Anne Nevins meet

Tue. Oct. 1, 1946 Anne seduces Ted.

Sat. May 8, 1948 Stephen and Ted become motorcycle policemen

Sat. Dec. 24, 1949 Steve drunk on duty

Thu. Mar. 2, 1950 Ted buys lot on Pembroke Lake from Rabbi Waterman.

Tue. Aug. 8, 1950 Stanley becomes V. A. Hospital out-patient for therapy

Mon. Sept. 4, 1950 Blue Haven Lodge finished. Ted Meets ex-Navy cook Fred Banks

Fri. Sept. 8, 1950 Ted buys Freeport Motors used car company from Johnny di Birtallo who has been drafted for the Korean conflict.

Wed. Oct. 4, 1950 Claudia gets her driver's license.

Sat. Oct. 7, 1950 Ted seduces Claudia's mother Ruth Demarest.

Sun. Oct. 15, 1950 Ted seduces Claudia.

Thu. Nov. 23, 1950 Catherine Brooks Ryler needs Ted's help with her abusive husband the alcoholic Stephen.

Sun. Nov. 26, 1950 Catherine seduces Ted. He changes the name of the lodge to the *Blue Haven*

Fri. Dec.1, 1950 Funeral for Stephen '*Steve*' Ryler

Sun. Apr.18, 1951 Claudia goes to live with Aunt Beatrice in N.Y.C.

Sun. Feb. 3, 1952 Claudia and Virginia 'Ginny' meet and discuss Ted. Virginia reveals that she is bi-sexual.

Wed. Dec. 2, 1953 Teddy is promoted to Sergeant.

Sat. Dec. 19, 1953 an ill Claudia comes to Freeport Motors office. Stanley insists upon immediately acquiring a dialysis machine for her.

Wed. Dec. 23, 1953 Brink's Holdup brains Joe McInnis & Tony Pino picked up for questioning.

Thu. May 4, 1954 Jeanne Marie Brooks graduates from Wellesley and becomes a stewardess for North East Airways.

Sun. June 20, 1954 Stanley donates a kidney to Claudia.

Fri. July 30, 1954 Claudia proposes to Stanley

Sun. Dec. 18, 1954 Claudia becomes Mrs. Stanley Sheerin

Mon. July 4, 1955 Jeanne Marie Brooks is seduced by Tito Mangino

Sun. Aug. 7, 1955 Jeanne meets Sergio Canalejo with cocaine money, beds Captain Patrick Eden

Sun. Mar. 8, 1956 Jeanne seduces Sergio

Sun. May 6, 1956 Jeanne and Sergio are busted by New Jersey State Police Narco Lt. Carmen '*Bruto*' Colizzi, they jump bail and flee to join the Canalejo family in Naples.

Mon. June 4, 1956. Brinks' loot, paid by Gold Dust Twins to Fats Buccelli, recovered hidden in a water cooler behind the wall of Fats' Tremont St. Construction Co.

Wed. Sept. 12, 1956 Cathy tells Ted that she is going to marry Cameron

Sat. Oct. 6, 1956 Fr. Tim marries Catherine Brooks Ryler to Lawrence Cameron.

Tue. Nov. 6, 1956 on the same ballot as Ike is re-elected President, Lawrence Cameron is defeated in his first time bid to be elected to the position of the Suffolk County (Boston area) District Attorney.

Wed. Nov. 14, 1956 Jeanne meets Lucky Luciano

Fri. Nov. 23, 1956 Cathy tells Ted that she is pregnant from him.

Sun. Dec 22, 1956 Claudia seeks sex advice from Virginia Bushnell.

Fri. Feb. 4, 1957 Jeanne is interrogated by British Immigration Officer in London

Fri. Apr. 19, 1957 Bernice 'Bunny' Carroll seduces Teddy at his birthday party. Fr. Tim brings 18 yr old Mary Margaret Mitchell to party.

Fri. June 7, 1957 Jeanne Marie sentenced 3 to 5 years in British Columbia prison.

Tue. June 18, 1957 Cathy births Lawrence Edward Cameron, her and Ted's son.

Sat. Aug. 3, 1957 52 year old Eamon Sheerin marries 44 year old Ruth Demarest while in Seabrook Beach, N.H. Teddy now has a step-mom

Tue. Aug. 13, 1957 Ted plays French sex with Mary Margaret Mitchell.

Mon. Sep. 2, 1957 Fr. Tim makes Novena to St. Jude, and then decides to resigns from Catholic priesthood and move to Blue Haven. He plans to marry Mary Margaret Mitchell

Mon. Jan. 1, 1958 Bunny gives birth to 6 lb. daughter Edwina

Thu. Jan. 4, 1958 Edwina is adopted by Stanley & Claudia.

Mon. Mar. 17, 1958 Ted brings money to I.R.A. in Belfast Erin

Fri. March 28, 1958 Stanley goes for his quarterly check-up at the V. A. Hospital.

Wed. April 2, 1958, Doctors tell Stanley he has multiple myeloma cancer and he has up to eighteen months to live.

Sat. Apr. 19, 1958 Fr. Tim enters Episcopal Seminary

Thu. June 19, 1958 Wimpy Bennett kills Buccelli

Sun. July 13, 1958 Fr. Tim is inducted into the Episcopal Ministries

Tues. July 22, 1958 Mary Margaret leaves Fr. Tim and returns to Erin

Wed. Oct. 8, 1958 Stanley Sheerin dies.

Fri. Dec. 19, 1958 Claudia & Edwina move to Hingham to live with Aunt Philomena Buchannan

Sun. Dec. 21, 1958 Jeanne Marie Brooks extradited from B.C. to New Jersey

Sun. Feb. 8, 1959 Claudia agrees to go to work for Ferber's Office supply.

Mon. Mar. 8, 1959 Jeanne Marie Brooks sentenced 6 to 8 yrs in Newark Federal prison

Sat. May 21, 1960 Matthew Ferber proposes to Claudia Sheerin

Sat. June 25, 1960 Claudia marries Matthew Ferber at St. Patrick Cathedral.

Wed. Feb. 15, 1961 Birth control pill introduce to world.

Mon. May 15, 1961 Teddy sets up Joaquim 'Jockey' Ayaho in Gloucester bookie operation for Jazz Kelley and enjoys nymphet Donna Louise Broes.

Thu. May 18, 1961 Teddy is promoted to Lieutenant in B.P.D.

Sun. May 28, 1961 Teddy meets Jazz and gives him a section of land next to him on the lake. Jazz gets Teddy the powerful position of Assistant to Police Superintendent Hanratty.

Sat. June 17, 1961 Parker House tryst. Next day the Camerons meet with J.F.K.

Sun. Aug. 6, 1961 The Camerons off to Erin as Assistant to Ambassador McCloskey

Thu. Aug. 10, 1961 Baby boy born to Claudia and Matthew and they adopt Edwina. On the 19th Edward *Teddy* Sheerin & Virginia Bushnell are named God Parents at Baptism of John 'Fitzy' Fitzgerald Ferber.

Thu. Aug. 17, 1961 Freddy Banks is given the Ayaho account with all its fringe benefits.

Fri. Sept. 22, 1961 Freddy marries Jackie.

Wed. Nov. 15, 1961 Cardinal Cruikshank blesses Hibernia House

Fri. Nov. 22, 1963 Lawrence and Catherine back from Ireland, return to Boston.

Tue. Dec. 24, 1963 Claudia diagnosed breast cancer.

Sun. April 19, 1964 Claudia Ferber dies of breast cancer. Bay boy Claude Shane Ferber is born.
Grandma Ruth Demarest Sheerin will raise the baby
Tue. Aug. 4, 1964 Little Larry kidnapped

Wed. Aug. 5, 1964 Eamon beaten and sent to B.C.H.

Thu. Aug. 6, 1964 Ted forces Captain Lombardo to retired

Friday Aug. 7, 1964 Ted kills, and sea buries, two of Sonny's hit men.

Thur. Aug. 13, 1964 Kidnapped Lawrence Edward Cameron is returned to his mother.

Mon. Sept. 7, 1964 Marion Frazier seduces Matthew Ferber

Thu. Oct. 8, 1964 Eamon, crippled, is released from B.C.H.

Thu, April 1, 1965 42 year old Matthew marries 37 year old divorcee Marion Frazier mother of two boys, 11 year old Randolph and 7 year old Mark, in a ceremony at Judge Casey's Court room.

Tue. September 21, 1965 Beatrice Elizabeth Ferber is born to Marion.

Mon. Nov. 22, 1965 the night of Cassius Clay TKO of Floyd Patterson, Cathy brings Lawrence Edward to Blue Haven Lodge.

Sat. May 14, 1966 Cathy and Teddy are married by Cardinal Richard Cruikshank at Holy Name Cathedral

Fri. May 20, 1966 Jeanne Brooks released after doing 7 years, moves in with Ted & Cathy

Sat. May 28, 1966 Cathy & Donna accompany Eamon Sheerin when he retires to cousin Malachy "Mickey" Fallon's Clinic in Erin. Jeanne seduces Teddy while Cathy is in Ireland with Eamon

Sat. May 28, 1966 Andrew Palmer McLaughlin born

Sun. June 12, 1966 Anne tries to ram water skiing Ruth.

Thu. Jan. 19, 1967 'Rifleman' Flemmi kills 'Wimpy' Bennett.

Sat. Mar. 16, 1968 Randolph rapes Edwina

Wed. Sept. 4, 1968 Randolph incarcerated until he is 21.

Mon. Oct. 21, 1968 Matthew divorces Marion. Gets custody of Edwina, Claude Shane & John 'Fitzy' Fitzgerald

Sat. May 31, 1969 Fred Banks drowned on orders of Jazz

Tue. Aug. 26, 1969 Thugs of Vic Damone threaten Teddy

Sun. Aug. 31, 1969 Jackie shoots Teddy

Mon. Oct. 13, 1969 the now crippled Teddy leaves B.C.H.

Friday June 2, 1972 Eddy Cameron enrolled in Phillips Exeter Academy

Sat. June 3, 1972 Alvan in Cincinnati at ordination of first American female Rabbi

Tue. Aug. 8, 1972 Southie Irish gives Jazz an ultimatum

Mon. Sept. 4, 1972 Southies fail in attempt to kill Jazz

Friday Sept. 8, 1972 Cathy moves in with Lawrence Cameron

Tue. Dec. 9, 1972 Sean murders 'Jockey' Ayaho

Wed. Dec. 17, 1972 Sean & Ruth sent to Gloucester operations

Tue. Dec. 23, 1972 Donna Louise moves in to Blue Haven Lodge

Thu. Dec. 25, 1972 Kelley moves to Las Vegas

Tue. July 10, 1973 Edwina meets her half brother Jamison

Fri. Oct. 5, 1973 Anthony Pino dies

Sat. Oct. 6, 1973 Yom Kippur 6 day war begins

Sun. Oct. 8, 1973 Jazz Kelley moves his operations to Las Vegas

Sat. Oct. 20, 1973 Alvan & Phyllis leave for Israel

Sat. July 5, 1975 while they visit N.Y.C. Edwina seduces Jamison

Sun. Oct. 26, 1975 Edwina unknowingly meets her mother for the first time in her life.

Sun. Nov. 23, 1975 Edwina enters convent of Saint Theresa of the Little Flower in Erin.

Thu. Nov. 25, 1976 Anne Nevins dies in Federal Prison.

Sat. Nov. 13, 1977 50 yr old Bernice marries 54 yr old Matthew

Mon. Feb.4, 1980 Edward 'Teddy' Sheerin enters his watery tomb.

Characters

Mondays child *Fair of face* Thursdays child – Has *far to go/wander1*
Tuesdays *Full of grace* Fridays *Loving and giving*
Wednesday s *Full of woe* Saturdays *Works hard*
Sundays child *Bonny & blithe or Good and happy*

Eamon Sheerin a day laborer, 5'11" at 170 lbs. born Sat. 3/4/1905 on the Aran Island of Inis Mor migrates to Boston. Marries French Canadian Margaret la Chappelle. They are the parents of Edward '*Ted/Teddy*' Sheerin and Stanley 'Stan' Vincent Sheerin. She dies birthing *Teddy.*

Edward 'Ted-Teddy' Sheerin born Sat. 4/19/24 a 6'1" 189lb fullback. WW2 U.S. Army Air Force Colonel. Irish Mafia boss from Southie.

Stanley Vincent '*Stan'* Sheerin born Wed. 1/4/23, 6', 174lbs. Marries Claudia on Sun. 12/18/54. He dies Wed. 10/8/58.

Catherine Jane '*Cathy'* Brooks Ryler born Fri. 9/9/27. 5'6", 129lbs. a braided blonde. Parents, Arthur '*Art'* & Marie Esposito Brooks marries Stephen Ryler Sat. 6/29/46. Marries Senator Lawrence Cameron Sat. Oct. 6,1956 Marries Ted Sheerin Tue. 5/24/66

Jeanne Marie Brooks, sister of Catherine. 5'8", 125lbs with wavy auburn hair. Born Thurs.5/4/32 a known heroin 'mule' for the mob.

Stephen *Steve* Ryler, born Wed. 6/10/25. 5'11" at 165lbs. with a waffle cut blonde haircut. Dies Mon. 11/27/50, Parents Donald & Eileen Ryler.

Lawrence Francis *'Larry'* Cameron, born Sat. 8/12/16. 6'2", 190lbs. Black hair sprinkled with gray. Marries Catherine Ryler Sat. Oct. 6, 1956. Divorces Cathy Tues. Nov 23, 1956. Marries Maev Bridget O'Toole Thu. May 23, 1957.

Lawrence Edward Cameron born Tue 6/18/57 to Lawrence Frances Cameron and Catherine Brooks Cameron but was fathered by Teddy Sheerin.

Claudia Theresa Demarest, born Wed. 10/5/32. 5'2" and 116lbs. A blue eyed blonde with long braided hair. Marries Stanley Sheerin Sun. 12/18/54. Marries Matthew Ferber Sat. June 25, 1960. Dies Sun. April 19, 1964.

Ruth Lillian Demarest, born Mon. 10/5/14, 5'4" at 134lbs. A dark auburn haired voluptuous divorcee and the mother of Claudia. Marries Eamon Sheerin Sat. 8/3/57

Alvan Joshua *'Al'* Waterman, born Sat. 3/3/23, 5'9", 170 lbs. A devout Ashkenazi Rabbi married to a Christian girl Phyllis born Sun 4/12/25, 5'4" 135lbs.

Anne Marie Nevins, born Fri. 5/12/22. 5'9", 145lbs a Liz Taylor type brunette wearing a short bob. A former U.S. Marine Captain Nurse at Iwo Jima. Dies 11/25/76

John *'Jack'* Carroll used car buyer at Southie Ford Dealership. Born Fri. 8/10/17. 6'2" 180lbs. blue eyes. Married to Bernice, *'Bunny'* Miller. After his divorce in 1958 marries Noreen Keenan

Bernice 'Bunny' Carroll, born Fri 11/11/27. 5'5" one hundred thirty five pounds petite blue eyed blonde wife of John Carroll. Seduces Ted Sheerin Fri. 4/19/57.

Brenda Carroll blue eyed daughter of John and Bernice, born Tue. 5/11/48

Jamison Carroll son of John and Bernice, born Thur. 4/9/53

Edwina Carroll Sheerin Ferber born Mon 1/1/58 daughter of Bunny Carroll and Ted Sheerin adopted by Stanley and Claudia Sheerin

Noreen Jean Keenan, office secretary at the South Boston Ford Dealership. Born Mon. 8/8/38. A 5'7", 139 lb. with alabaster white skin accented by her black eyes and wavy black hair. A divorcee mistress of John Carroll. She marries Carroll in 1958.

Virginia Jane 'Ginny' Bushnell born Tue. 7/16/29. A brown eyed brunette, of 5'6" and at 135 lbs. Lesbian friend of Claudia.

Frederic Xavier *'Fred/Freddy'* Banks born Sat. 3/6/33. 5'10" 170lbs, a U.S. Navy Vet. Delivery man for the local Sears. Meets Ted on Thu. 9/7/50. Marries Jacquelyn Coleman Fri. 9/22/61. He is murdered Fri. 5/30/69

Jacquelyn *'Jackie'* Coleman, born Wed. 11/1/33. 5'5" and 119lbs. A black haired blue eyed aphrodisiac quadroon. Brought to a party at Blue Haven, by Fred Banks. Marries Fred Fri. 9/22/61

Matthew 'Matty' Ferber born Mon. 6/18/23. 6'1" 175 lbs. Ruddy complexion. Owner of Ferber's Office Supply store. Marries Claudia Sheerin Sat. 6/25/60.

John 'Fitzy' Fitzgerald Ferber born Thu. 8/10/61 son of Claudia & Matthew Ferber

Claude Shane Ferber born Sun 4/19/64 son of Claudia and Matthew Ferber.

After Claudia's death, Matthew, on Thu 4/1/65 marries Marion Frazier born Mon. 5/14/28 a brown eye, gregarious petite brunette female, the mother of Randolph and Mark Frazier. They divorce Mon. 10/7/68.

Randolph Frazier born Tues. 3/23/54 son of Marion Frazier

Mark Frazier born Fri. 8/8/58 son of Marion Frazier

Beatrice Elizabeth Ferber born Tue. 9/21/65. Daughter of Marion and Matthew Ferber

Father Timothy Coughlin, Pastor of St. Columba Catholic Church, born Mon. May 1, 1922. 5'10" and 170 lbs, he could be mistaken for a full-back instead of a priest.

Mary Margaret Mitchell born Sun. 4/23/39 in Galway Ireland, a mischievous seductive Irish pixy. Came to U.S. in 1955. Altar Flower arranger at St. Columba Church. Has an illicit affair with Fr. Timothy. Returns to Ireland Tues. 7/22/58.

Giovanni 'Johnny', '*Dago*' di Birtallo 5'9" 180lbs.Born Thu. 10/17/29. Black hair, dark completion.

Tito 'Bruno' Mangino, Owner of the East Boston Hotel *Amicizia Italiano* (Friendly Italian) located in the little Italy section of Boston. He is 5'8" and 165 lbs. Born in Naples Italy in 1918.

Sergio '*Bello*' Canalejas born Sat. 5/7/32. Brown eyed dark hair, 5'10" and 175lbs. in a weight lifters frame.

Thomas 'Jazz' Kelley, 5'7" 175 lb born Thu. 10/9/19 in Southie. Always meticulously dressed in the latest businessman's attire. He is the head of the Irish Mafia that controls Massachusetts with the permission of and contributor too, Mafia Don Raymond Patriarca.

Seamus McMann, born Fri. 2/10/22. An Ex-Marine Gunnery Sgt. Former middle weight boxer @ 6', 165 lbs. Henchman of Kelley.

Sean 'Johnny three strikes' McLaughlin, born Sat. 9/19/36, 5'10" 180 lbs. married to Norma Palmer. Hit man for Kelley and or Ted Sheerin.

Norma Palmer McLaughlin wife of Sean. Born Mon 5/29/33. Their son Andrew born Sat. 5/28/66

Donna Maria Broes, born Thu. 10/12/44 dark complexioned, raven-haired, red-lipped, *Portigy*, aphrodisiac.

Maev Bridget O'Toole born Thu. 7/13/33. Illegal Irish immigrant smuggled into U.S. by Lawrence Cameron.

Gaelach 'Gale' O'Toole born Tue. 2/10/30 brother of Maev also smuggled into the U.S. by Cameron.

Paulo 'Tip-toe' Ferrara muscle man for Ted Sheerin.

Meredith 'Baldie' Jason Muscle man for Ted Sheerin.

Vincenzo 'Sonny' Paraviccino, Sicilian born owner of Vincenzo's Luogo. Mob boss gangster who runs the North End area of Boston. –

Gaeta & Joey Petrocci, Vick Damone thugs.